Federico Rossi Edrighi

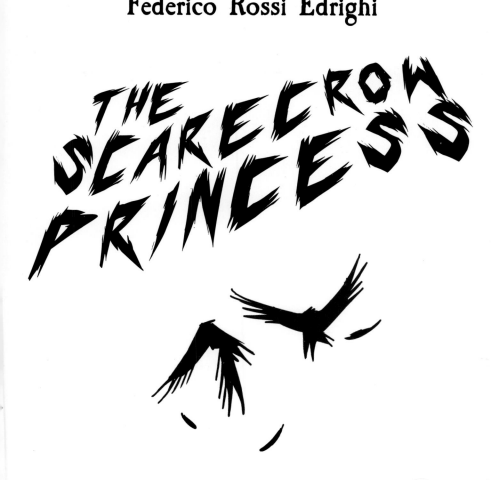

THE SCARECROW PRINCESS

ROAR

Writer and Artist
FEDERICO ROSSI EDRIGHI

Letters, Lion Forge edition
DERON BENNETT

Editor, Lion Forge edition
HAZEL NEWLEVANT

ROAR

Publisher's Cataloging-In-Publication Data

(Prepared by The Donohue Group, Inc.)

Names: Rossi Edrighi, Federico, author, illustrator. | Bennett, Deron, letterer. | Newlevant, Hazel, editor. | Roncalli di Montorio, Carla, translator.

Title: The scarecrow princess / writer and artist, Federico Rossi Edrighi ; letters, Lion Forge edition, Deron Bennett ; editor, Lion Forge edition, Hazel Newlevant ; [translator, Carla Roncalli Di Montorio].

Other Titles: Principessa spaventapasseri. English

Description: [St. Louis, Missouri] : ROAR, [an imprint of] The Lion Forge, LLC, [2017] | Translation of: La principessa spaventapasseri. Milano : BAO Publishing, ©2016.

Identifiers: ISBN 978-1-941302-42-2

Subjects: LCSH: Teenage girls--Comic books, strips, etc. | Disappeared persons--Comic books, strips, etc. | Strangers--Comic books, strips, etc. | Revenge--Comic books, strips, etc. | LCGFT: Graphic novels.

Classification: LCC PN6767.R67 P7513 2017 | DDC 741.5945--dc23

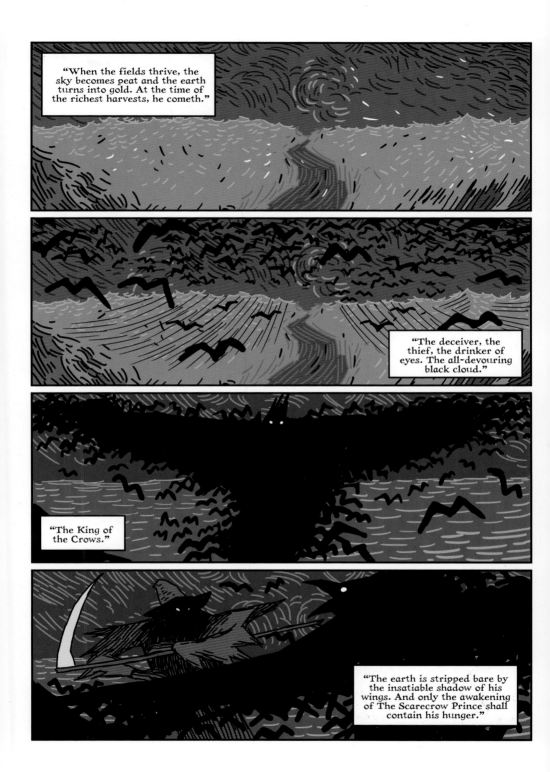

"When the fields thrive, the sky becomes peat and the earth turns into gold. At the time of the richest harvests, he cometh."

"The deceiver, the thief, the drinker of eyes. The all-devouring black cloud."

"The King of the Crows."

"The earth is stripped bare by the insatiable shadow of his wings. And only the awakening of The Scarecrow Prince shall contain his hunger."

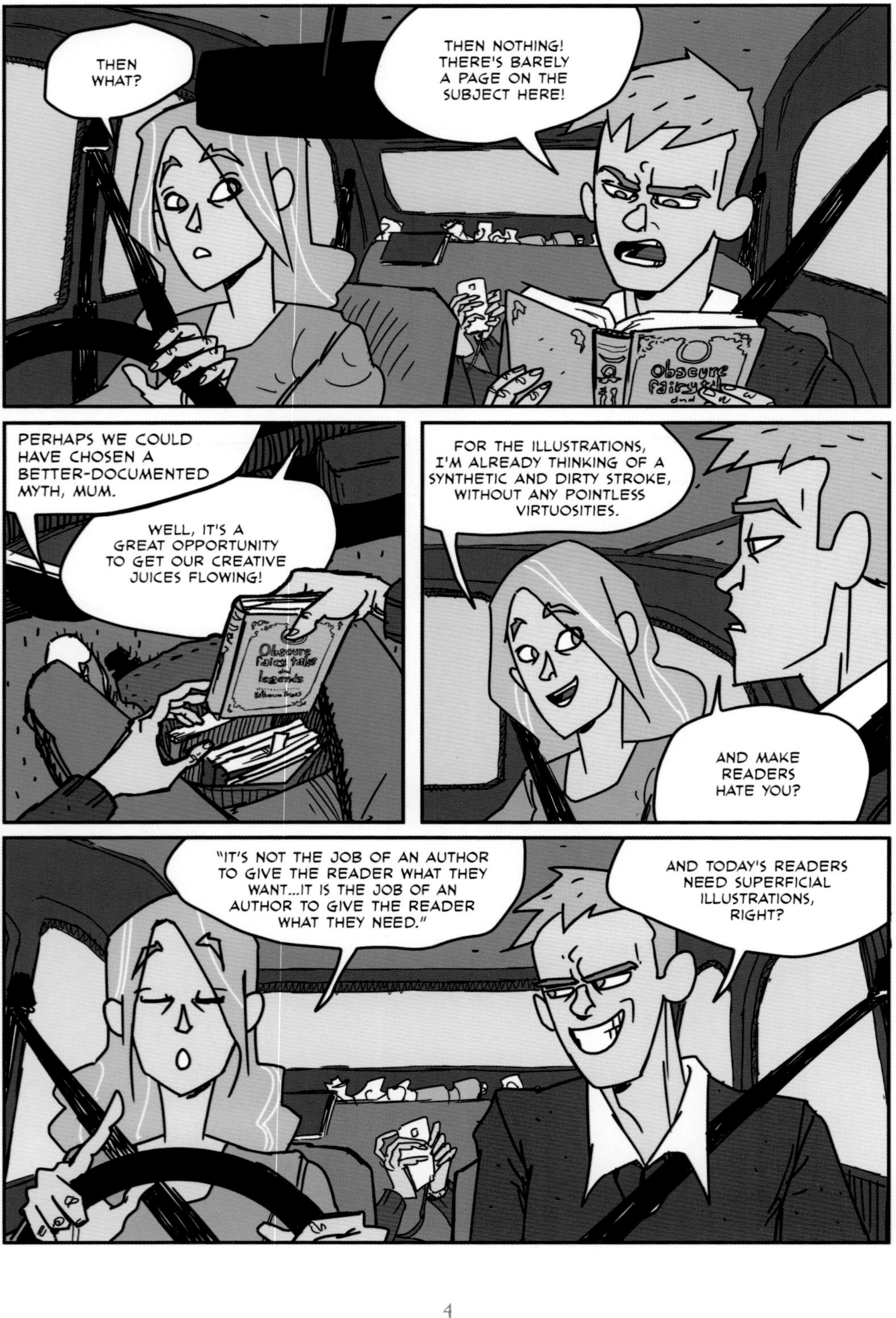
THEN WHAT?
THEN NOTHING! THERE'S BARELY A PAGE ON THE SUBJECT HERE!
PERHAPS WE COULD HAVE CHOSEN A BETTER-DOCUMENTED MYTH, MUM.
WELL, IT'S A GREAT OPPORTUNITY TO GET OUR CREATIVE JUICES FLOWING!
Obscure fairy tales and legends
FOR THE ILLUSTRATIONS, I'M ALREADY THINKING OF A SYNTHETIC AND DIRTY STROKE, WITHOUT ANY POINTLESS VIRTUOSITIES.
AND MAKE READERS HATE YOU?
"IT'S NOT THE JOB OF AN AUTHOR TO GIVE THE READER WHAT THEY WANT...IT IS THE JOB OF AN AUTHOR TO GIVE THE READER WHAT THEY NEED."
AND TODAY'S READERS NEED SUPERFICIAL ILLUSTRATIONS, RIGHT?

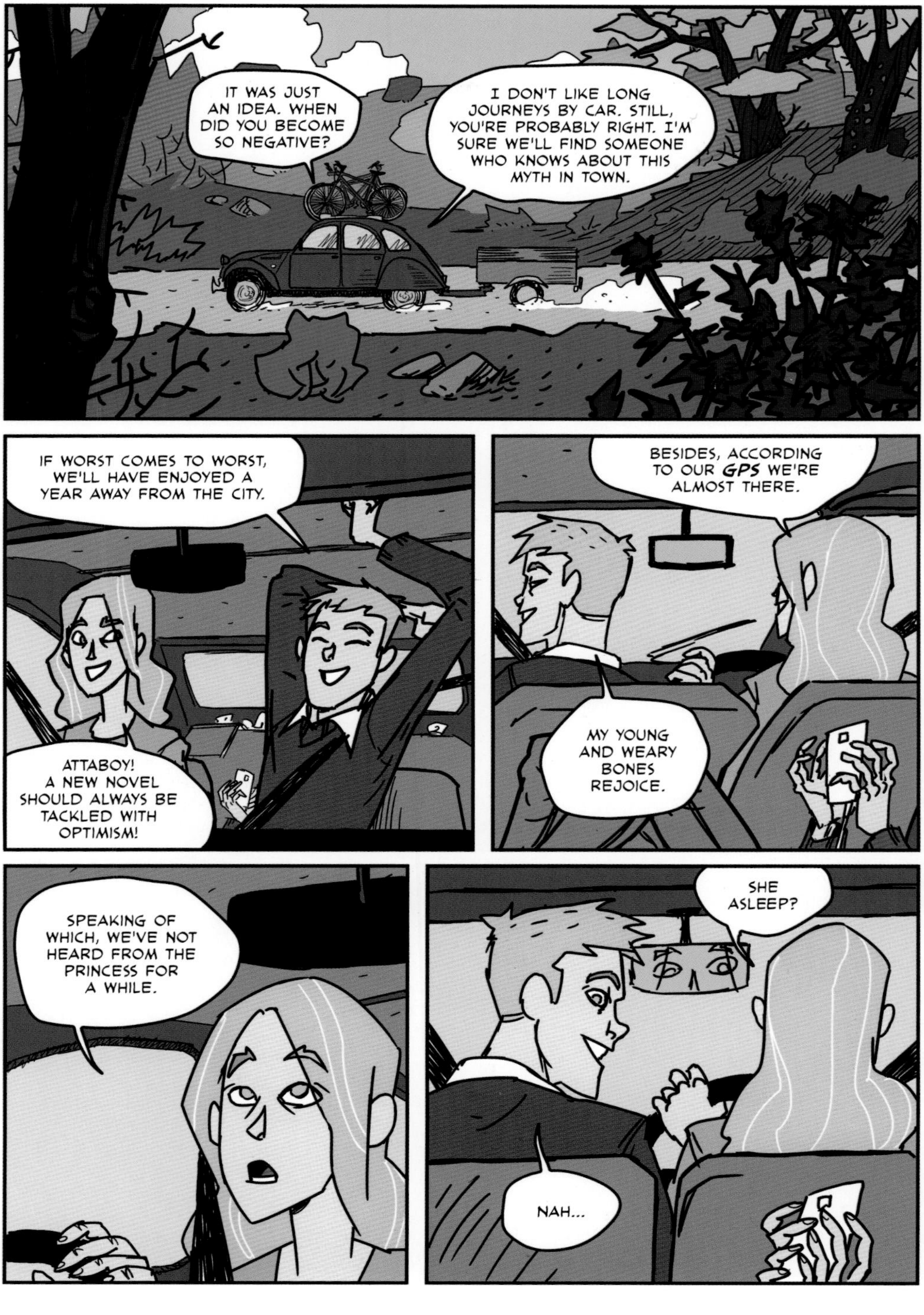
IT WAS JUST AN IDEA. WHEN DID YOU BECOME SO NEGATIVE?
I DON'T LIKE LONG JOURNEYS BY CAR. STILL, YOU'RE PROBABLY RIGHT. I'M SURE WE'LL FIND SOMEONE WHO KNOWS ABOUT THIS MYTH IN TOWN.
IF WORST COMES TO WORST, WE'LL HAVE ENJOYED A YEAR AWAY FROM THE CITY.
ATTABOY! A NEW NOVEL SHOULD ALWAYS BE TACKLED WITH OPTIMISM!
BESIDES, ACCORDING TO OUR GPS WE'RE ALMOST THERE.
MY YOUNG AND WEARY BONES REJOICE.
SPEAKING OF WHICH, WE'VE NOT HEARD FROM THE PRINCESS FOR A WHILE.
SHE ASLEEP?
NAH...

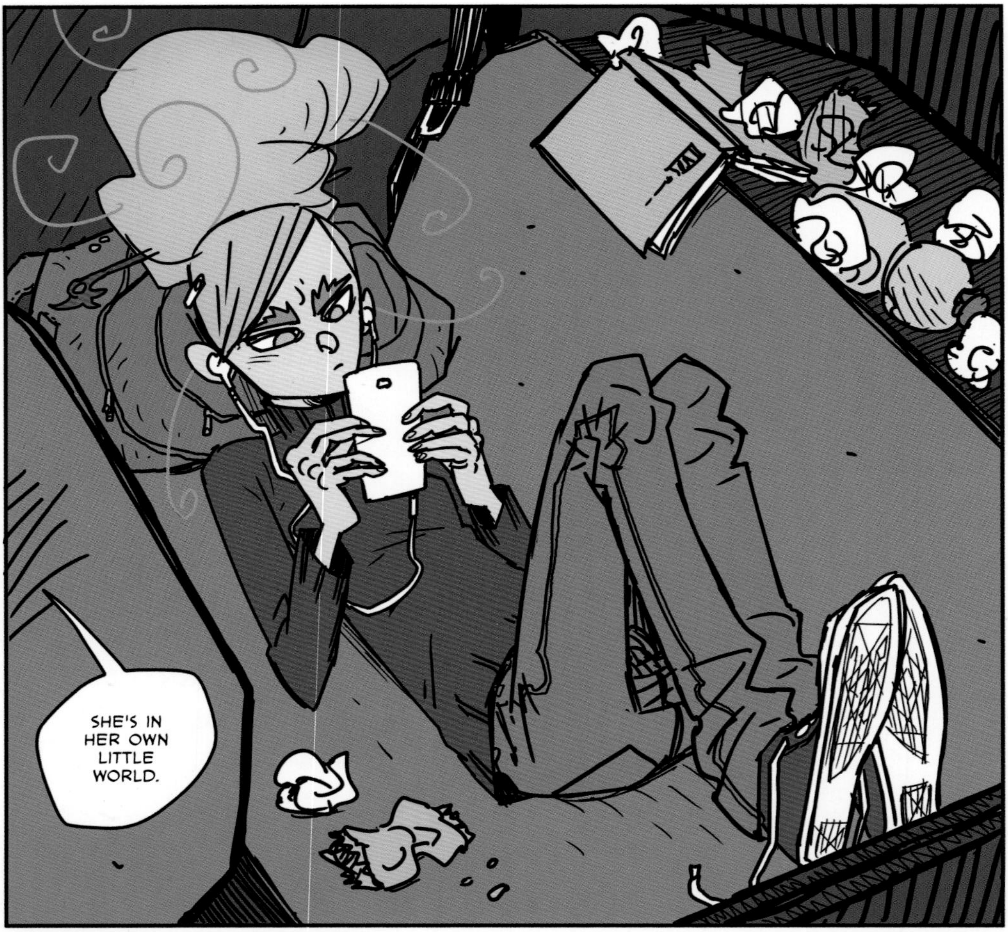
SHE'S IN HER OWN LITTLE WORLD.

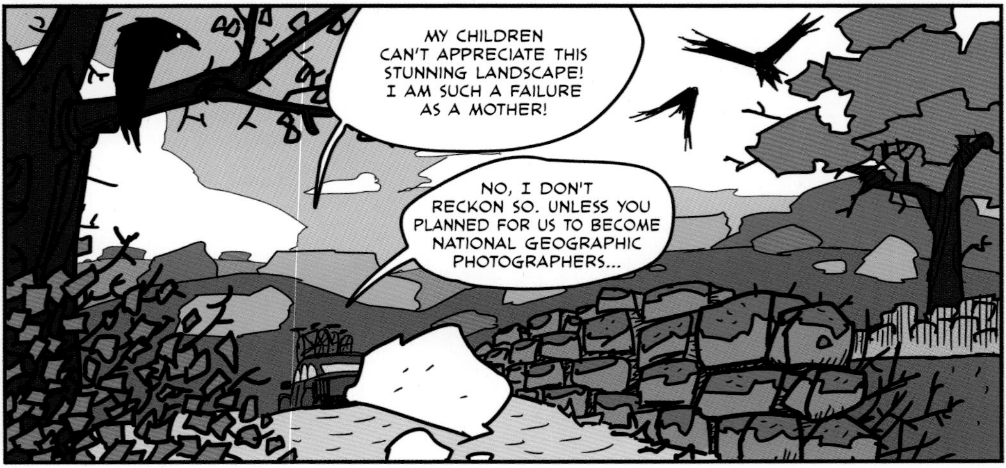
MY CHILDREN CAN'T APPRECIATE THIS STUNNING LANDSCAPE! I AM SUCH A FAILURE AS A MOTHER!
NO, I DON'T RECKON SO. UNLESS YOU PLANNED FOR US TO BECOME NATIONAL GEOGRAPHIC PHOTOGRAPHERS...

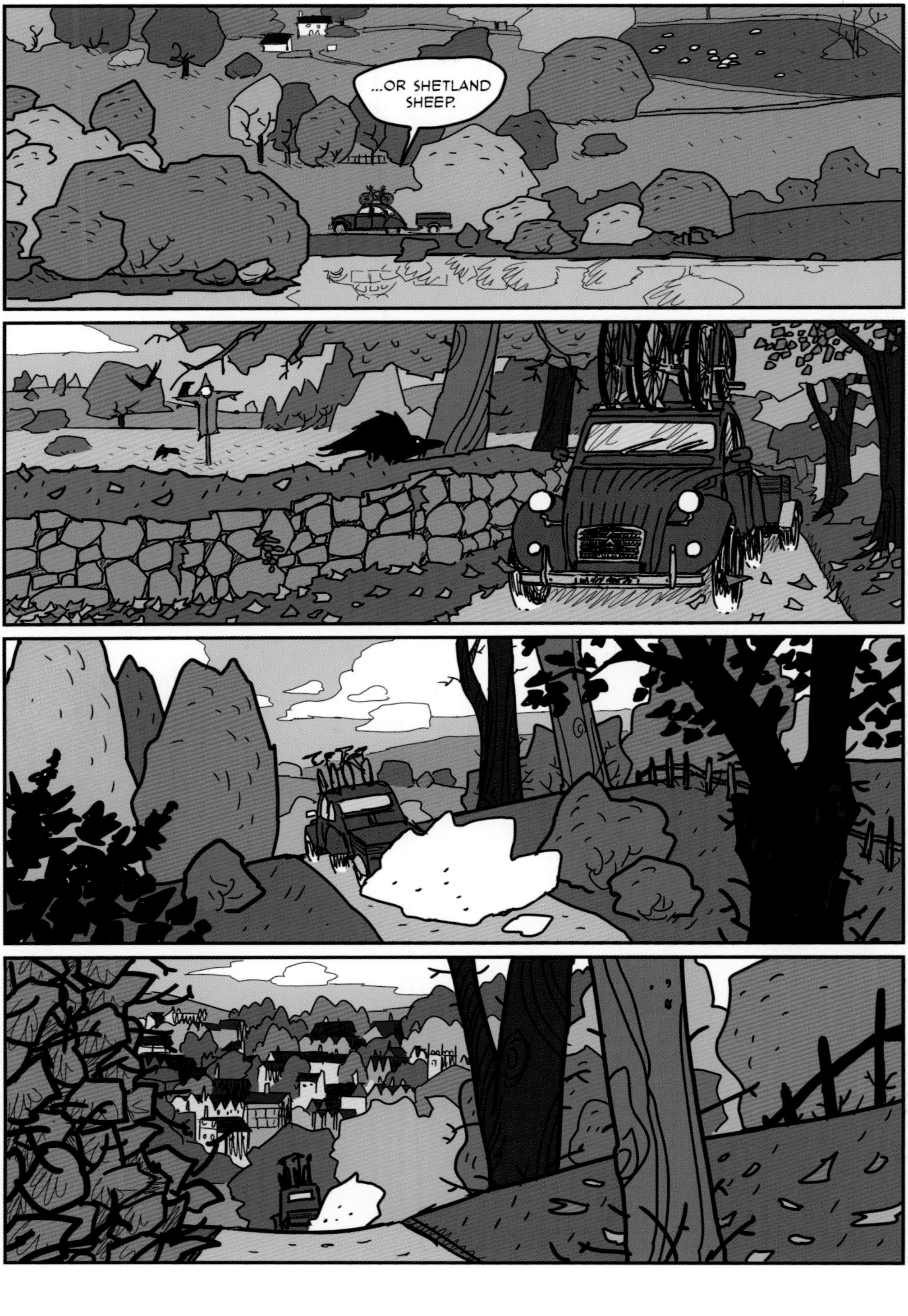
...OR SHETLAND SHEEP.

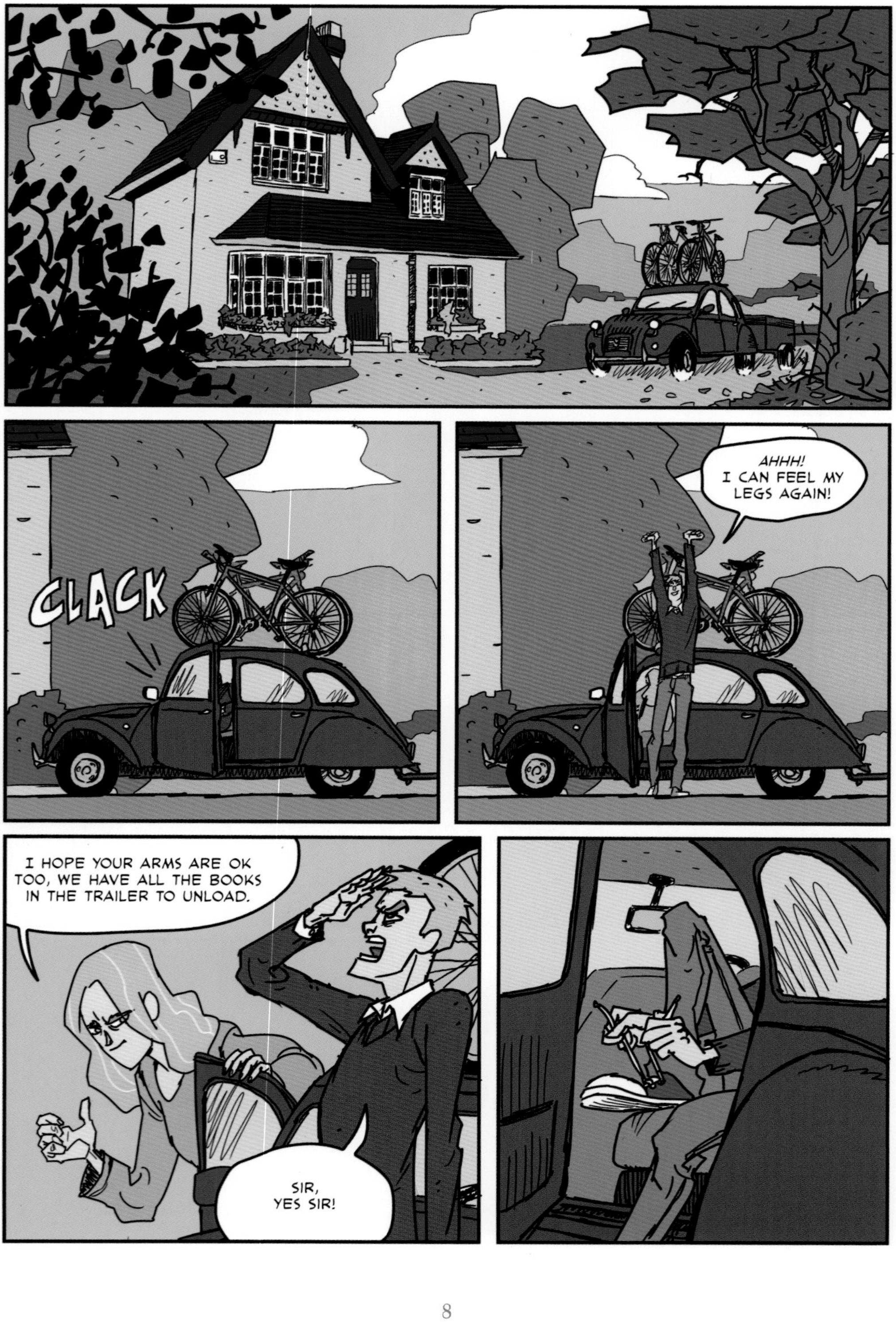
CLACK
AHHH! I CAN FEEL MY LEGS AGAIN!
I HOPE YOUR ARMS ARE OK TOO, WE HAVE ALL THE BOOKS IN THE TRAILER TO UNLOAD.
SIR, YES SIR!

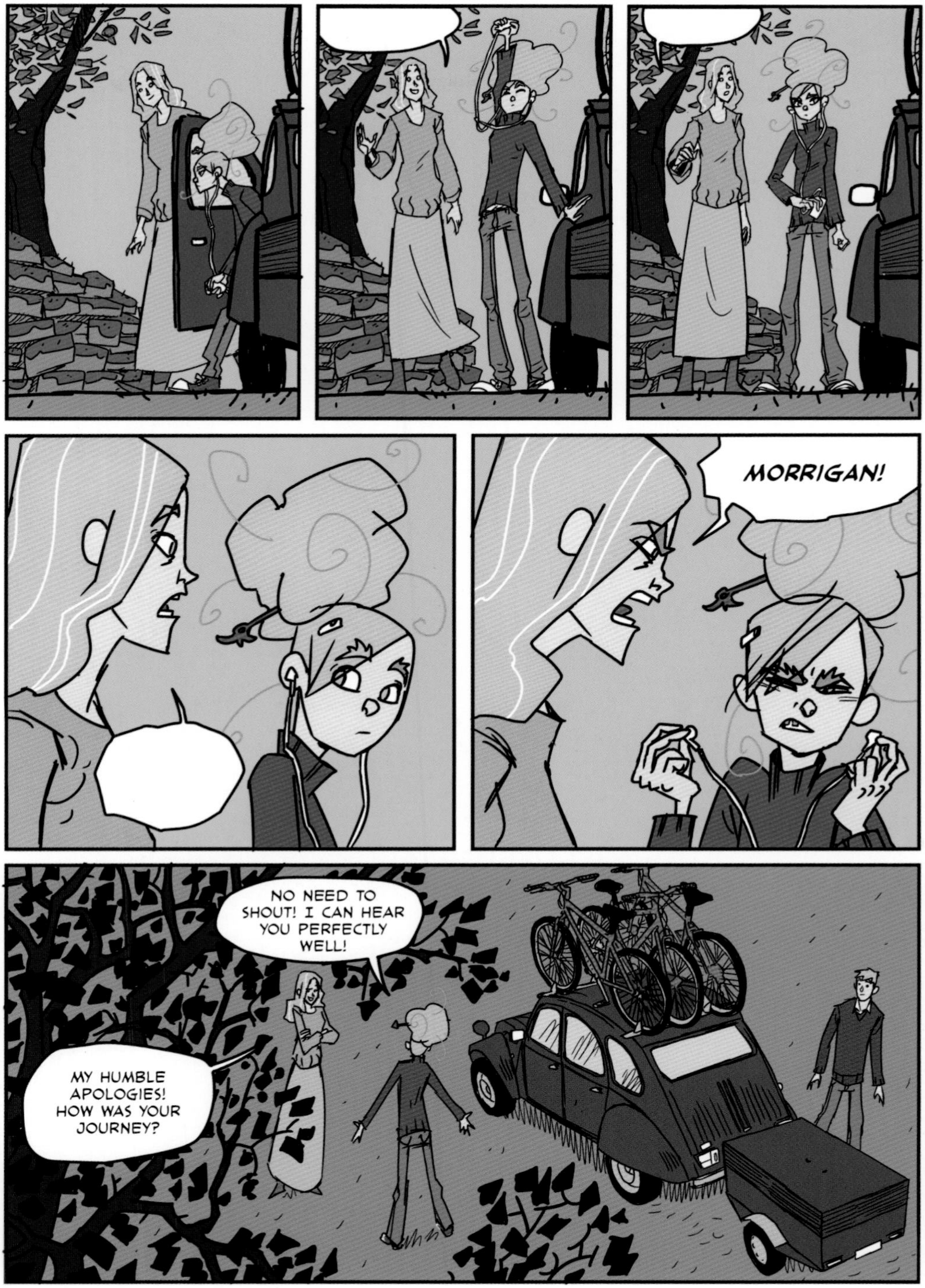
MORRIGAN!
NO NEED TO SHOUT! I CAN HEAR YOU PERFECTLY WELL!
MY HUMBLE APOLOGIES! HOW WAS YOUR JOURNEY?

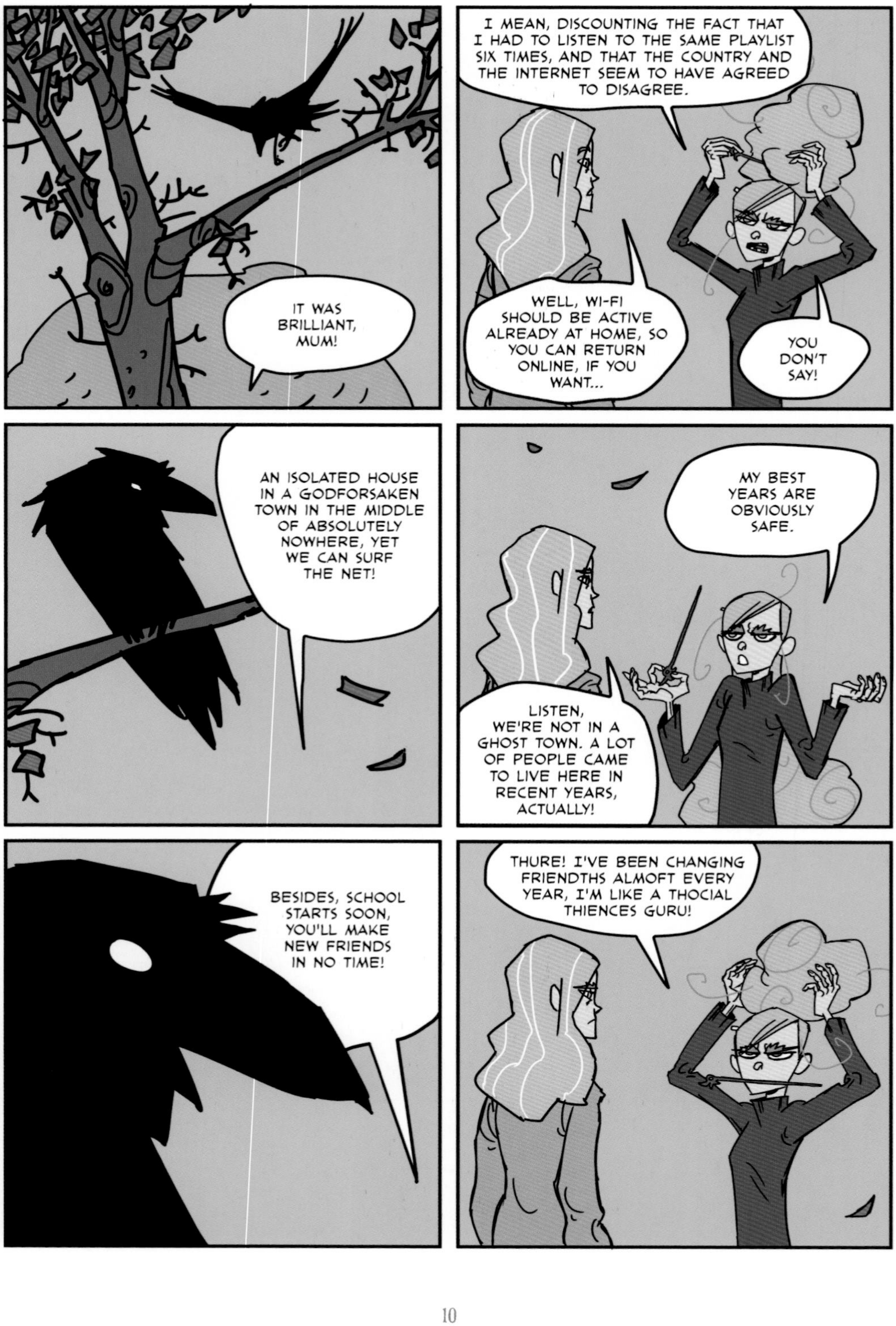
IT WAS BRILLIANT, MUM!
I MEAN, DISCOUNTING THE FACT THAT I HAD TO LISTEN TO THE SAME PLAYLIST SIX TIMES, AND THAT THE COUNTRY AND THE INTERNET SEEM TO HAVE AGREED TO DISAGREE.
WELL, WI-FI SHOULD BE ACTIVE ALREADY AT HOME, SO YOU CAN RETURN ONLINE, IF YOU WANT...
YOU DON'T SAY!
AN ISOLATED HOUSE IN A GODFORSAKEN TOWN IN THE MIDDLE OF ABSOLUTELY NOWHERE, YET WE CAN SURF THE NET!
MY BEST YEARS ARE OBVIOUSLY SAFE.
LISTEN, WE'RE NOT IN A GHOST TOWN. A LOT OF PEOPLE CAME TO LIVE HERE IN RECENT YEARS, ACTUALLY!
BESIDES, SCHOOL STARTS SOON, YOU'LL MAKE NEW FRIENDS IN NO TIME!
THURE! I'VE BEEN CHANGING FRIENDTHS ALMOFT EVERY YEAR, I'M LIKE A THOCIAL THIENCES GURU!

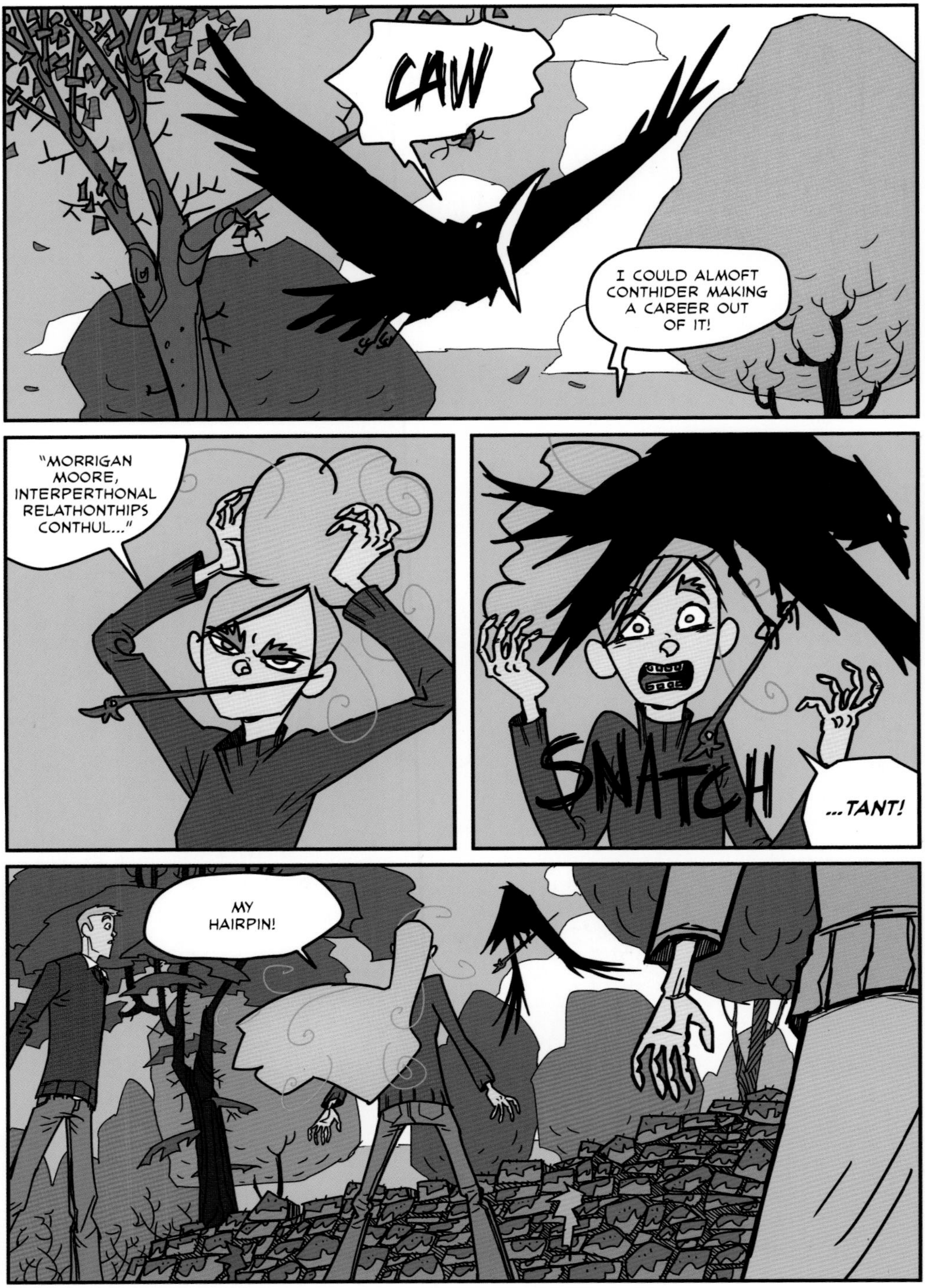
CAW
I COULD ALMOFT CONTHIDER MAKING A CAREER OUT OF IT!
"MORRIGAN MOORE, INTERPERTHONAL RELATHONTHIPS CONTHUL..."
SNATCH
...TANT!
MY HAIRPIN!

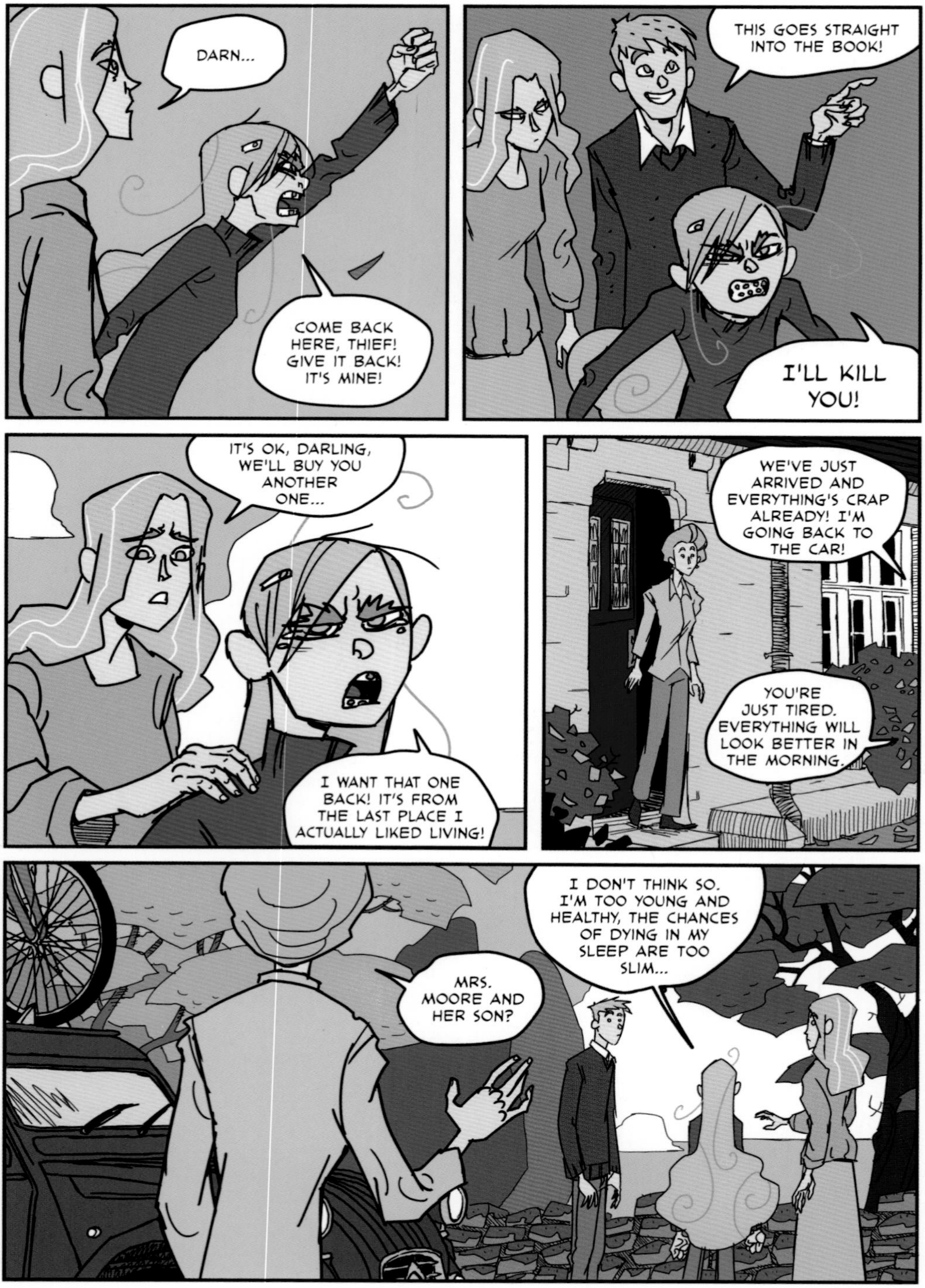
DARN...
COME BACK HERE, THIEF! GIVE IT BACK! IT'S MINE!
THIS GOES STRAIGHT INTO THE BOOK!
I'LL KILL YOU!
IT'S OK, DARLING, WE'LL BUY YOU ANOTHER ONE...
I WANT THAT ONE BACK! IT'S FROM THE LAST PLACE I ACTUALLY LIKED LIVING!
WE'VE JUST ARRIVED AND EVERYTHING'S CRAP ALREADY! I'M GOING BACK TO THE CAR!
YOU'RE JUST TIRED. EVERYTHING WILL LOOK BETTER IN THE MORNING.
MRS. MOORE AND HER SON?
I DON'T THINK SO. I'M TOO YOUNG AND HEALTHY, THE CHANCES OF DYING IN MY SLEEP ARE TOO SLIM...

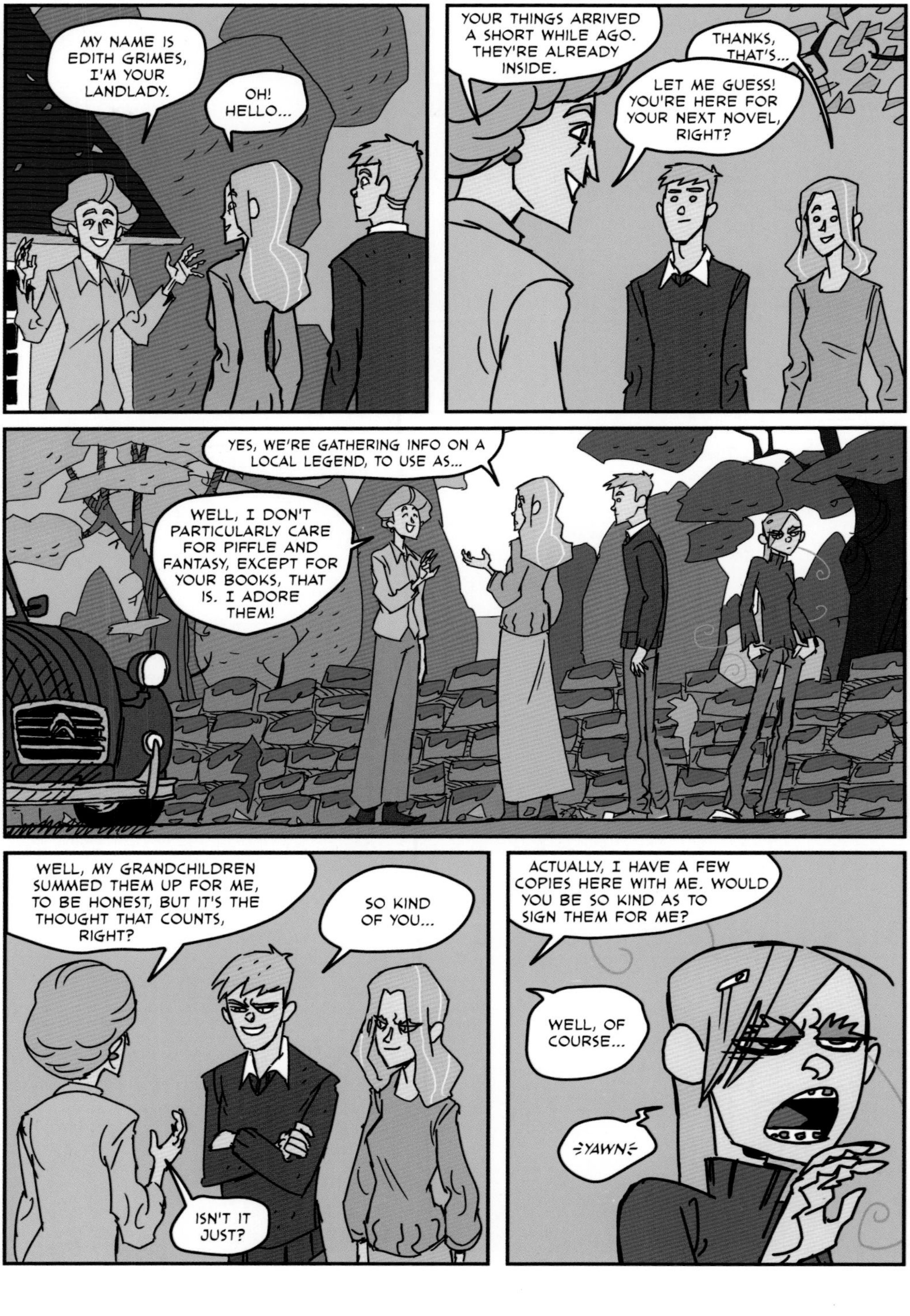
MY NAME IS EDITH GRIMES, I'M YOUR LANDLADY.
OH! HELLO...
YOUR THINGS ARRIVED A SHORT WHILE AGO. THEY'RE ALREADY INSIDE.
THANKS, THAT'S...
LET ME GUESS! YOU'RE HERE FOR YOUR NEXT NOVEL, RIGHT?
YES, WE'RE GATHERING INFO ON A LOCAL LEGEND, TO USE AS...
WELL, I DON'T PARTICULARLY CARE FOR PIFFLE AND FANTASY, EXCEPT FOR YOUR BOOKS, THAT IS. I ADORE THEM!
WELL, MY GRANDCHILDREN SUMMED THEM UP FOR ME, TO BE HONEST, BUT IT'S THE THOUGHT THAT COUNTS, RIGHT?
SO KIND OF YOU...
ISN'T IT JUST?
ACTUALLY, I HAVE A FEW COPIES HERE WITH ME. WOULD YOU BE SO KIND AS TO SIGN THEM FOR ME?
WELL, OF COURSE...
YAWN

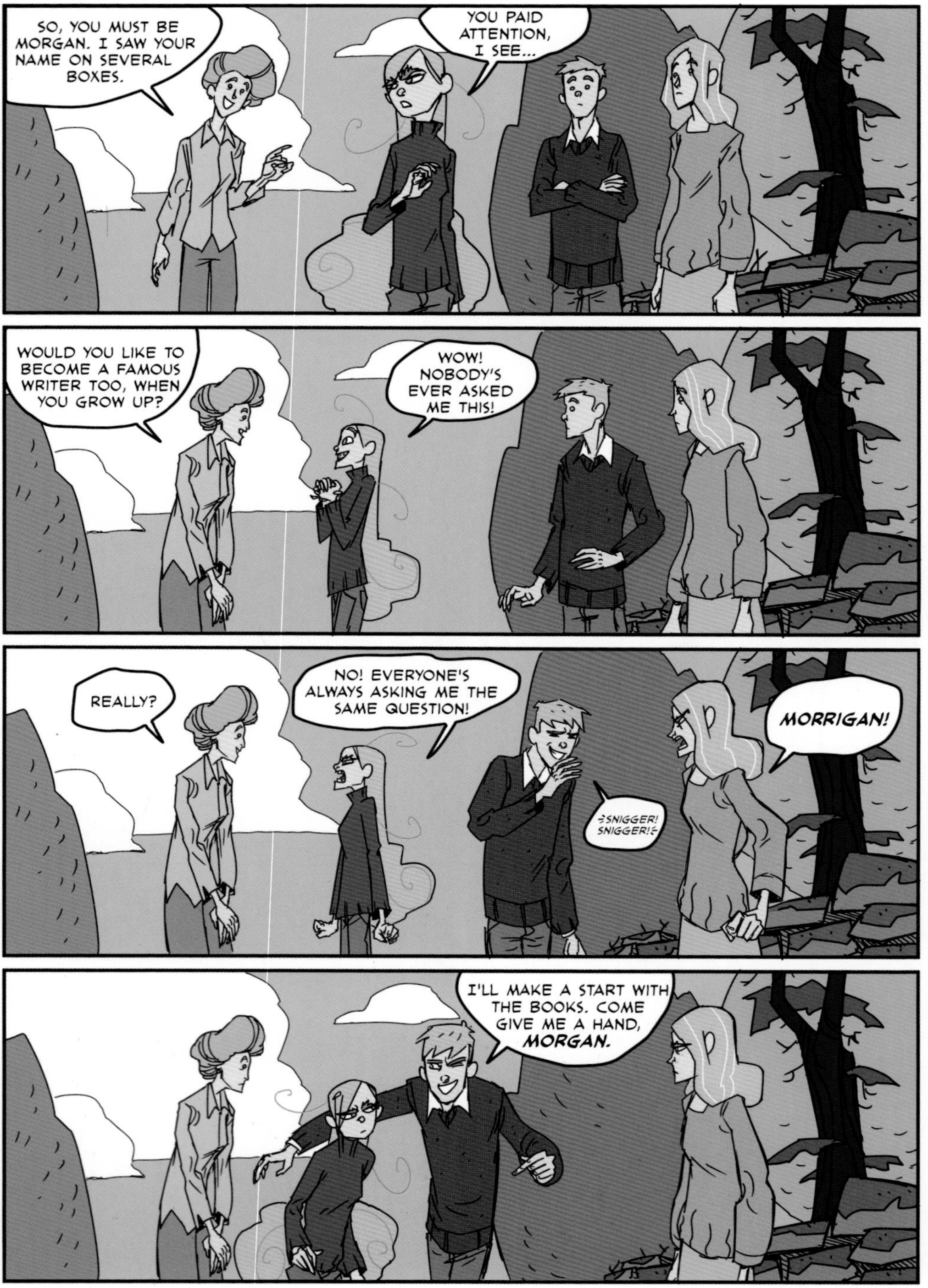
SO, YOU MUST BE MORGAN. I SAW YOUR NAME ON SEVERAL BOXES.
YOU PAID ATTENTION, I SEE...
WOULD YOU LIKE TO BECOME A FAMOUS WRITER TOO, WHEN YOU GROW UP?
WOW! NOBODY'S EVER ASKED ME THIS!
REALLY?
NO! EVERYONE'S ALWAYS ASKING ME THE SAME QUESTION!
SNIGGER! SNIGGER!
MORRIGAN!
I'LL MAKE A START WITH THE BOOKS. COME GIVE ME A HAND, MORGAN.

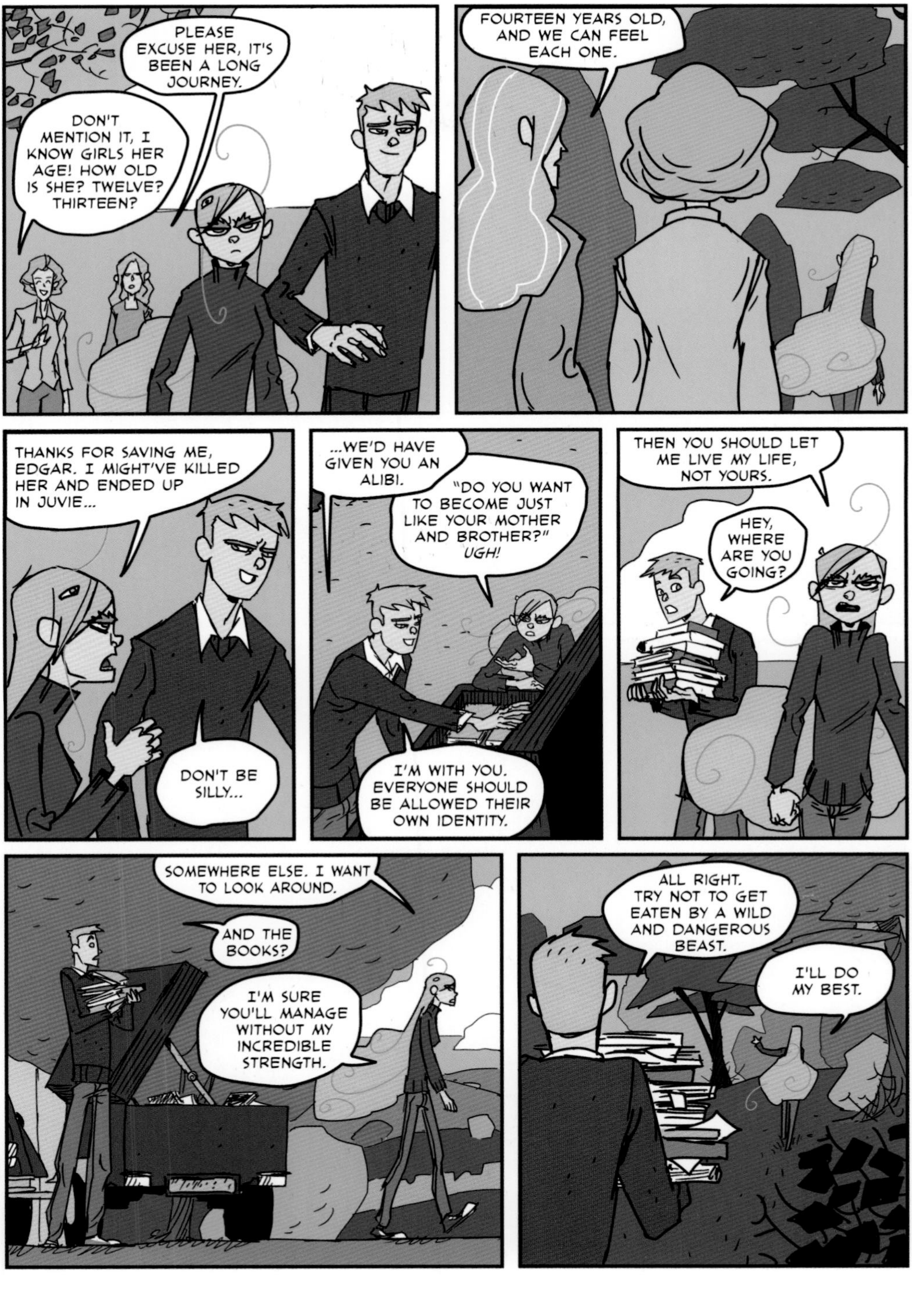
PLEASE EXCUSE HER, IT'S BEEN A LONG JOURNEY.
DON'T MENTION IT, I KNOW GIRLS HER AGE! HOW OLD IS SHE? TWELVE? THIRTEEN?
FOURTEEN YEARS OLD, AND WE CAN FEEL EACH ONE.
THANKS FOR SAVING ME, EDGAR. I MIGHT'VE KILLED HER AND ENDED UP IN JUVIE...
DON'T BE SILLY...
...WE'D HAVE GIVEN YOU AN ALIBI.
"DO YOU WANT TO BECOME JUST LIKE YOUR MOTHER AND BROTHER?" UGH!
I'M WITH YOU. EVERYONE SHOULD BE ALLOWED THEIR OWN IDENTITY.
THEN YOU SHOULD LET ME LIVE MY LIFE, NOT YOURS.
HEY, WHERE ARE YOU GOING?
SOMEWHERE ELSE. I WANT TO LOOK AROUND.
AND THE BOOKS?
I'M SURE YOU'LL MANAGE WITHOUT MY INCREDIBLE STRENGTH.
ALL RIGHT. TRY NOT TO GET EATEN BY A WILD AND DANGEROUS BEAST.
I'LL DO MY BEST.

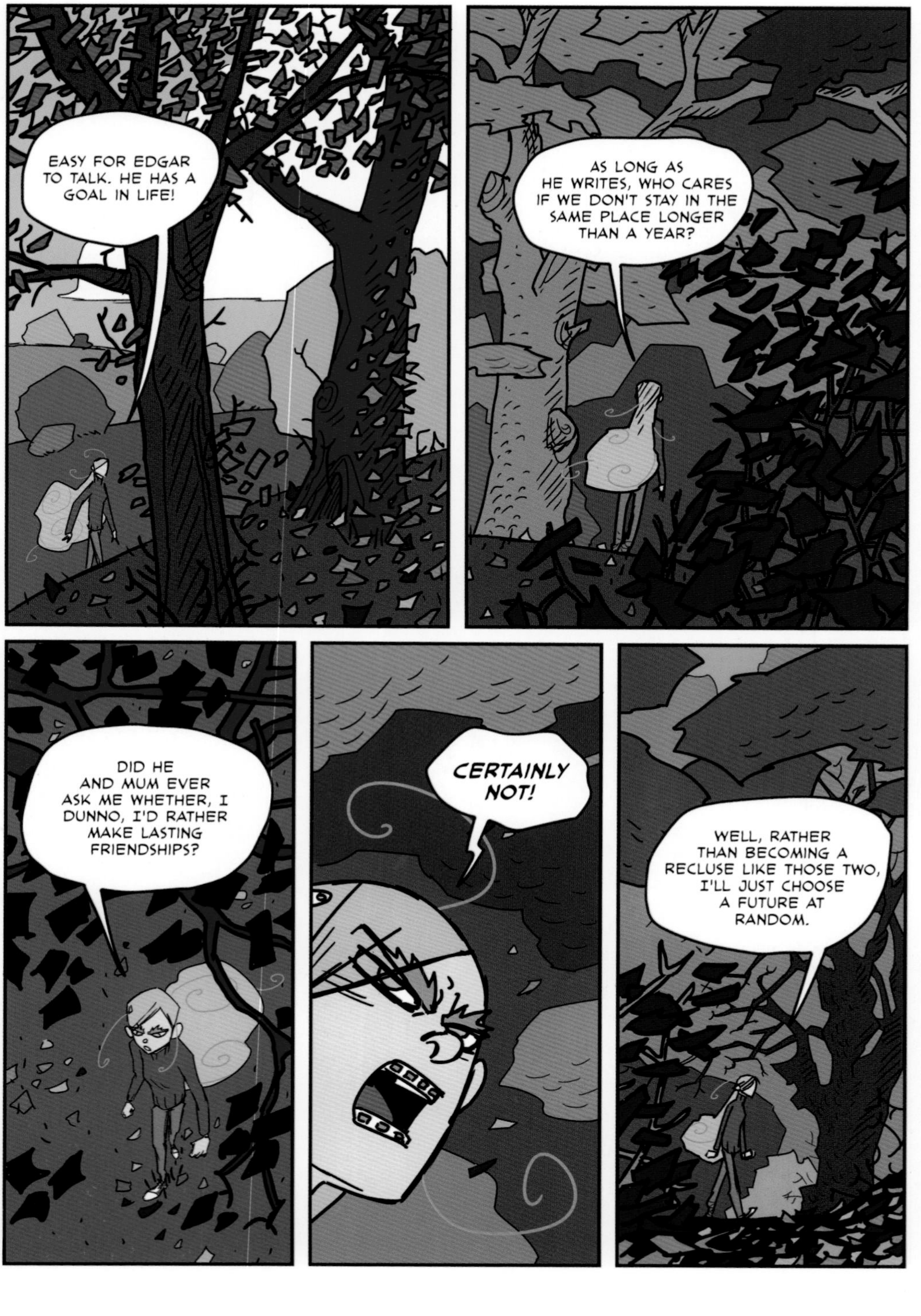
EASY FOR EDGAR TO TALK. HE HAS A GOAL IN LIFE!
AS LONG AS HE WRITES, WHO CARES IF WE DON'T STAY IN THE SAME PLACE LONGER THAN A YEAR?
DID HE AND MUM EVER ASK ME WHETHER, I DUNNO, I'D RATHER MAKE LASTING FRIENDSHIPS?
CERTAINLY NOT!
WELL, RATHER THAN BECOMING A RECLUSE LIKE THOSE TWO, I'LL JUST CHOOSE A FUTURE AT RANDOM.

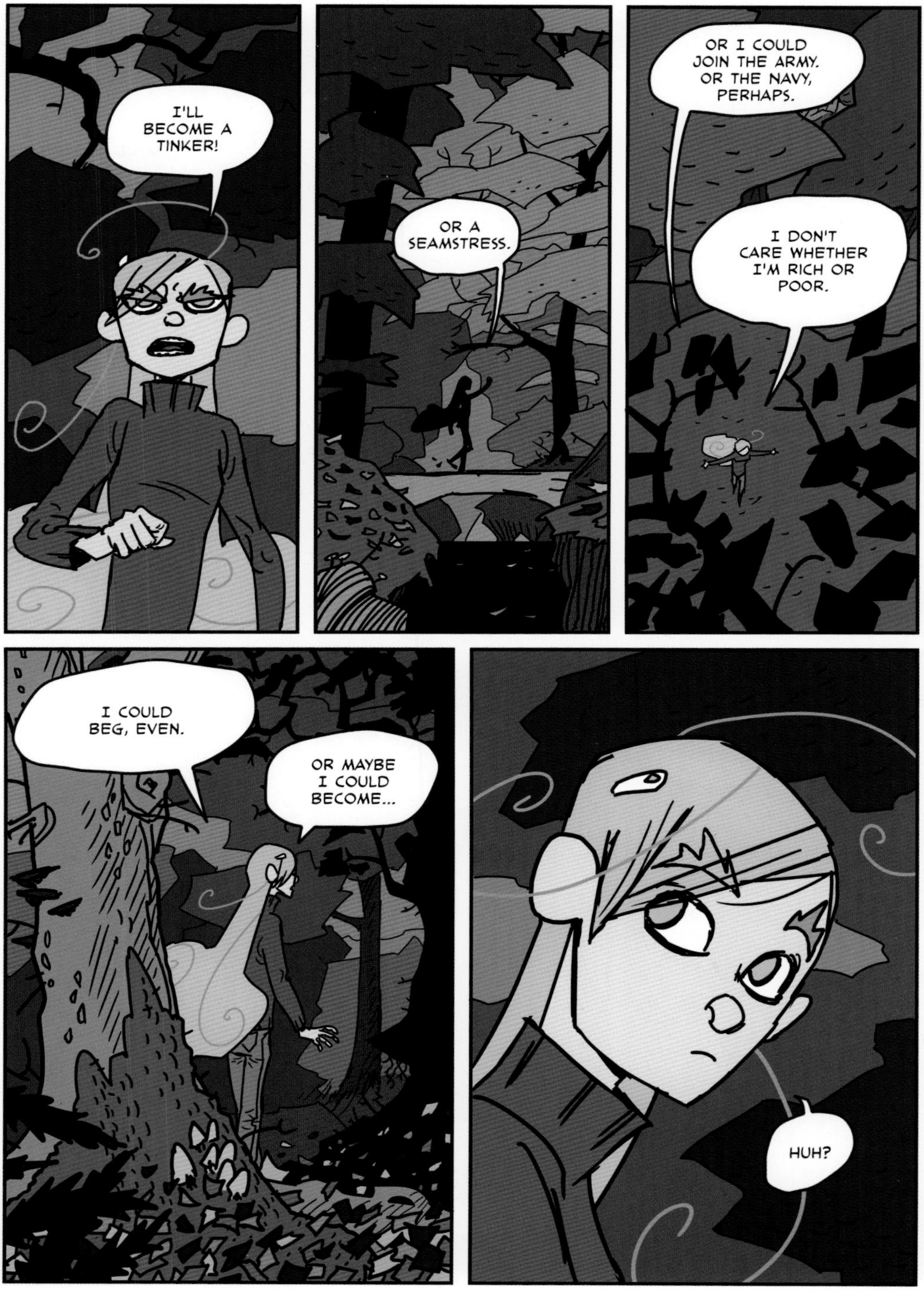
I'LL BECOME A TINKER!
OR A SEAMSTRESS.
OR I COULD JOIN THE ARMY. OR THE NAVY, PERHAPS.
I DON'T CARE WHETHER I'M RICH OR POOR.
I COULD BEG, EVEN.
OR MAYBE I COULD BECOME...
HUH?

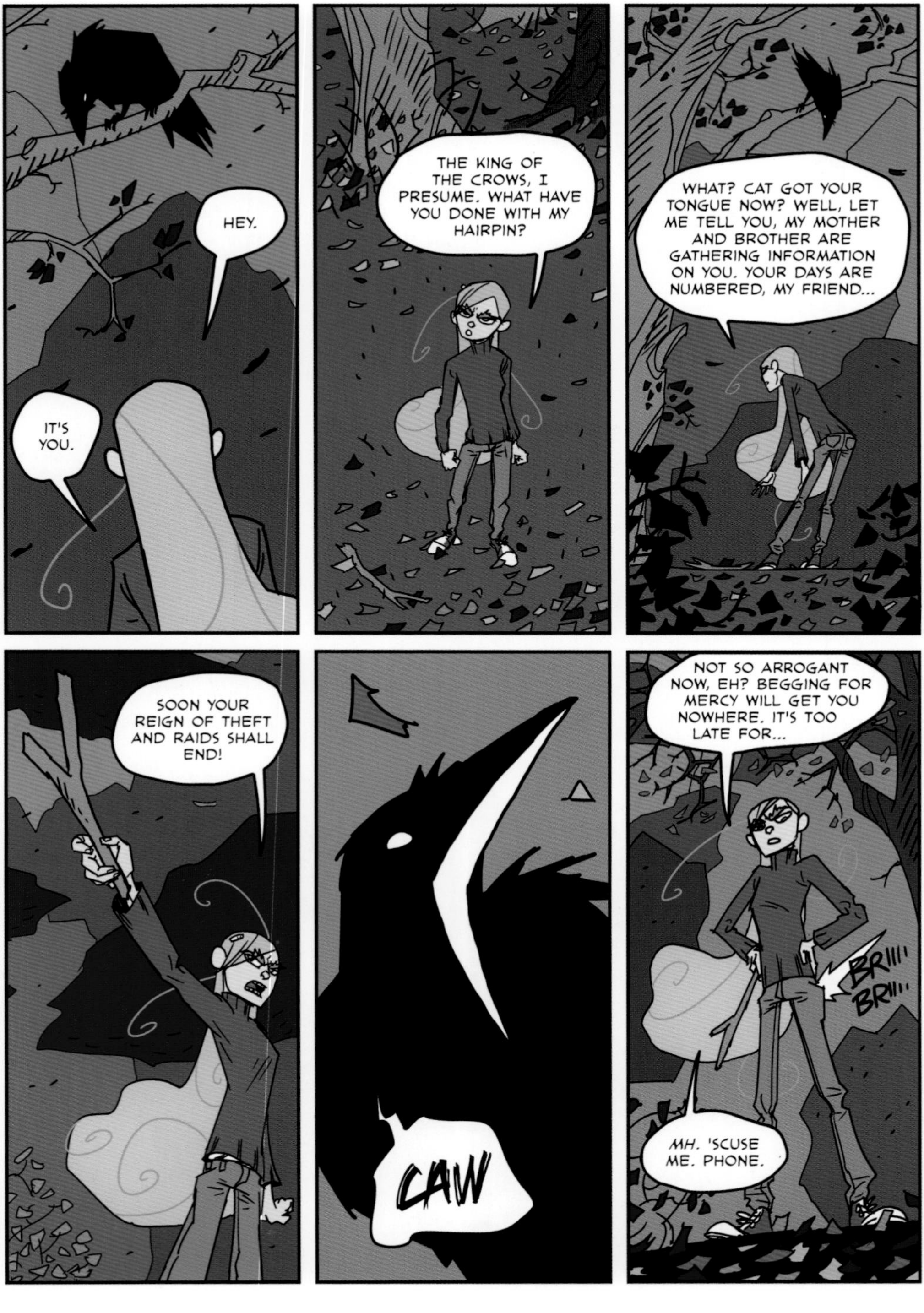
HEY.
IT'S YOU.
THE KING OF THE CROWS, I PRESUME. WHAT HAVE YOU DONE WITH MY HAIRPIN?
WHAT? CAT GOT YOUR TONGUE NOW? WELL, LET ME TELL YOU, MY MOTHER AND BROTHER ARE GATHERING INFORMATION ON YOU. YOUR DAYS ARE NUMBERED, MY FRIEND...
SOON YOUR REIGN OF THEFT AND RAIDS SHALL END!
CAW
NOT SO ARROGANT NOW, EH? BEGGING FOR MERCY WILL GET YOU NOWHERE. IT'S TOO LATE FOR...
BR BR
MH. 'SCUSE ME. PHONE.

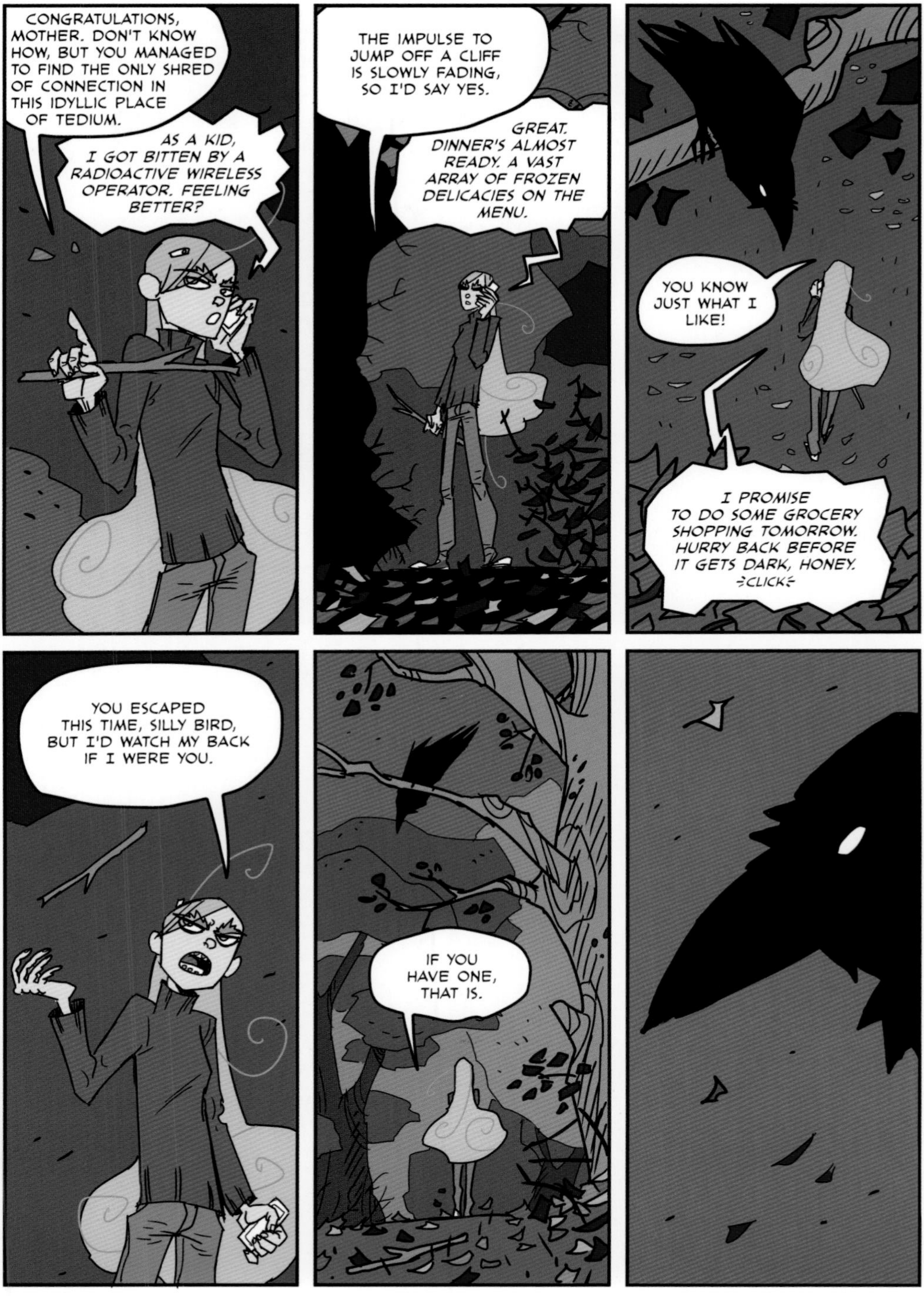
CONGRATULATIONS, MOTHER. DON'T KNOW HOW, BUT YOU MANAGED TO FIND THE ONLY SHRED OF CONNECTION IN THIS IDYLLIC PLACE OF TEDIUM.
AS A KID, I GOT BITTEN BY A RADIOACTIVE WIRELESS OPERATOR. FEELING BETTER?
THE IMPULSE TO JUMP OFF A CLIFF IS SLOWLY FADING, SO I'D SAY YES.
GREAT. DINNER'S ALMOST READY. A VAST ARRAY OF FROZEN DELICACIES ON THE MENU.
YOU KNOW JUST WHAT I LIKE!
I PROMISE TO DO SOME GROCERY SHOPPING TOMORROW. HURRY BACK BEFORE IT GETS DARK, HONEY.
CLICK
YOU ESCAPED THIS TIME, SILLY BIRD, BUT I'D WATCH MY BACK IF I WERE YOU.
IF YOU HAVE ONE, THAT IS.

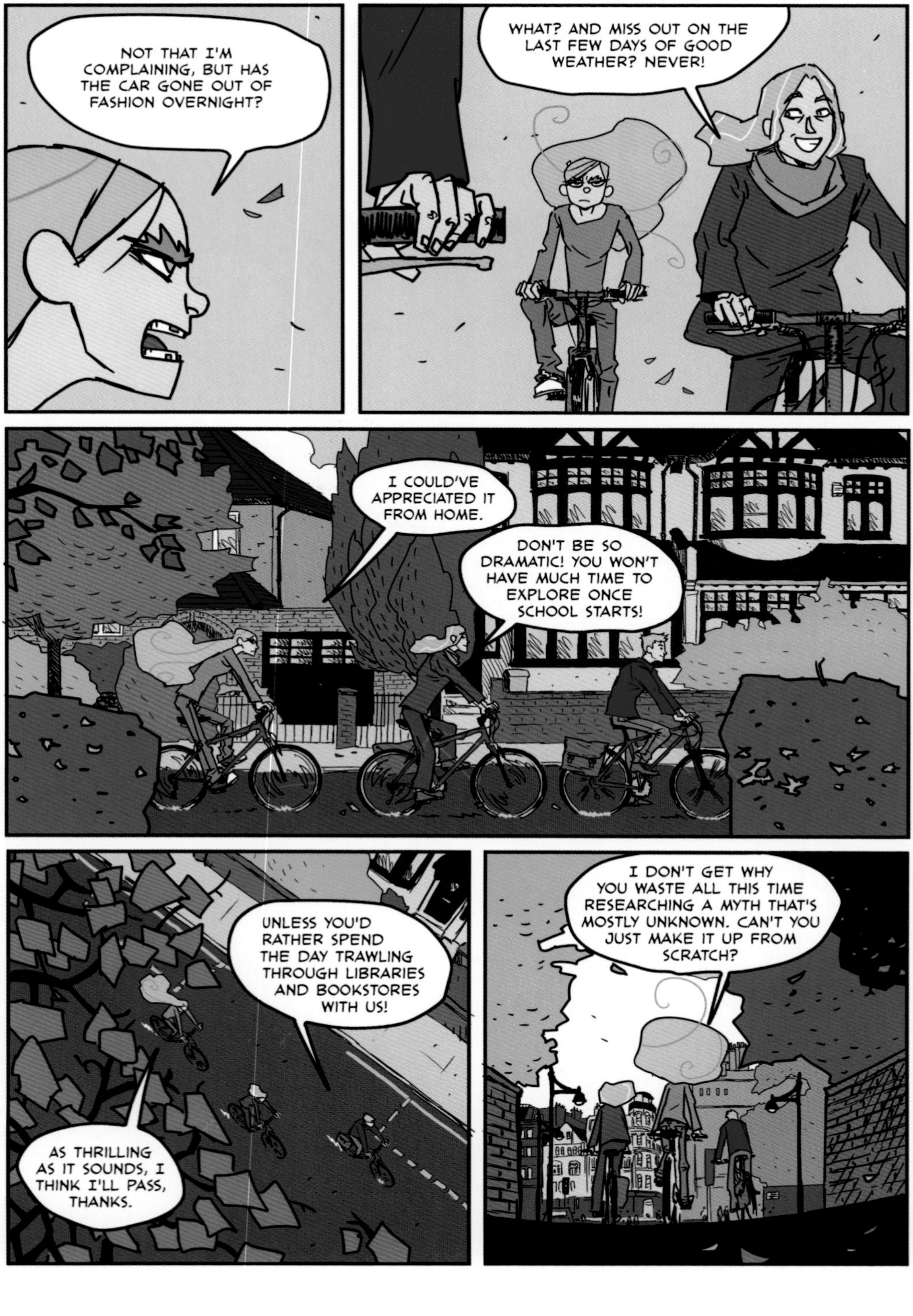
NOT THAT I'M COMPLAINING, BUT HAS THE CAR GONE OUT OF FASHION OVERNIGHT?
WHAT? AND MISS OUT ON THE LAST FEW DAYS OF GOOD WEATHER? NEVER!
I COULD'VE APPRECIATED IT FROM HOME.
DON'T BE SO DRAMATIC! YOU WON'T HAVE MUCH TIME TO EXPLORE ONCE SCHOOL STARTS!
UNLESS YOU'D RATHER SPEND THE DAY TRAWLING THROUGH LIBRARIES AND BOOKSTORES WITH US!
AS THRILLING AS IT SOUNDS, I THINK I'LL PASS, THANKS.
I DON'T GET WHY YOU WASTE ALL THIS TIME RESEARCHING A MYTH THAT'S MOSTLY UNKNOWN. CAN'T YOU JUST MAKE IT UP FROM SCRATCH?

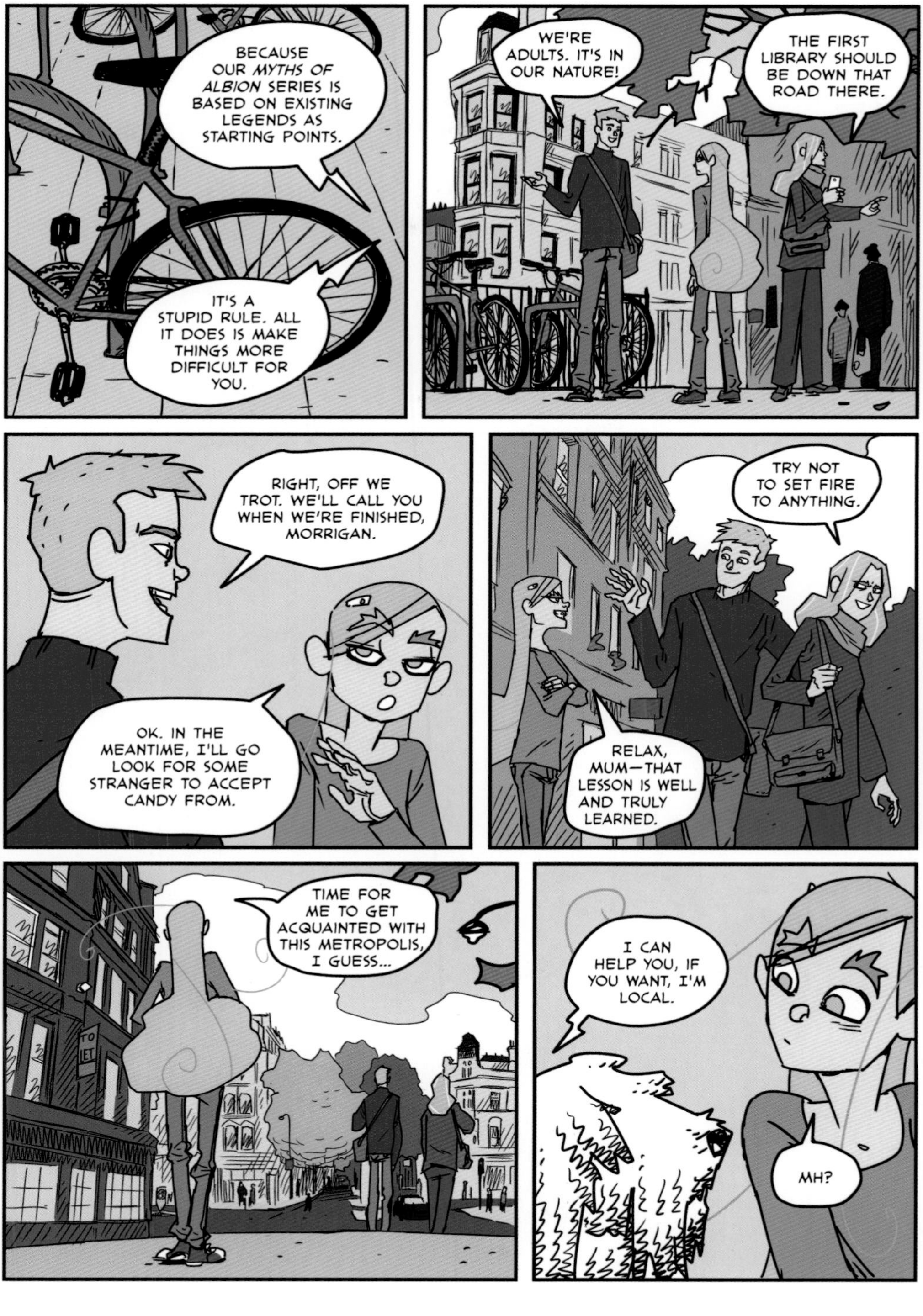
BECAUSE OUR *MYTHS OF ALBION* SERIES IS BASED ON EXISTING LEGENDS AS STARTING POINTS.
IT'S A STUPID RULE. ALL IT DOES IS MAKE THINGS MORE DIFFICULT FOR YOU.
WE'RE ADULTS. IT'S IN OUR NATURE!
THE FIRST LIBRARY SHOULD BE DOWN THAT ROAD THERE.
RIGHT, OFF WE TROT. WE'LL CALL YOU WHEN WE'RE FINISHED, MORRIGAN.
OK. IN THE MEANTIME, I'LL GO LOOK FOR SOME STRANGER TO ACCEPT CANDY FROM.
TRY NOT TO SET FIRE TO ANYTHING.
RELAX, MUM—THAT LESSON IS WELL AND TRULY LEARNED.
TIME FOR ME TO GET ACQUAINTED WITH THIS METROPOLIS, I GUESS...
TO LET
I CAN HELP YOU, IF YOU WANT, I'M LOCAL.
MH?

HI, I'M ALMA. AND THIS ONE HEAVILY TESTING MY ARMS IS DANDELION.
OH, HI, I'M MORRIGAN...
HELLO, DANDELION!
LOOK, I WOULDN'T GET THAT HAND TOO CLOSE...
DOES SHE BITE?
NO.
EWWW!
SLAPP
HEY, AREN'T THOSE SOPHIE AND EDGAR MOORE, THE WRITERS? ARE YOU A RELATIVE?
MM-HM, I HAVE THAT UNPARALLELED HONOR.

YOU DON'T SOUND TOO THRILLED, MORRIGAN. IT SEEMS SO COOL TO ME...

IF WE WERE CHARACTERS IN A FANTASY SAGA, MAYBE. IN REAL LIFE, BEING KNOWN FOR YOUR FAMILY IS JUST SAD.

SO, YOU'LL BE UPSET IF I ASK YOU FOR THEIR AUTOGRAPH? I'M SUCH A BIG FAN. I HAVE ALL THEIR NOVELS, THEIR SHORT STORIES, AND EVEN THAT POP-UP BOOK THAT CAME OUT LAST YEAR...

NAH, NO SWEAT. IT DEPENDS ON HOW MUCH CASH YOU'RE WILLING TO PART FROM!

OH! ER...OK, HOW MUCH DO YOU THINK...

I'M JUST TEASING YOU! I SUPPOSE YOU COULD POINT ME IN THE DIRECTION OF A DRINK, THOUGH. I'VE BEEN RIDING FOR LIKE A ZILLION MILES.

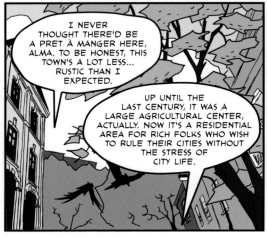

I NEVER THOUGHT THERE'D BE A PRET À MANGER HERE, ALMA. TO BE HONEST, THIS TOWN'S A LOT LESS... RUSTIC THAN I EXPECTED.

UP UNTIL THE LAST CENTURY, IT WAS A LARGE AGRICULTURAL CENTER, ACTUALLY. NOW IT'S A RESIDENTIAL AREA FOR RICH FOLKS WHO WISH TO RULE THEIR CITIES WITHOUT THE STRESS OF CITY LIFE.

DANDELION BELONGS TO THE WIFE OF A MEMBER OF PARLIAMENT, HIS PEDIGREE DATES BACK TO THE DAWN OF TIME. YOU'VE GOT NO IDEA HOW MUCH THEY PAY ME TO DOG-SIT, I FEEL ALMOST GUILTY.

THERE ARE WORSE WAYS TO EARN YOUR MONEY. WRITE NOVELS, FOR INSTANCE!

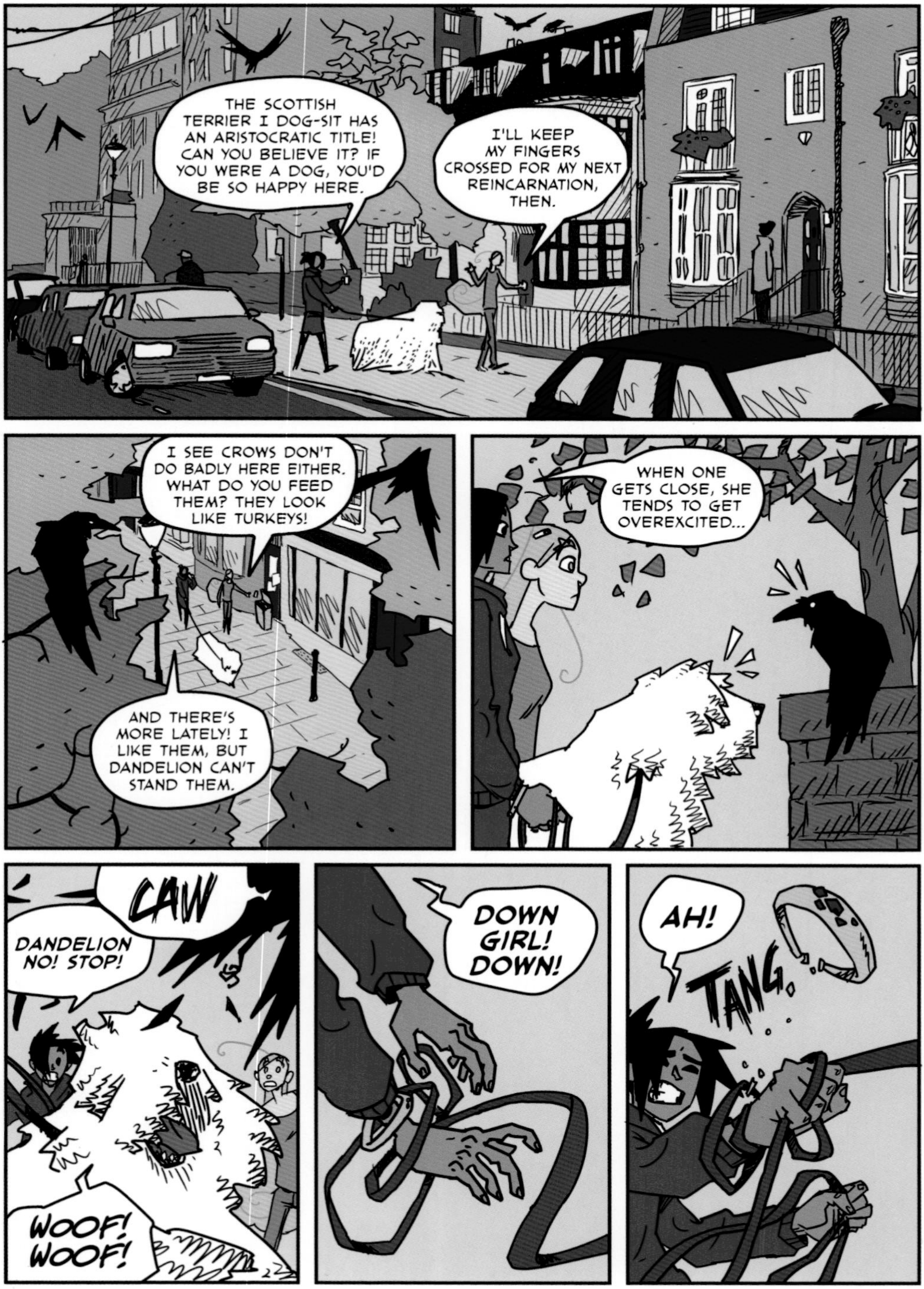
THE SCOTTISH TERRIER I DOG-SIT HAS AN ARISTOCRATIC TITLE! CAN YOU BELIEVE IT? IF YOU WERE A DOG, YOU'D BE SO HAPPY HERE.
I'LL KEEP MY FINGERS CROSSED FOR MY NEXT REINCARNATION, THEN.
I SEE CROWS DON'T DO BADLY HERE EITHER. WHAT DO YOU FEED THEM? THEY LOOK LIKE TURKEYS!
AND THERE'S MORE LATELY! I LIKE THEM, BUT DANDELION CAN'T STAND THEM.
WHEN ONE GETS CLOSE, SHE TENDS TO GET OVEREXCITED...
CAW
DANDELION NO! STOP!
WOOF! WOOF!
DOWN GIRL! DOWN!
AH!
TANG

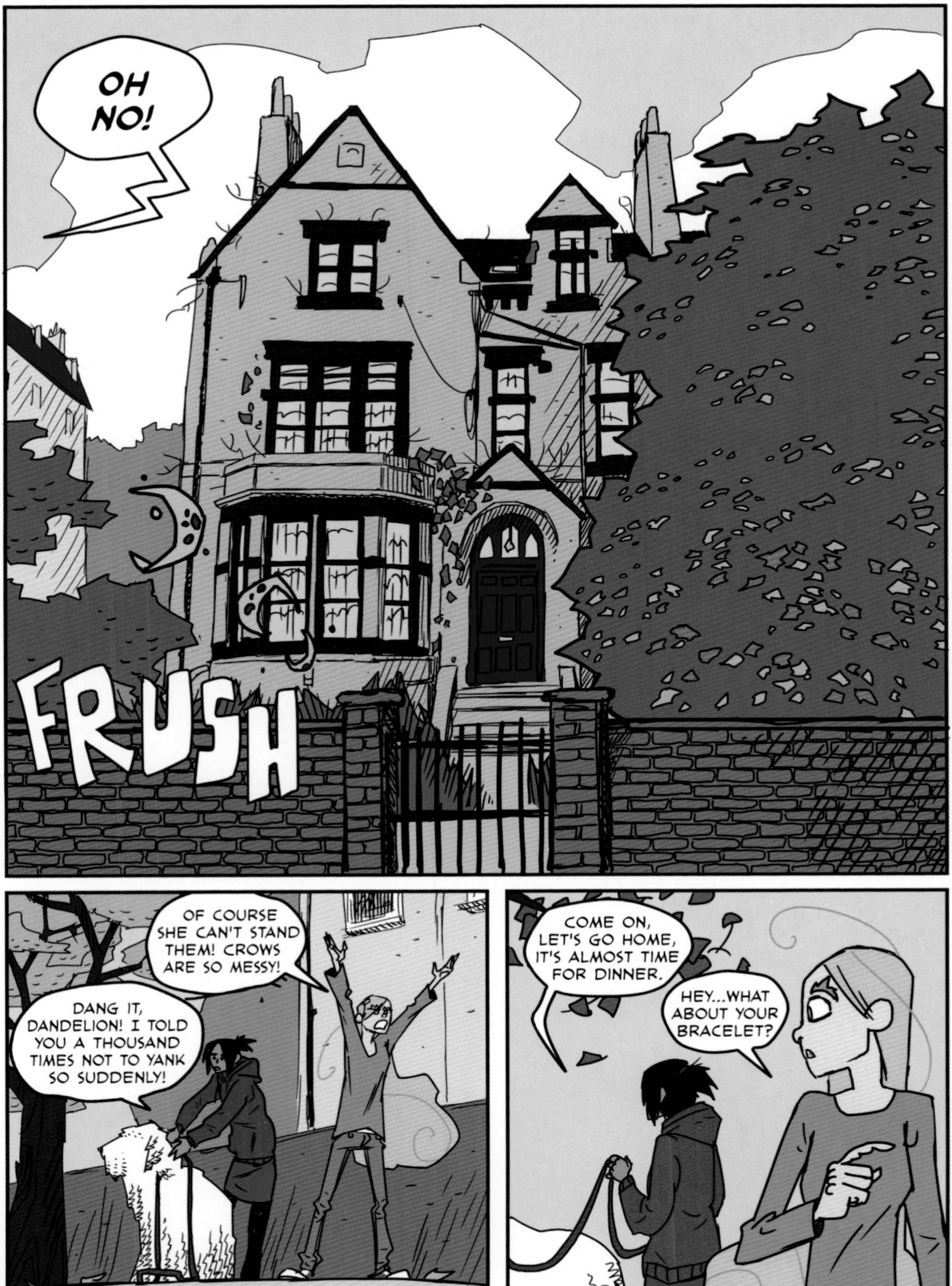
OH NO!
FRUSH
DANG IT, DANDELION! I TOLD YOU A THOUSAND TIMES NOT TO YANK SO SUDDENLY!
OF COURSE SHE CAN'T STAND THEM! CROWS ARE SO MESSY!
COME ON, LET'S GO HOME, IT'S ALMOST TIME FOR DINNER.
HEY...WHAT ABOUT YOUR BRACELET?

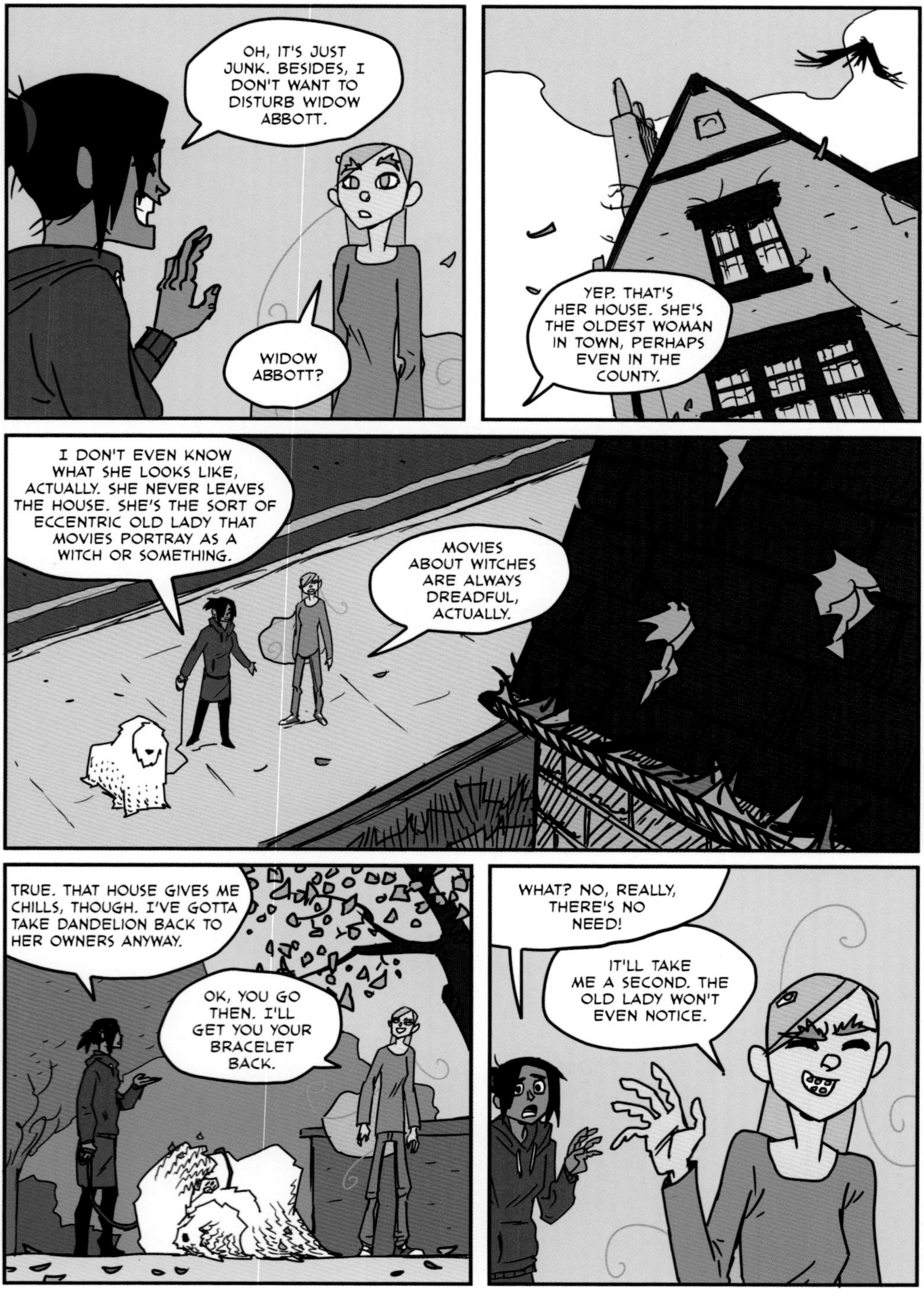
OH, IT'S JUST JUNK. BESIDES, I DON'T WANT TO DISTURB WIDOW ABBOTT.
WIDOW ABBOTT?
YEP. THAT'S HER HOUSE. SHE'S THE OLDEST WOMAN IN TOWN, PERHAPS EVEN IN THE COUNTY.
I DON'T EVEN KNOW WHAT SHE LOOKS LIKE, ACTUALLY. SHE NEVER LEAVES THE HOUSE. SHE'S THE SORT OF ECCENTRIC OLD LADY THAT MOVIES PORTRAY AS A WITCH OR SOMETHING.
MOVIES ABOUT WITCHES ARE ALWAYS DREADFUL, ACTUALLY.
TRUE. THAT HOUSE GIVES ME CHILLS, THOUGH. I'VE GOTTA TAKE DANDELION BACK TO HER OWNERS ANYWAY.
OK, YOU GO THEN. I'LL GET YOU YOUR BRACELET BACK.
WHAT? NO, REALLY, THERE'S NO NEED!
IT'LL TAKE ME A SECOND. THE OLD LADY WON'T EVEN NOTICE.

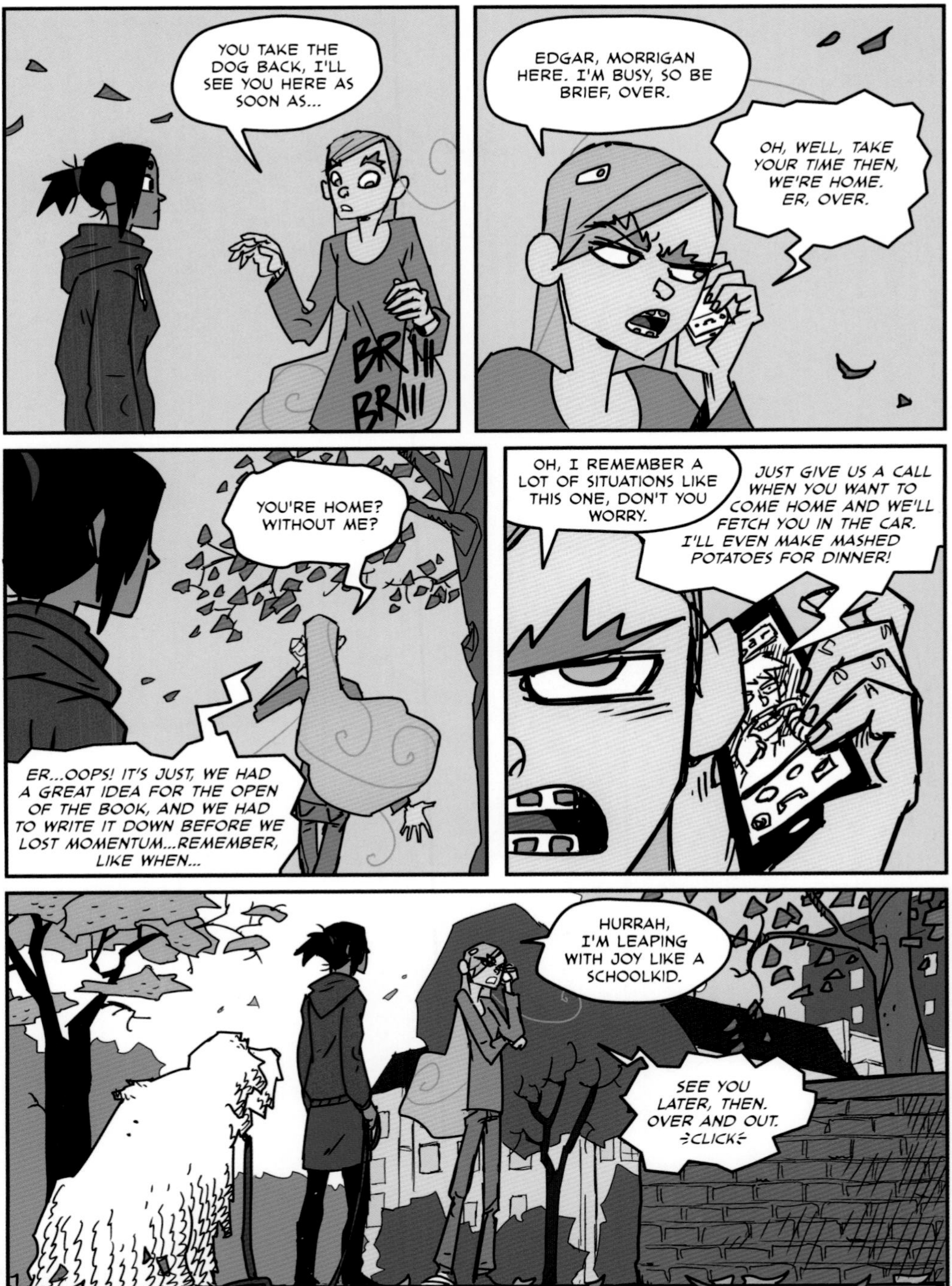

YOU TAKE THE DOG BACK, I'LL SEE YOU HERE AS SOON AS...
BRIII BRIII
EDGAR, MORRIGAN HERE. I'M BUSY, SO BE BRIEF, OVER.
OH, WELL, TAKE YOUR TIME THEN, WE'RE HOME. ER, OVER.
YOU'RE HOME? WITHOUT ME?
ER...OOPS! IT'S JUST, WE HAD A GREAT IDEA FOR THE OPEN OF THE BOOK, AND WE HAD TO WRITE IT DOWN BEFORE WE LOST MOMENTUM...REMEMBER, LIKE WHEN...
OH, I REMEMBER A LOT OF SITUATIONS LIKE THIS ONE, DON'T YOU WORRY.
JUST GIVE US A CALL WHEN YOU WANT TO COME HOME AND WE'LL FETCH YOU IN THE CAR. I'LL EVEN MAKE MASHED POTATOES FOR DINNER!
HURRAH, I'M LEAPING WITH JOY LIKE A SCHOOLKID.
SEE YOU LATER, THEN. OVER AND OUT.
CLICK

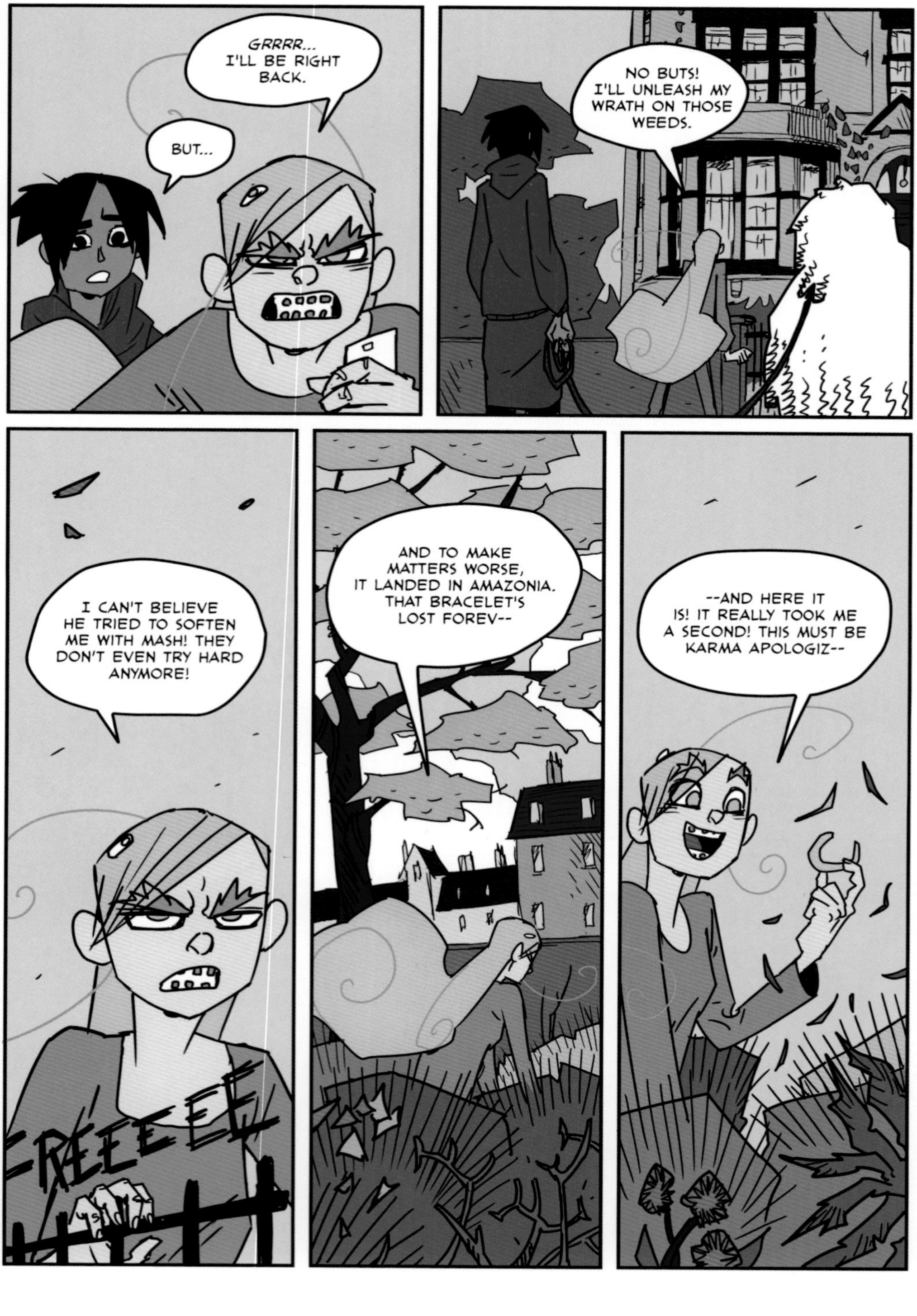
GRRRR... I'LL BE RIGHT BACK.
BUT...
NO BUTS! I'LL UNLEASH MY WRATH ON THOSE WEEDS.
I CAN'T BELIEVE HE TRIED TO SOFTEN ME WITH MASH! THEY DON'T EVEN TRY HARD ANYMORE!
FREEEEE
AND TO MAKE MATTERS WORSE, IT LANDED IN AMAZONIA. THAT BRACELET'S LOST FOREV--
--AND HERE IT IS! IT REALLY TOOK ME A SECOND! THIS MUST BE KARMA APOLOGIZ--

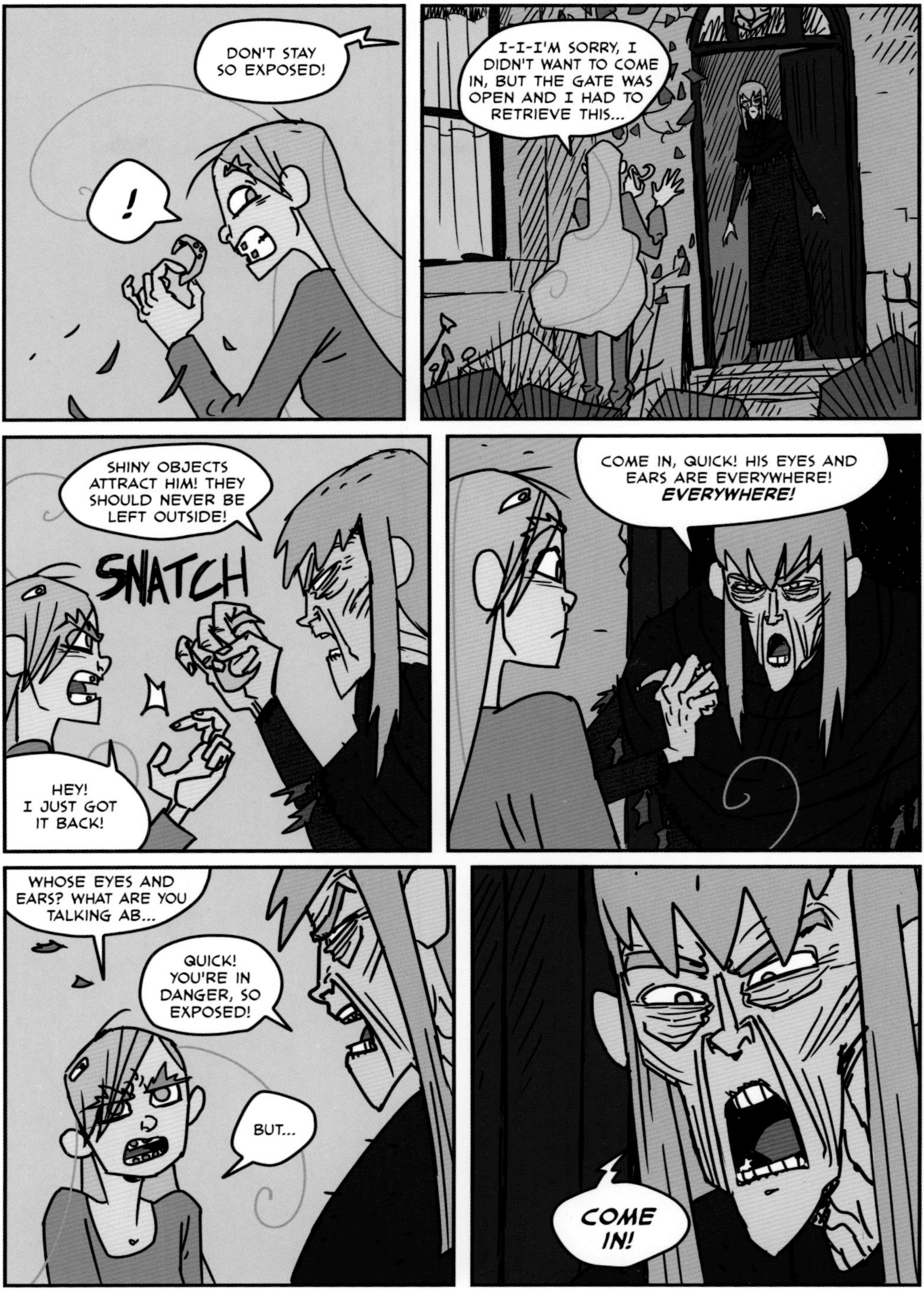
DON'T STAY SO EXPOSED!
!
I-I-I'M SORRY, I DIDN'T WANT TO COME IN, BUT THE GATE WAS OPEN AND I HAD TO RETRIEVE THIS...
SHINY OBJECTS ATTRACT HIM! THEY SHOULD NEVER BE LEFT OUTSIDE!
SNATCH
HEY! I JUST GOT IT BACK!
COME IN, QUICK! HIS EYES AND EARS ARE EVERYWHERE! ***EVERYWHERE!***
WHOSE EYES AND EARS? WHAT ARE YOU TALKING AB...
QUICK! YOU'RE IN DANGER, SO EXPOSED!
BUT...
COME IN!

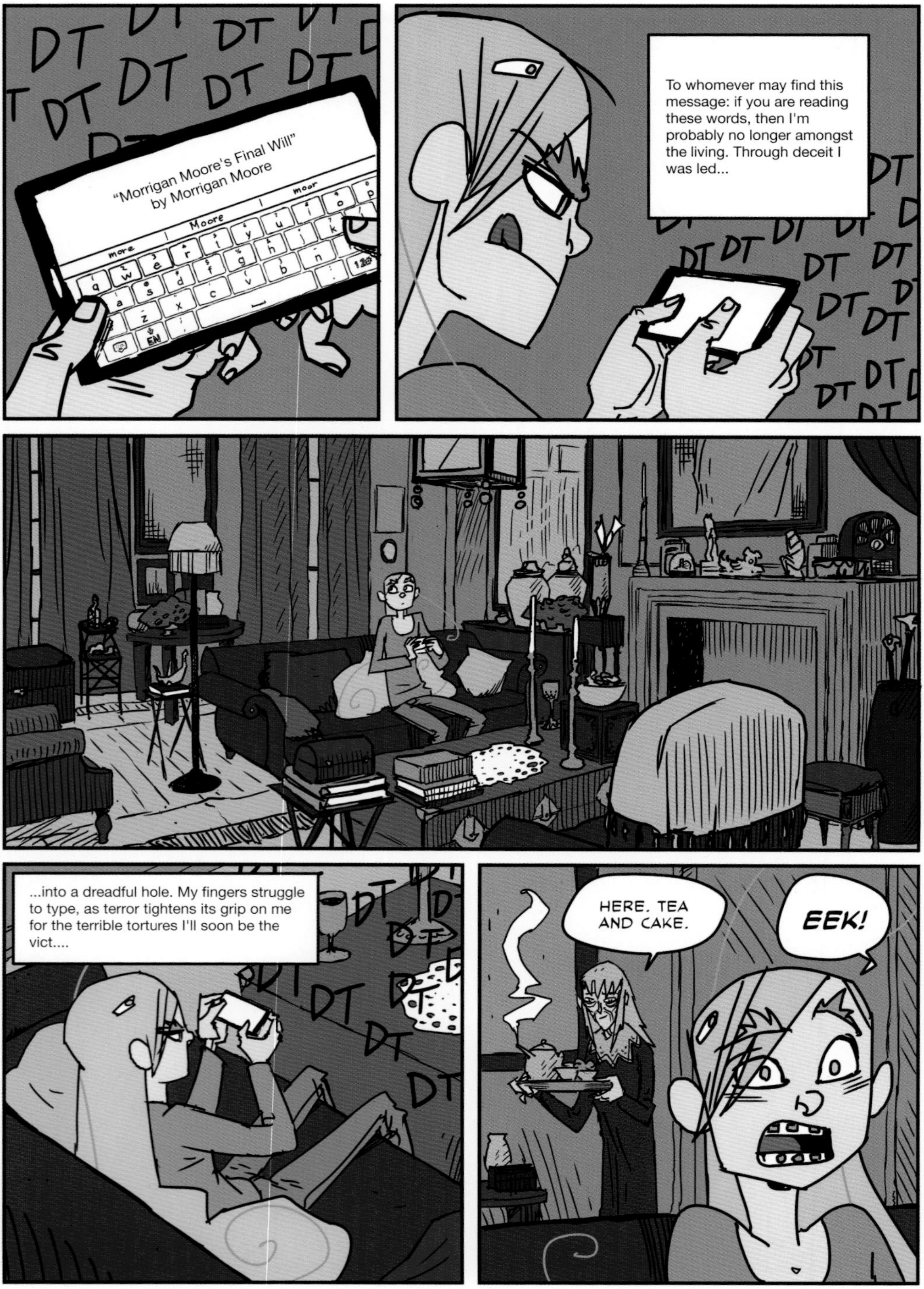
DT DT DT
"Morrigan Moore's Final Will"
by Morrigan Moore
To whomever may find this message: if you are reading these words, then I'm probably no longer amongst the living. Through deceit I was led...
DT DT DT
...into a dreadful hole. My fingers struggle to type, as terror tightens its grip on me for the terrible tortures I'll soon be the vict....
DT DT DT
HERE. TEA AND CAKE.
EEK!

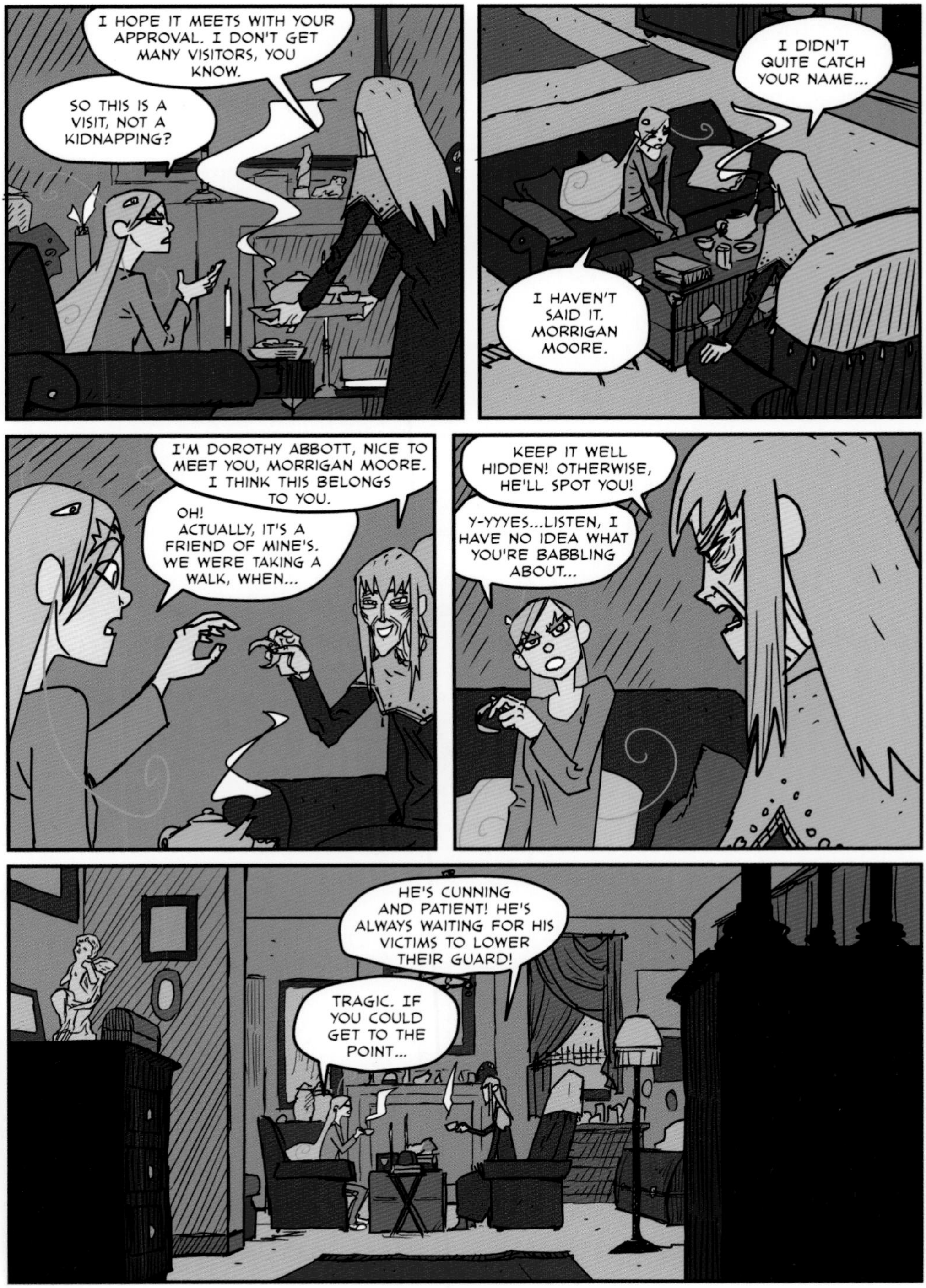
I HOPE IT MEETS WITH YOUR APPROVAL. I DON'T GET MANY VISITORS, YOU KNOW.
SO THIS IS A VISIT, NOT A KIDNAPPING?
I DIDN'T QUITE CATCH YOUR NAME...
I HAVEN'T SAID IT. MORRIGAN MOORE.
I'M DOROTHY ABBOTT, NICE TO MEET YOU, MORRIGAN MOORE. I THINK THIS BELONGS TO YOU.
OH! ACTUALLY, IT'S A FRIEND OF MINE'S. WE WERE TAKING A WALK, WHEN...
KEEP IT WELL HIDDEN! OTHERWISE, HE'LL SPOT YOU!
Y-YYYES...LISTEN, I HAVE NO IDEA WHAT YOU'RE BABBLING ABOUT...
HE'S CUNNING AND PATIENT! HE'S ALWAYS WAITING FOR HIS VICTIMS TO LOWER THEIR GUARD!
TRAGIC. IF YOU COULD GET TO THE POINT...

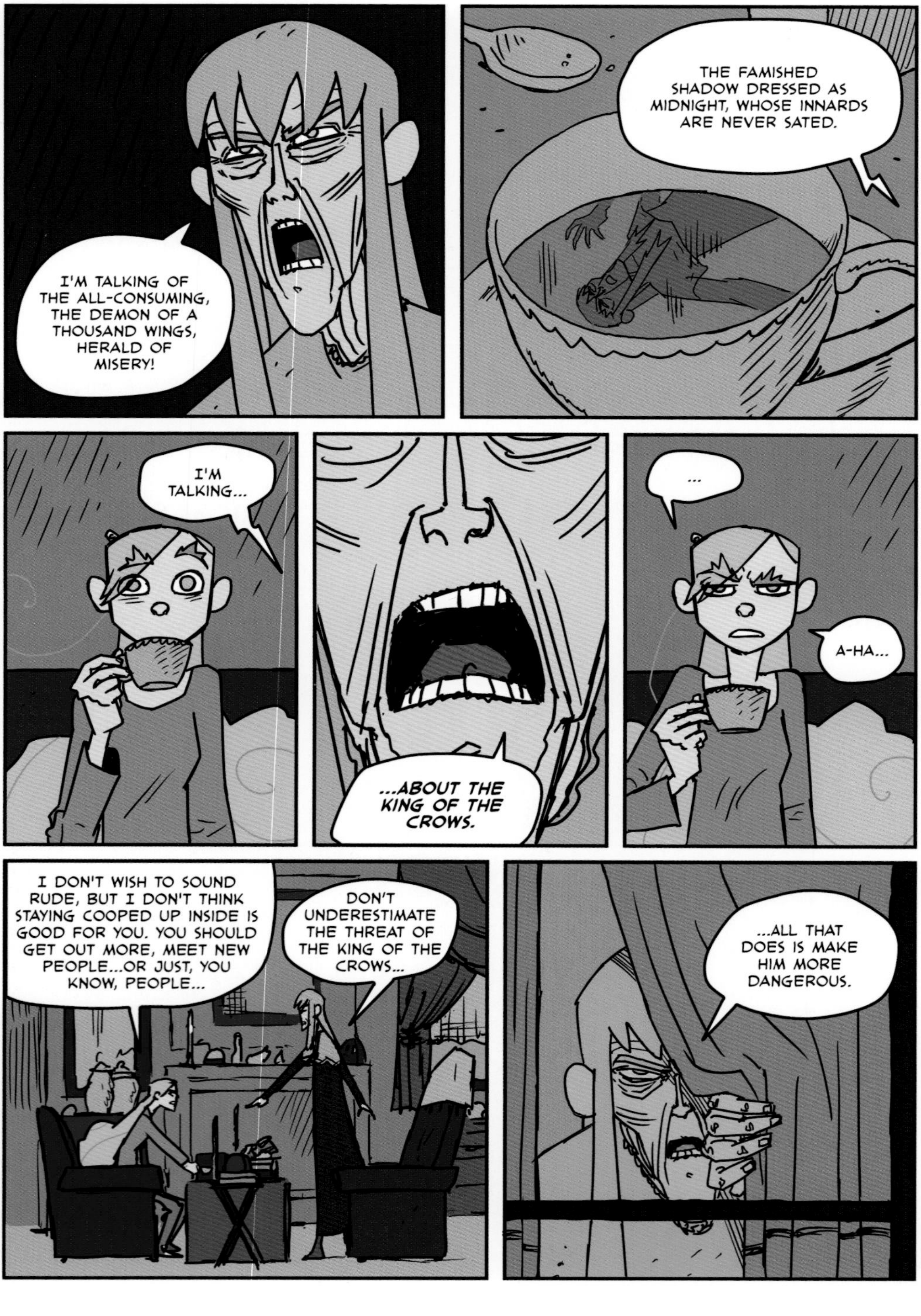
I'M TALKING OF THE ALL-CONSUMING, THE DEMON OF A THOUSAND WINGS, HERALD OF MISERY!
THE FAMISHED SHADOW DRESSED AS MIDNIGHT, WHOSE INNARDS ARE NEVER SATED.
I'M TALKING...
...ABOUT THE KING OF THE CROWS.
...
A-HA...
I DON'T WISH TO SOUND RUDE, BUT I DON'T THINK STAYING COOPED UP INSIDE IS GOOD FOR YOU. YOU SHOULD GET OUT MORE, MEET NEW PEOPLE...OR JUST, YOU KNOW, PEOPLE...
DON'T UNDERESTIMATE THE THREAT OF THE KING OF THE CROWS...
...ALL THAT DOES IS MAKE HIM MORE DANGEROUS.

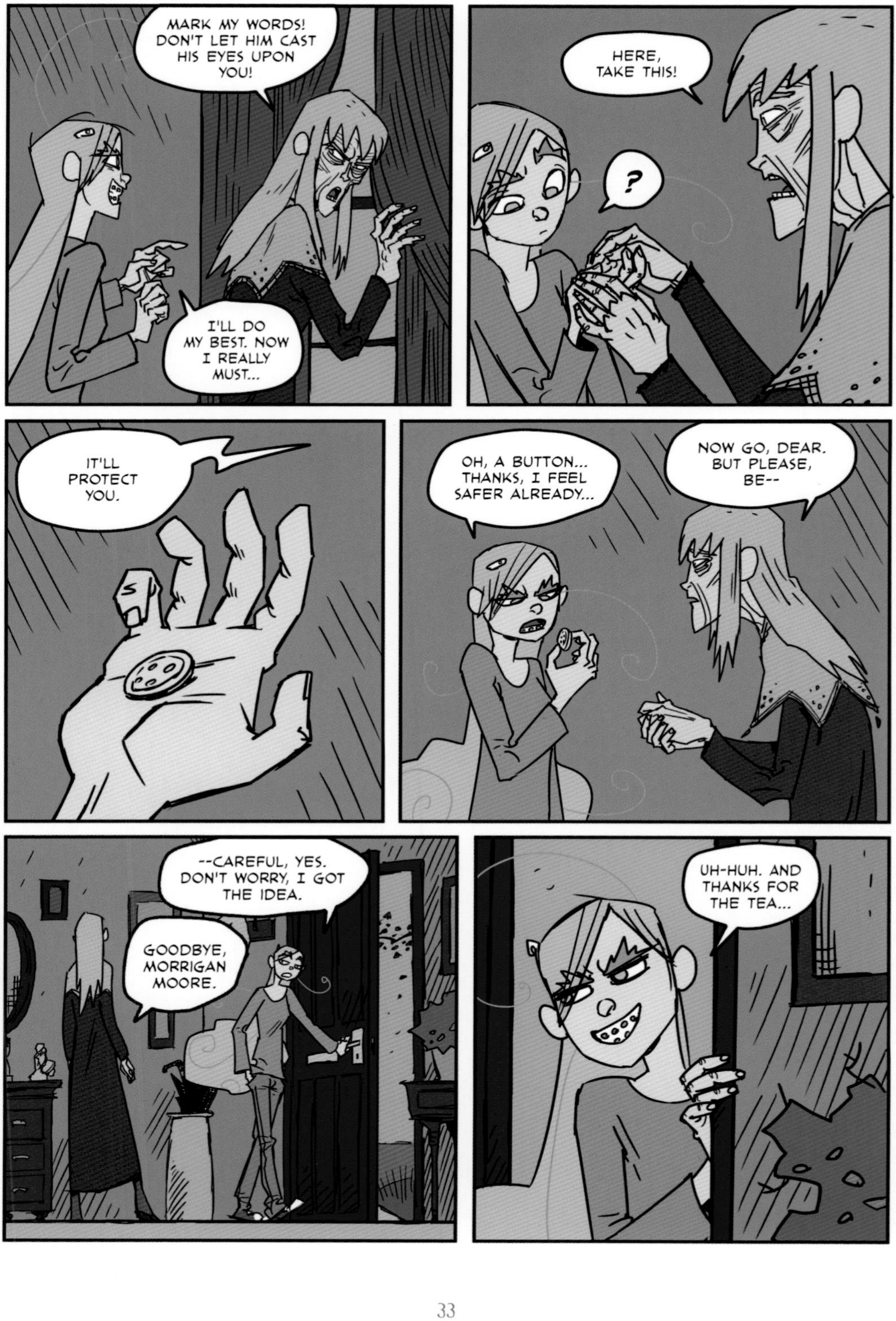
MARK MY WORDS! DON'T LET HIM CAST HIS EYES UPON YOU!
I'LL DO MY BEST. NOW I REALLY MUST...
HERE, TAKE THIS!
?
IT'LL PROTECT YOU.
OH, A BUTTON... THANKS, I FEEL SAFER ALREADY...
NOW GO, DEAR. BUT PLEASE, BE--
--CAREFUL, YES. DON'T WORRY, I GOT THE IDEA.
GOODBYE, MORRIGAN MOORE.
UH-HUH. AND THANKS FOR THE TEA...

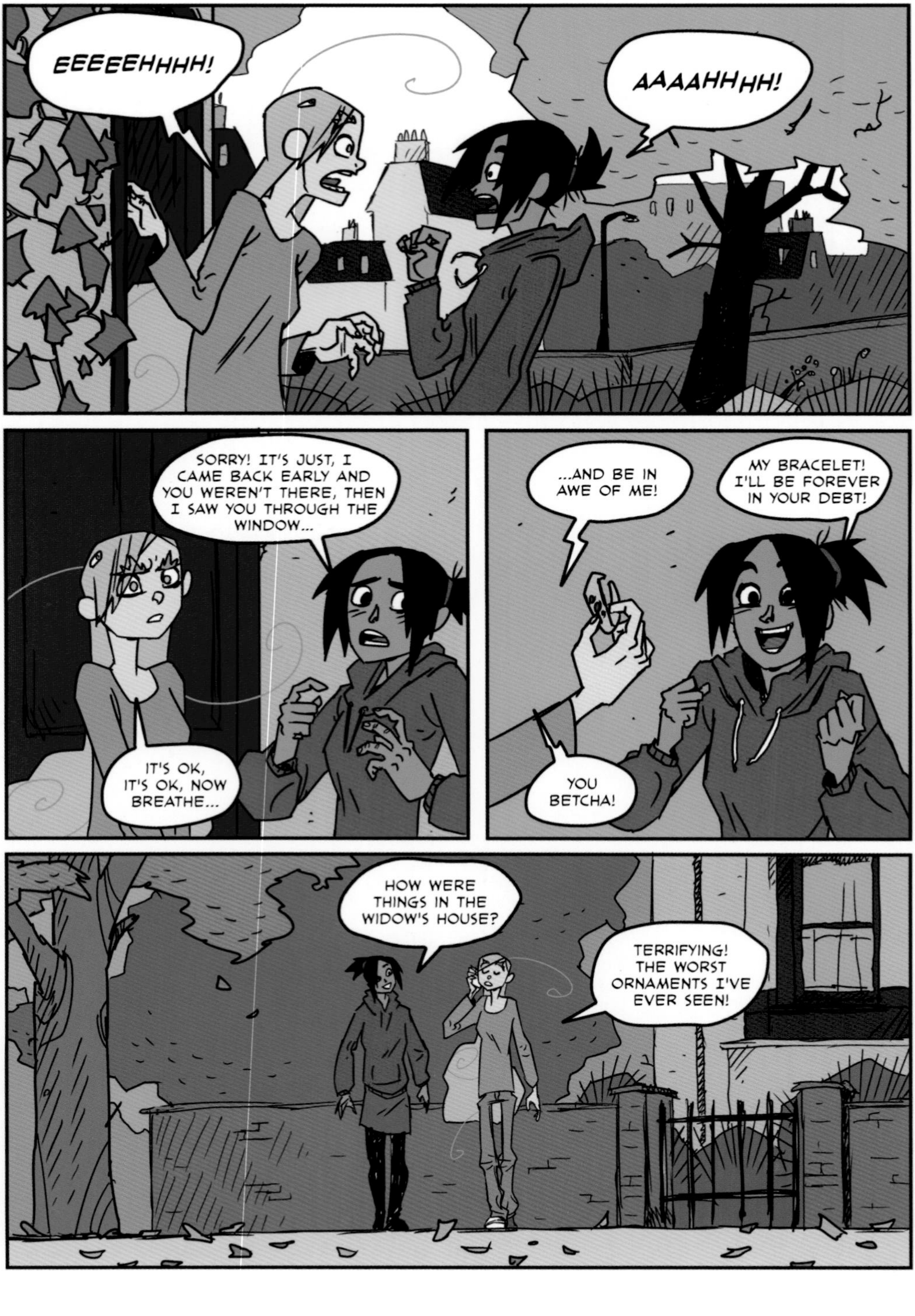
EEEEEHHHH!
AAAAHHHH!
SORRY! IT'S JUST, I CAME BACK EARLY AND YOU WEREN'T THERE, THEN I SAW YOU THROUGH THE WINDOW...
IT'S OK, IT'S OK, NOW BREATHE...
MY BRACELET! I'LL BE FOREVER IN YOUR DEBT!
YOU BETCHA!
...AND BE IN AWE OF ME!
HOW WERE THINGS IN THE WIDOW'S HOUSE?
TERRIFYING! THE WORST ORNAMENTS I'VE EVER SEEN!

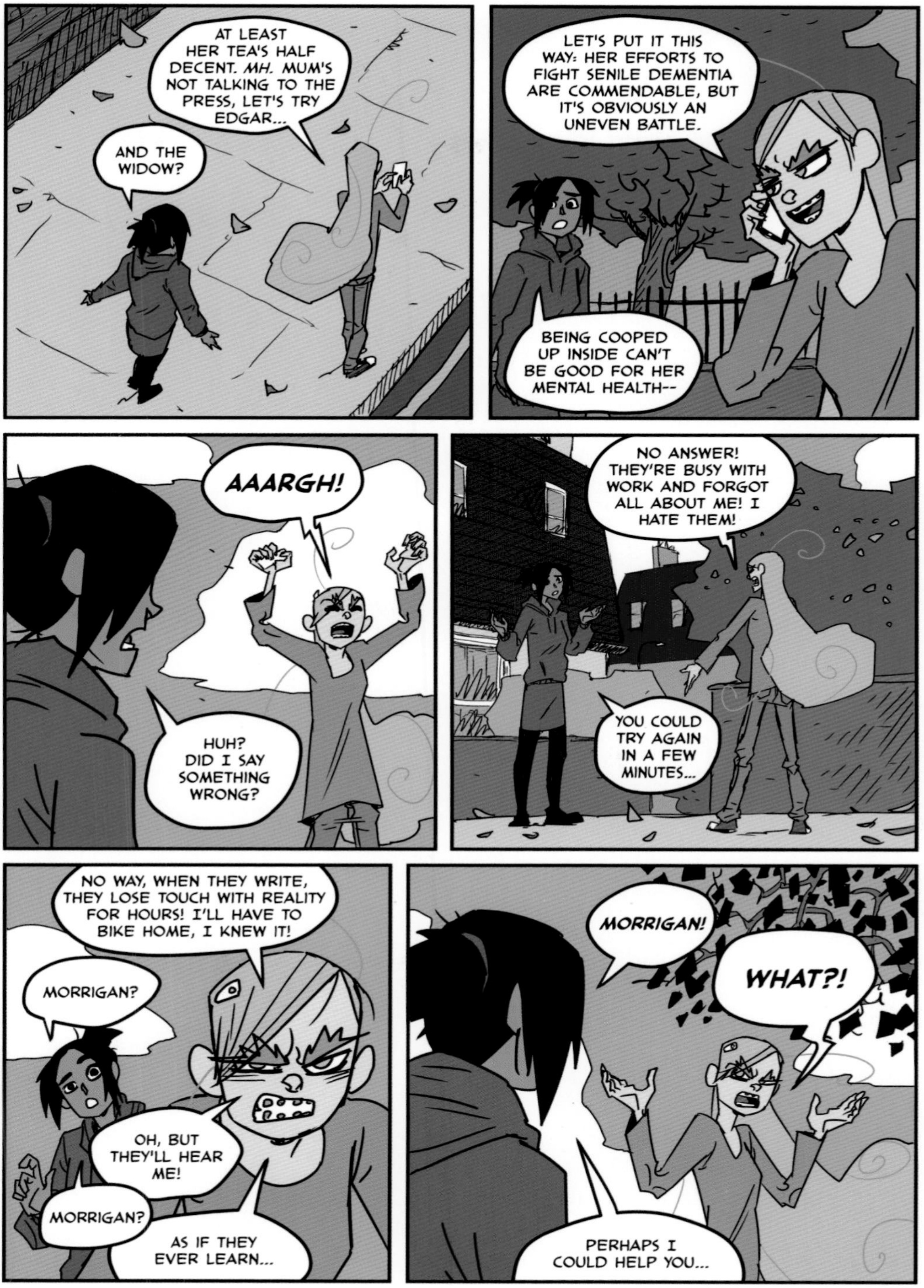
AT LEAST HER TEA'S HALF DECENT. *MH.* MUM'S NOT TALKING TO THE PRESS, LET'S TRY EDGAR...
AND THE WIDOW?
LET'S PUT IT THIS WAY: HER EFFORTS TO FIGHT SENILE DEMENTIA ARE COMMENDABLE, BUT IT'S OBVIOUSLY AN UNEVEN BATTLE.
BEING COOPED UP INSIDE CAN'T BE GOOD FOR HER MENTAL HEALTH--
AAARGH!
HUH? DID I SAY SOMETHING WRONG?
NO ANSWER! THEY'RE BUSY WITH WORK AND FORGOT ALL ABOUT ME! I HATE THEM!
YOU COULD TRY AGAIN IN A FEW MINUTES...
NO WAY, WHEN THEY WRITE, THEY LOSE TOUCH WITH REALITY FOR HOURS! I'LL HAVE TO BIKE HOME, I KNEW IT!
MORRIGAN?
OH, BUT THEY'LL HEAR ME!
MORRIGAN?
AS IF THEY EVER LEARN...
MORRIGAN!
WHAT?!
PERHAPS I COULD HELP YOU...

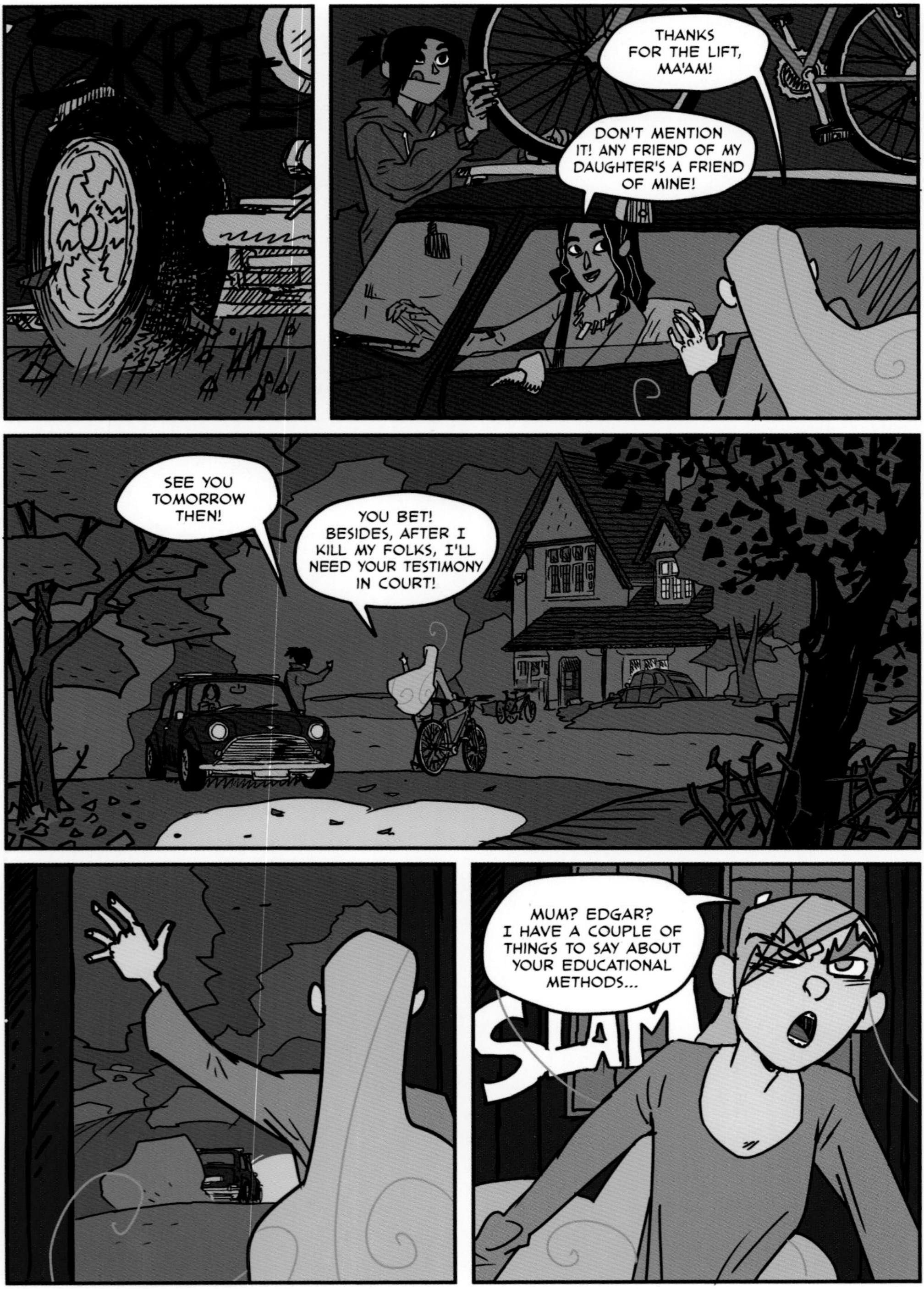
SKREE
THANKS FOR THE LIFT, MA'AM!
DON'T MENTION IT! ANY FRIEND OF MY DAUGHTER'S A FRIEND OF MINE!
SEE YOU TOMORROW THEN!
YOU BET! BESIDES, AFTER I KILL MY FOLKS, I'LL NEED YOUR TESTIMONY IN COURT!
MUM? EDGAR? I HAVE A COUPLE OF THINGS TO SAY ABOUT YOUR EDUCATIONAL METHODS...
SLAM

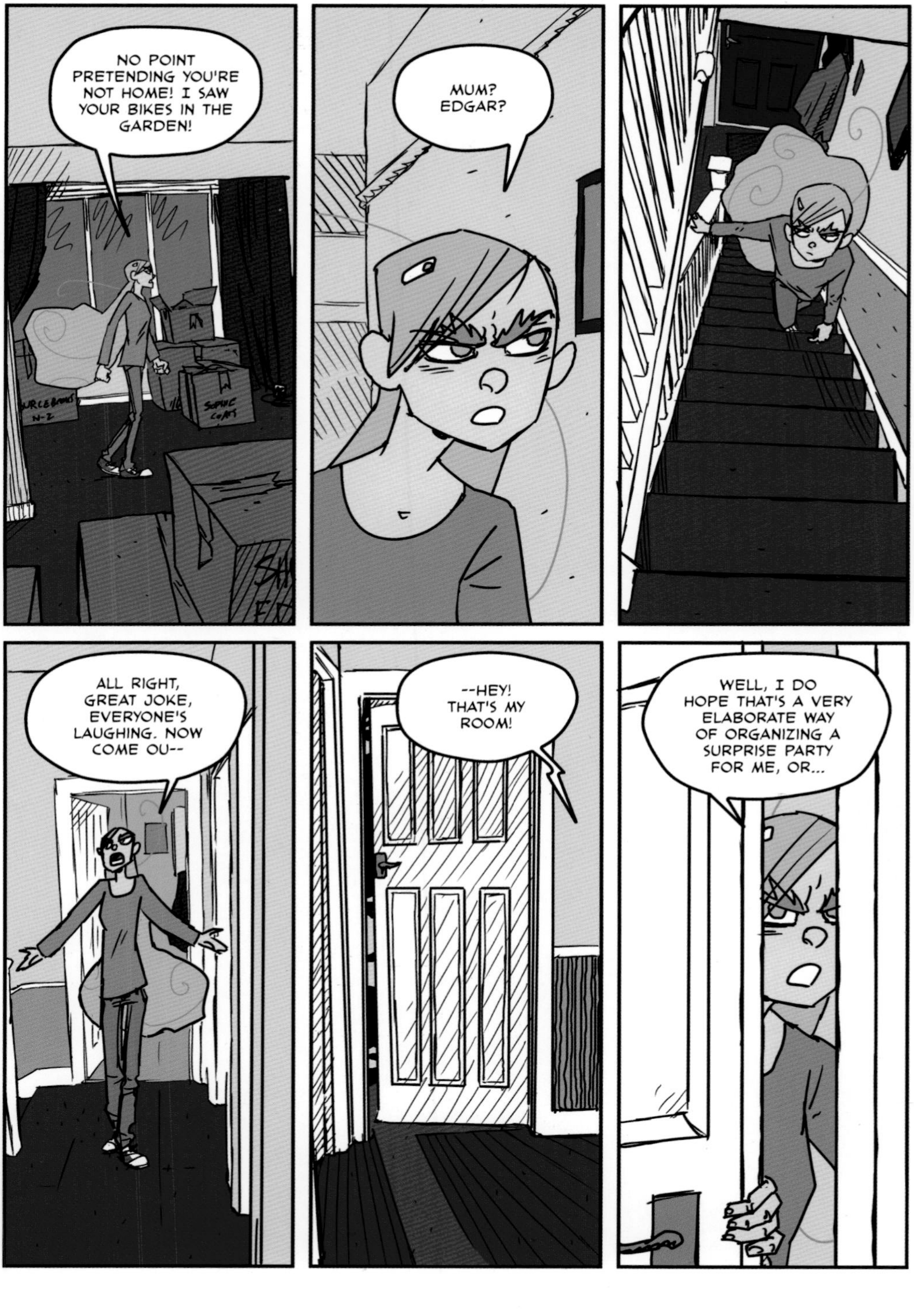
NO POINT PRETENDING YOU'RE NOT HOME! I SAW YOUR BIKES IN THE GARDEN!
MUM? EDGAR?
ALL RIGHT, GREAT JOKE, EVERYONE'S LAUGHING. NOW COME OU--
--HEY! THAT'S MY ROOM!
WELL, I DO HOPE THAT'S A VERY ELABORATE WAY OF ORGANIZING A SURPRISE PARTY FOR ME, OR...

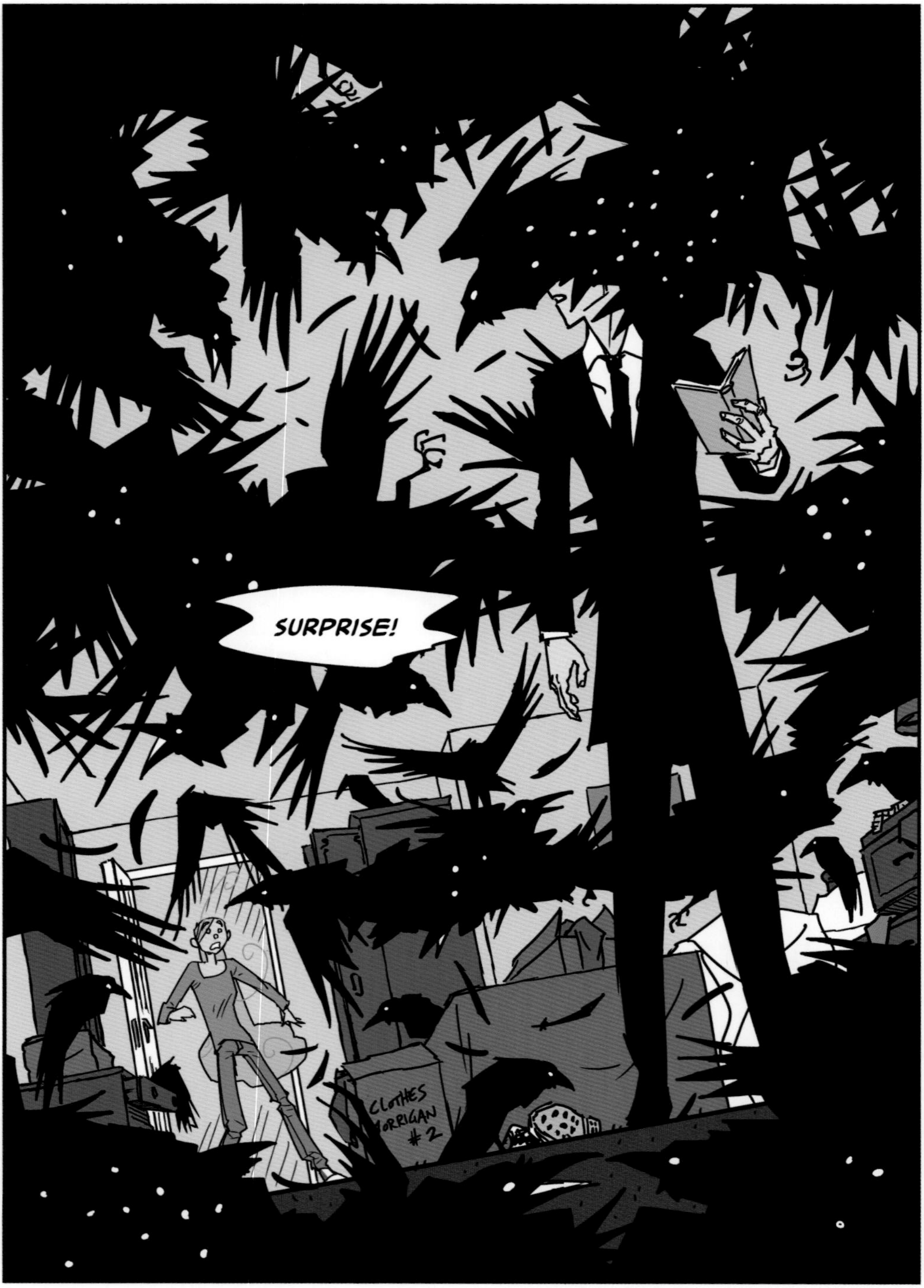
SURPRISE!
CLOTHES
MORRIGAN
#2

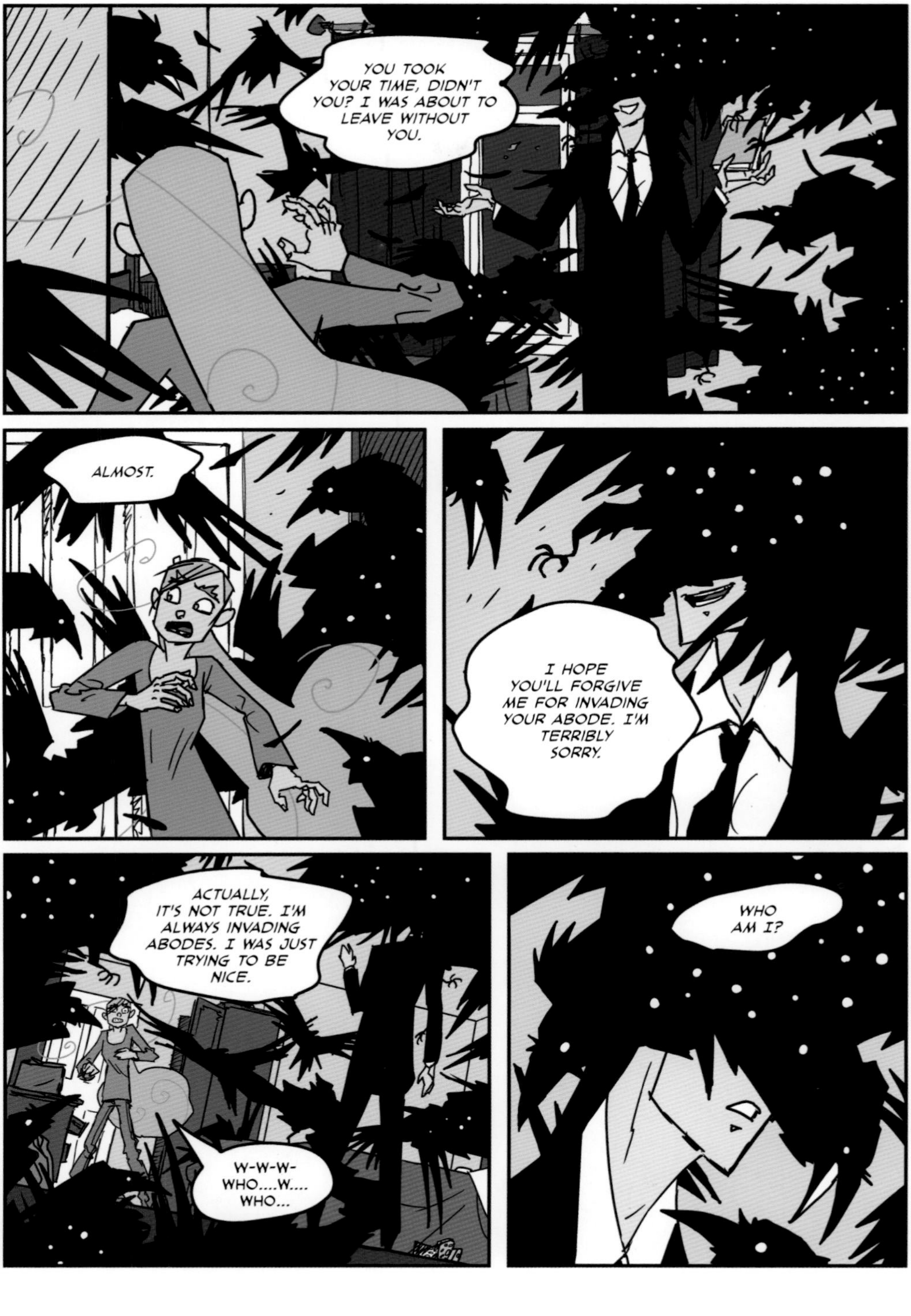
YOU TOOK YOUR TIME, DIDN'T YOU? I WAS ABOUT TO LEAVE WITHOUT YOU.
ALMOST.
I HOPE YOU'LL FORGIVE ME FOR INVADING YOUR ABODE. I'M TERRIBLY SORRY.
ACTUALLY, IT'S NOT TRUE. I'M ALWAYS INVADING ABODES. I WAS JUST TRYING TO BE NICE.
W-W-W- WHO....W.... WHO...
WHO AM I?

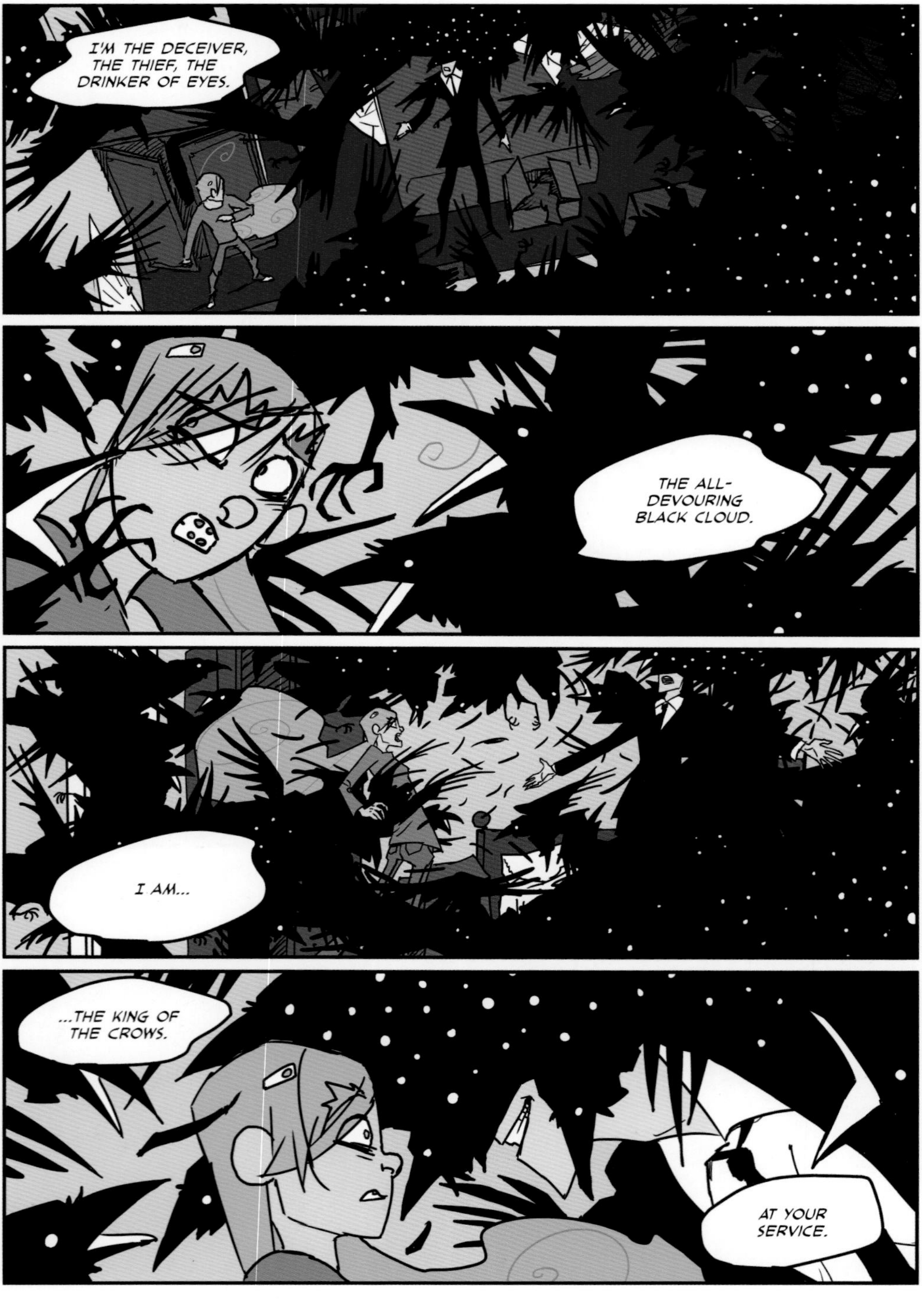
I'M THE DECEIVER, THE THIEF, THE DRINKER OF EYES.
THE ALL-DEVOURING BLACK CLOUD.
I AM...
...THE KING OF THE CROWS.
AT YOUR SERVICE.

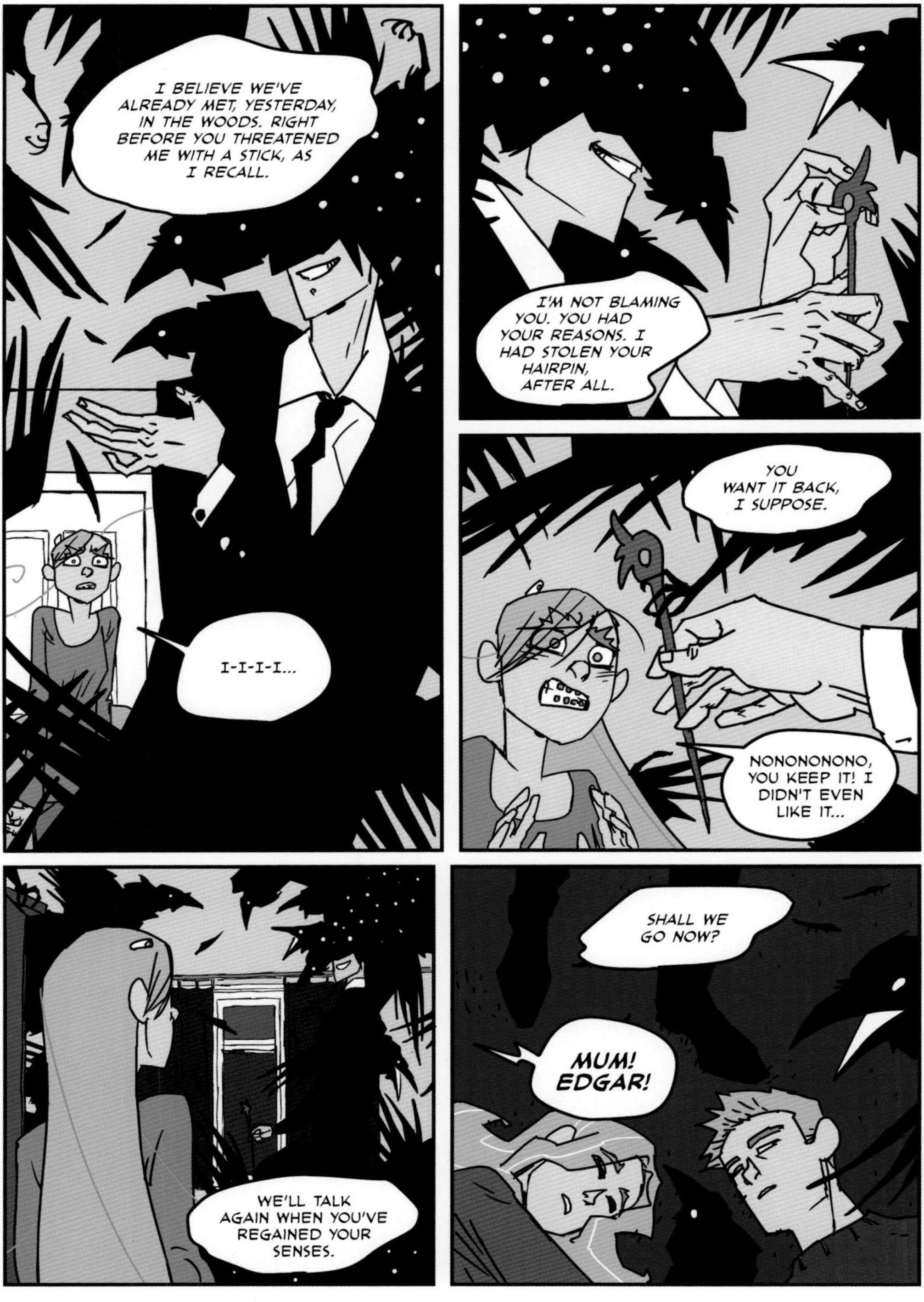
I BELIEVE WE'VE ALREADY MET, YESTERDAY, IN THE WOODS. RIGHT BEFORE YOU THREATENED ME WITH A STICK, AS I RECALL.
I-I-I-I...
I'M NOT BLAMING YOU. YOU HAD YOUR REASONS. I HAD STOLEN YOUR HAIRPIN, AFTER ALL.
YOU WANT IT BACK, I SUPPOSE.
NONONONONO, YOU KEEP IT! I DIDN'T EVEN LIKE IT...
WE'LL TALK AGAIN WHEN YOU'VE REGAINED YOUR SENSES.
SHALL WE GO NOW?
MUM! EDGAR!

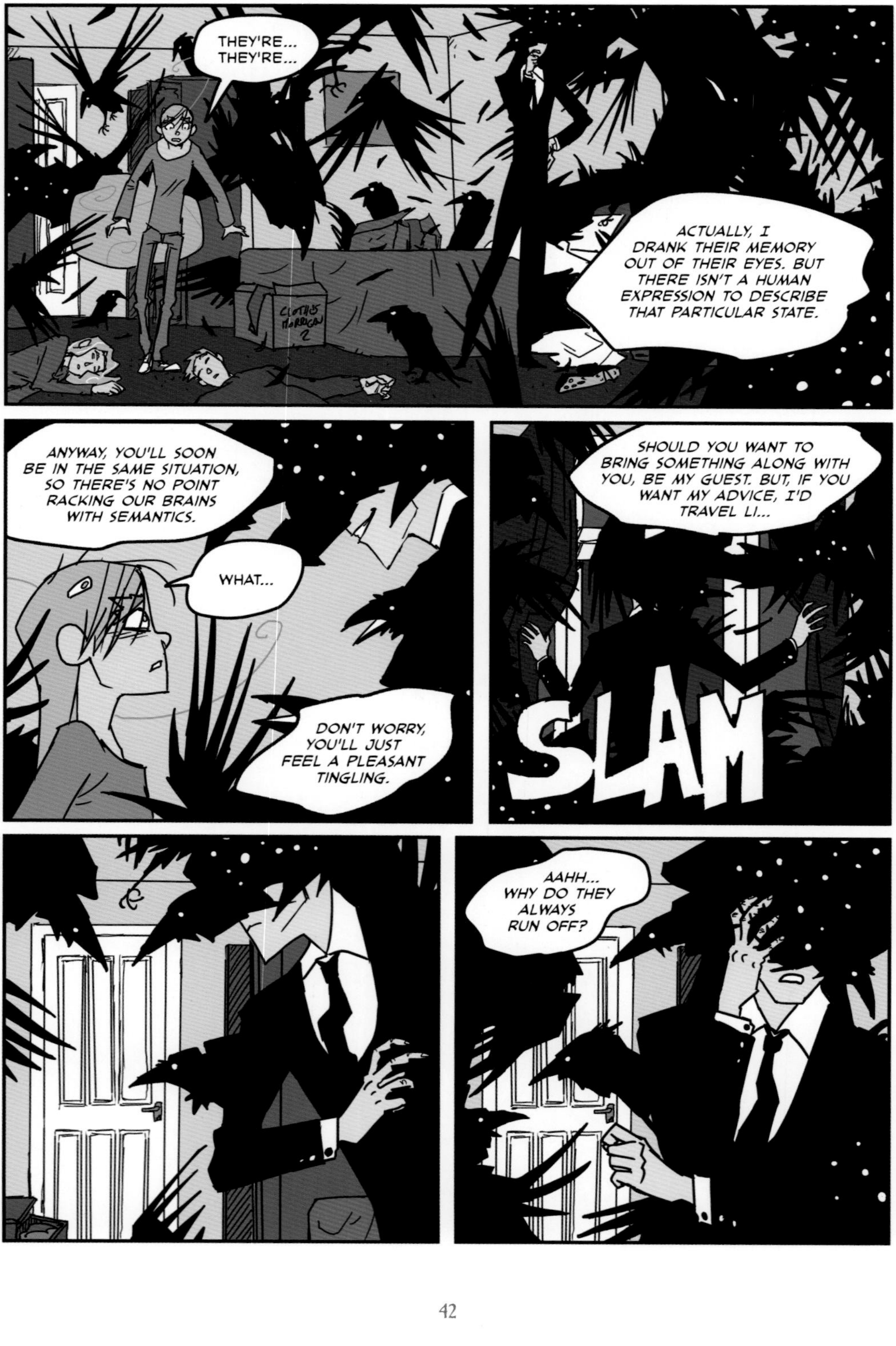
THEY'RE... THEY'RE...
ACTUALLY, I DRANK THEIR MEMORY OUT OF THEIR EYES. BUT THERE ISN'T A HUMAN EXPRESSION TO DESCRIBE THAT PARTICULAR STATE.
CLOTHES MORRIGAN 2
ANYWAY, YOU'LL SOON BE IN THE SAME SITUATION, SO THERE'S NO POINT RACKING OUR BRAINS WITH SEMANTICS.
WHAT...
DON'T WORRY, YOU'LL JUST FEEL A PLEASANT TINGLING.
SHOULD YOU WANT TO BRING SOMETHING ALONG WITH YOU, BE MY GUEST. BUT, IF YOU WANT MY ADVICE, I'D TRAVEL LI...
SLAM
AAHH... WHY DO THEY ALWAYS RUN OFF?

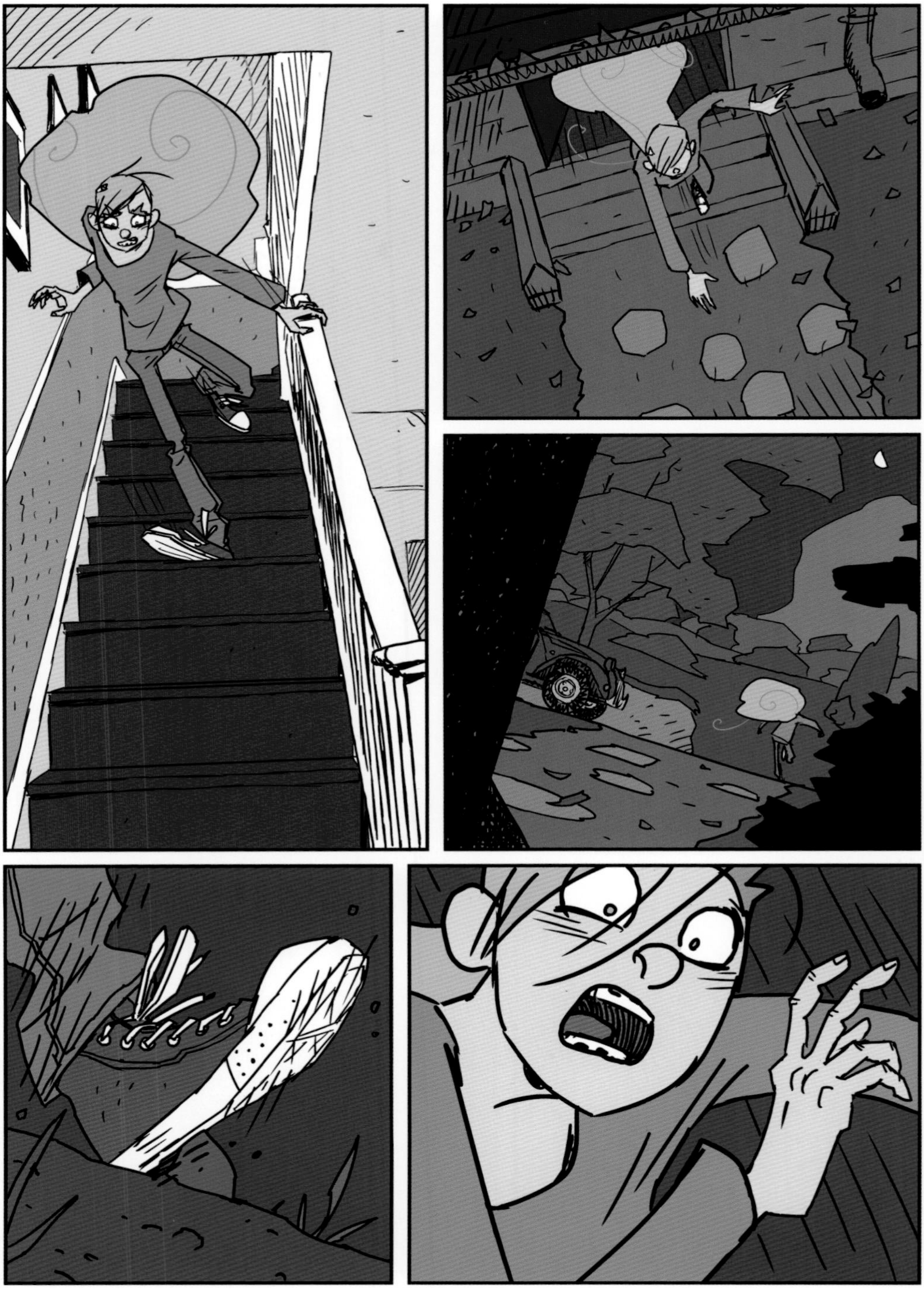

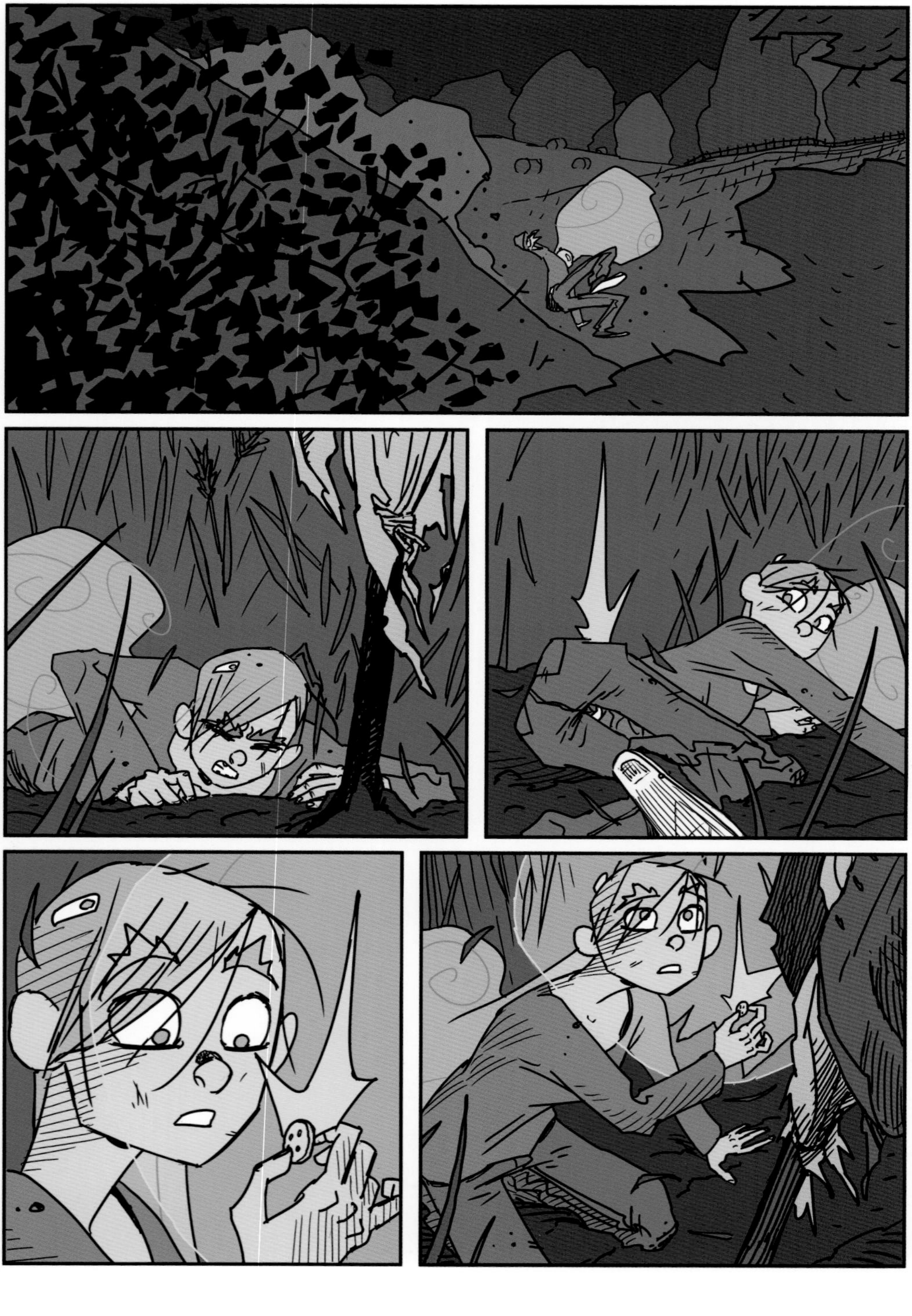

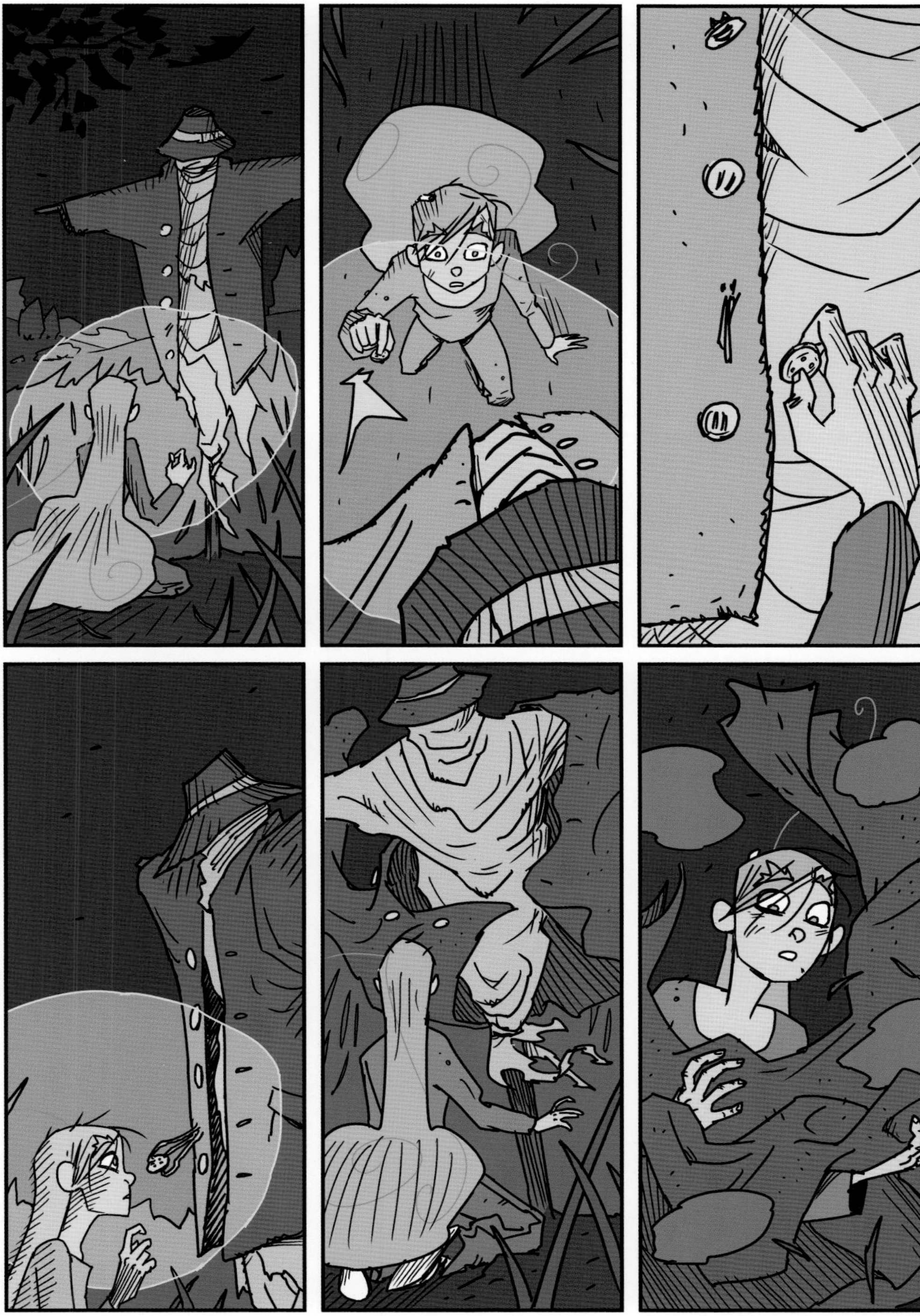

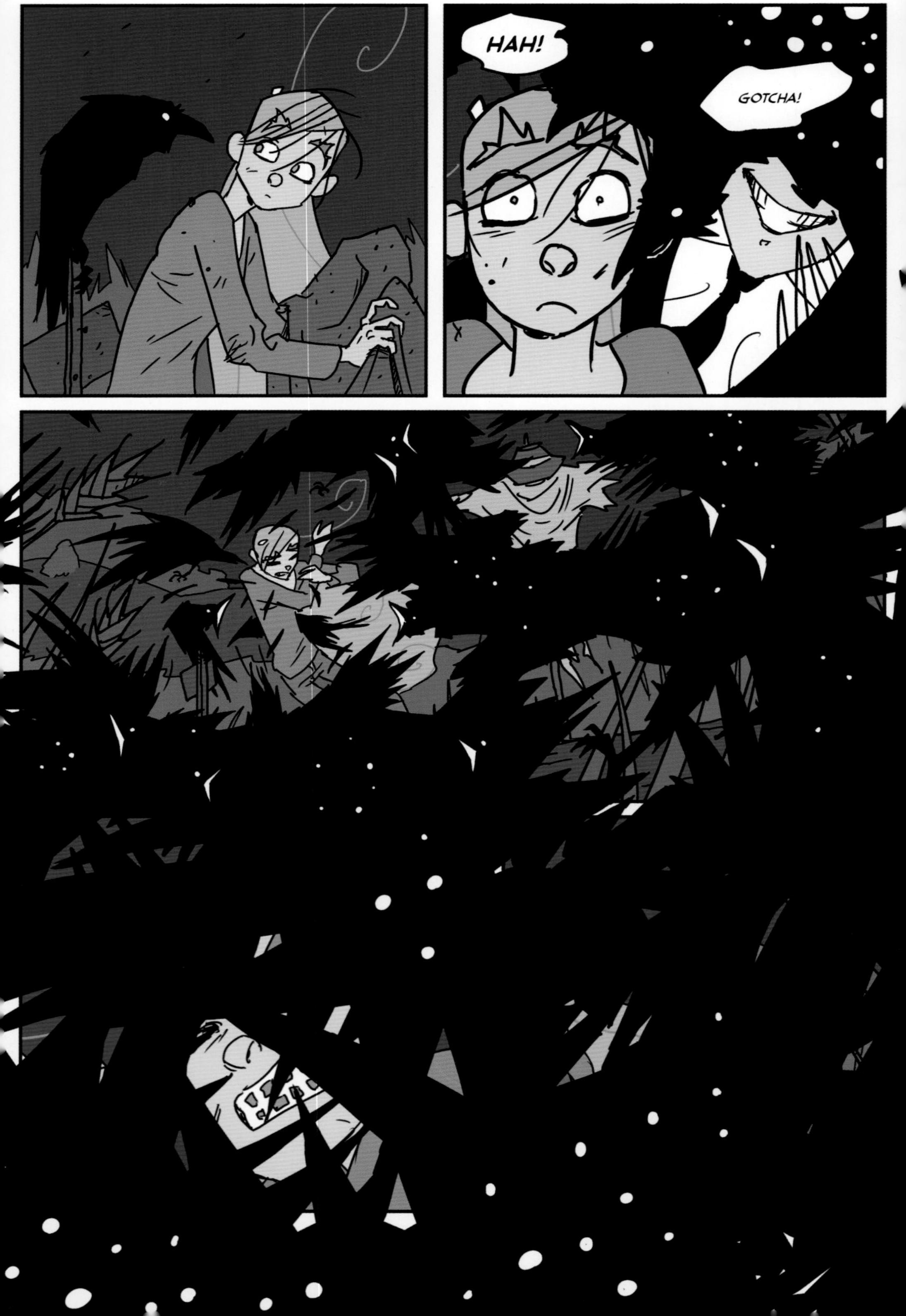
HAH!
GOTCHA!

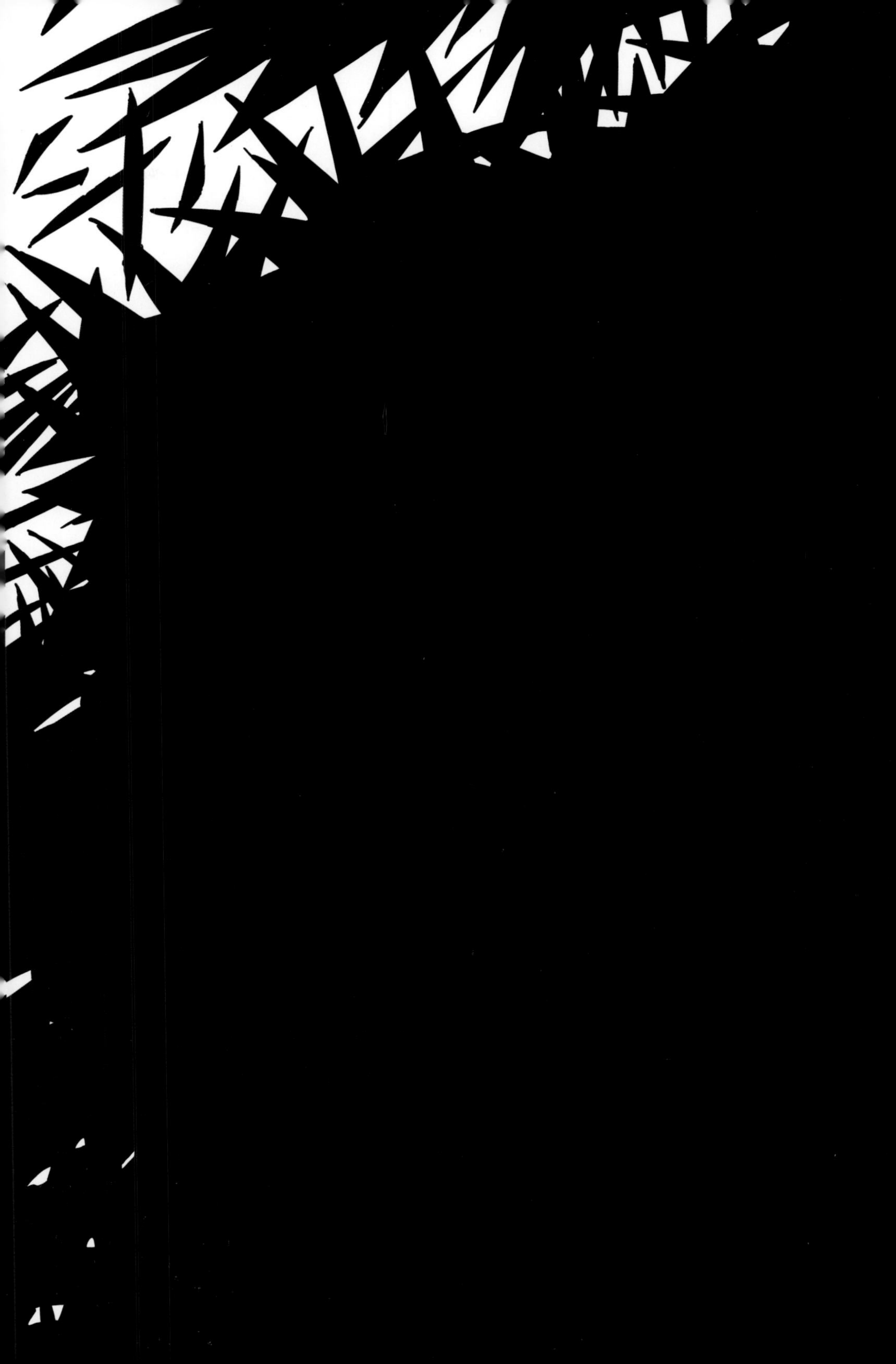

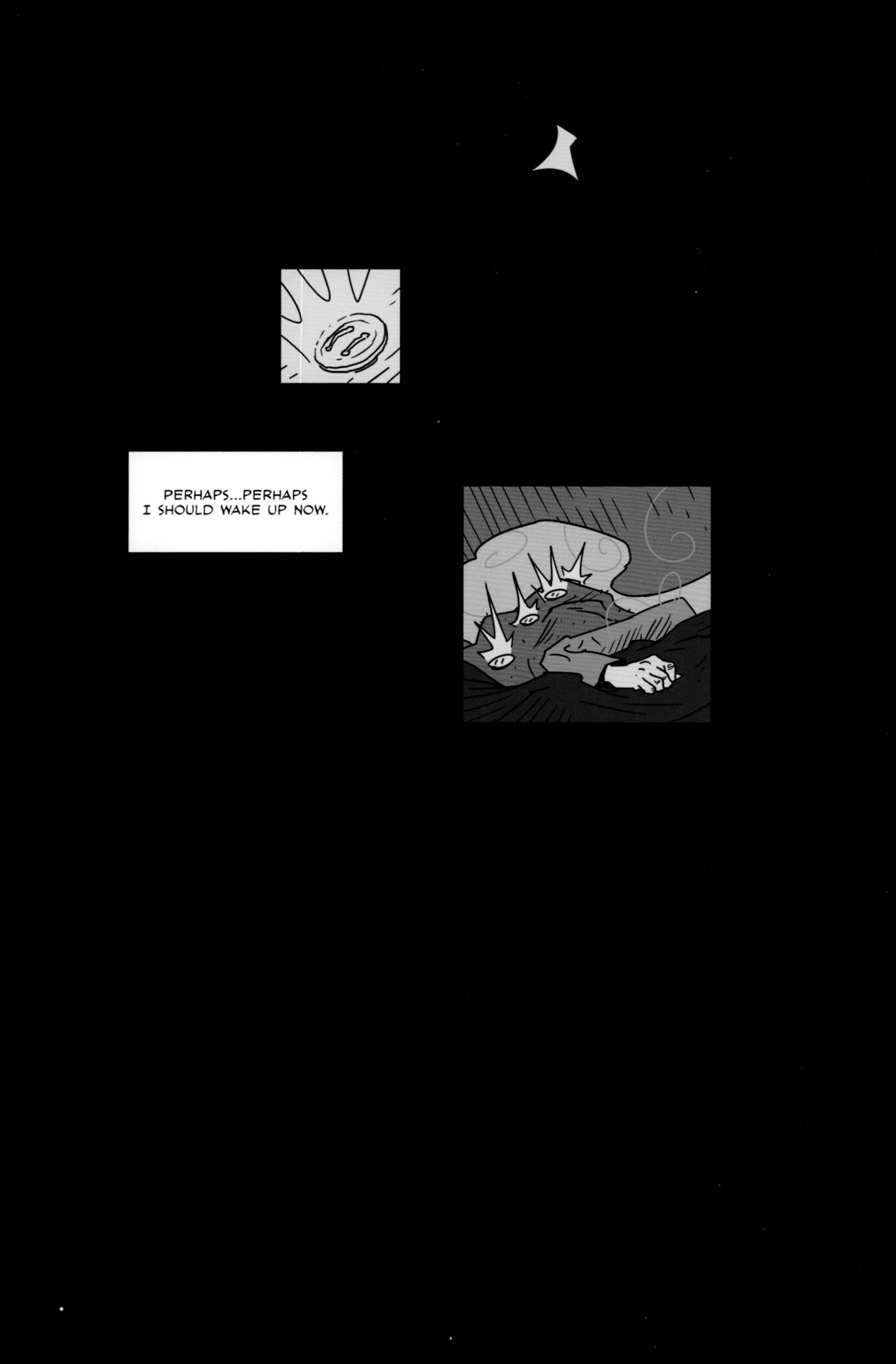
PERHAPS...PERHAPS
I SHOULD WAKE UP NOW.

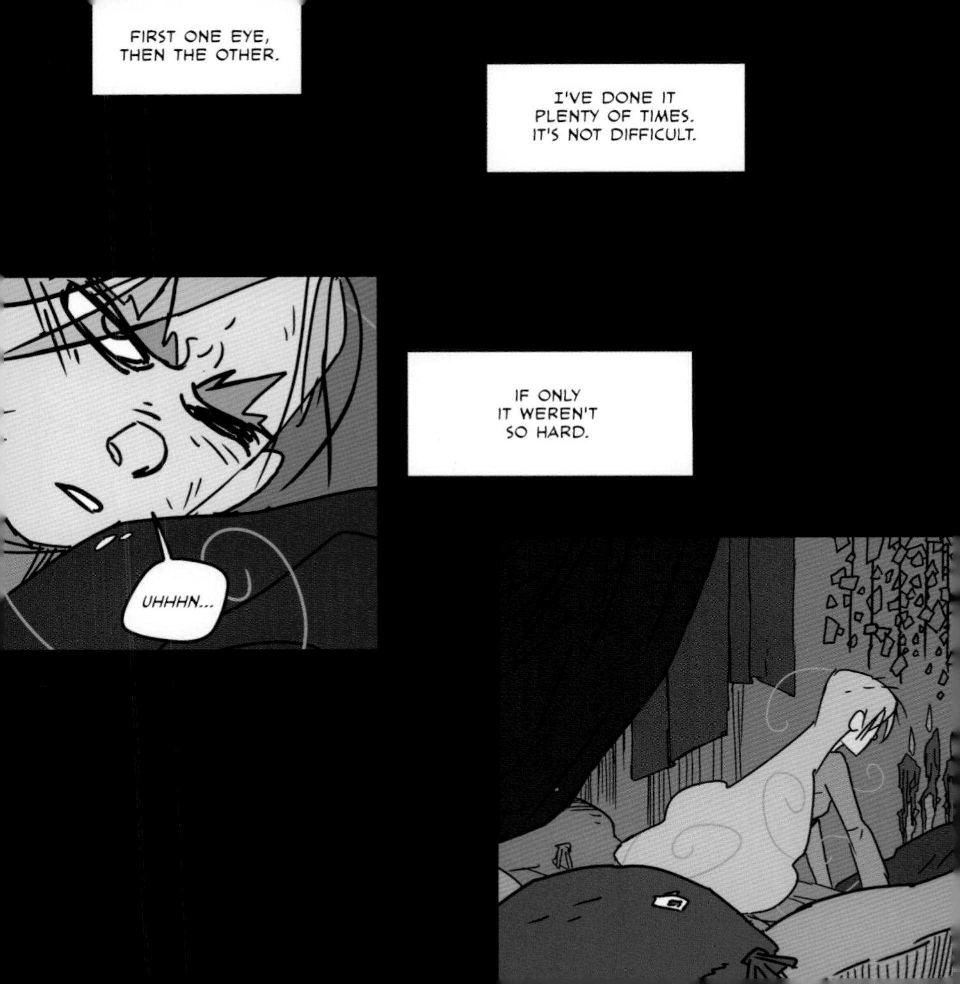
FIRST ONE EYE, THEN THE OTHER.
I'VE DONE IT PLENTY OF TIMES. IT'S NOT DIFFICULT.
IF ONLY IT WEREN'T SO HARD.
UHHHN...

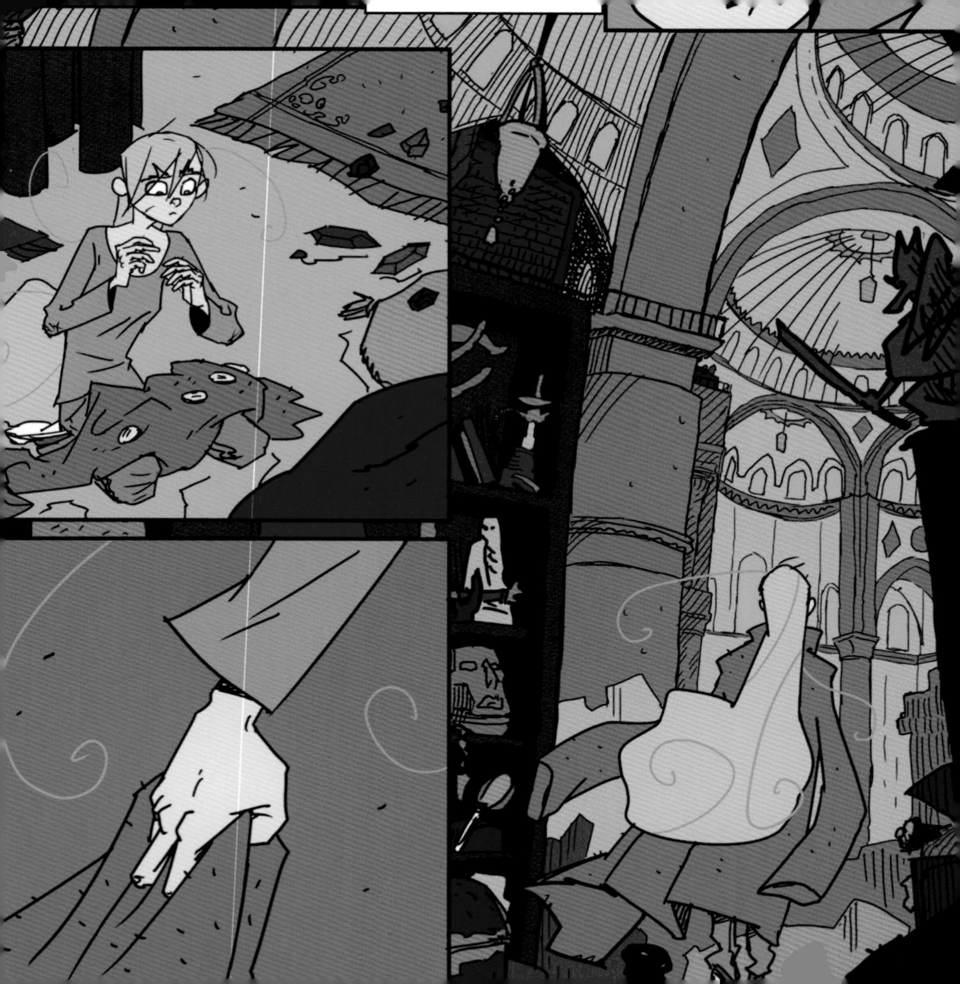

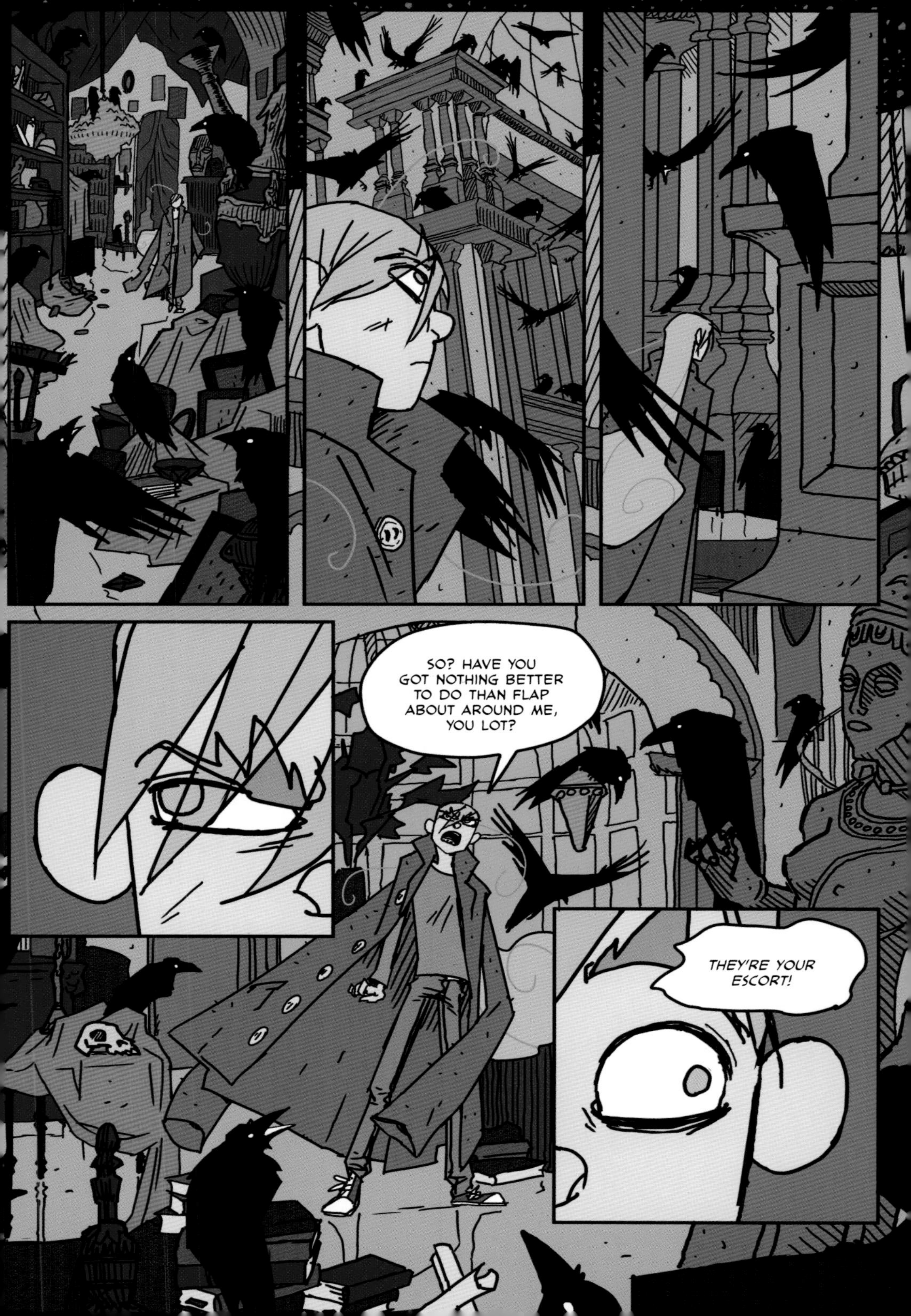
SO? HAVE YOU GOT NOTHING BETTER TO DO THAN FLAP ABOUT AROUND ME, YOU LOT?
THEY'RE YOUR ESCORT!

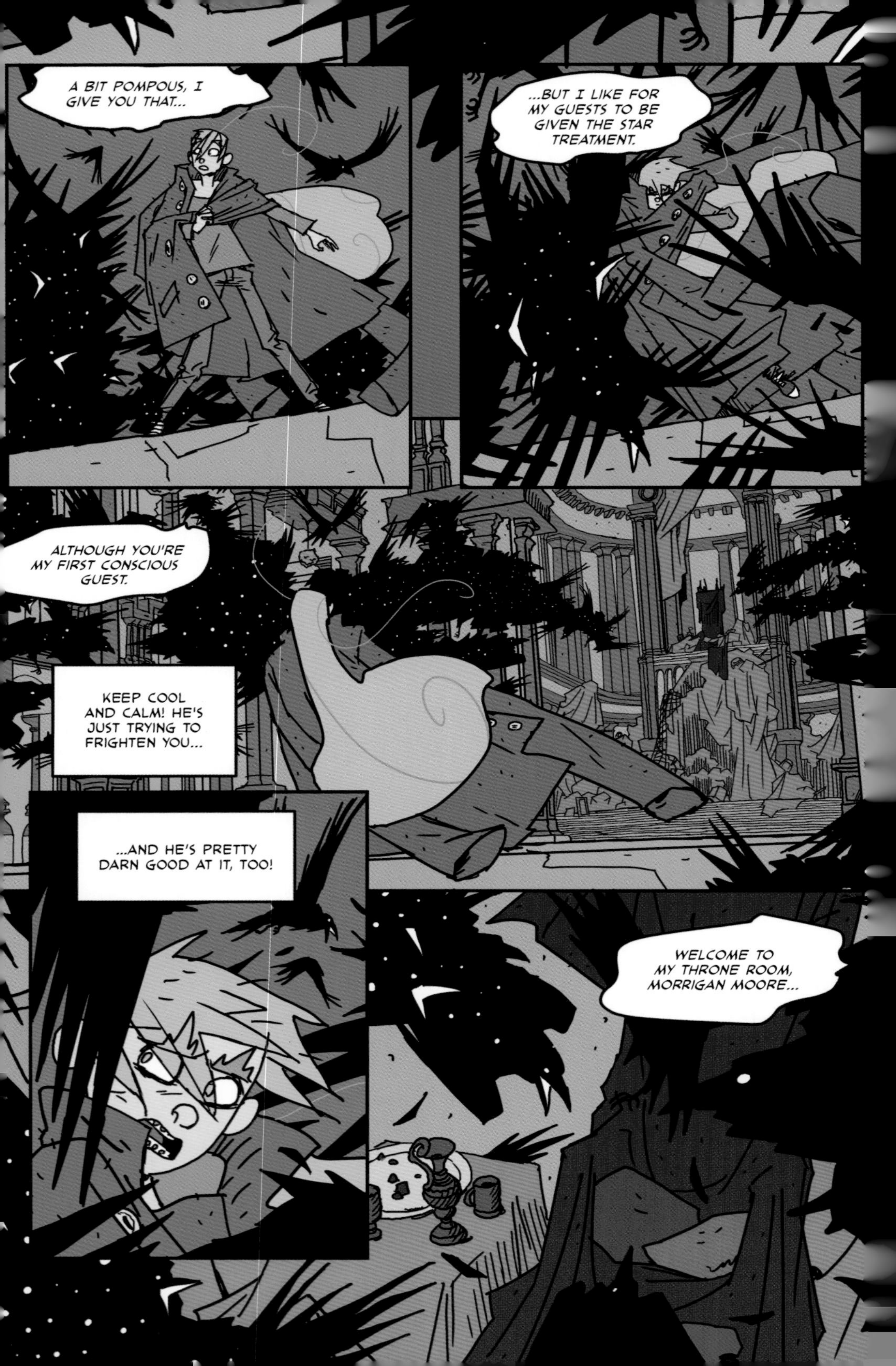
A BIT POMPOUS, I GIVE YOU THAT...
...BUT I LIKE FOR MY GUESTS TO BE GIVEN THE STAR TREATMENT.
ALTHOUGH YOU'RE MY FIRST CONSCIOUS GUEST.
KEEP COOL AND CALM! HE'S JUST TRYING TO FRIGHTEN YOU...
...AND HE'S PRETTY DARN GOOD AT IT, TOO!
WELCOME TO MY THRONE ROOM, MORRIGAN MOORE...

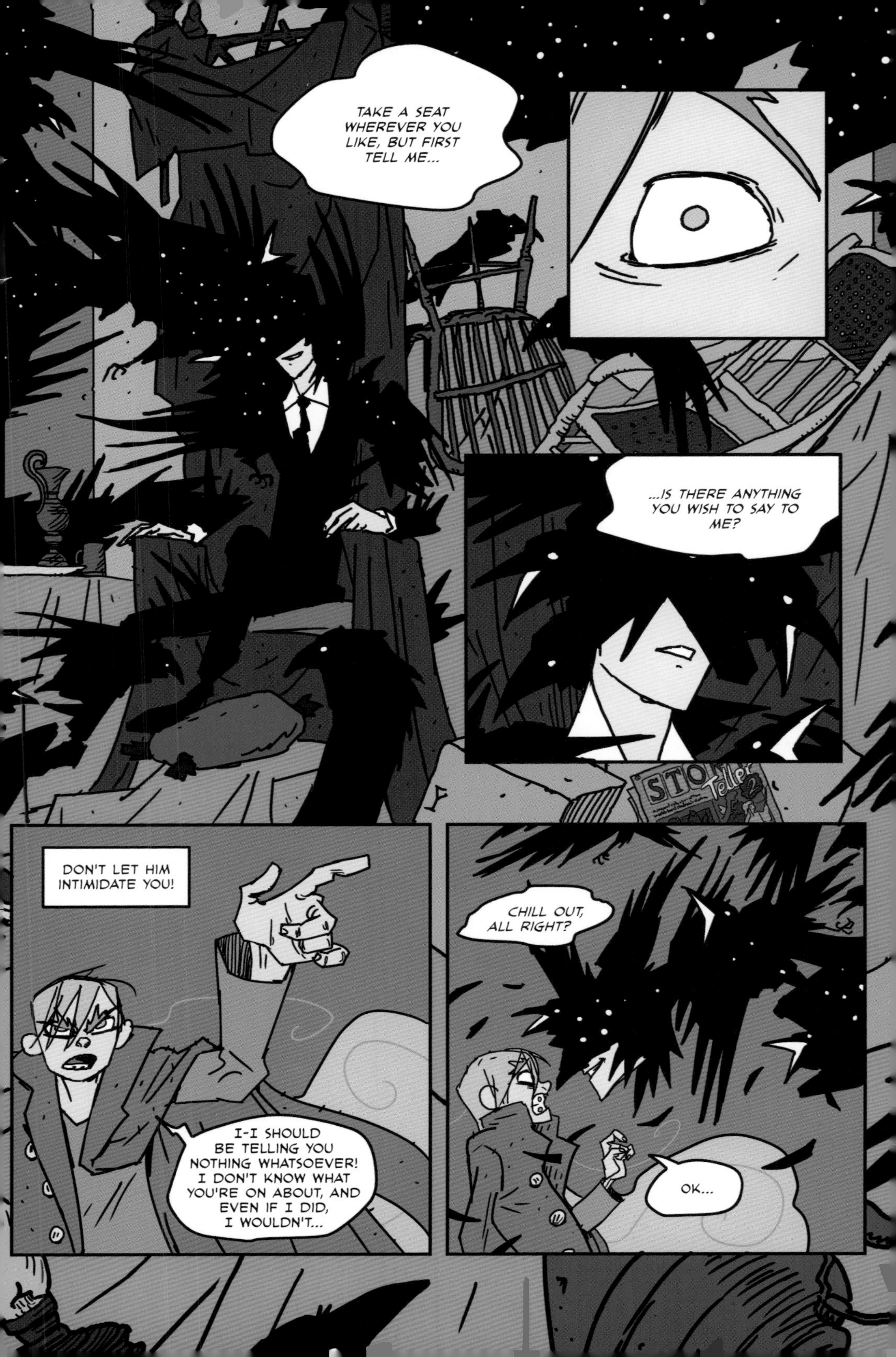
TAKE A SEAT WHEREVER YOU LIKE, BUT FIRST TELL ME...
...IS THERE ANYTHING YOU WISH TO SAY TO ME?
DON'T LET HIM INTIMIDATE YOU!
I-I SHOULD BE TELLING YOU NOTHING WHATSOEVER! I DON'T KNOW WHAT YOU'RE ON ABOUT, AND EVEN IF I DID, I WOULDN'T...
CHILL OUT, ALL RIGHT?
OK...

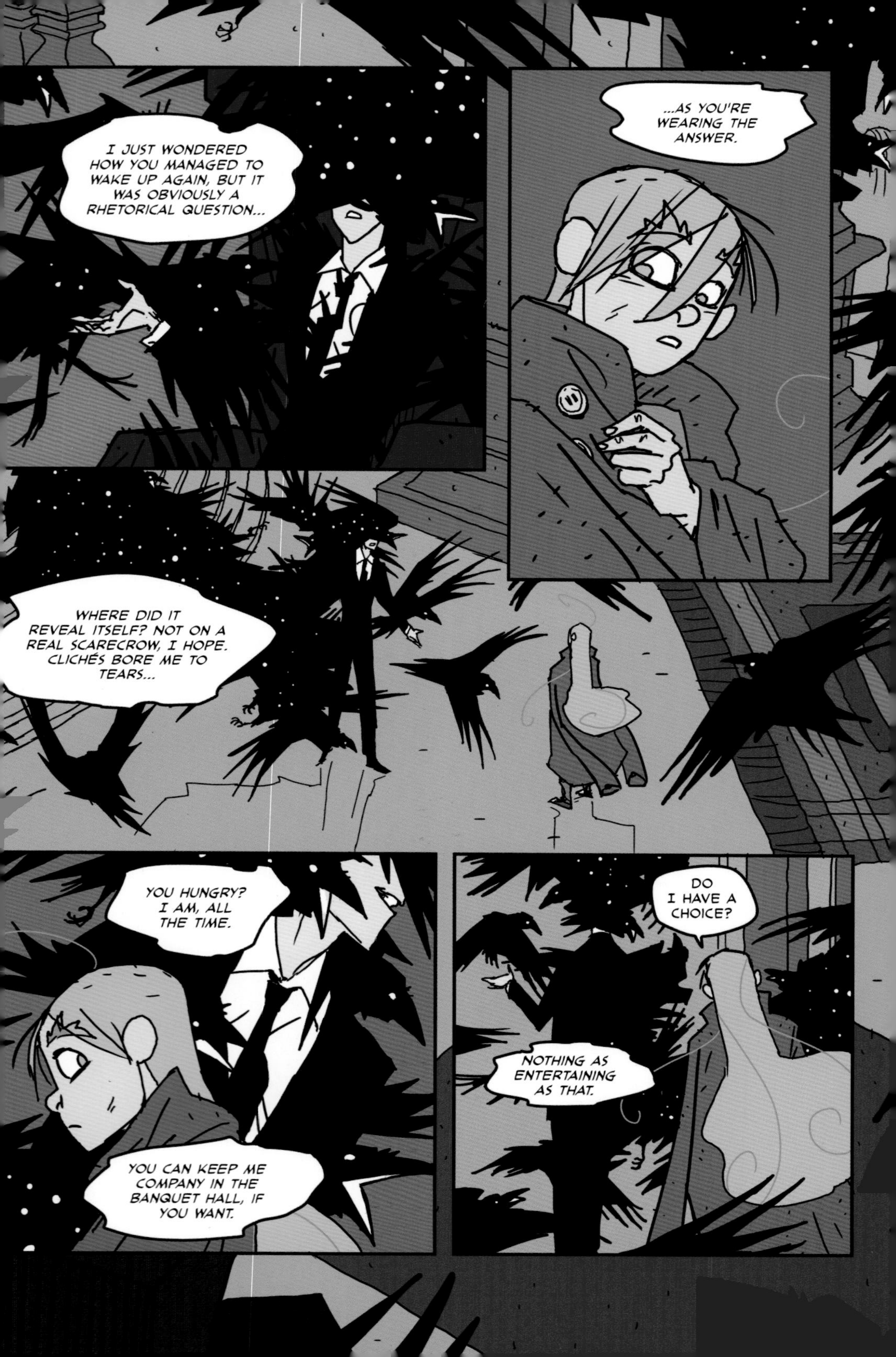
I JUST WONDERED HOW YOU MANAGED TO WAKE UP AGAIN, BUT IT WAS OBVIOUSLY A RHETORICAL QUESTION...
...AS YOU'RE WEARING THE ANSWER.
WHERE DID IT REVEAL ITSELF? NOT ON A REAL SCARECROW, I HOPE. CLICHÉS BORE ME TO TEARS...
YOU HUNGRY? I AM, ALL THE TIME.
YOU CAN KEEP ME COMPANY IN THE BANQUET HALL, IF YOU WANT.
DO I HAVE A CHOICE?
NOTHING AS ENTERTAINING AS THAT.

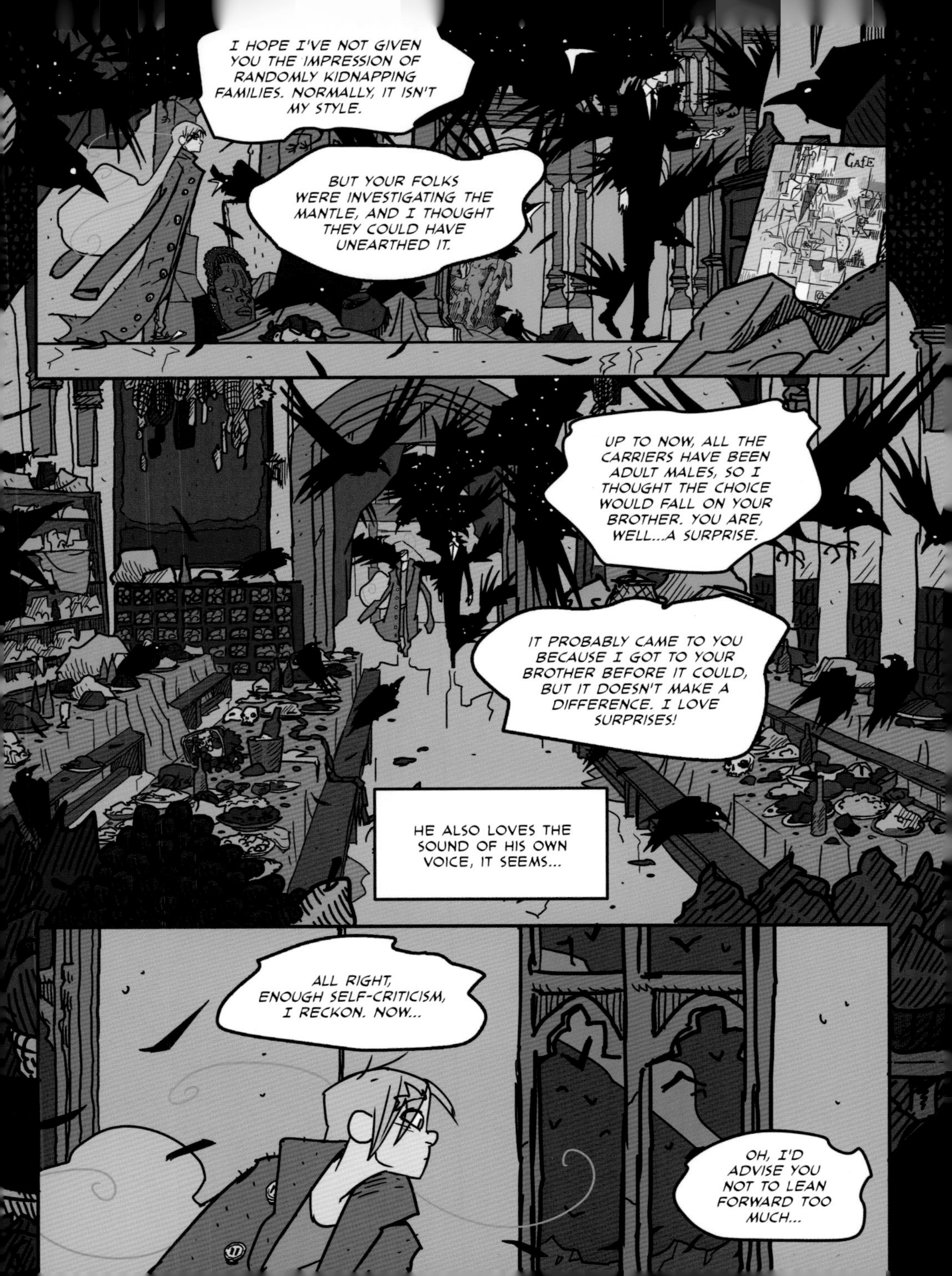
I HOPE I'VE NOT GIVEN YOU THE IMPRESSION OF RANDOMLY KIDNAPPING FAMILIES. NORMALLY, IT ISN'T MY STYLE.
BUT YOUR FOLKS WERE INVESTIGATING THE MANTLE, AND I THOUGHT THEY COULD HAVE UNEARTHED IT.
CAFE
UP TO NOW, ALL THE CARRIERS HAVE BEEN ADULT MALES, SO I THOUGHT THE CHOICE WOULD FALL ON YOUR BROTHER. YOU ARE, WELL...A SURPRISE.
IT PROBABLY CAME TO YOU BECAUSE I GOT TO YOUR BROTHER BEFORE IT COULD, BUT IT DOESN'T MAKE A DIFFERENCE. I LOVE SURPRISES!
HE ALSO LOVES THE SOUND OF HIS OWN VOICE, IT SEEMS...
ALL RIGHT, ENOUGH SELF-CRITICISM, I RECKON. NOW...
OH, I'D ADVISE YOU NOT TO LEAN FORWARD TOO MUCH...

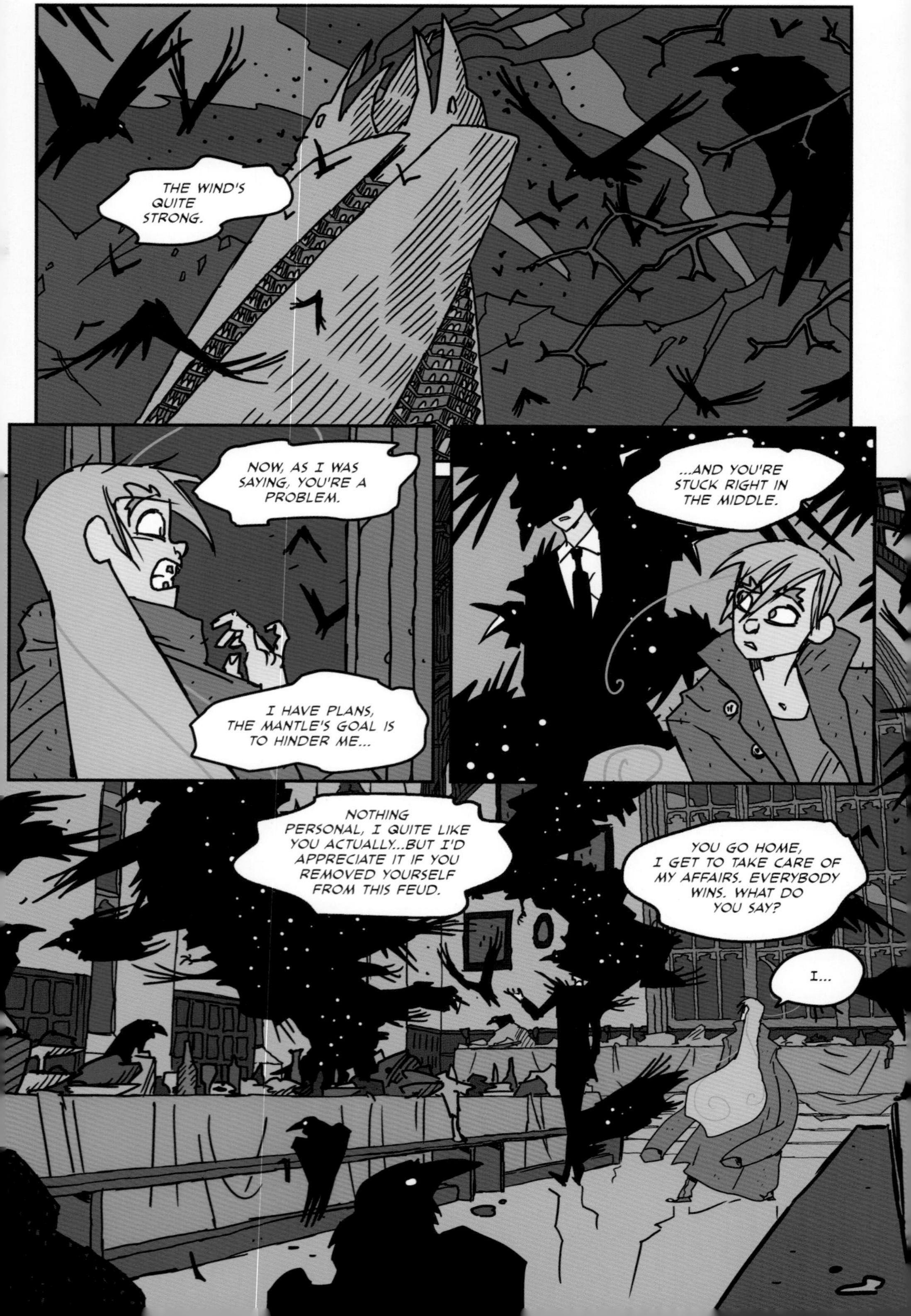
THE WIND'S QUITE STRONG.
NOW, AS I WAS SAYING, YOU'RE A PROBLEM.
I HAVE PLANS, THE MANTLE'S GOAL IS TO HINDER ME...
...AND YOU'RE STUCK RIGHT IN THE MIDDLE.
NOTHING PERSONAL, I QUITE LIKE YOU ACTUALLY...BUT I'D APPRECIATE IT IF YOU REMOVED YOURSELF FROM THIS FEUD.
YOU GO HOME, I GET TO TAKE CARE OF MY AFFAIRS. EVERYBODY WINS. WHAT DO YOU SAY?
I...

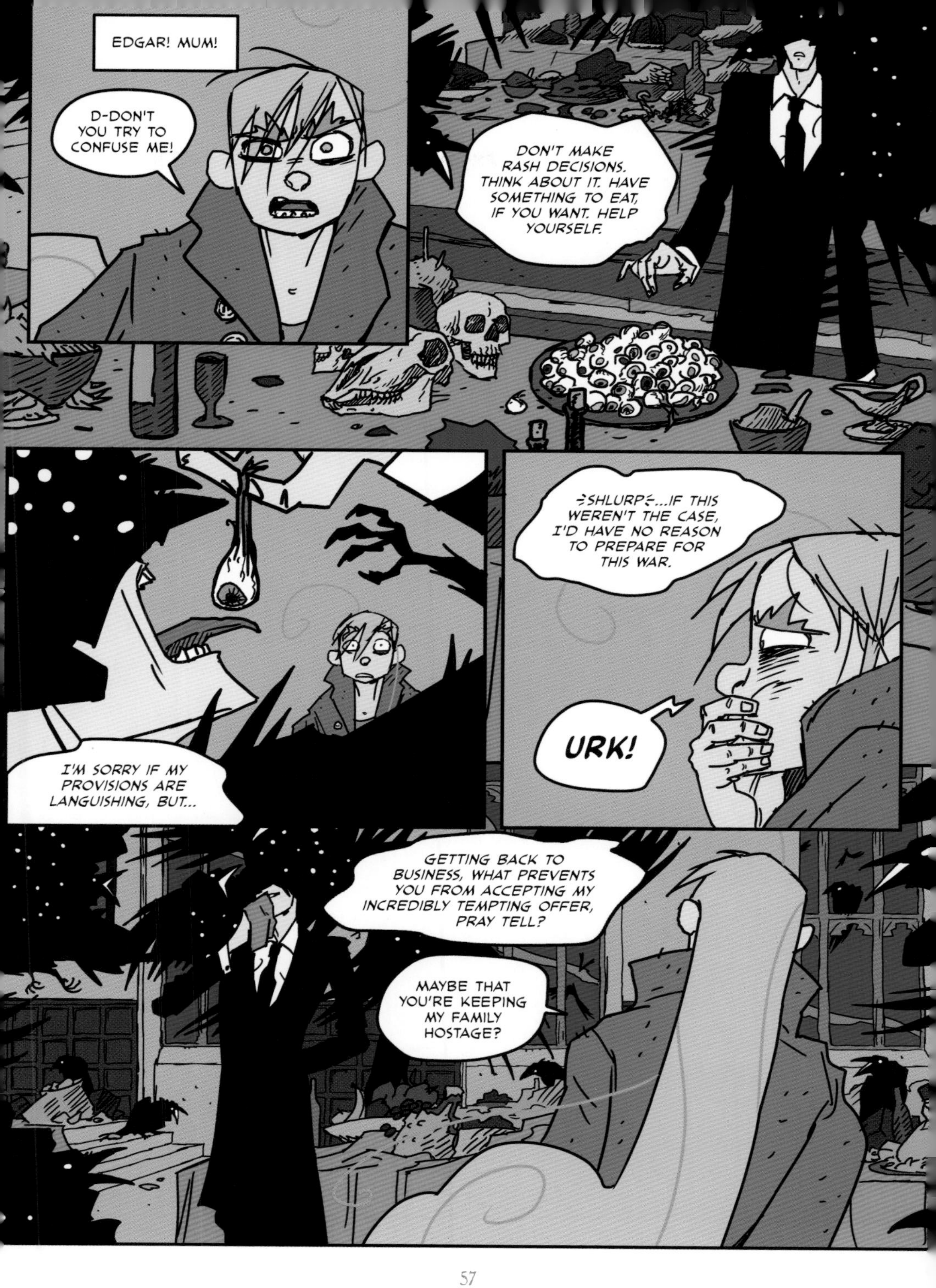
EDGAR! MUM!
D-DON'T YOU TRY TO CONFUSE ME!
DON'T MAKE RASH DECISIONS. THINK ABOUT IT. HAVE SOMETHING TO EAT, IF YOU WANT. HELP YOURSELF.
I'M SORRY IF MY PROVISIONS ARE LANGUISHING, BUT...
⸗SHLURP⸗...IF THIS WEREN'T THE CASE, I'D HAVE NO REASON TO PREPARE FOR THIS WAR.
URK!
GETTING BACK TO BUSINESS, WHAT PREVENTS YOU FROM ACCEPTING MY INCREDIBLY TEMPTING OFFER, PRAY TELL?
MAYBE THAT YOU'RE KEEPING MY FAMILY HOSTAGE?

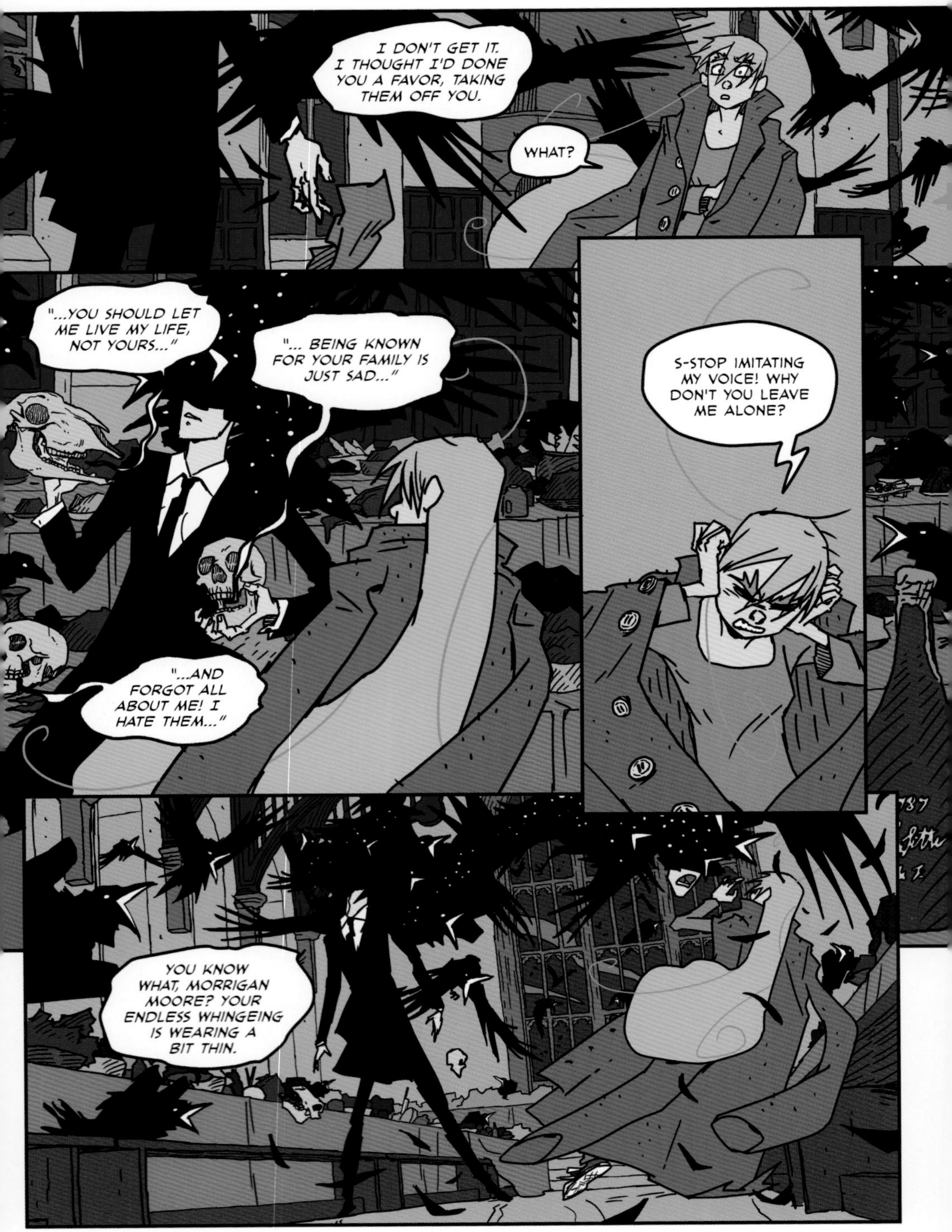
I DON'T GET IT. I THOUGHT I'D DONE YOU A FAVOR, TAKING THEM OFF YOU.
WHAT?
"...YOU SHOULD LET ME LIVE MY LIFE, NOT YOURS..."
"... BEING KNOWN FOR YOUR FAMILY IS JUST SAD..."
"...AND FORGOT ALL ABOUT ME! I HATE THEM..."
S-STOP IMITATING MY VOICE! WHY DON'T YOU LEAVE ME ALONE?
YOU KNOW WHAT, MORRIGAN MOORE? YOUR ENDLESS WHINGEING IS WEARING A BIT THIN.

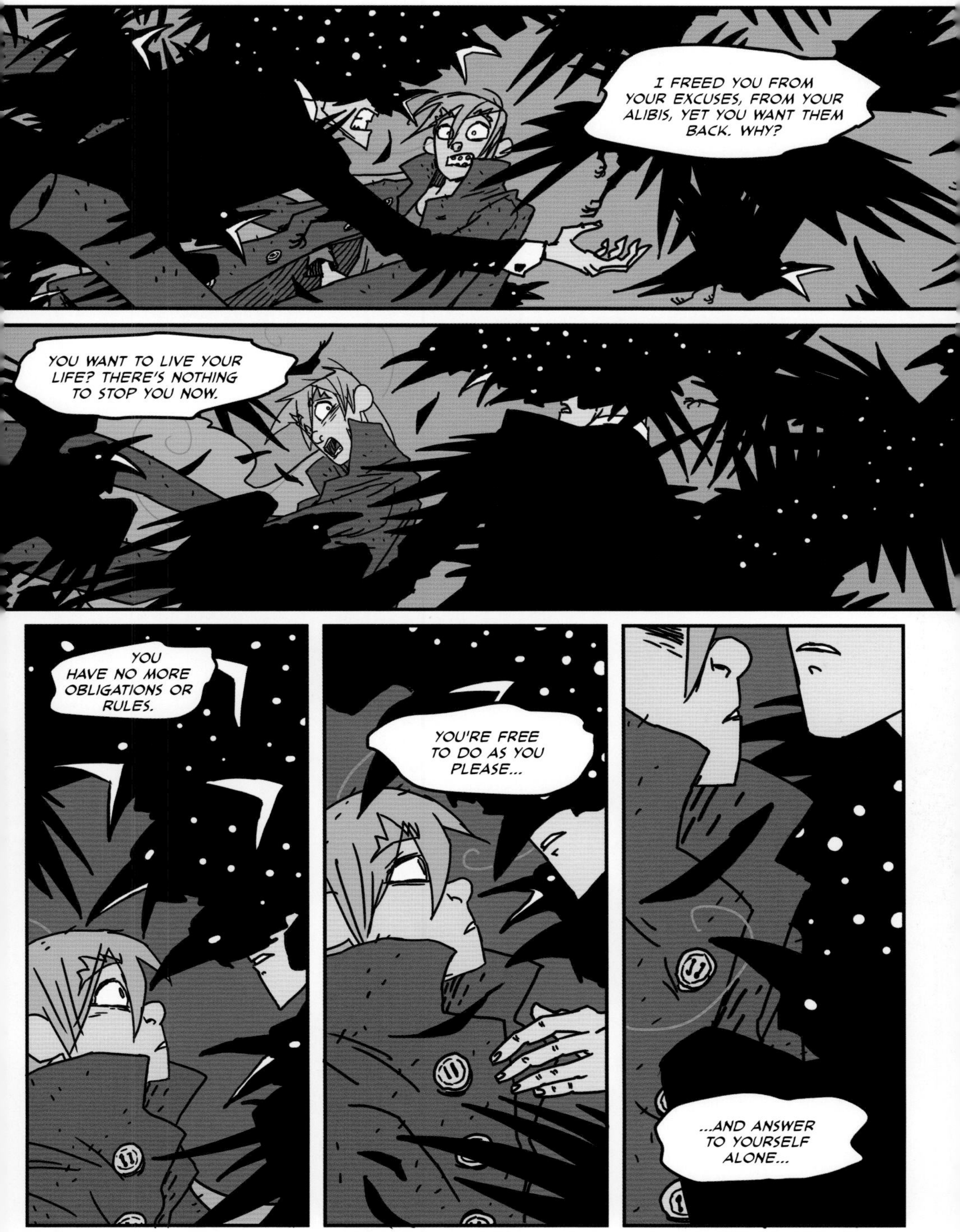
I FREED YOU FROM YOUR EXCUSES, FROM YOUR ALIBIS, YET YOU WANT THEM BACK. WHY?
YOU WANT TO LIVE YOUR LIFE? THERE'S NOTHING TO STOP YOU NOW.
YOU HAVE NO MORE OBLIGATIONS OR RULES.
YOU'RE FREE TO DO AS YOU PLEASE...
...AND ANSWER TO YOURSELF ALONE...

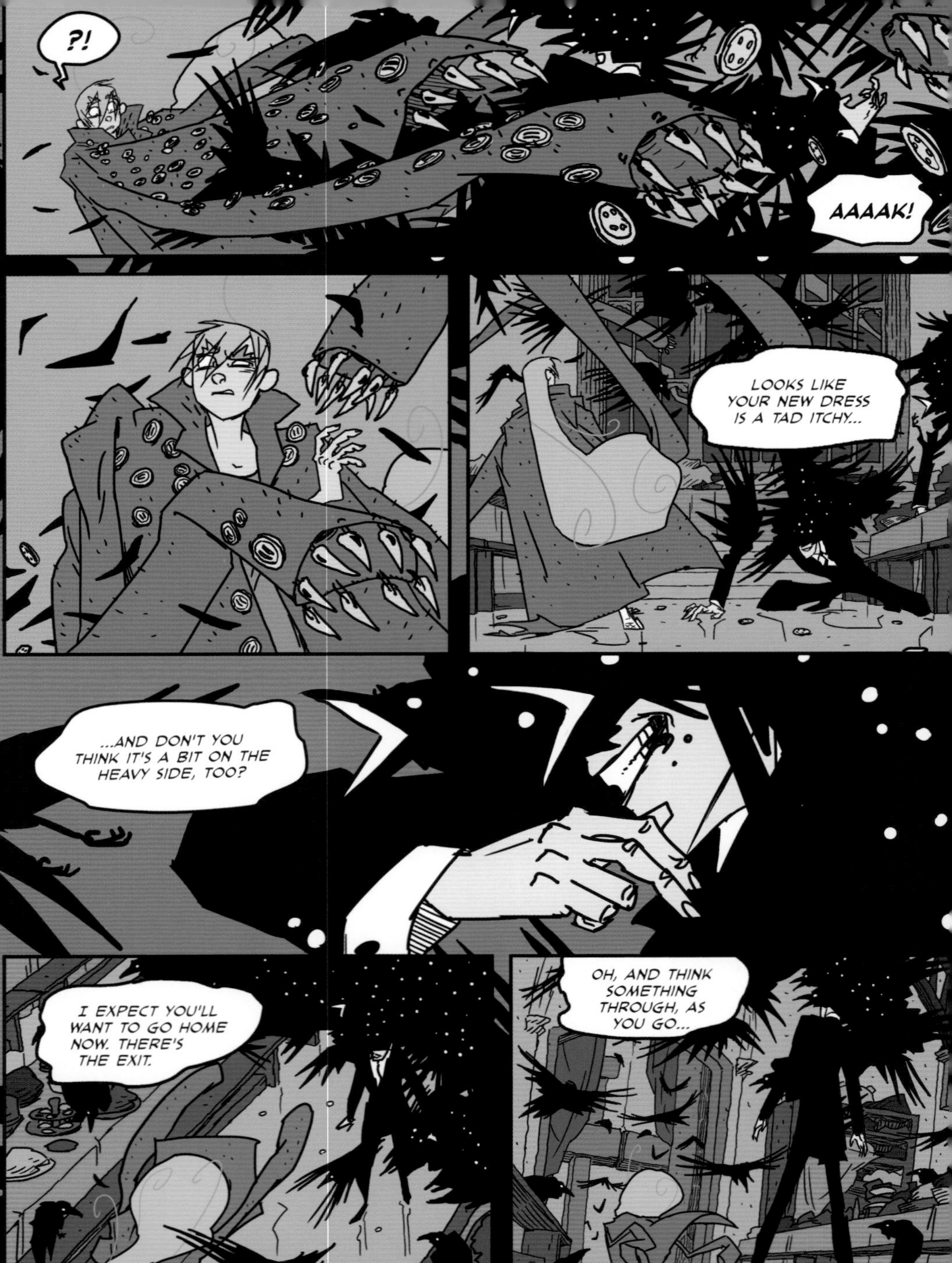
?!
AAAAK!
LOOKS LIKE YOUR NEW DRESS IS A TAD ITCHY...
...AND DON'T YOU THINK IT'S A BIT ON THE HEAVY SIDE, TOO?
I EXPECT YOU'LL WANT TO GO HOME NOW. THERE'S THE EXIT.
OH, AND THINK SOMETHING THROUGH, AS YOU GO...

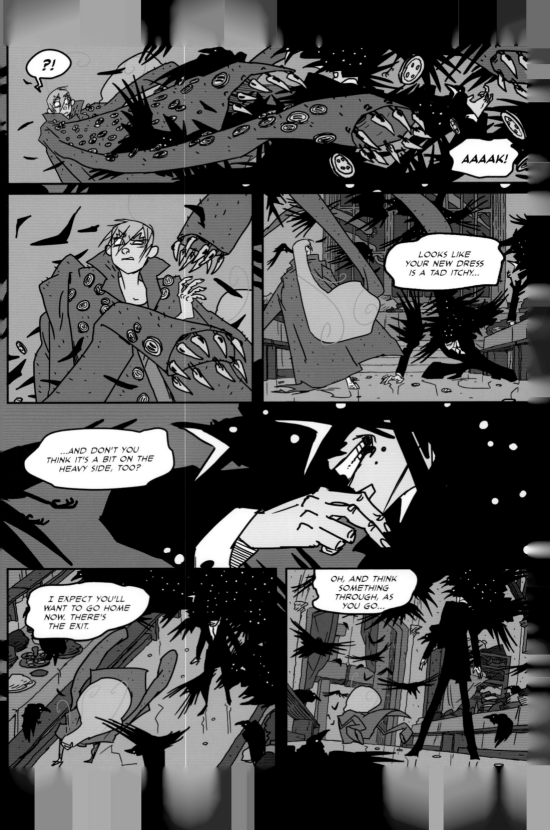

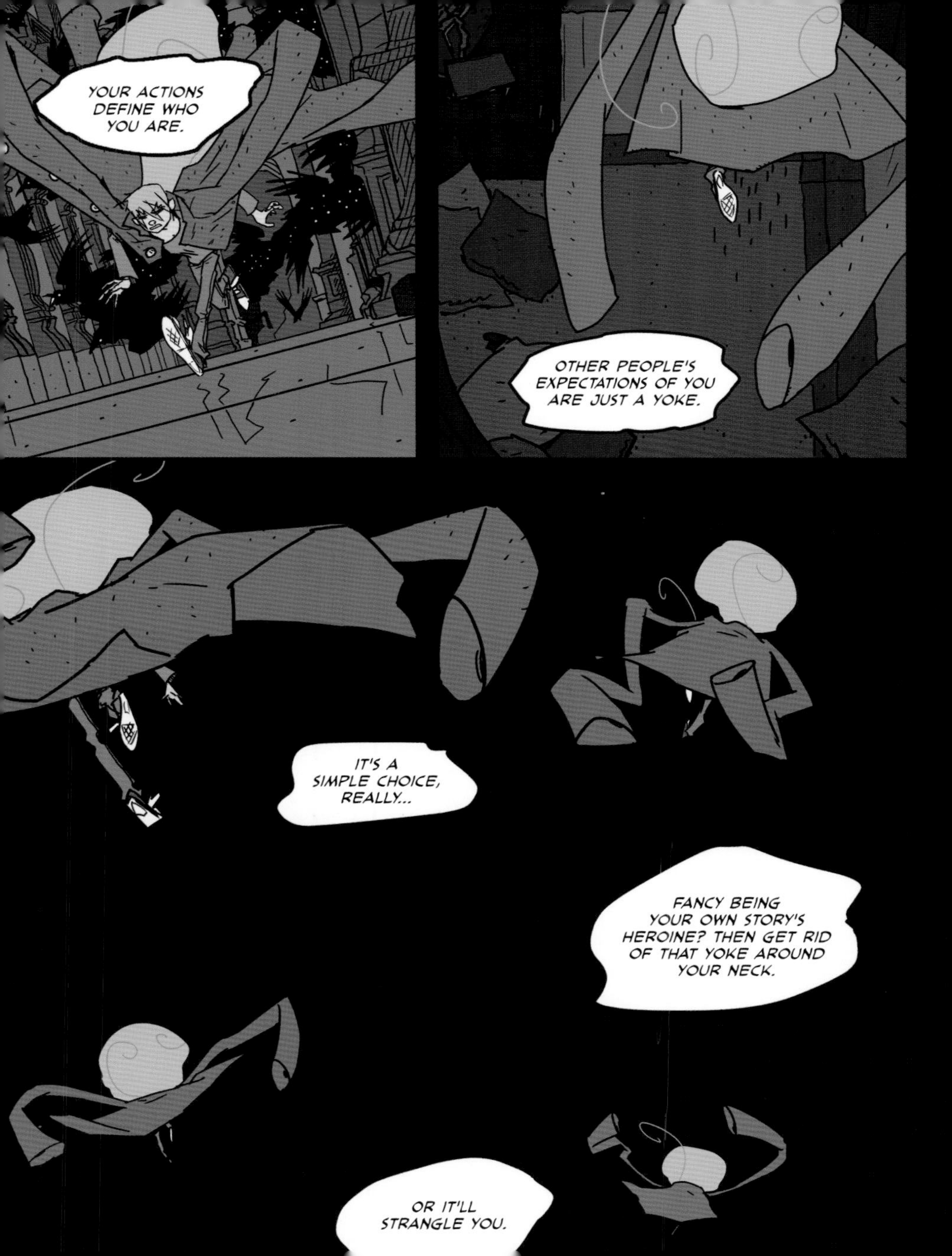
YOUR ACTIONS DEFINE WHO YOU ARE.
OTHER PEOPLE'S EXPECTATIONS OF YOU ARE JUST A YOKE.
IT'S A SIMPLE CHOICE, REALLY...
FANCY BEING YOUR OWN STORY'S HEROINE? THEN GET RID OF THAT YOKE AROUND YOUR NECK.
OR IT'LL STRANGLE YOU.

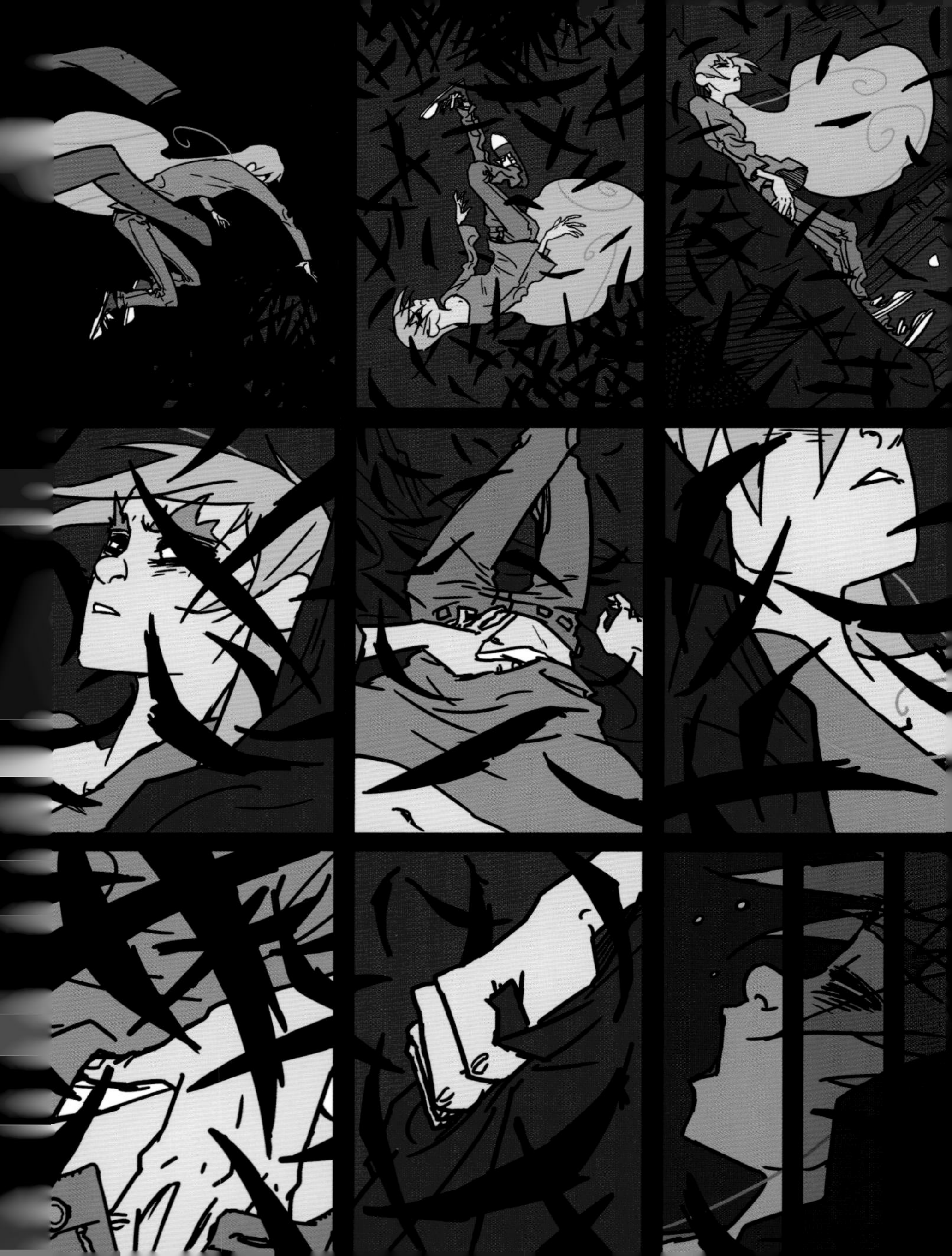

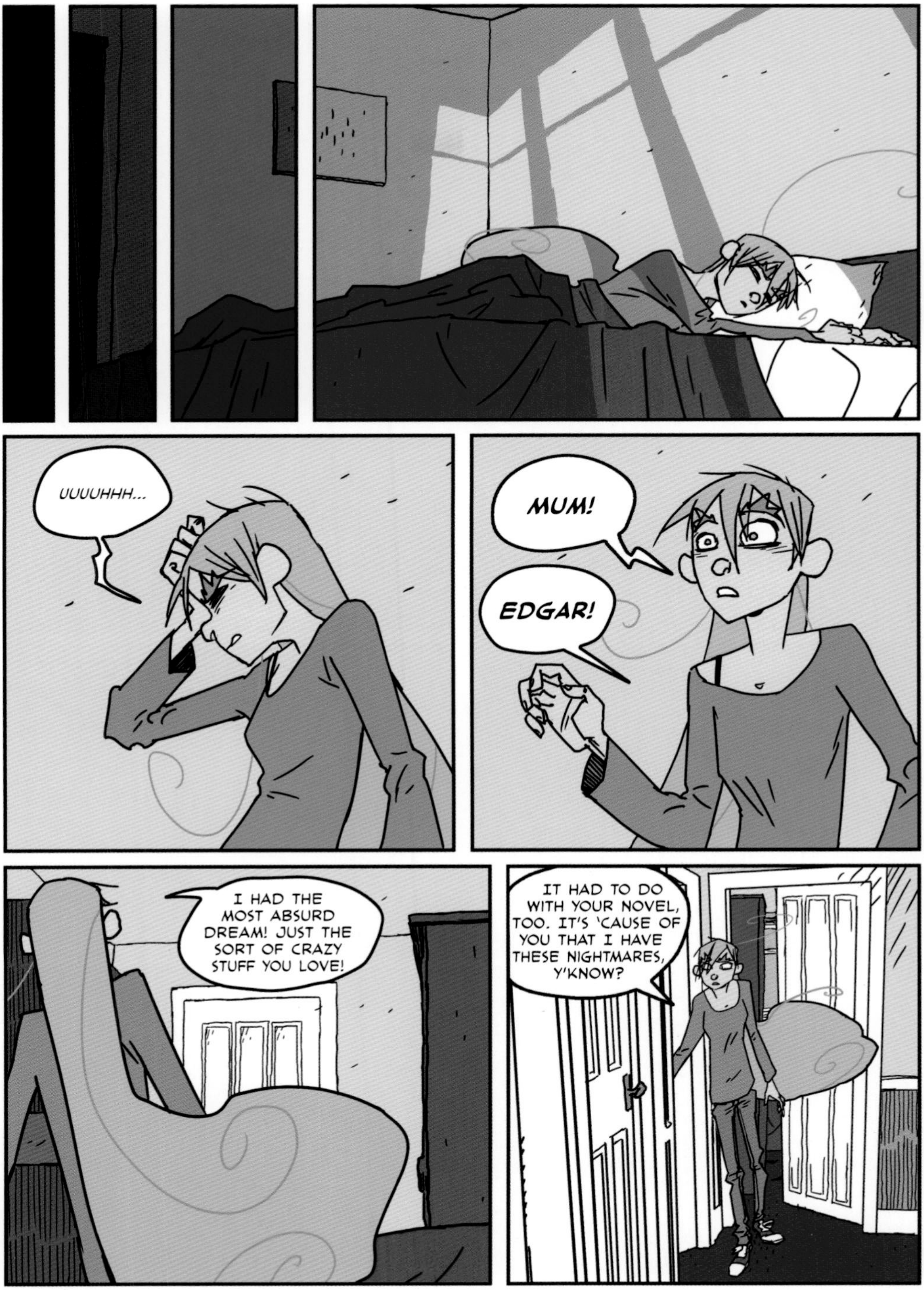
UUUUHHH...
MUM!
EDGAR!
I HAD THE MOST ABSURD DREAM! JUST THE SORT OF CRAZY STUFF YOU LOVE!
IT HAD TO DO WITH YOUR NOVEL, TOO. IT'S 'CAUSE OF YOU THAT I HAVE THESE NIGHTMARES, Y'KNOW?

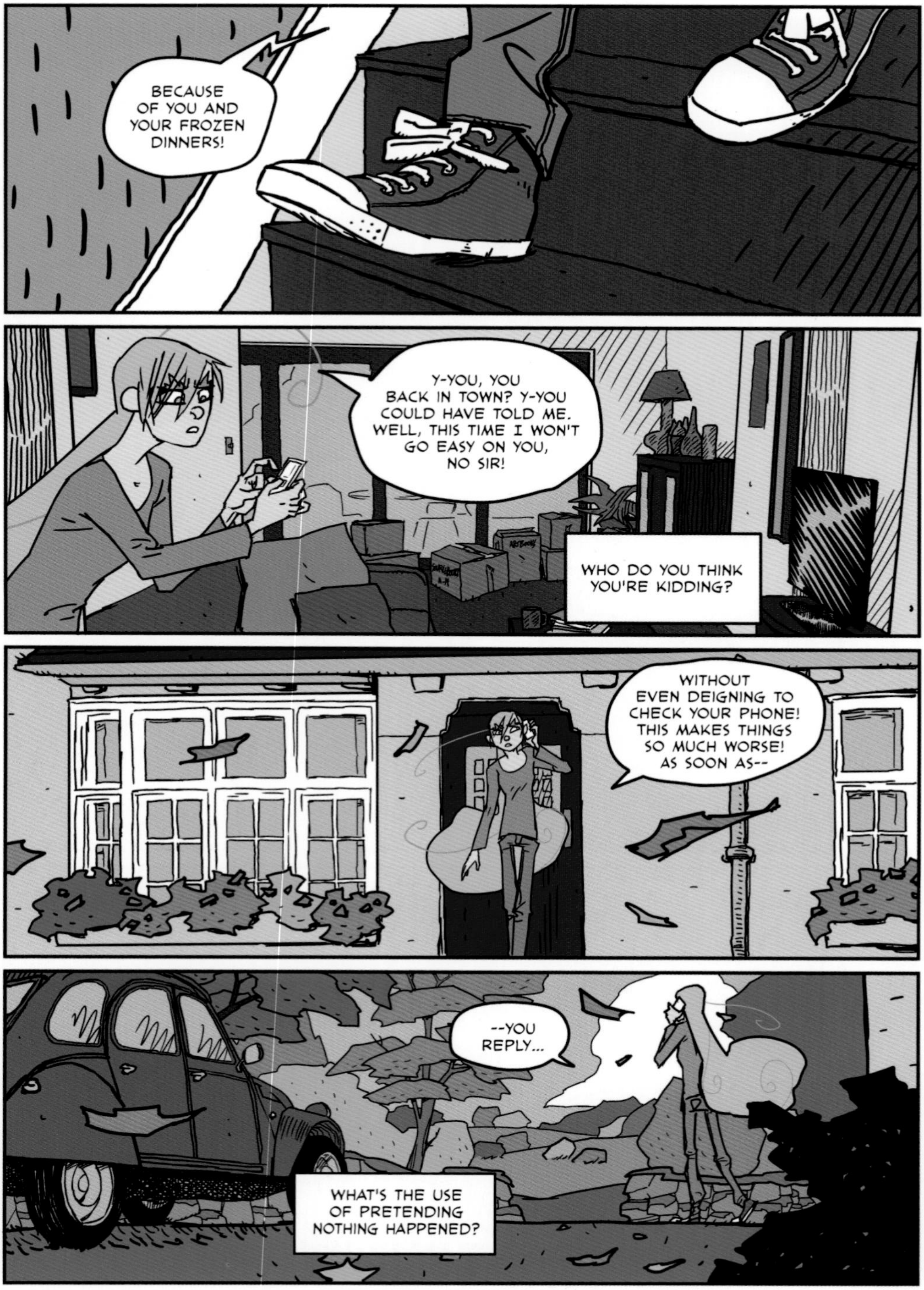
BECAUSE OF YOU AND YOUR FROZEN DINNERS!
Y-YOU, YOU BACK IN TOWN? Y-YOU COULD HAVE TOLD ME. WELL, THIS TIME I WON'T GO EASY ON YOU, NO SIR!
WHO DO YOU THINK YOU'RE KIDDING?
WITHOUT EVEN DEIGNING TO CHECK YOUR PHONE! THIS MAKES THINGS SO MUCH WORSE! AS SOON AS--
--YOU REPLY...
WHAT'S THE USE OF PRETENDING NOTHING HAPPENED?

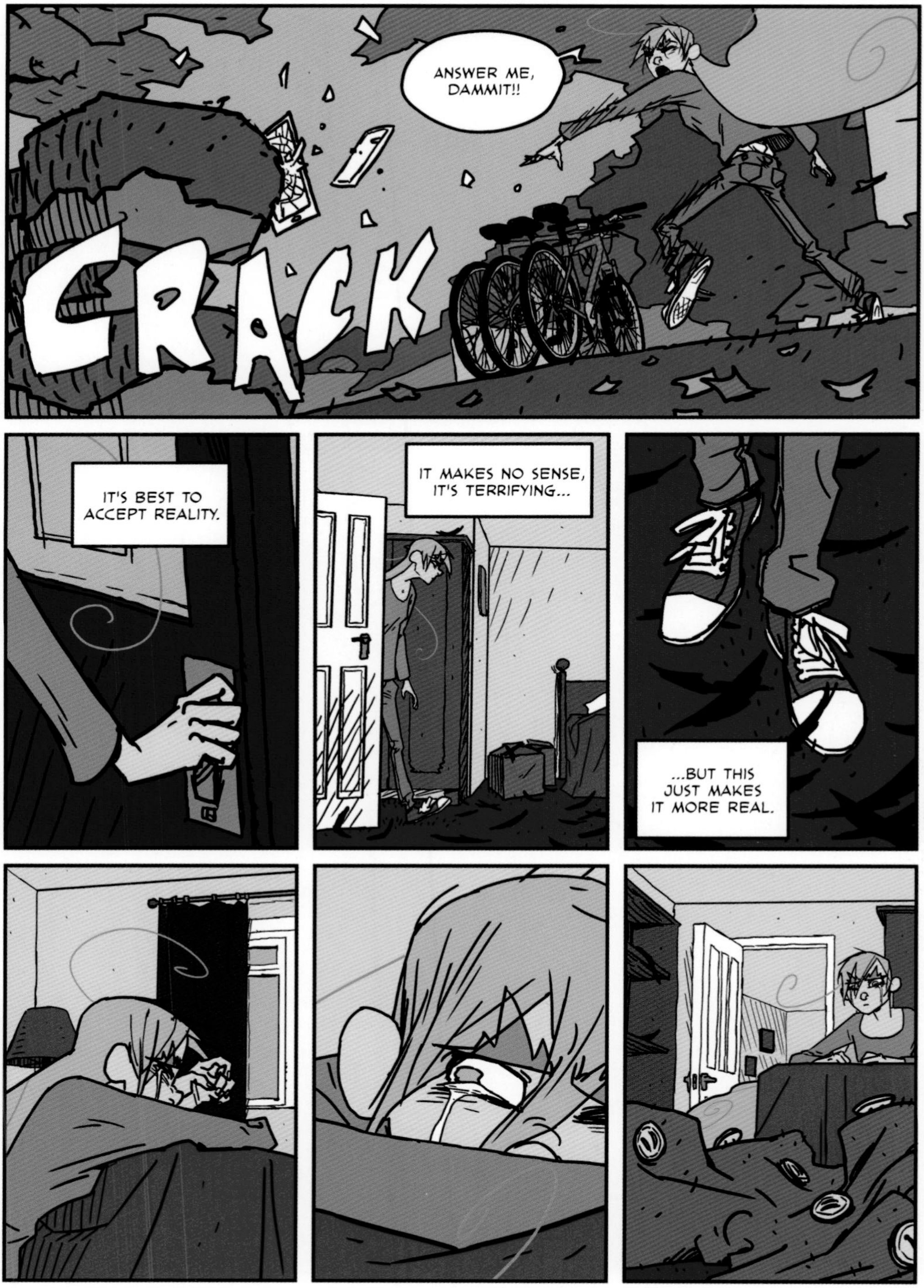
ANSWER ME, DAMMIT!!
CRACK
IT'S BEST TO ACCEPT REALITY.
IT MAKES NO SENSE, IT'S TERRIFYING...
...BUT THIS JUST MAKES IT MORE REAL.

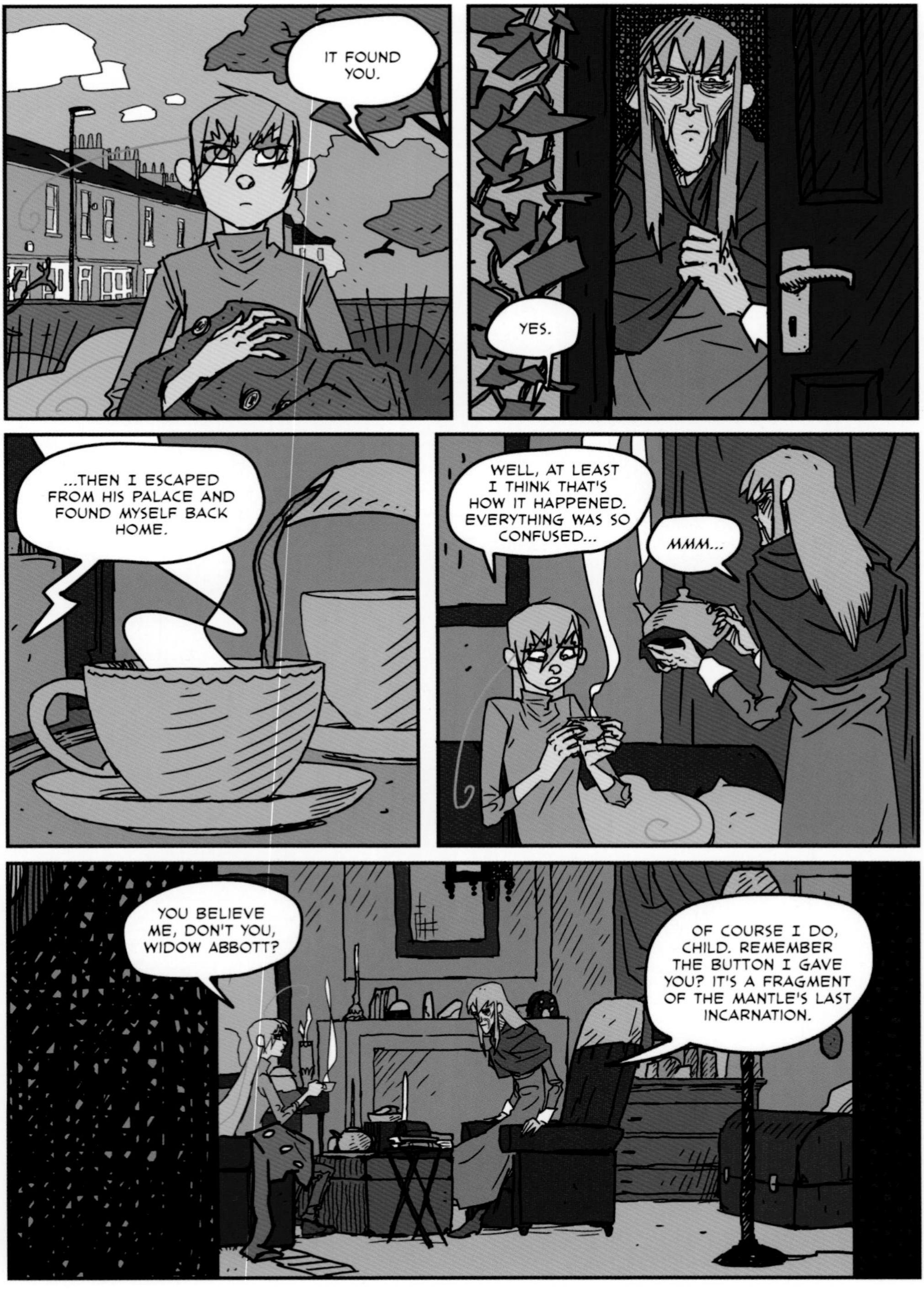
IT FOUND YOU.
YES.
...THEN I ESCAPED FROM HIS PALACE AND FOUND MYSELF BACK HOME.
WELL, AT LEAST I THINK THAT'S HOW IT HAPPENED. EVERYTHING WAS SO CONFUSED...
MMM...
YOU BELIEVE ME, DON'T YOU, WIDOW ABBOTT?
OF COURSE I DO, CHILD. REMEMBER THE BUTTON I GAVE YOU? IT'S A FRAGMENT OF THE MANTLE'S LAST INCARNATION.

ARE YOU TELLING ME THAT YOU PASSED IT ON TO ME, LIKE SOME KIND OF VIRUS?

OH, NOT AT ALL. THE BUTTON'S JUST A TALISMAN, A LUCKY CHARM. A RELIC, IF YOU WILL...

IT'S THE SCARECROW'S MANTLE ITSELF WHO CHOOSES ITS WEARER.

ALRIGHT, WHAT IS THE SCARECROW'S MANTLE, NOW? WHO CREATED IT? HOW...

THESE ARE NOT THE RIGHT QUESTIONS. ALL THEY DO IS GENERATE DOUBT AND FEAR. ONLY TRUST IN THE MANTLE'S POWERS WILL HELP YOU.

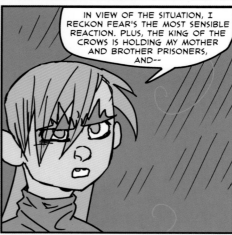

IN VIEW OF THE SITUATION, I RECKON FEAR'S THE MOST SENSIBLE REACTION. PLUS, THE KING OF THE CROWS IS HOLDING MY MOTHER AND BROTHER PRISONERS, AND--

YOUR LOVED ONES ARE IN NO DANGER, FOR NOW. HIS COWARDLY NATURE LEADS HIM TO STEAL RATHER THAN DESTROY.

BUT...

DON'T GET ME WRONG, THIS DOESN'T MEAN KILLING'S AN ISSUE FOR HIM. IT'S JUST THAT IT'S BETTER FOR HIM TO KEEP THEM HOSTAGE, AS IT GRANTS HIM POWER OVER YOU.

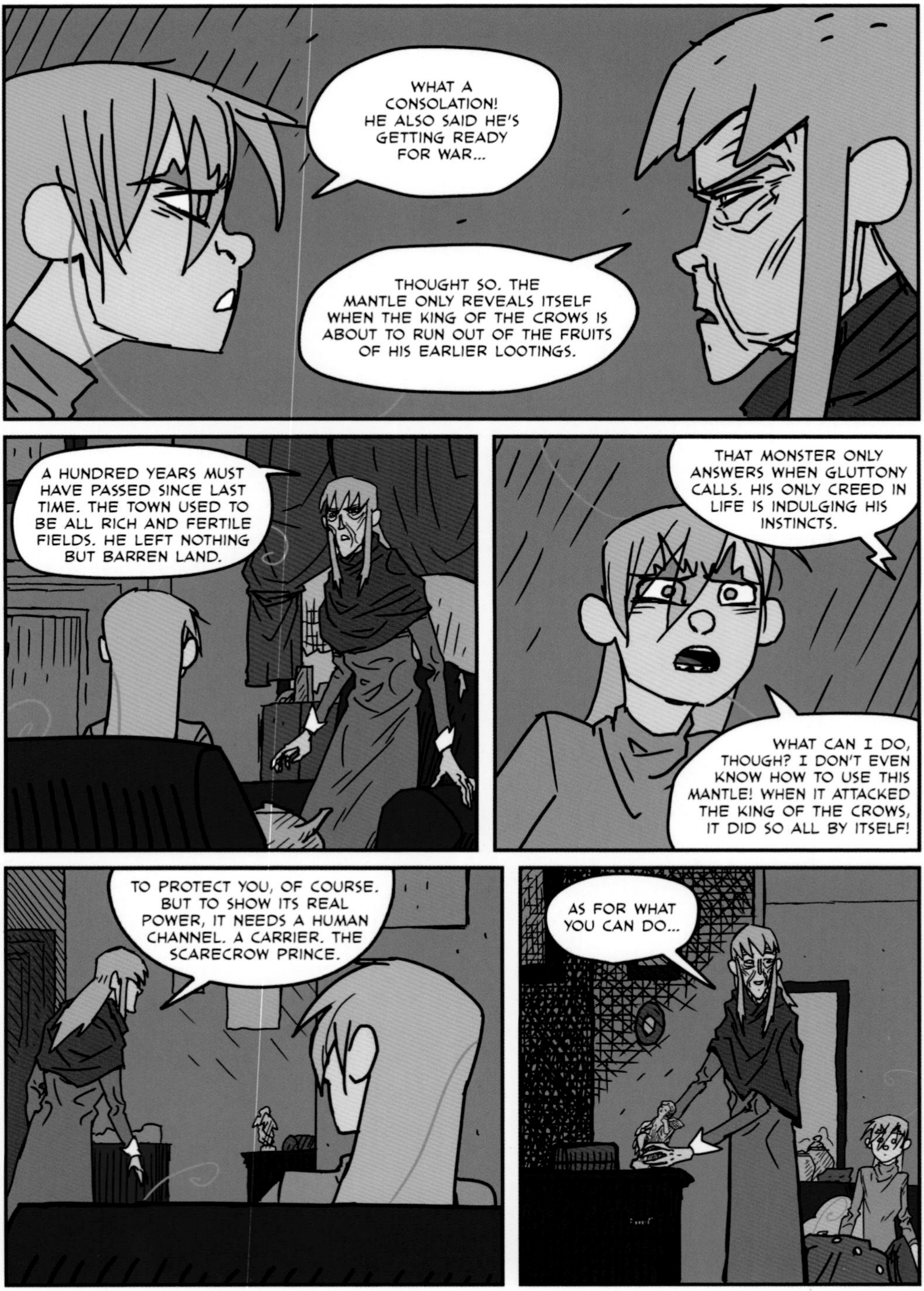
WHAT A CONSOLATION! HE ALSO SAID HE'S GETTING READY FOR WAR...
THOUGHT SO. THE MANTLE ONLY REVEALS ITSELF WHEN THE KING OF THE CROWS IS ABOUT TO RUN OUT OF THE FRUITS OF HIS EARLIER LOOTINGS.
A HUNDRED YEARS MUST HAVE PASSED SINCE LAST TIME. THE TOWN USED TO BE ALL RICH AND FERTILE FIELDS. HE LEFT NOTHING BUT BARREN LAND.
THAT MONSTER ONLY ANSWERS WHEN GLUTTONY CALLS. HIS ONLY CREED IN LIFE IS INDULGING HIS INSTINCTS.
WHAT CAN I DO, THOUGH? I DON'T EVEN KNOW HOW TO USE THIS MANTLE! WHEN IT ATTACKED THE KING OF THE CROWS, IT DID SO ALL BY ITSELF!
TO PROTECT YOU, OF COURSE. BUT TO SHOW ITS REAL POWER, IT NEEDS A HUMAN CHANNEL. A CARRIER. THE SCARECROW PRINCE.
AS FOR WHAT YOU CAN DO...

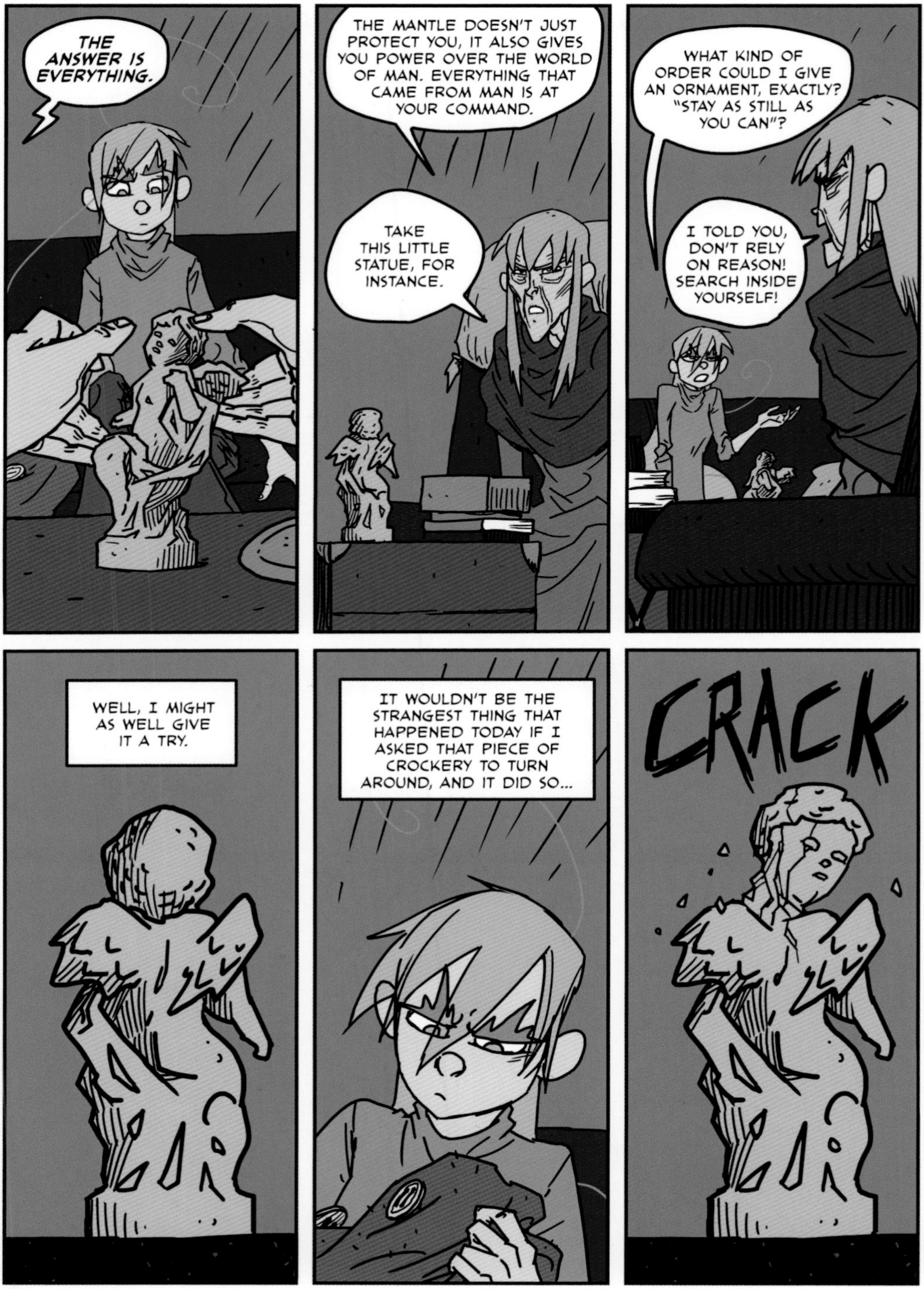

THE ANSWER IS EVERYTHING.
THE MANTLE DOESN'T JUST PROTECT YOU, IT ALSO GIVES YOU POWER OVER THE WORLD OF MAN. EVERYTHING THAT CAME FROM MAN IS AT YOUR COMMAND.
TAKE THIS LITTLE STATUE, FOR INSTANCE.
WHAT KIND OF ORDER COULD I GIVE AN ORNAMENT, EXACTLY? "STAY AS STILL AS YOU CAN"?
I TOLD YOU, DON'T RELY ON REASON! SEARCH INSIDE YOURSELF!
WELL, I MIGHT AS WELL GIVE IT A TRY.
IT WOULDN'T BE THE STRANGEST THING THAT HAPPENED TODAY IF I ASKED THAT PIECE OF CROCKERY TO TURN AROUND, AND IT DID SO...
CRACK

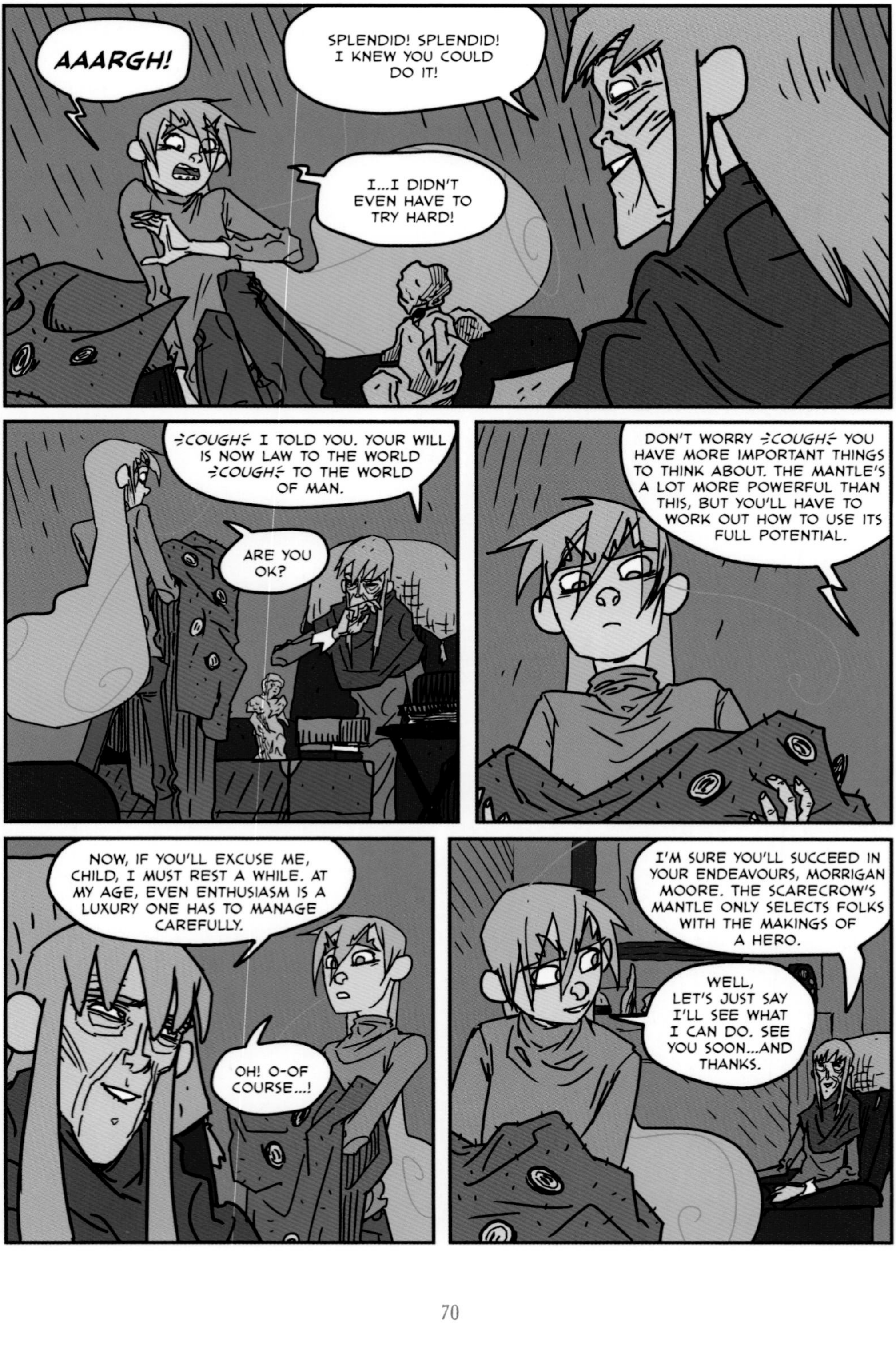
AAARGH!
SPLENDID! SPLENDID! I KNEW YOU COULD DO IT!
I...I DIDN'T EVEN HAVE TO TRY HARD!
⸗COUGH⸗ I TOLD YOU. YOUR WILL IS NOW LAW TO THE WORLD ⸗COUGH⸗ TO THE WORLD OF MAN.
ARE YOU OK?
DON'T WORRY ⸗COUGH⸗ YOU HAVE MORE IMPORTANT THINGS TO THINK ABOUT. THE MANTLE'S A LOT MORE POWERFUL THAN THIS, BUT YOU'LL HAVE TO WORK OUT HOW TO USE ITS FULL POTENTIAL.
NOW, IF YOU'LL EXCUSE ME, CHILD, I MUST REST A WHILE. AT MY AGE, EVEN ENTHUSIASM IS A LUXURY ONE HAS TO MANAGE CAREFULLY.
OH! O-OF COURSE...!
I'M SURE YOU'LL SUCCEED IN YOUR ENDEAVOURS, MORRIGAN MOORE. THE SCARECROW'S MANTLE ONLY SELECTS FOLKS WITH THE MAKINGS OF A HERO.
WELL, LET'S JUST SAY I'LL SEE WHAT I CAN DO. SEE YOU SOON...AND THANKS.

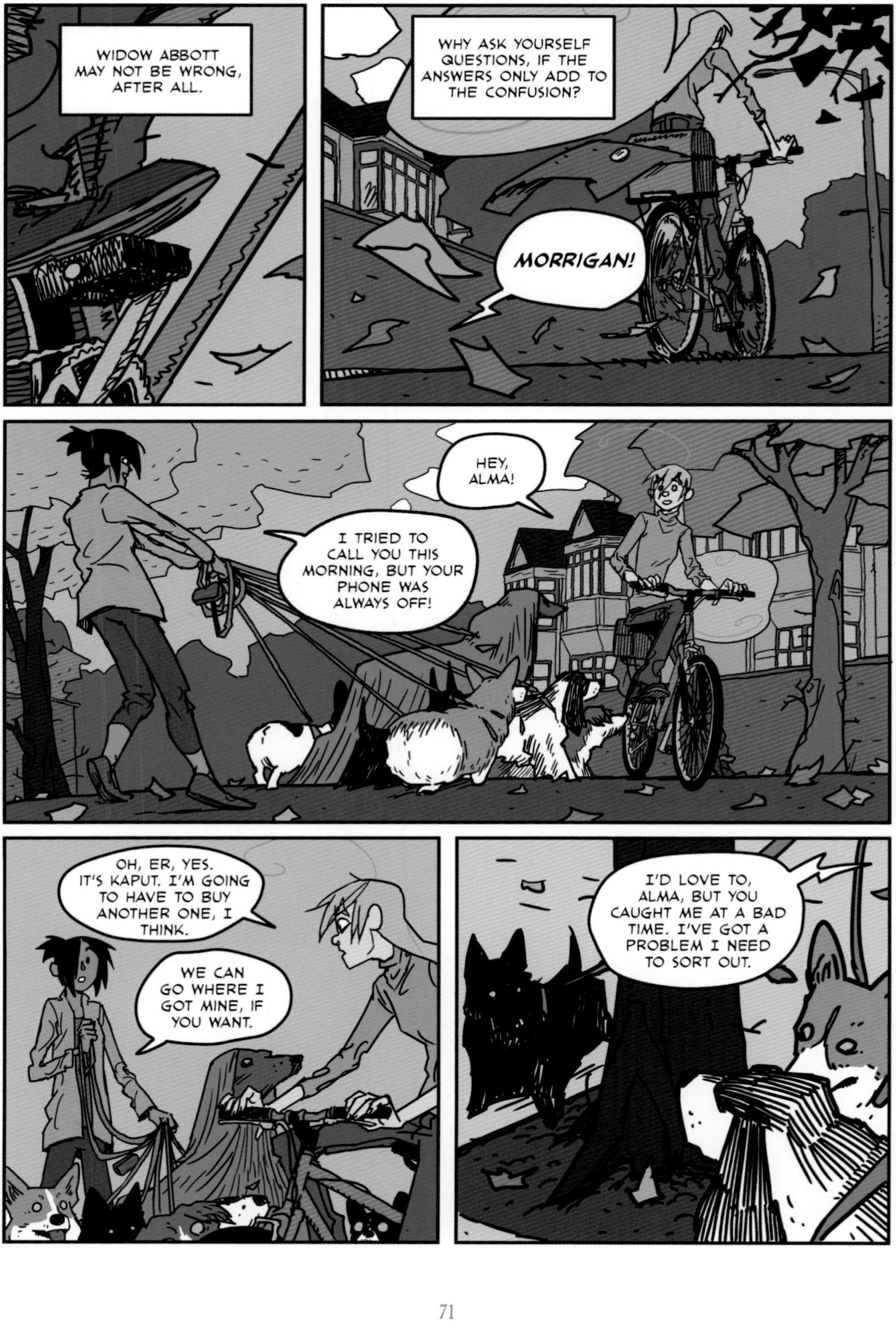
WIDOW ABBOTT MAY NOT BE WRONG, AFTER ALL.
WHY ASK YOURSELF QUESTIONS, IF THE ANSWERS ONLY ADD TO THE CONFUSION?
MORRIGAN!
HEY, ALMA!
I TRIED TO CALL YOU THIS MORNING, BUT YOUR PHONE WAS ALWAYS OFF!
OH, ER, YES. IT'S KAPUT. I'M GOING TO HAVE TO BUY ANOTHER ONE, I THINK.
WE CAN GO WHERE I GOT MINE, IF YOU WANT.
I'D LOVE TO, ALMA, BUT YOU CAUGHT ME AT A BAD TIME. I'VE GOT A PROBLEM I NEED TO SORT OUT.

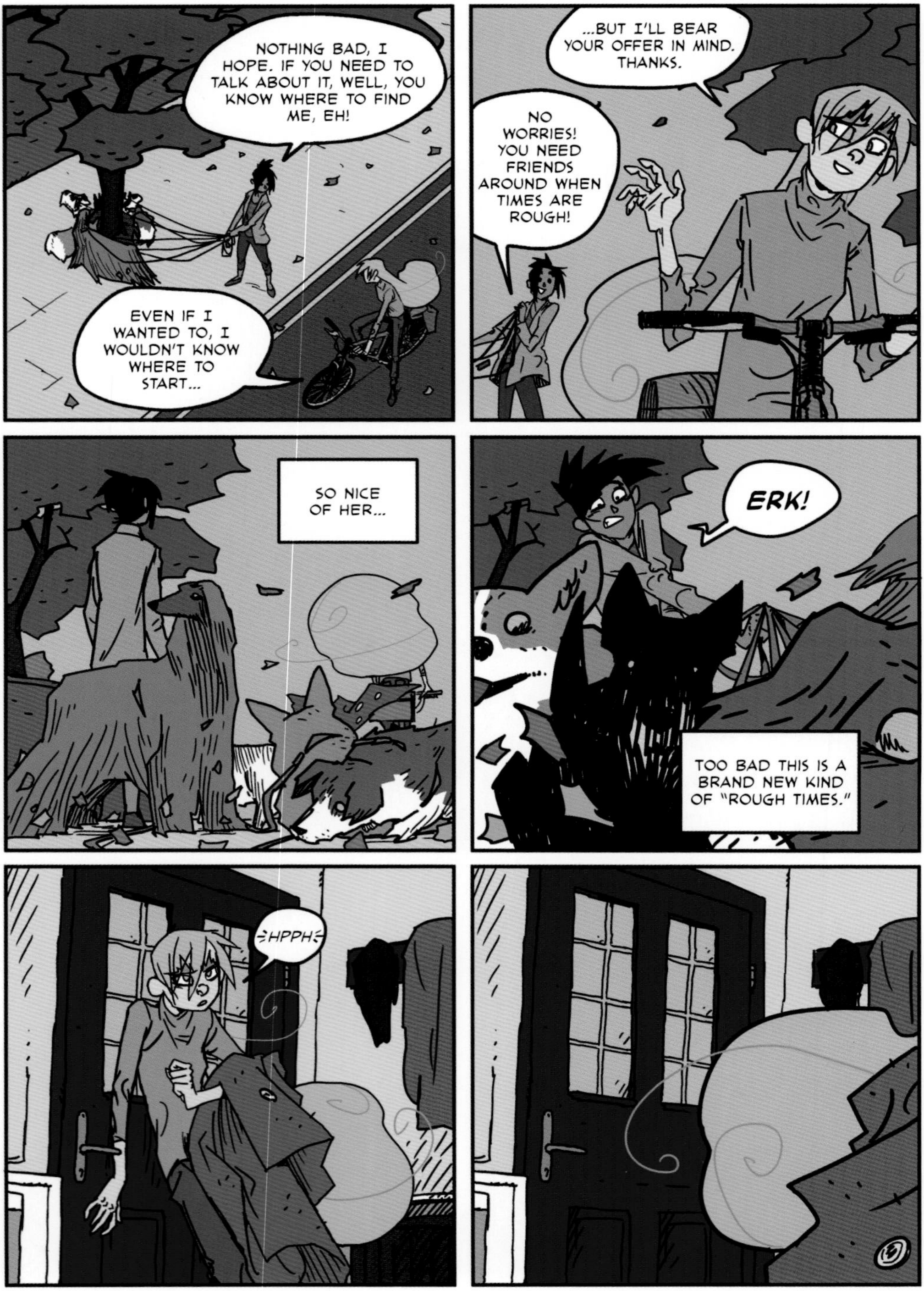
NOTHING BAD, I HOPE. IF YOU NEED TO TALK ABOUT IT, WELL, YOU KNOW WHERE TO FIND ME, EH!
EVEN IF I WANTED TO, I WOULDN'T KNOW WHERE TO START...
...BUT I'LL BEAR YOUR OFFER IN MIND. THANKS.
NO WORRIES! YOU NEED FRIENDS AROUND WHEN TIMES ARE ROUGH!
SO NICE OF HER...
ERK!
TOO BAD THIS IS A BRAND NEW KIND OF "ROUGH TIMES."
HPPH

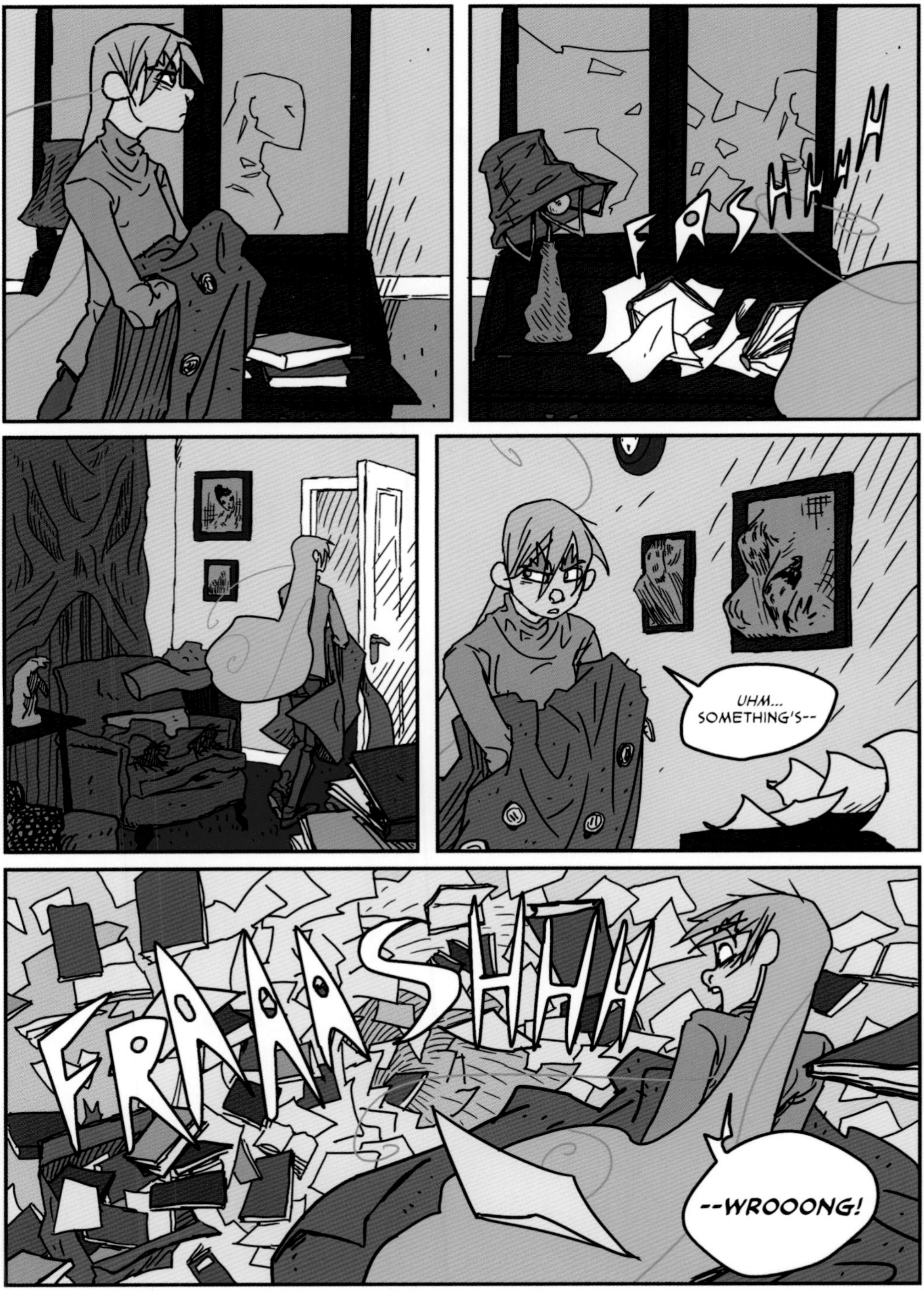
FRASHHHHH
UHM... SOMETHING'S--
FRAAAASHHHH
--WROOONG!

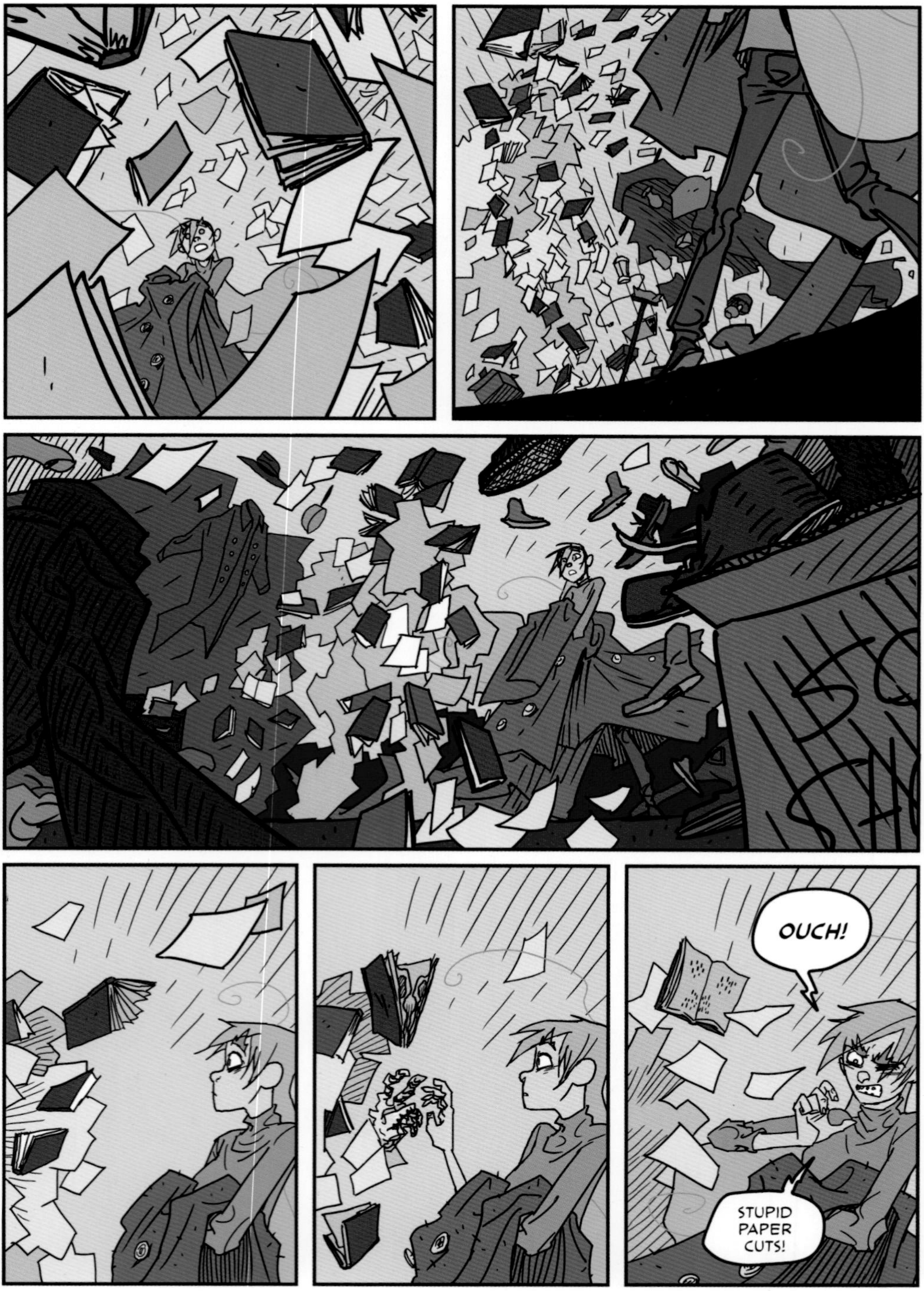
OUCH!
STUPID PAPER CUTS!

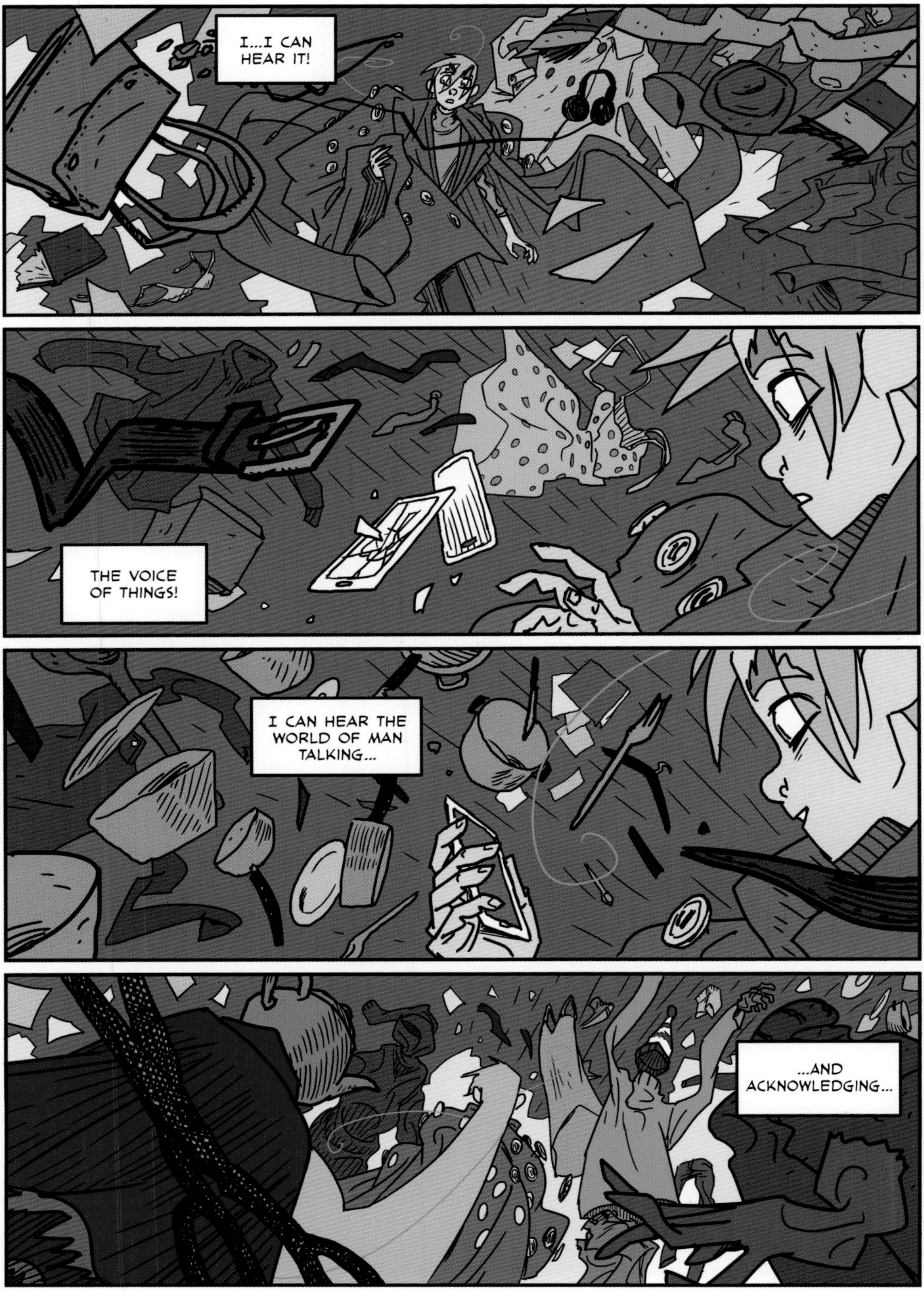

I...I CAN HEAR IT!
THE VOICE OF THINGS!
I CAN HEAR THE WORLD OF MAN TALKING...
...AND ACKNOWLEDGING...

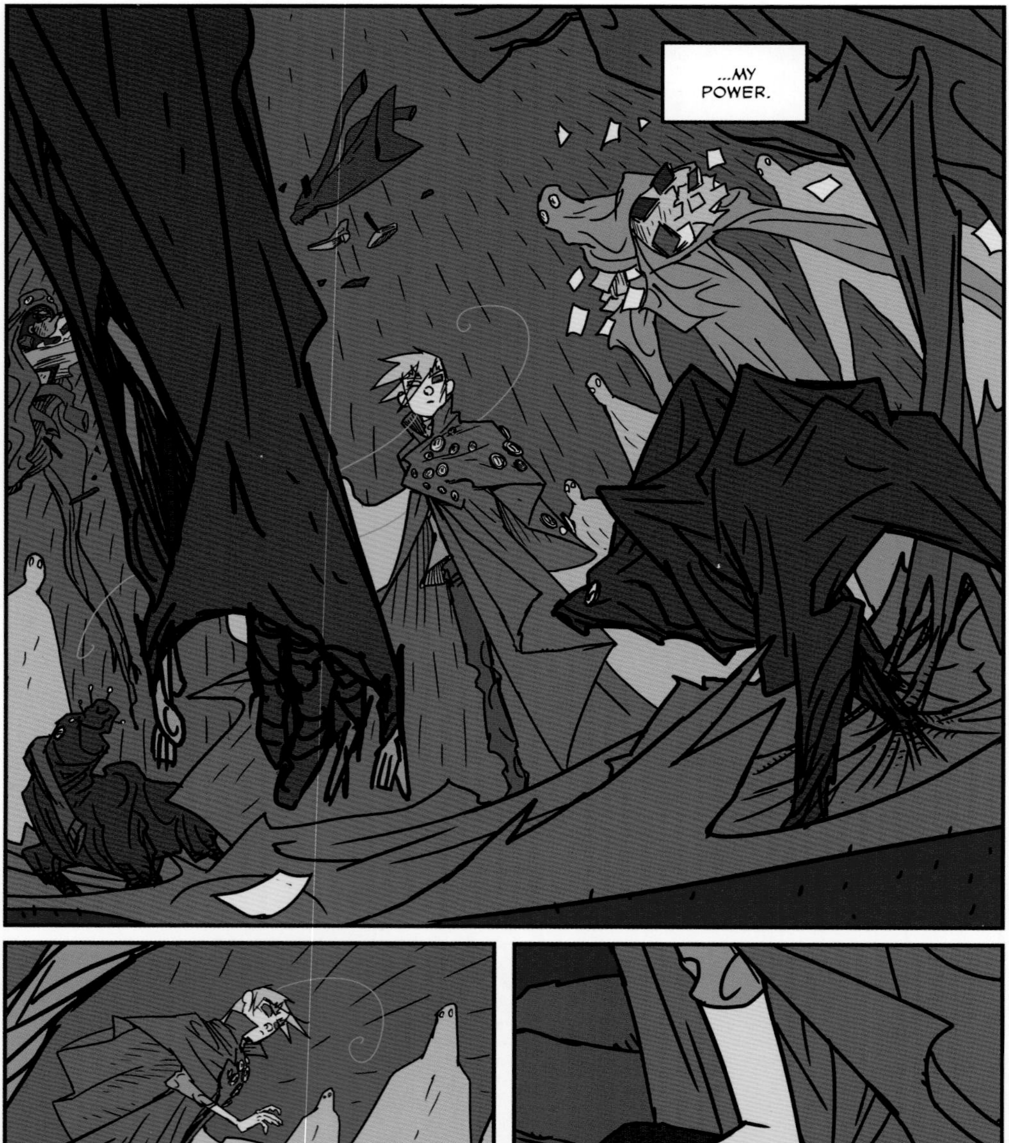
...MY POWER.

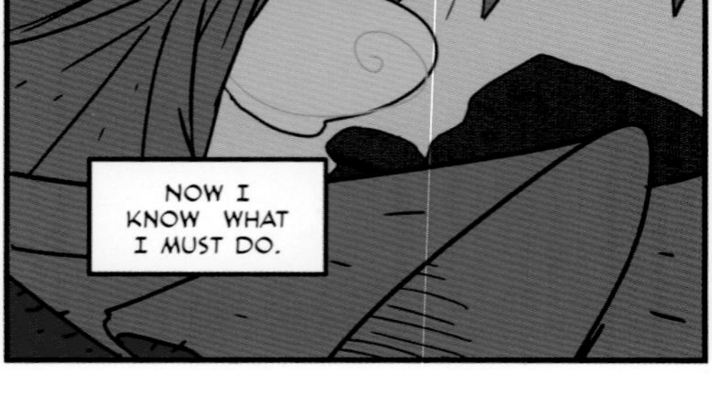
NOW I KNOW WHAT I MUST DO.

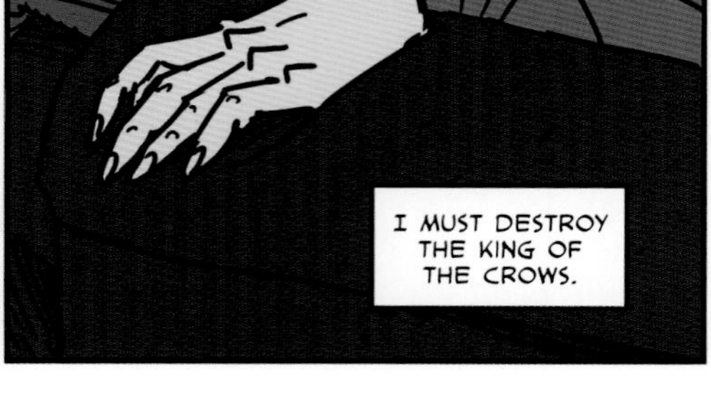
I MUST DESTROY THE KING OF THE CROWS.

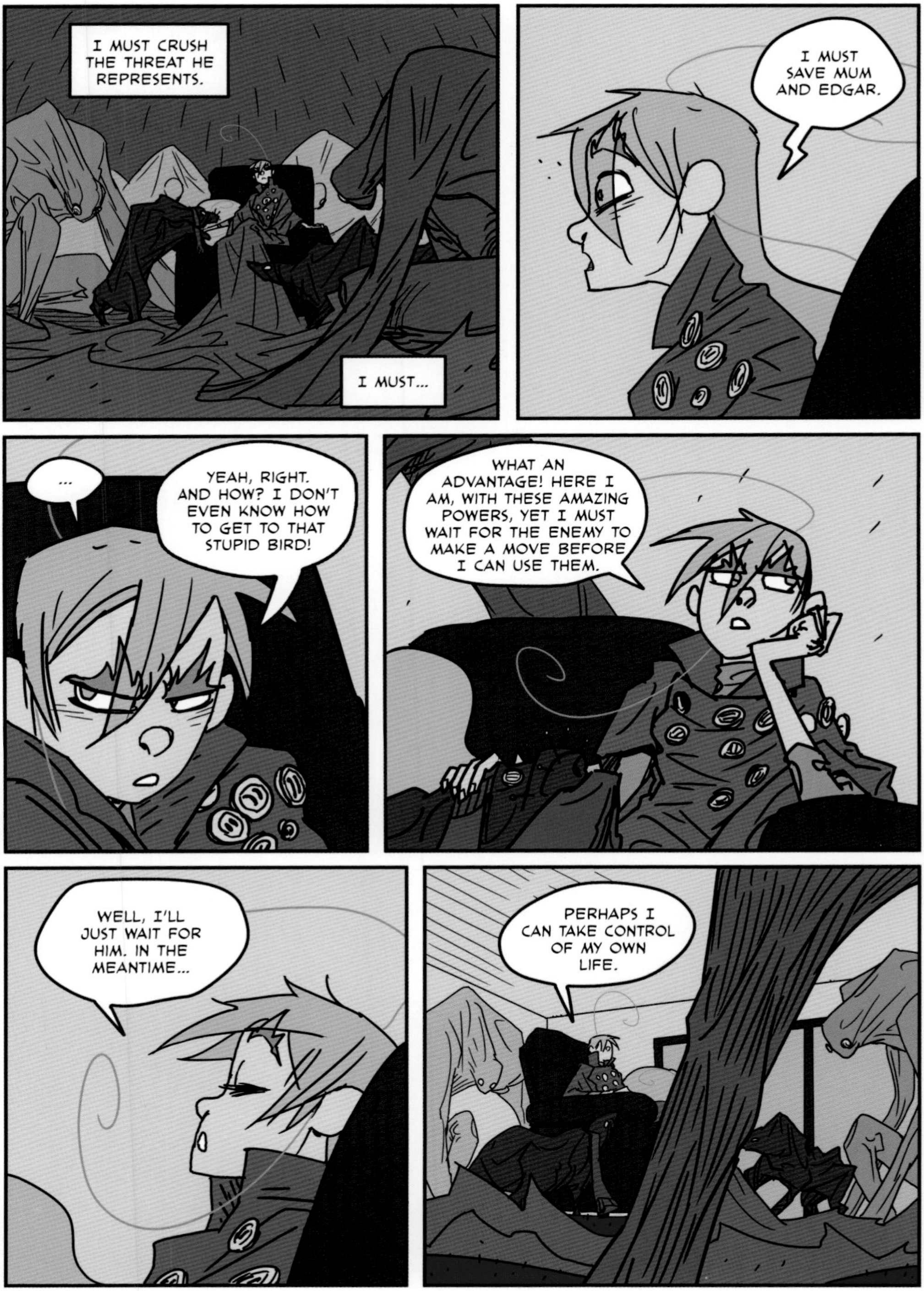
I MUST CRUSH THE THREAT HE REPRESENTS.
I MUST...
I MUST SAVE MUM AND EDGAR.
...
YEAH, RIGHT. AND HOW? I DON'T EVEN KNOW HOW TO GET TO THAT STUPID BIRD!
WHAT AN ADVANTAGE! HERE I AM, WITH THESE AMAZING POWERS, YET I MUST WAIT FOR THE ENEMY TO MAKE A MOVE BEFORE I CAN USE THEM.
WELL, I'LL JUST WAIT FOR HIM. IN THE MEANTIME...
PERHAPS I CAN TAKE CONTROL OF MY OWN LIFE.

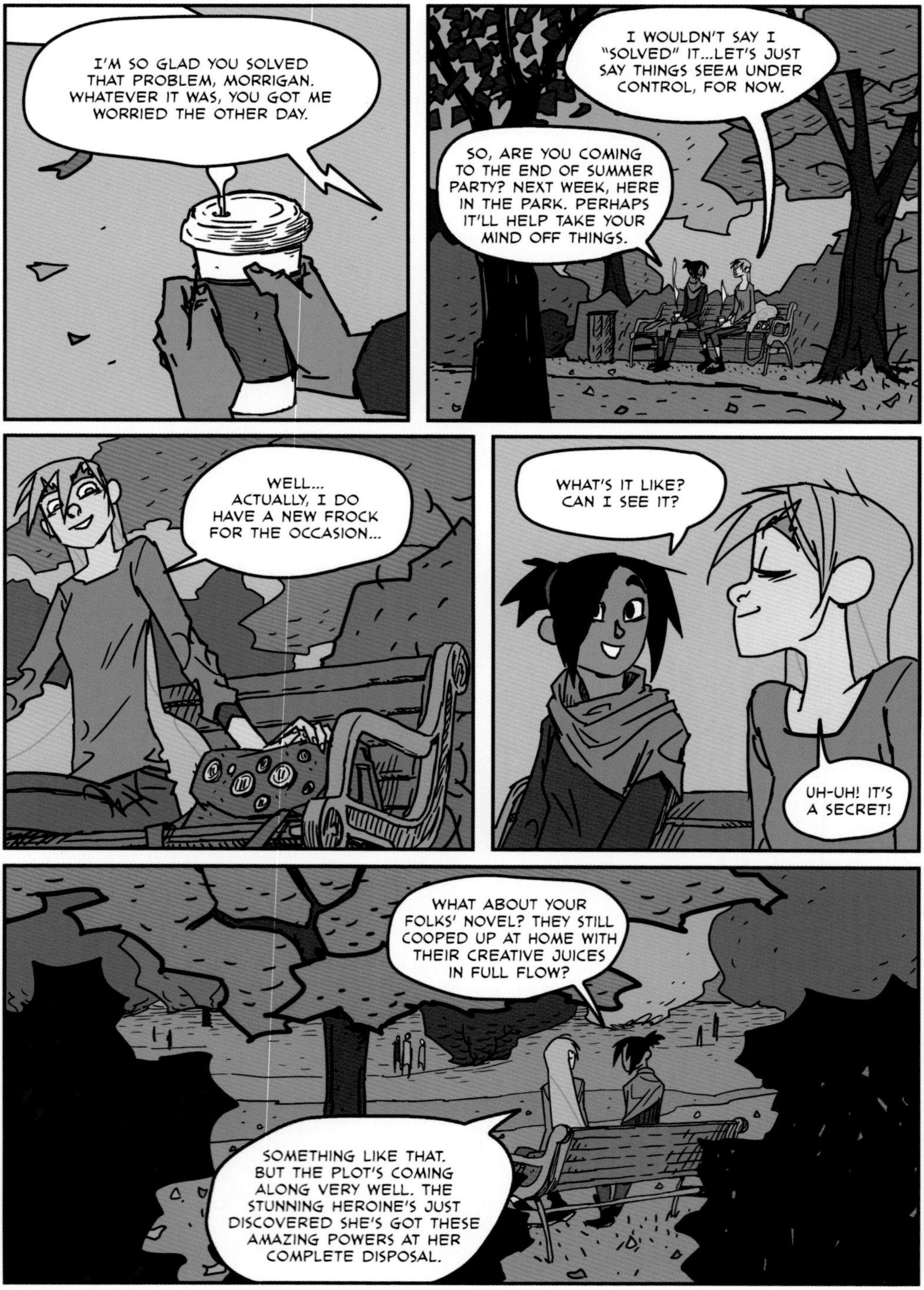
I'M SO GLAD YOU SOLVED THAT PROBLEM, MORRIGAN. WHATEVER IT WAS, YOU GOT ME WORRIED THE OTHER DAY.
I WOULDN'T SAY I "SOLVED" IT...LET'S JUST SAY THINGS SEEM UNDER CONTROL, FOR NOW.
SO, ARE YOU COMING TO THE END OF SUMMER PARTY? NEXT WEEK, HERE IN THE PARK. PERHAPS IT'LL HELP TAKE YOUR MIND OFF THINGS.
WELL... ACTUALLY, I DO HAVE A NEW FROCK FOR THE OCCASION...
WHAT'S IT LIKE? CAN I SEE IT?
UH-UH! IT'S A SECRET!
WHAT ABOUT YOUR FOLKS' NOVEL? THEY STILL COOPED UP AT HOME WITH THEIR CREATIVE JUICES IN FULL FLOW?
SOMETHING LIKE THAT. BUT THE PLOT'S COMING ALONG VERY WELL. THE STUNNING HEROINE'S JUST DISCOVERED SHE'S GOT THESE AMAZING POWERS AT HER COMPLETE DISPOSAL.

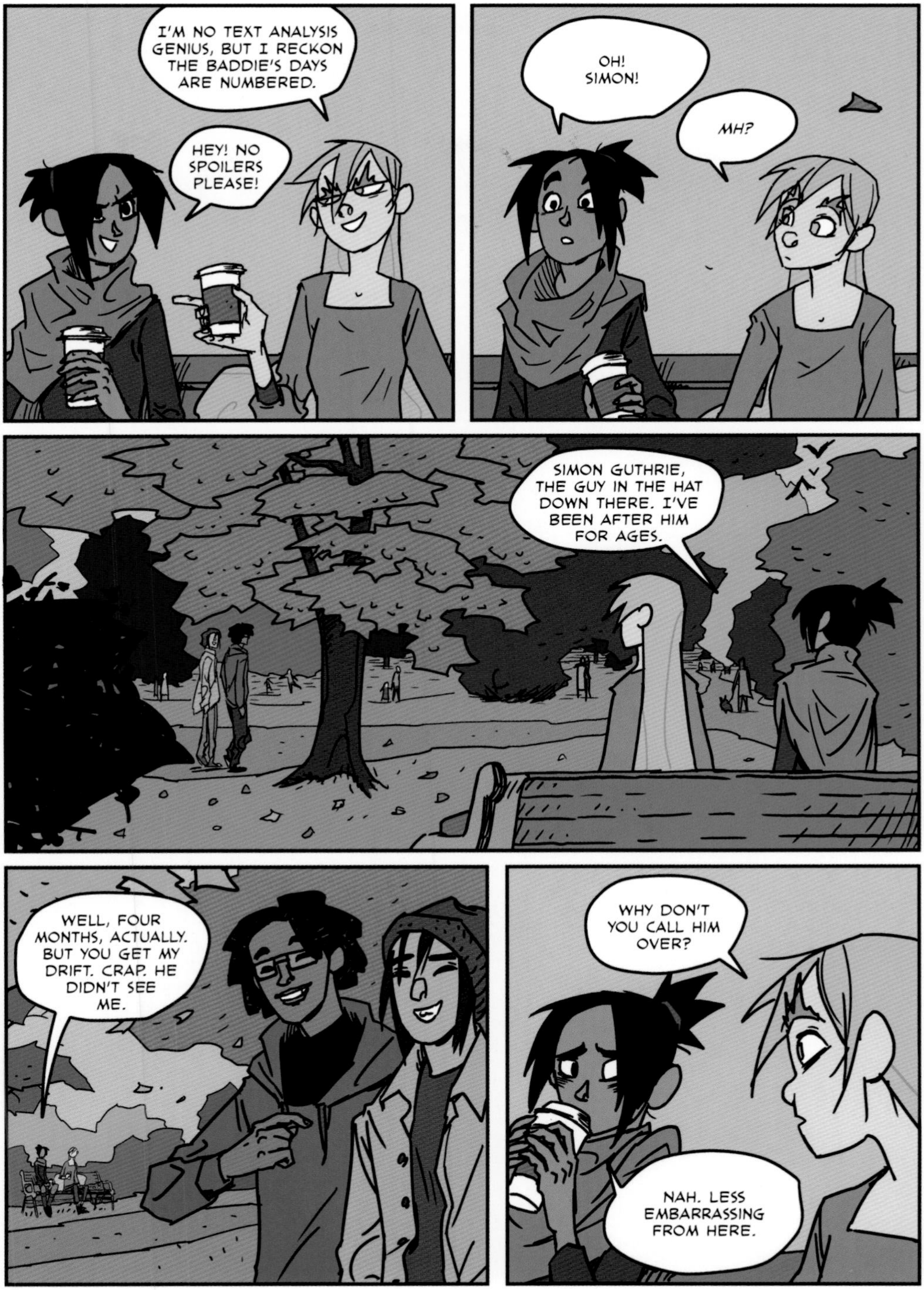
I'M NO TEXT ANALYSIS GENIUS, BUT I RECKON THE BADDIE'S DAYS ARE NUMBERED.
HEY! NO SPOILERS PLEASE!
OH! SIMON!
MH?
SIMON GUTHRIE, THE GUY IN THE HAT DOWN THERE. I'VE BEEN AFTER HIM FOR AGES.
WELL, FOUR MONTHS, ACTUALLY. BUT YOU GET MY DRIFT. CRAP. HE DIDN'T SEE ME.
WHY DON'T YOU CALL HIM OVER?
NAH. LESS EMBARRASSING FROM HERE.

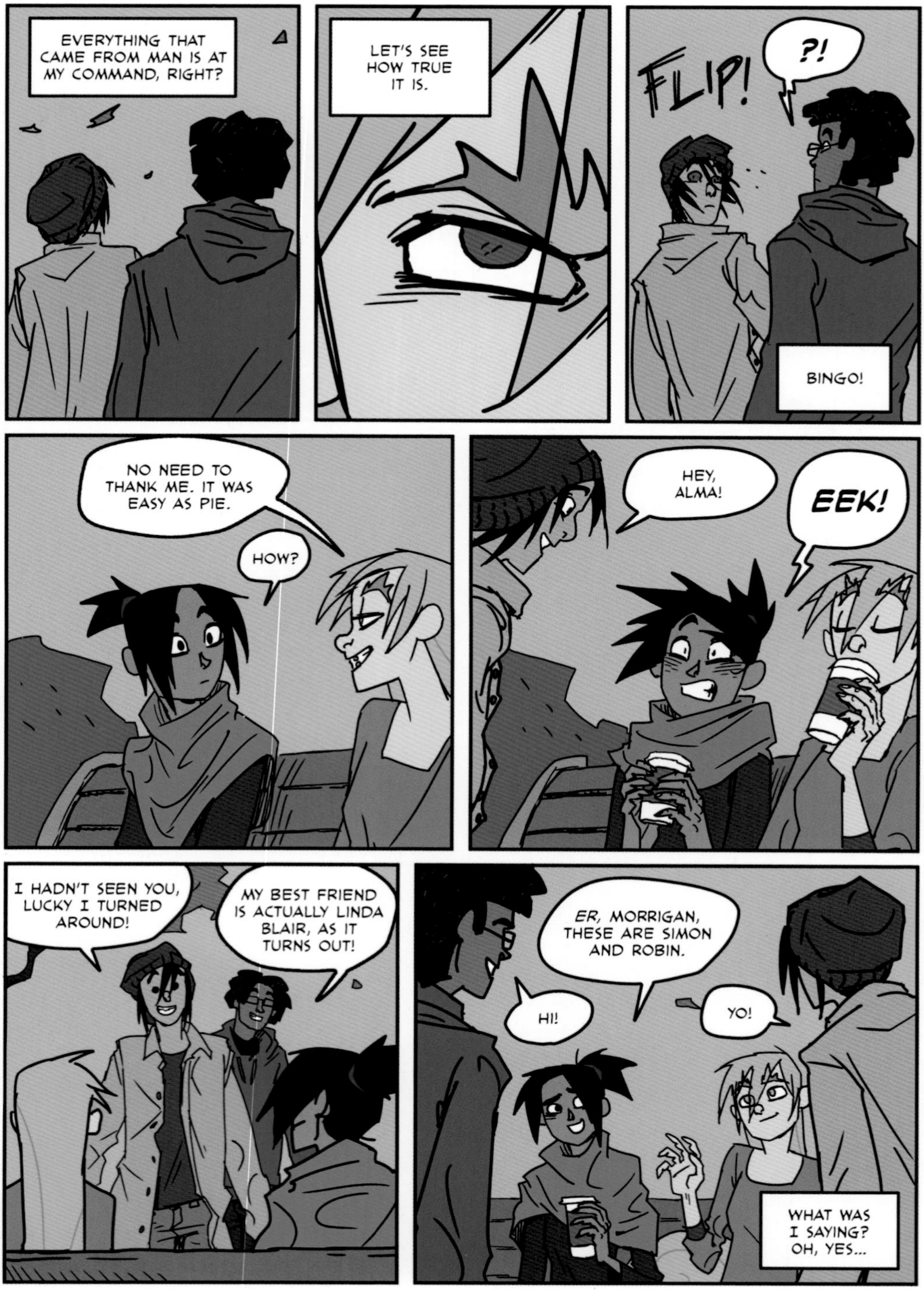
EVERYTHING THAT CAME FROM MAN IS AT MY COMMAND, RIGHT?
LET'S SEE HOW TRUE IT IS.
FLIP!
?!
BINGO!
NO NEED TO THANK ME. IT WAS EASY AS PIE.
HOW?
HEY, ALMA!
EEK!
I HADN'T SEEN YOU, LUCKY I TURNED AROUND!
MY BEST FRIEND IS ACTUALLY LINDA BLAIR, AS IT TURNS OUT!
ER, MORRIGAN, THESE ARE SIMON AND ROBIN.
HI!
YO!
WHAT WAS I SAYING? OH, YES...

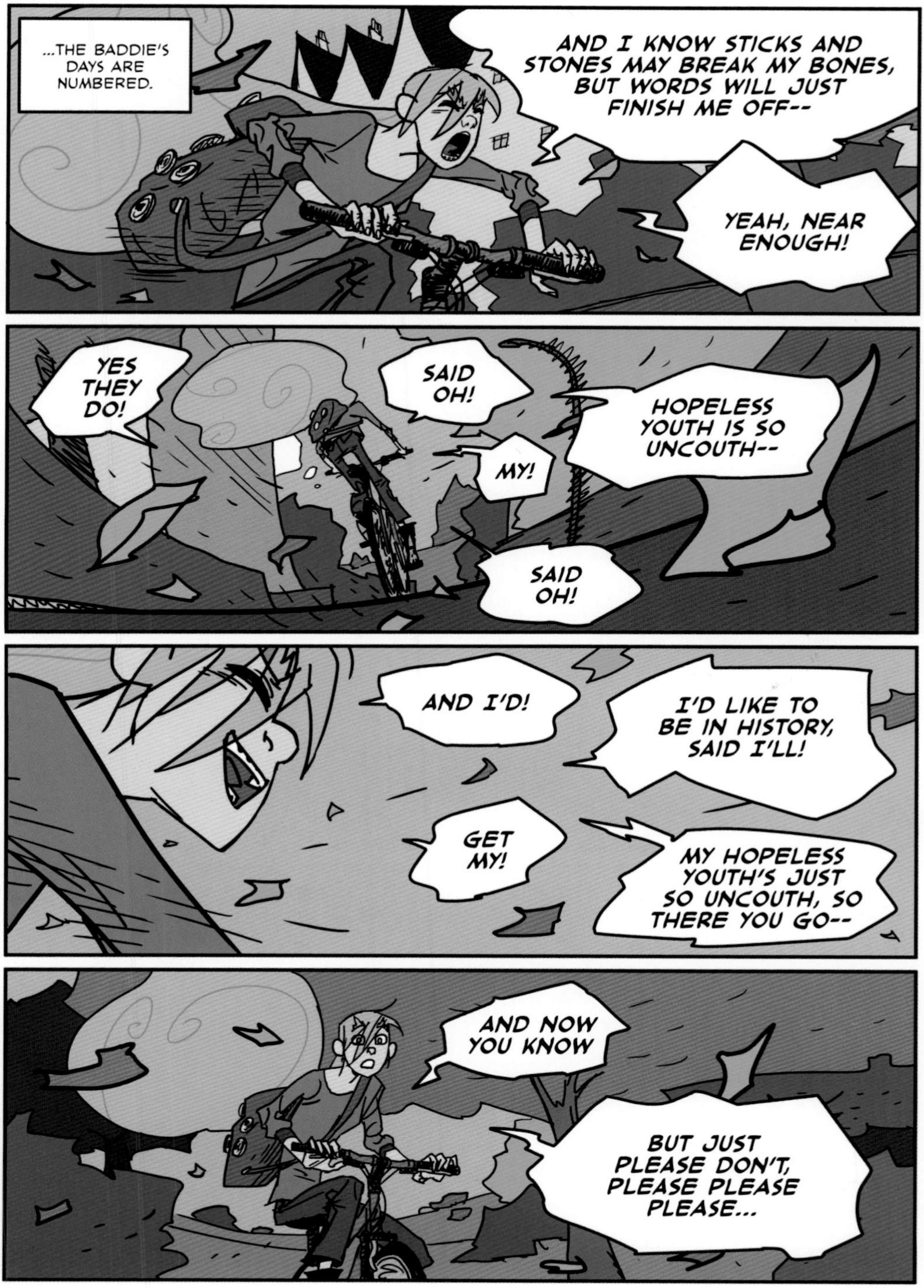
...THE BADDIE'S DAYS ARE NUMBERED.
AND I KNOW STICKS AND STONES MAY BREAK MY BONES, BUT WORDS WILL JUST FINISH ME OFF--
YEAH, NEAR ENOUGH!
YES THEY DO!
SAID OH!
MY!
HOPELESS YOUTH IS SO UNCOUTH--
SAID OH!
AND I'D!
I'D LIKE TO BE IN HISTORY, SAID I'LL!
GET MY!
MY HOPELESS YOUTH'S JUST SO UNCOUTH, SO THERE YOU GO--
AND NOW YOU KNOW
BUT JUST PLEASE DON'T, PLEASE PLEASE PLEASE...

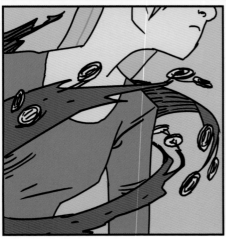

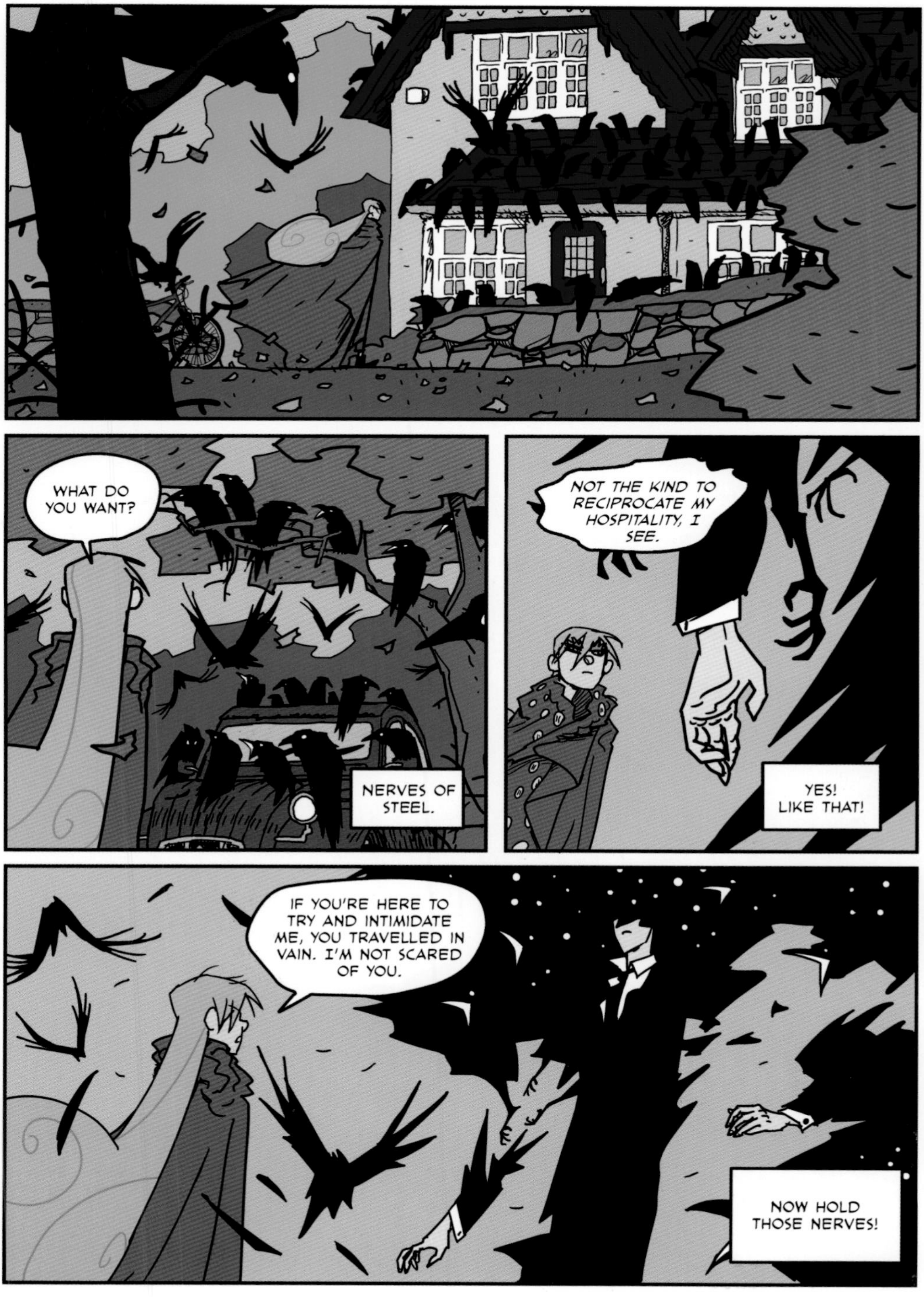
WHAT DO YOU WANT?
NERVES OF STEEL.
NOT THE KIND TO RECIPROCATE MY HOSPITALITY, I SEE.
YES! LIKE THAT!
IF YOU'RE HERE TO TRY AND INTIMIDATE ME, YOU TRAVELLED IN VAIN. I'M NOT SCARED OF YOU.
NOW HOLD THOSE NERVES!

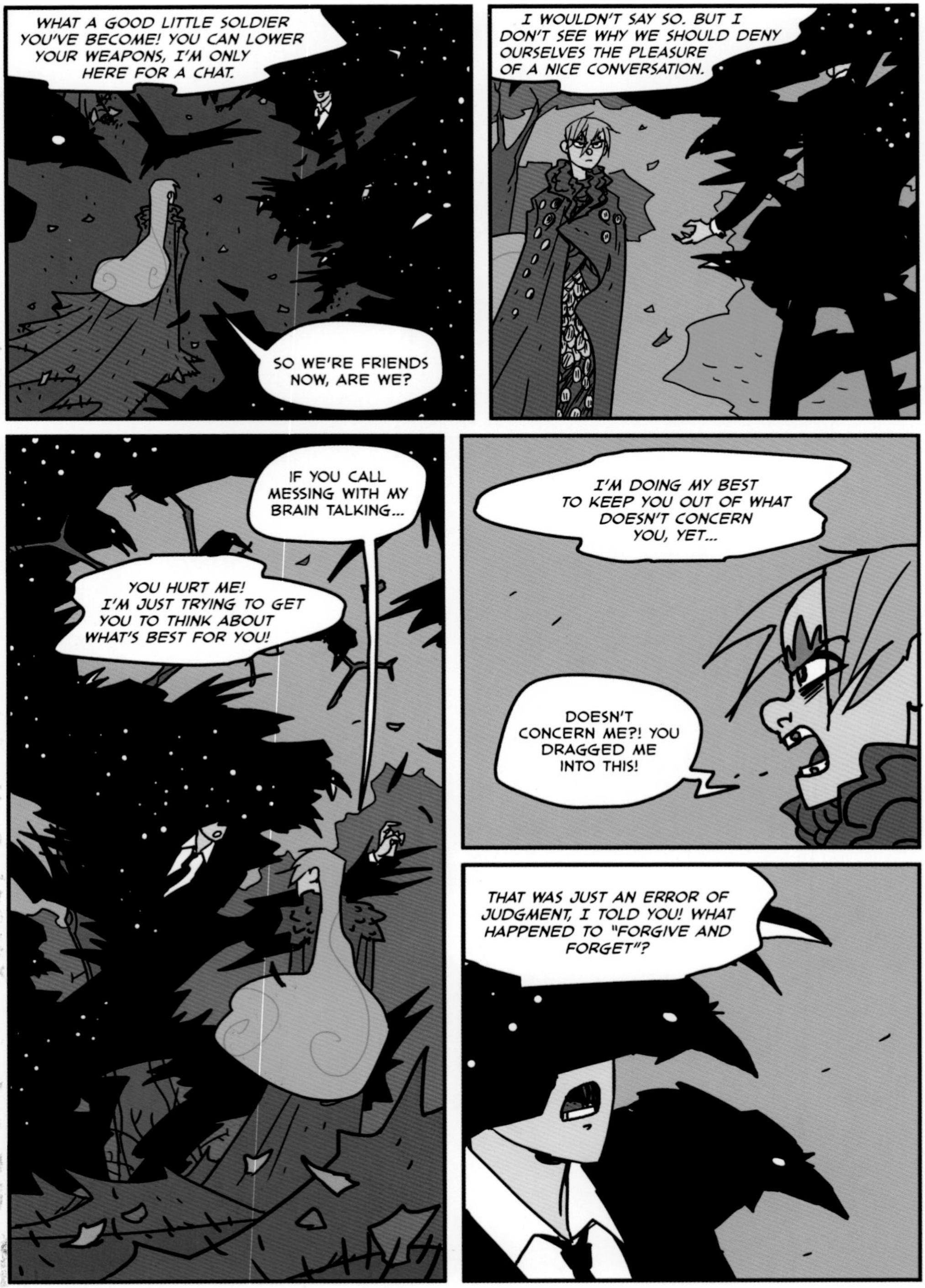
WHAT A GOOD LITTLE SOLDIER YOU'VE BECOME! YOU CAN LOWER YOUR WEAPONS, I'M ONLY HERE FOR A CHAT.
SO WE'RE FRIENDS NOW, ARE WE?
I WOULDN'T SAY SO. BUT I DON'T SEE WHY WE SHOULD DENY OURSELVES THE PLEASURE OF A NICE CONVERSATION.
IF YOU CALL MESSING WITH MY BRAIN TALKING...
YOU HURT ME! I'M JUST TRYING TO GET YOU TO THINK ABOUT WHAT'S BEST FOR YOU!
I'M DOING MY BEST TO KEEP YOU OUT OF WHAT DOESN'T CONCERN YOU, YET...
DOESN'T CONCERN ME?! YOU DRAGGED ME INTO THIS!
THAT WAS JUST AN ERROR OF JUDGMENT, I TOLD YOU! WHAT HAPPENED TO "FORGIVE AND FORGET"?

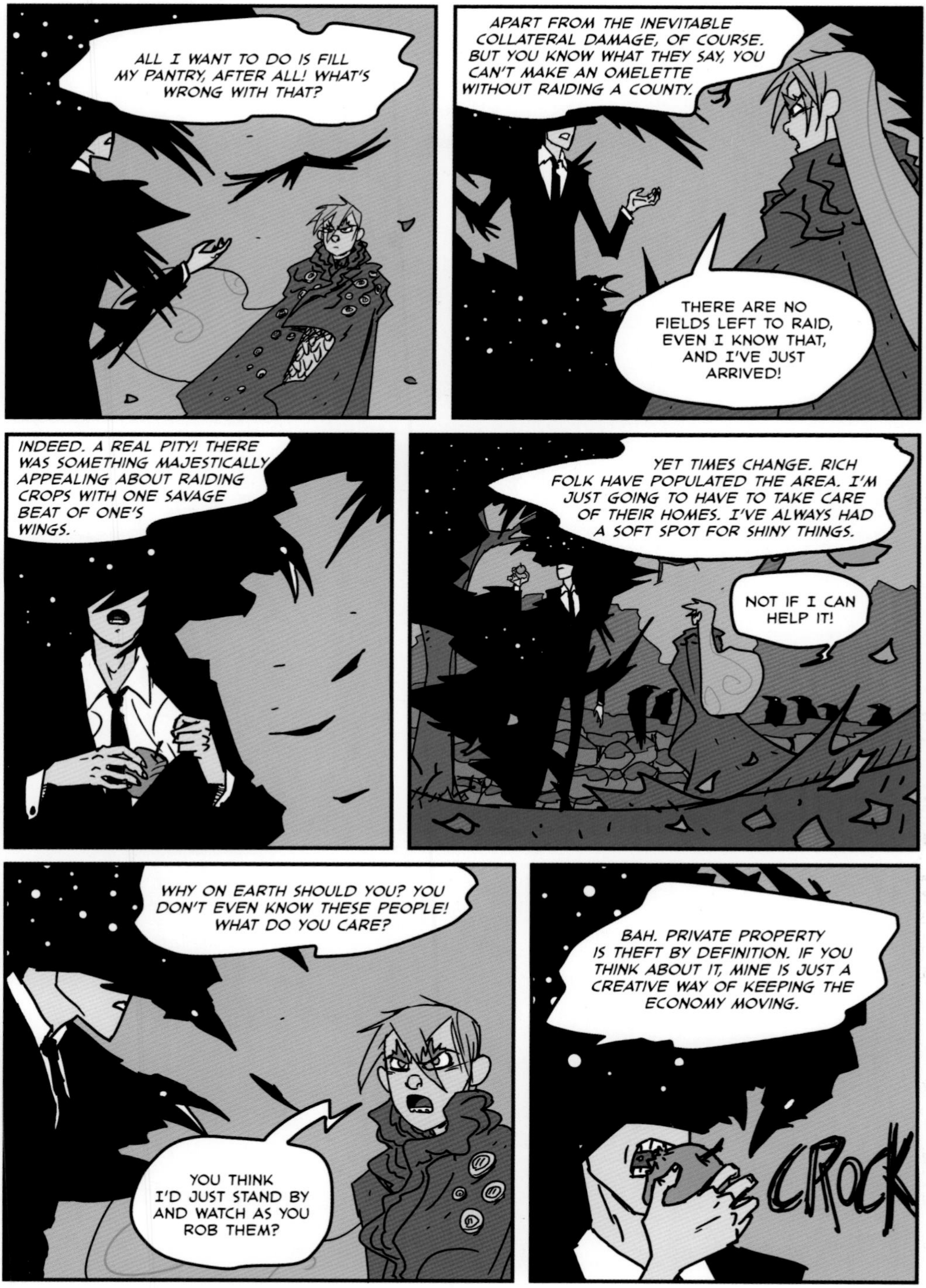
ALL I WANT TO DO IS FILL MY PANTRY, AFTER ALL! WHAT'S WRONG WITH THAT?
APART FROM THE INEVITABLE COLLATERAL DAMAGE, OF COURSE. BUT YOU KNOW WHAT THEY SAY, YOU CAN'T MAKE AN OMELETTE WITHOUT RAIDING A COUNTY.
THERE ARE NO FIELDS LEFT TO RAID, EVEN I KNOW THAT, AND I'VE JUST ARRIVED!
INDEED. A REAL PITY! THERE WAS SOMETHING MAJESTICALLY APPEALING ABOUT RAIDING CROPS WITH ONE SAVAGE BEAT OF ONE'S WINGS.
YET TIMES CHANGE. RICH FOLK HAVE POPULATED THE AREA. I'M JUST GOING TO HAVE TO TAKE CARE OF THEIR HOMES. I'VE ALWAYS HAD A SOFT SPOT FOR SHINY THINGS.
NOT IF I CAN HELP IT!
WHY ON EARTH SHOULD YOU? YOU DON'T EVEN KNOW THESE PEOPLE! WHAT DO YOU CARE?
YOU THINK I'D JUST STAND BY AND WATCH AS YOU ROB THEM?
BAH. PRIVATE PROPERTY IS THEFT BY DEFINITION. IF YOU THINK ABOUT IT, MINE IS JUST A CREATIVE WAY OF KEEPING THE ECONOMY MOVING.
CROCK

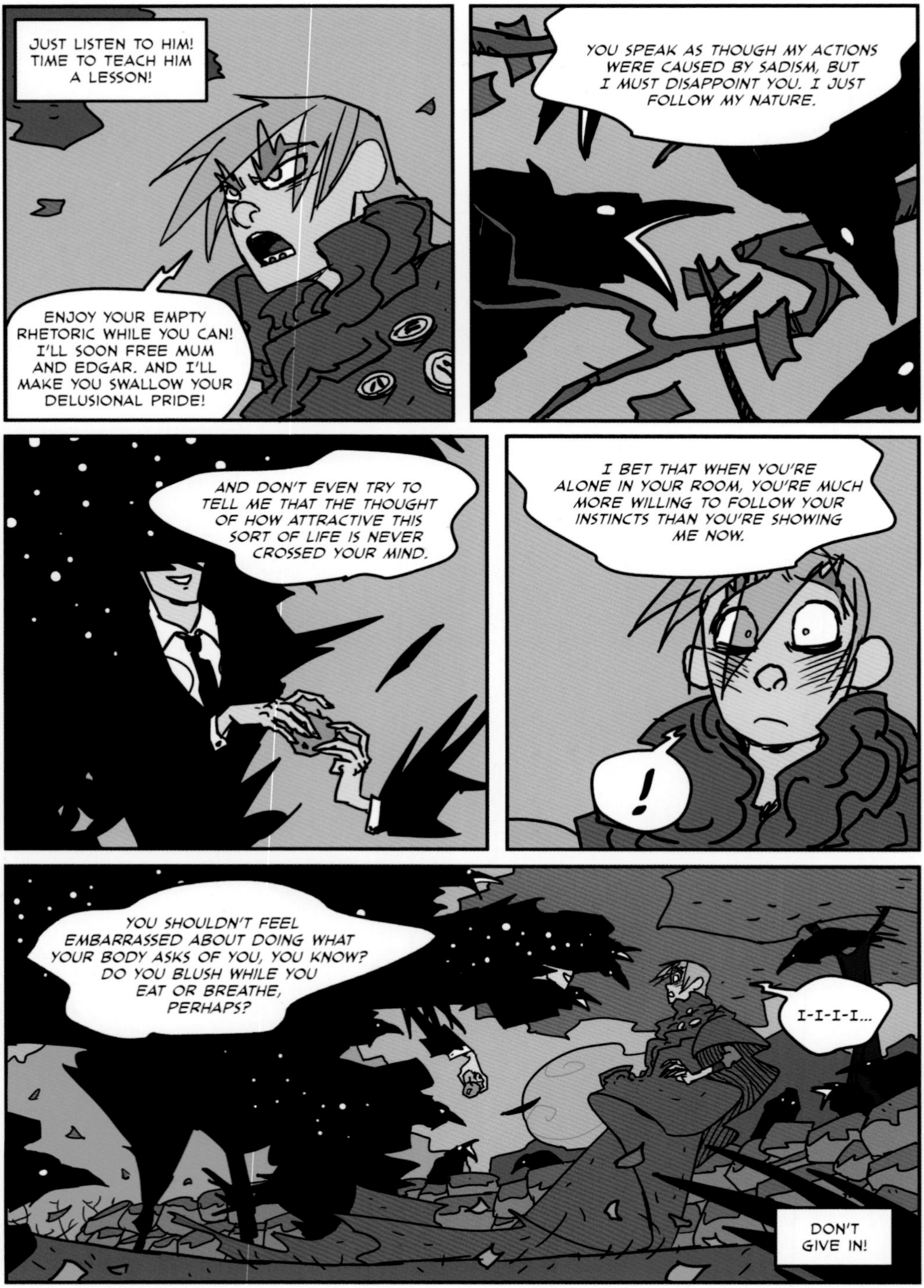
JUST LISTEN TO HIM! TIME TO TEACH HIM A LESSON!
ENJOY YOUR EMPTY RHETORIC WHILE YOU CAN! I'LL SOON FREE MUM AND EDGAR. AND I'LL MAKE YOU SWALLOW YOUR DELUSIONAL PRIDE!
YOU SPEAK AS THOUGH MY ACTIONS WERE CAUSED BY SADISM, BUT I MUST DISAPPOINT YOU. I JUST FOLLOW MY NATURE.
AND DON'T EVEN TRY TO TELL ME THAT THE THOUGHT OF HOW ATTRACTIVE THIS SORT OF LIFE IS NEVER CROSSED YOUR MIND.
I BET THAT WHEN YOU'RE ALONE IN YOUR ROOM, YOU'RE MUCH MORE WILLING TO FOLLOW YOUR INSTINCTS THAN YOU'RE SHOWING ME NOW.
!
YOU SHOULDN'T FEEL EMBARRASSED ABOUT DOING WHAT YOUR BODY ASKS OF YOU, YOU KNOW? DO YOU BLUSH WHILE YOU EAT OR BREATHE, PERHAPS?
I-I-I-I...
DON'T GIVE IN!

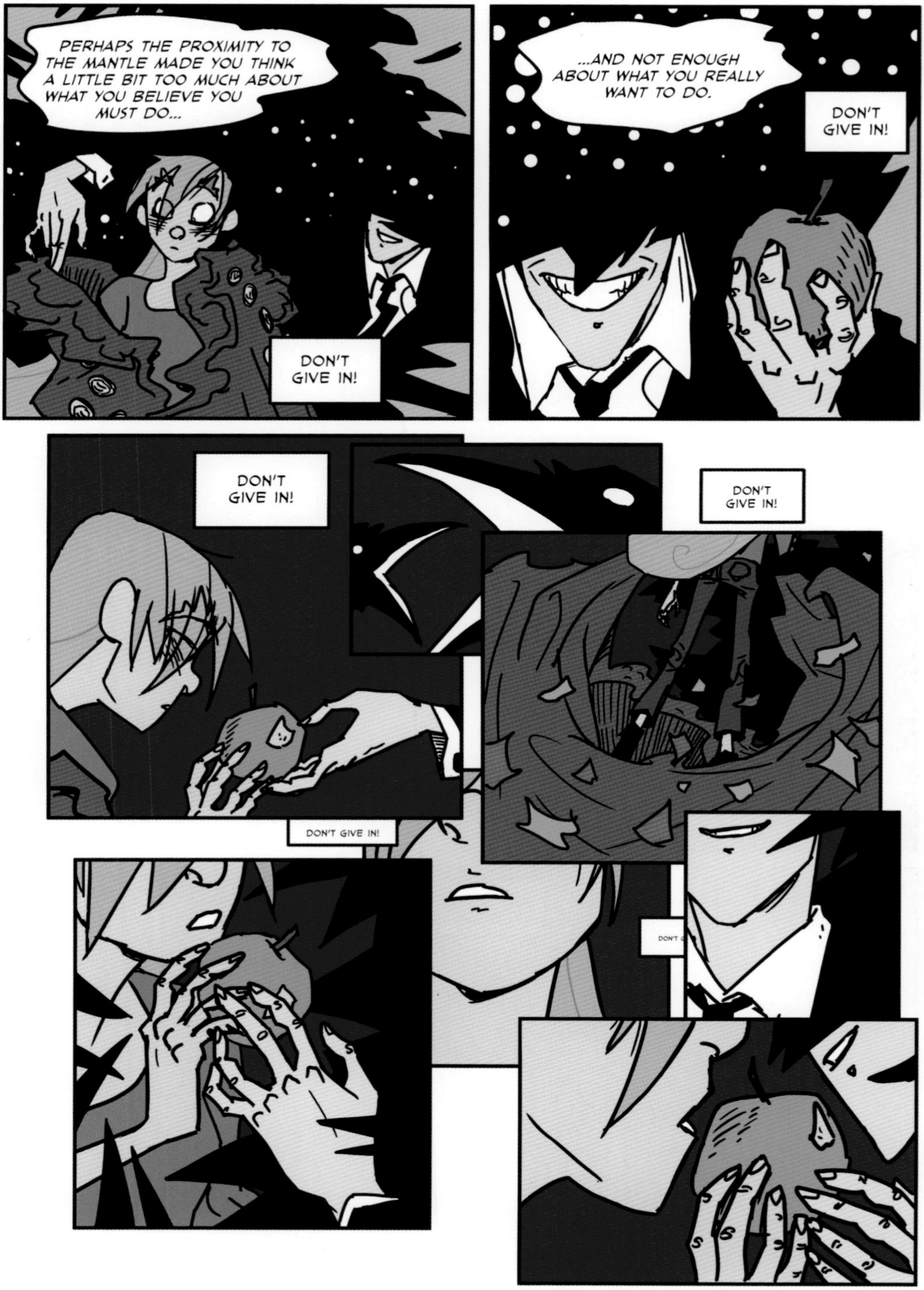
PERHAPS THE PROXIMITY TO THE MANTLE MADE YOU THINK A LITTLE BIT TOO MUCH ABOUT WHAT YOU BELIEVE YOU MUST DO...
DON'T GIVE IN!
...AND NOT ENOUGH ABOUT WHAT YOU REALLY WANT TO DO.
DON'T GIVE IN!
DON'T GIVE IN!
DON'T GIVE IN!
DON'T GIVE IN!
DON'T

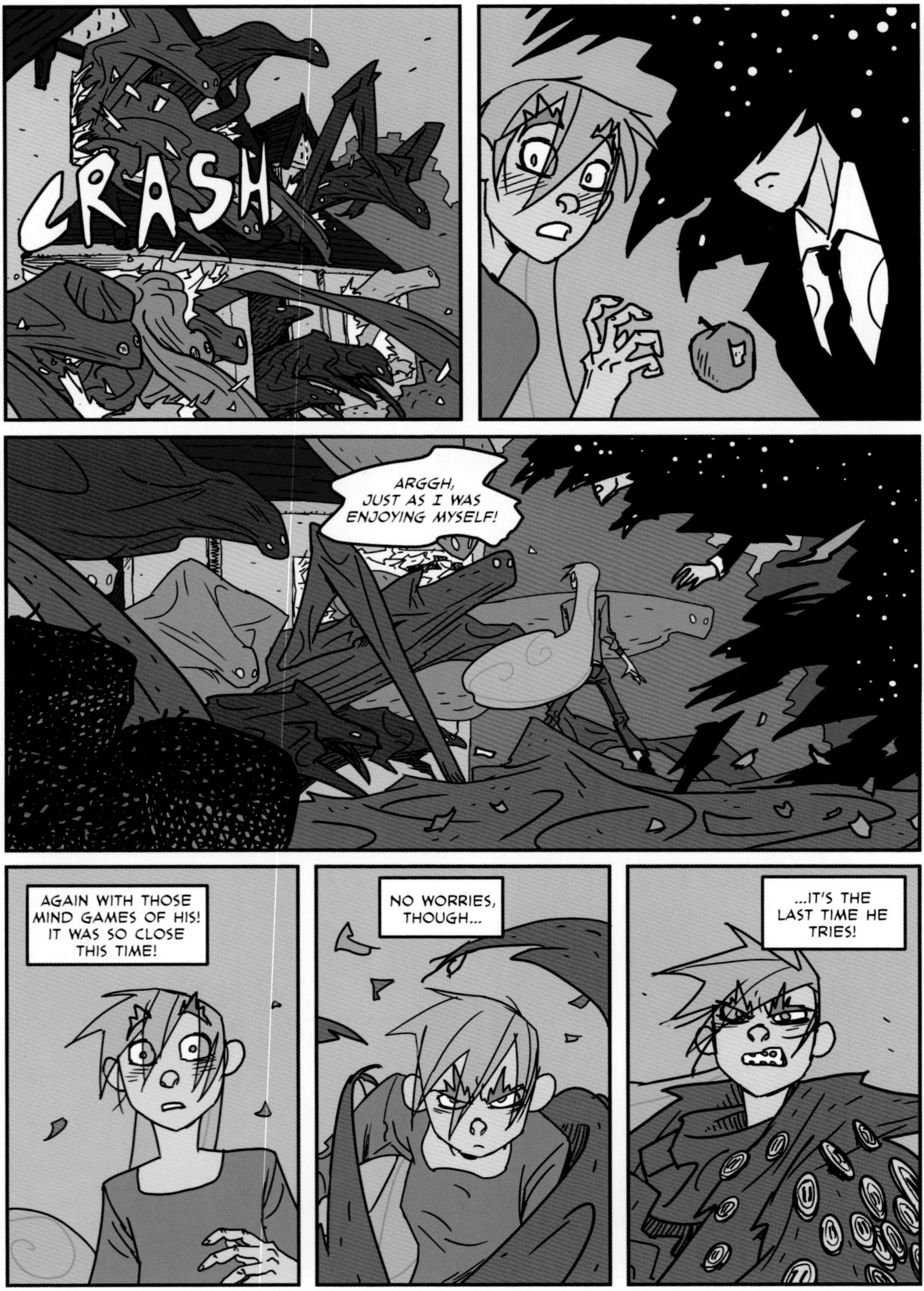
CRASH
ARGGH, JUST AS I WAS ENJOYING MYSELF!
AGAIN WITH THOSE MIND GAMES OF HIS! IT WAS SO CLOSE THIS TIME!
NO WORRIES, THOUGH...
...IT'S THE LAST TIME HE TRIES!

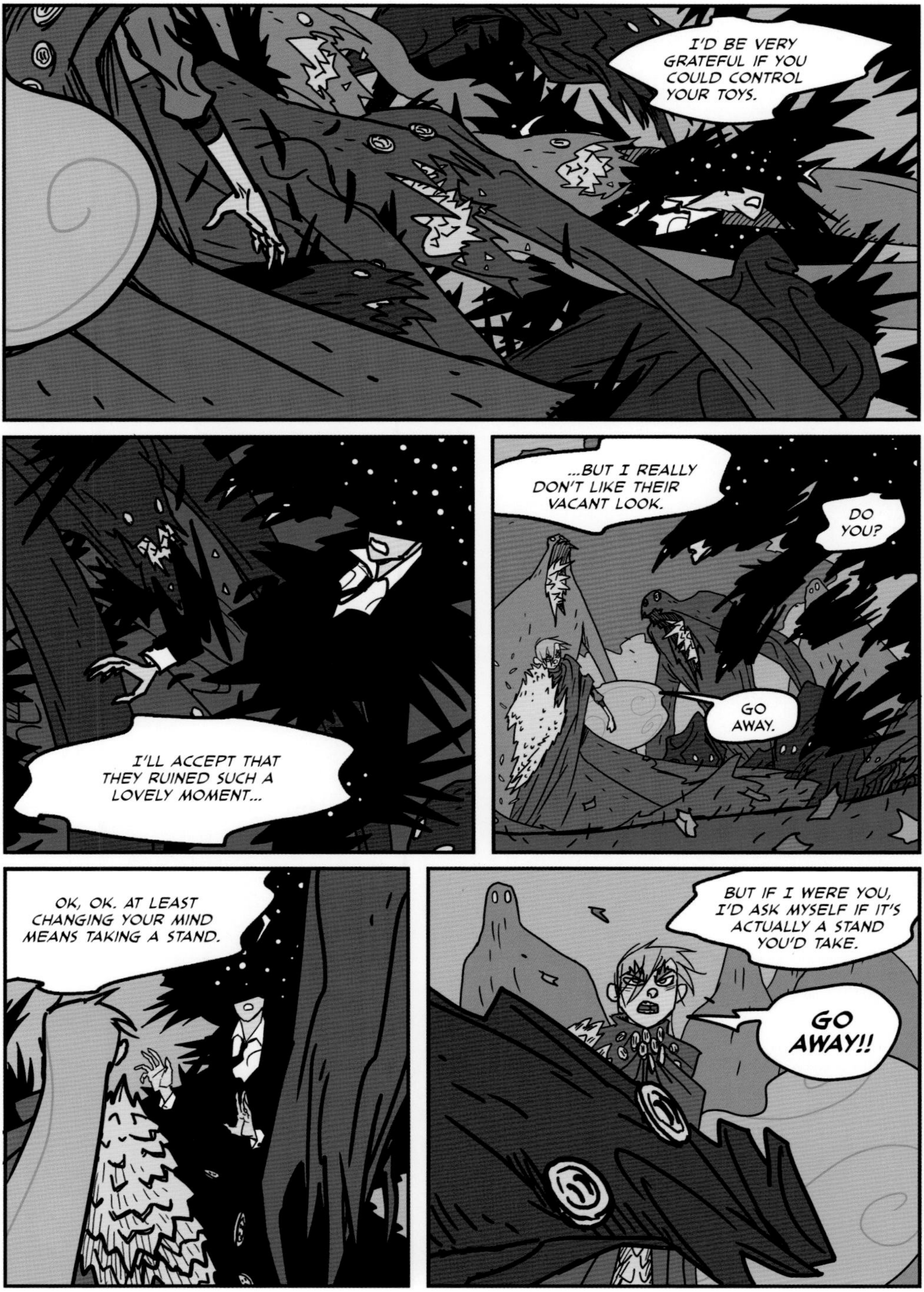
I'D BE VERY GRATEFUL IF YOU COULD CONTROL YOUR TOYS.
I'LL ACCEPT THAT THEY RUINED SUCH A LOVELY MOMENT...
...BUT I REALLY DON'T LIKE THEIR VACANT LOOK.
DO YOU?
GO AWAY.
OK, OK. AT LEAST CHANGING YOUR MIND MEANS TAKING A STAND.
BUT IF I WERE YOU, I'D ASK MYSELF IF IT'S ACTUALLY A STAND YOU'D TAKE.
GO AWAY!!

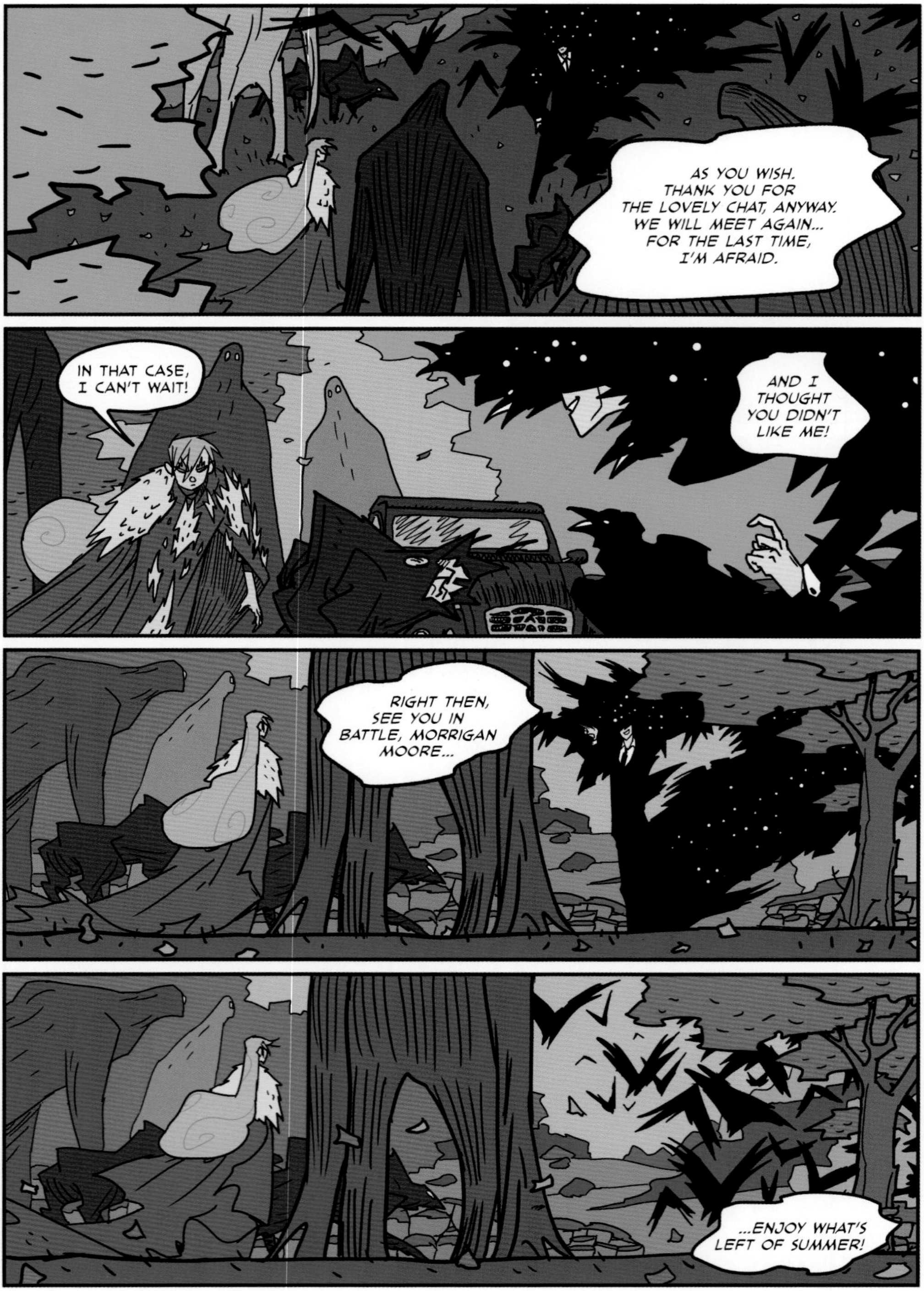
AS YOU WISH. THANK YOU FOR THE LOVELY CHAT, ANYWAY. WE WILL MEET AGAIN... ...FOR THE LAST TIME, I'M AFRAID.
IN THAT CASE, I CAN'T WAIT!
AND I THOUGHT YOU DIDN'T LIKE ME!
RIGHT THEN, SEE YOU IN BATTLE, MORRIGAN MOORE...
...ENJOY WHAT'S LEFT OF SUMMER!

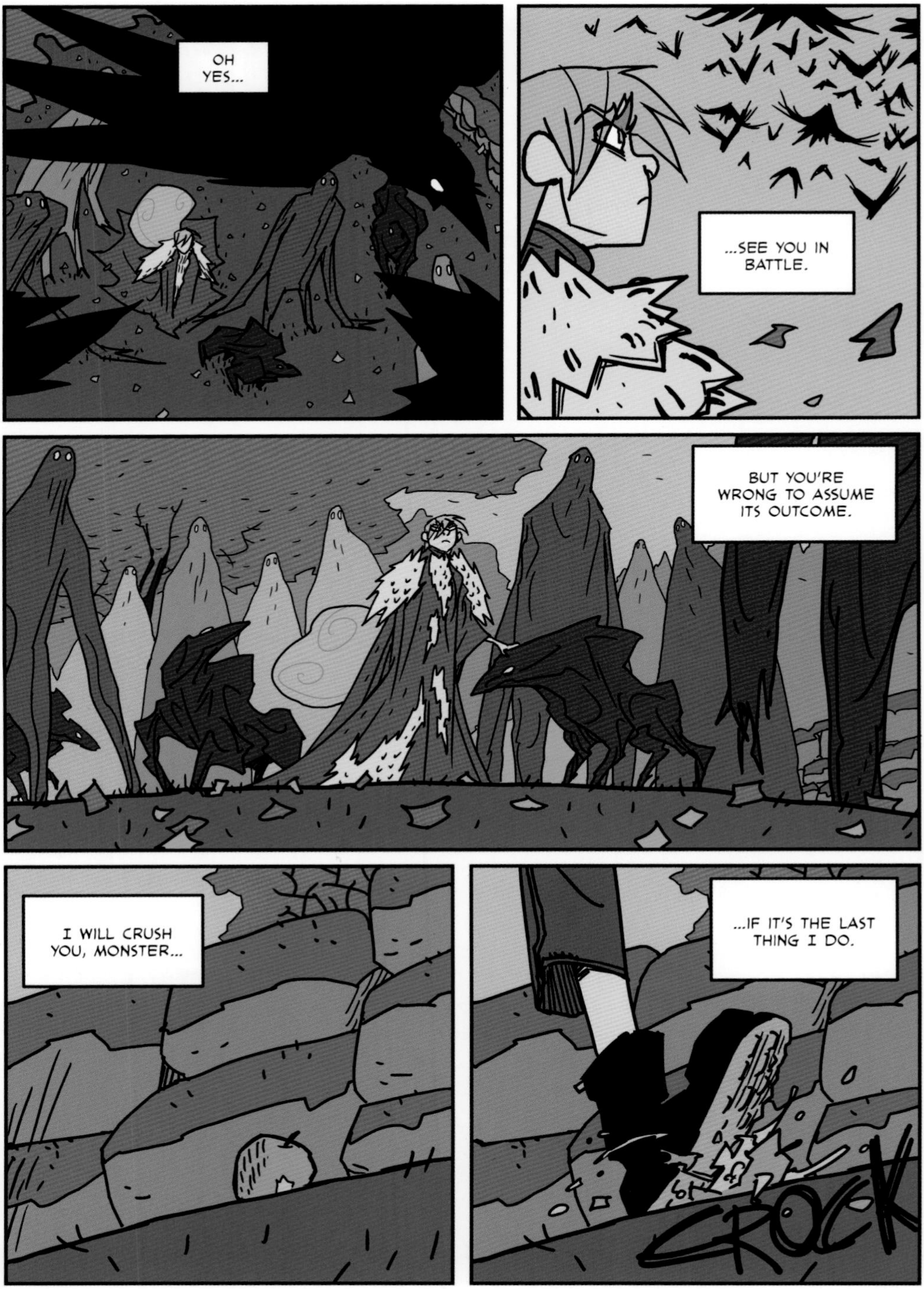

OH YES...
...SEE YOU IN BATTLE.
BUT YOU'RE WRONG TO ASSUME ITS OUTCOME.
I WILL CRUSH YOU, MONSTER...
...IF IT'S THE LAST THING I DO.
CROCK

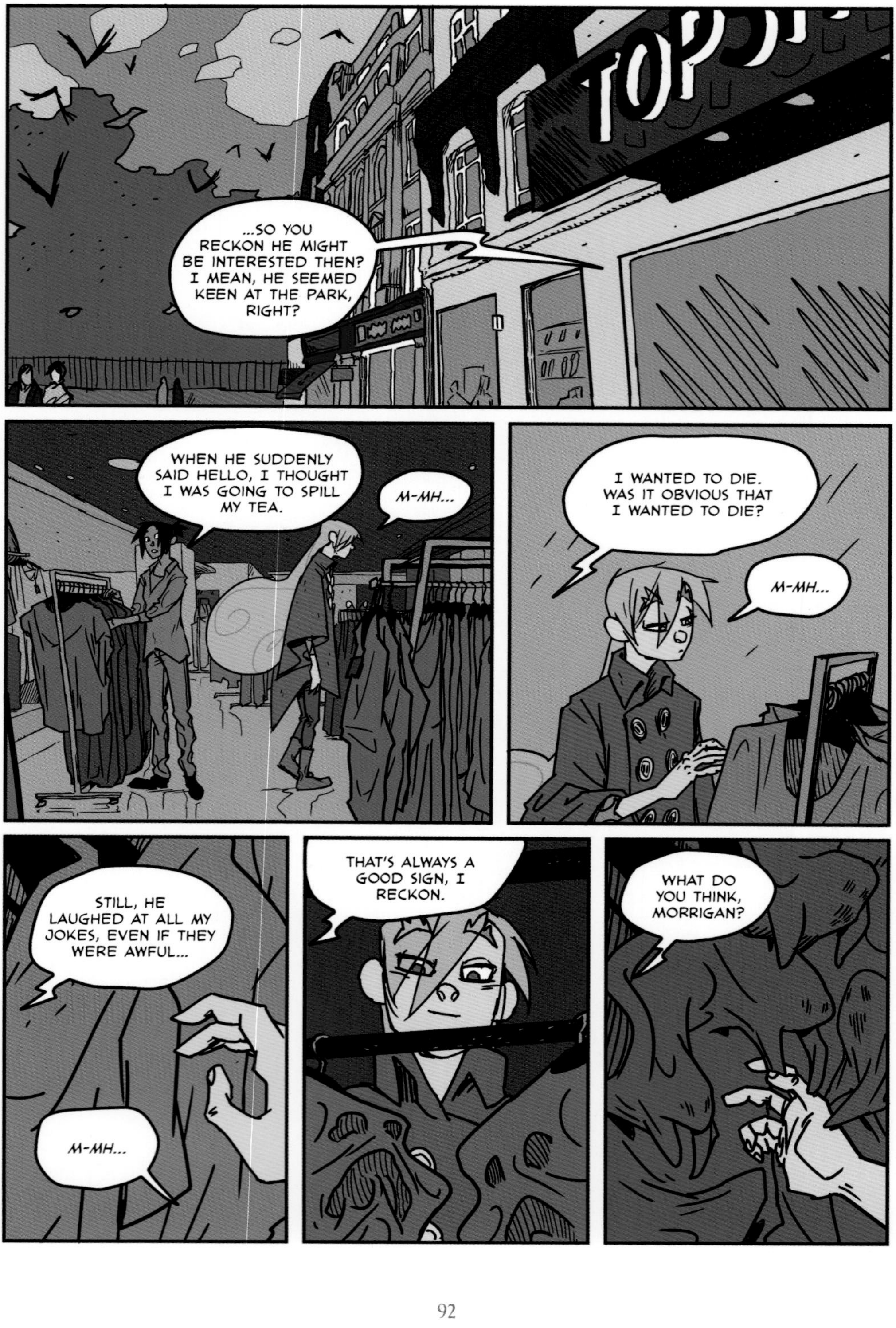
TOPSH
...SO YOU RECKON HE MIGHT BE INTERESTED THEN? I MEAN, HE SEEMED KEEN AT THE PARK, RIGHT?
WHEN HE SUDDENLY SAID HELLO, I THOUGHT I WAS GOING TO SPILL MY TEA.
M-MH...
I WANTED TO DIE. WAS IT OBVIOUS THAT I WANTED TO DIE?
M-MH...
STILL, HE LAUGHED AT ALL MY JOKES, EVEN IF THEY WERE AWFUL...
M-MH...
THAT'S ALWAYS A GOOD SIGN, I RECKON.
WHAT DO YOU THINK, MORRIGAN?

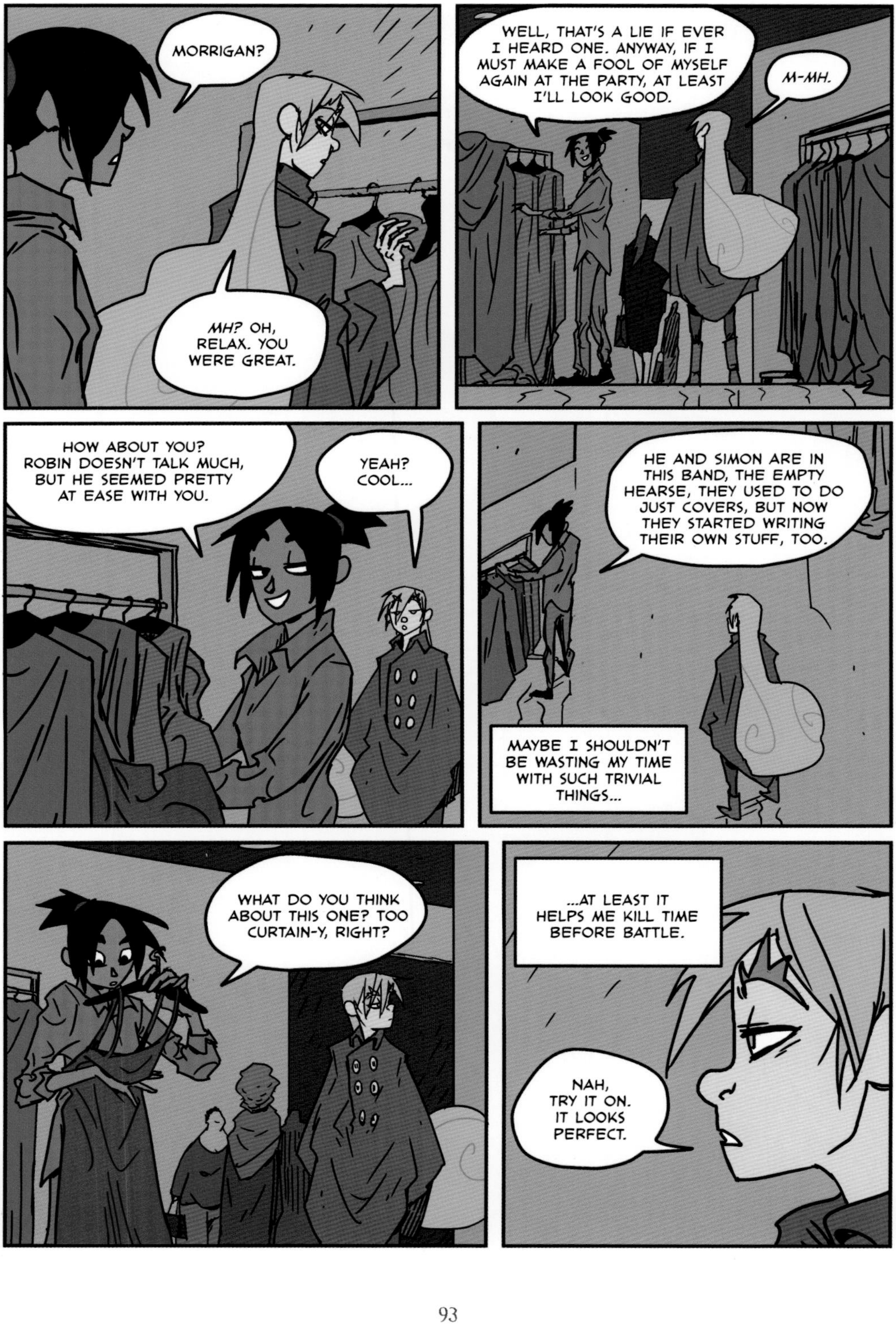
MORRIGAN?
MH? OH, RELAX. YOU WERE GREAT.
WELL, THAT'S A LIE IF EVER I HEARD ONE. ANYWAY, IF I MUST MAKE A FOOL OF MYSELF AGAIN AT THE PARTY, AT LEAST I'LL LOOK GOOD.
M-MH.
HOW ABOUT YOU? ROBIN DOESN'T TALK MUCH, BUT HE SEEMED PRETTY AT EASE WITH YOU.
YEAH? COOL...
HE AND SIMON ARE IN THIS BAND, THE EMPTY HEARSE, THEY USED TO DO JUST COVERS, BUT NOW THEY STARTED WRITING THEIR OWN STUFF, TOO.
MAYBE I SHOULDN'T BE WASTING MY TIME WITH SUCH TRIVIAL THINGS...
WHAT DO YOU THINK ABOUT THIS ONE? TOO CURTAIN-Y, RIGHT?
...AT LEAST IT HELPS ME KILL TIME BEFORE BATTLE.
NAH, TRY IT ON. IT LOOKS PERFECT.

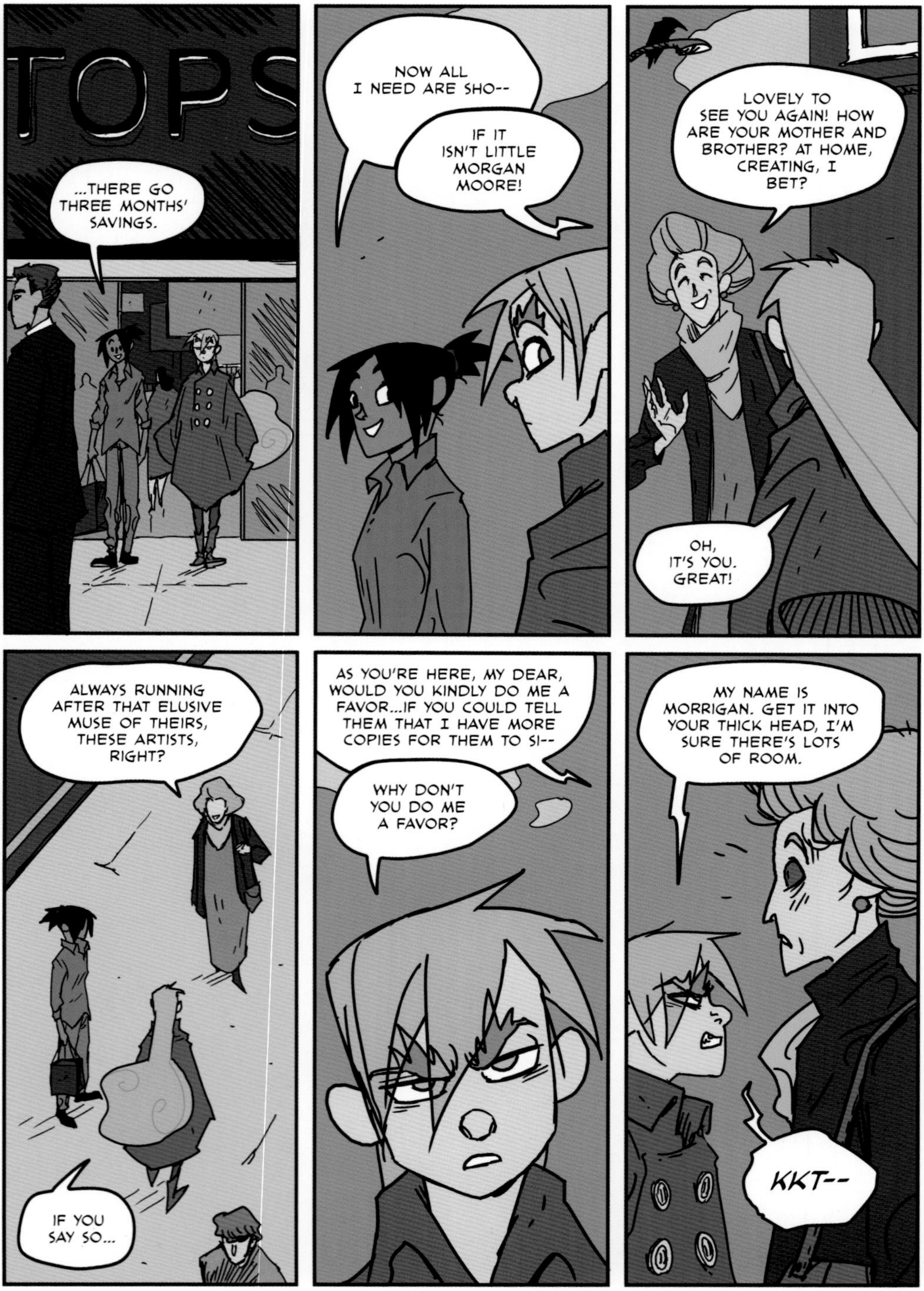
TOPS
...THERE GO THREE MONTHS' SAVINGS.
NOW ALL I NEED ARE SHO--
IF IT ISN'T LITTLE MORGAN MOORE!
LOVELY TO SEE YOU AGAIN! HOW ARE YOUR MOTHER AND BROTHER? AT HOME, CREATING, I BET?
OH, IT'S YOU. GREAT!
ALWAYS RUNNING AFTER THAT ELUSIVE MUSE OF THEIRS, THESE ARTISTS, RIGHT?
IF YOU SAY SO...
AS YOU'RE HERE, MY DEAR, WOULD YOU KINDLY DO ME A FAVOR...IF YOU COULD TELL THEM THAT I HAVE MORE COPIES FOR THEM TO SI--
WHY DON'T YOU DO ME A FAVOR?
MY NAME IS MORRIGAN. GET IT INTO YOUR THICK HEAD, I'M SURE THERE'S LOTS OF ROOM.
KKT--

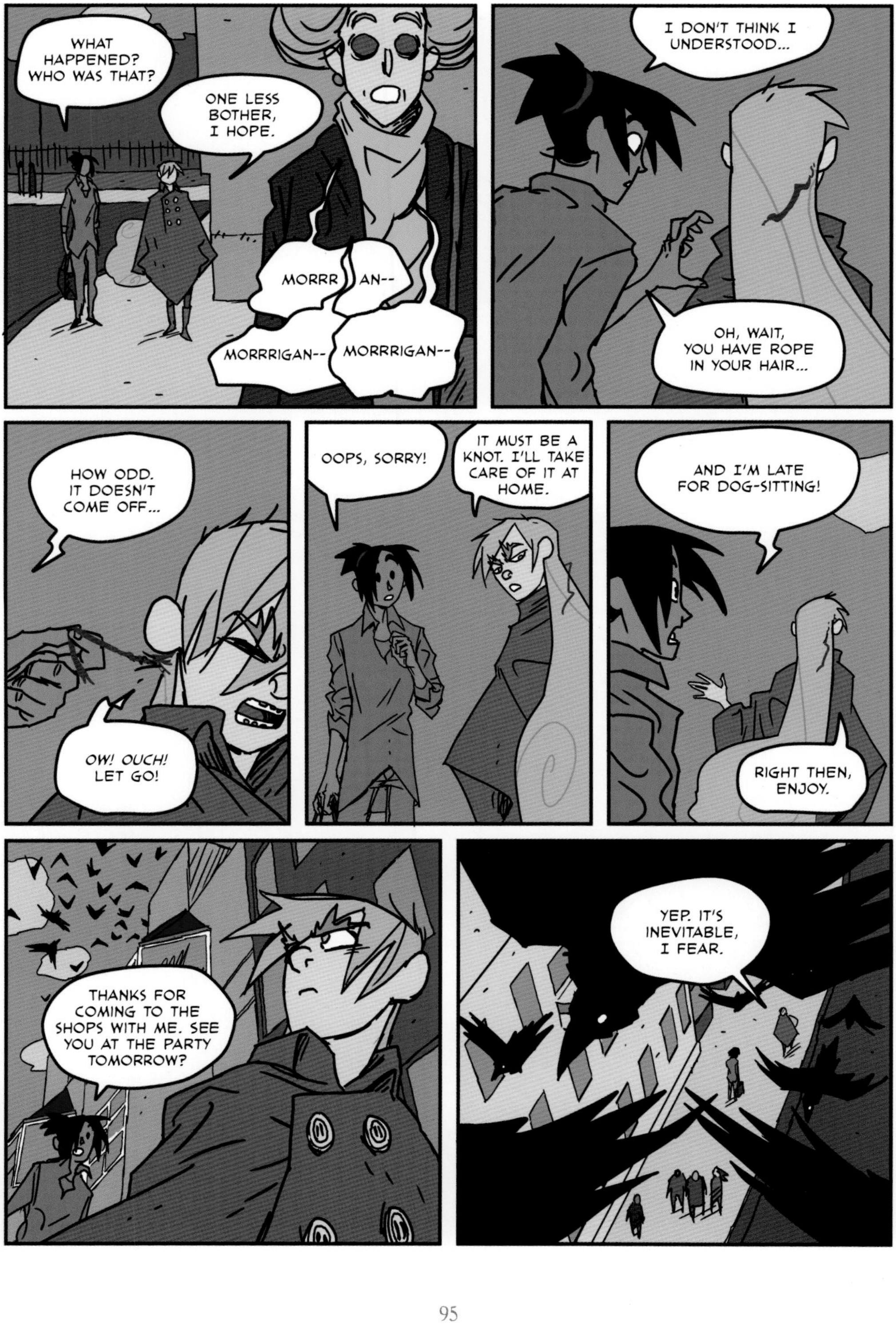
WHAT HAPPENED? WHO WAS THAT?
ONE LESS BOTHER, I HOPE.
MORRR AN--
MORRRIGAN--
MORRRIGAN--
I DON'T THINK I UNDERSTOOD...
OH, WAIT, YOU HAVE ROPE IN YOUR HAIR...
HOW ODD. IT DOESN'T COME OFF...
OW! OUCH! LET GO!
OOPS, SORRY!
IT MUST BE A KNOT. I'LL TAKE CARE OF IT AT HOME.
AND I'M LATE FOR DOG-SITTING!
RIGHT THEN, ENJOY.
THANKS FOR COMING TO THE SHOPS WITH ME. SEE YOU AT THE PARTY TOMORROW?
YEP. IT'S INEVITABLE, I FEAR.

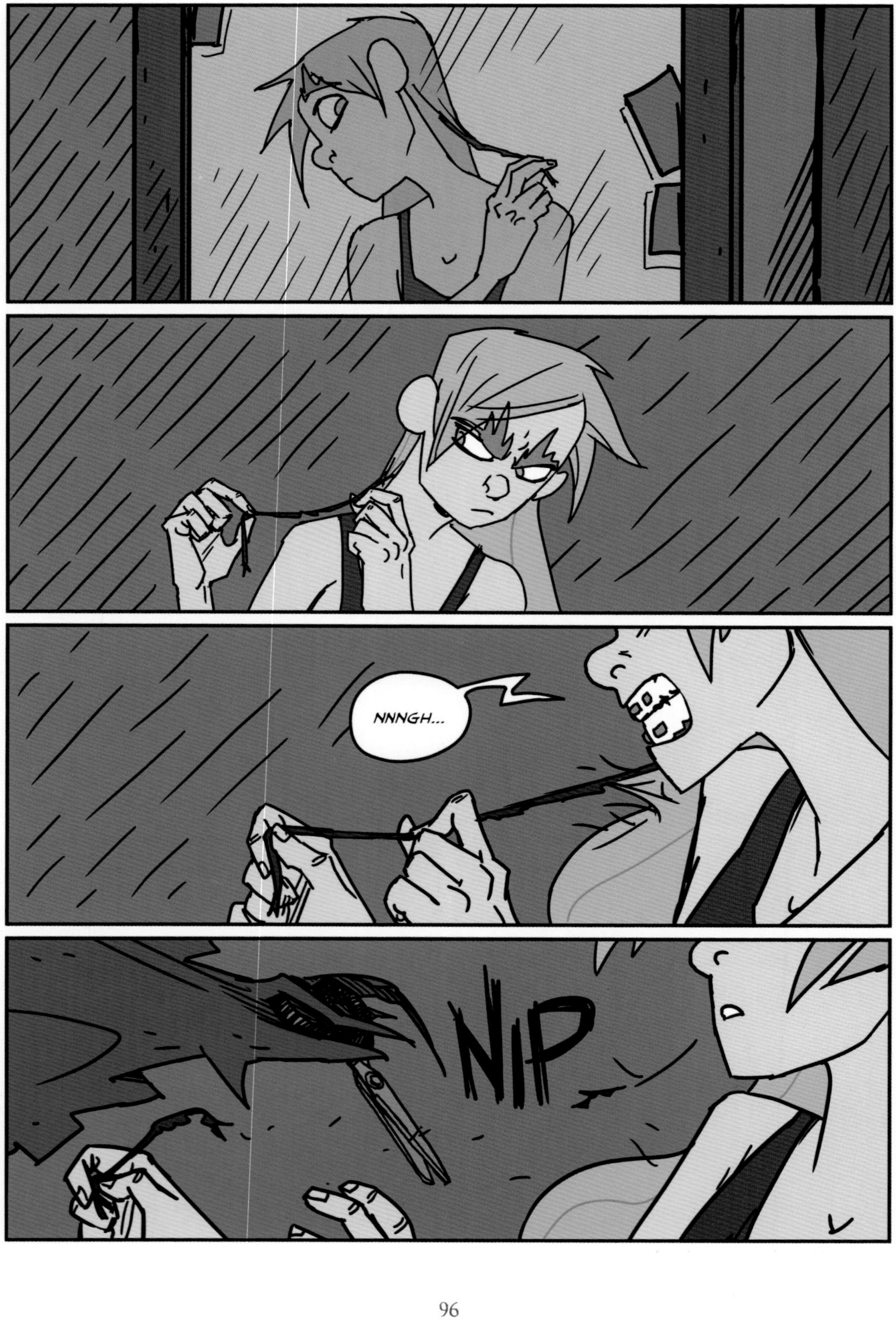
NNNGH...
NIP

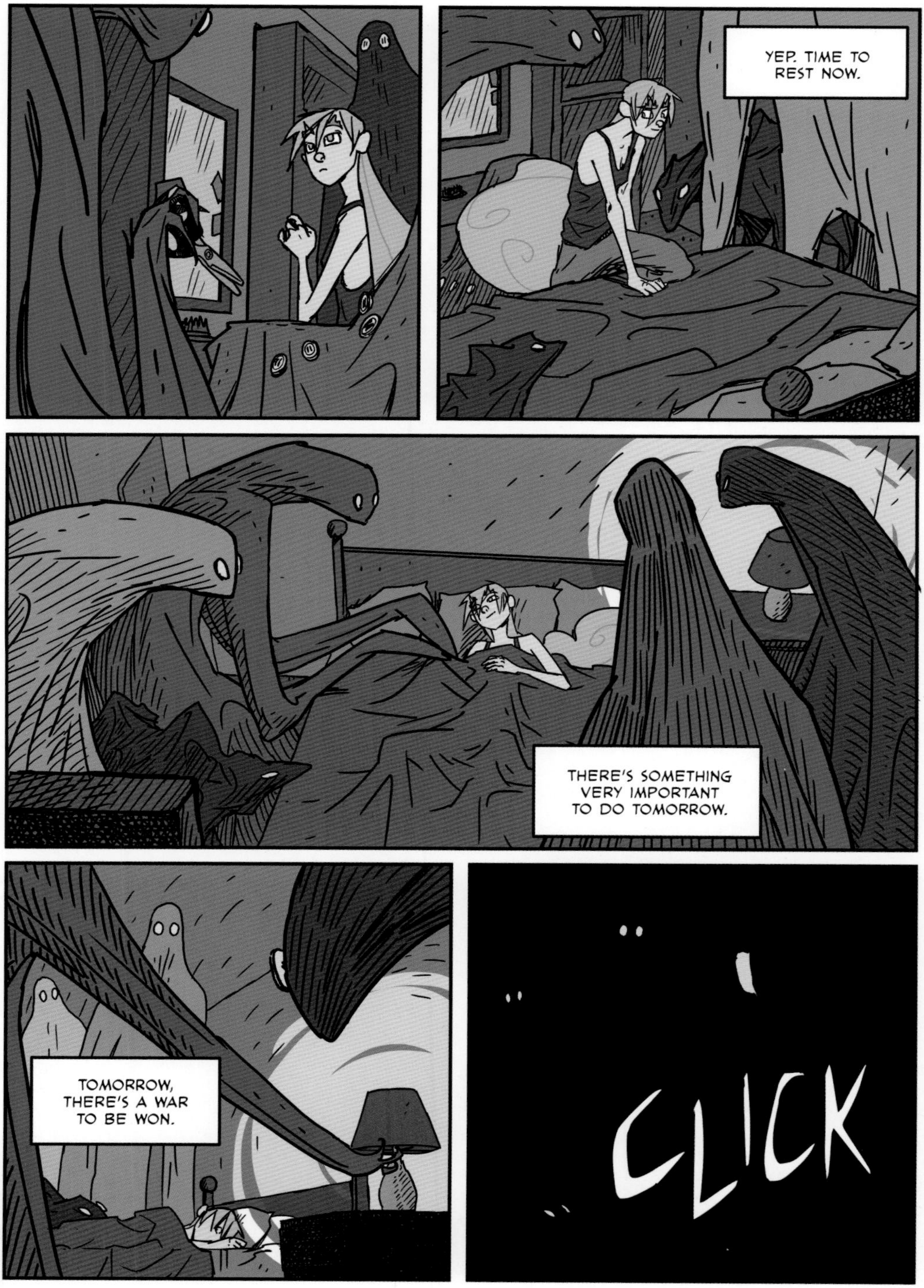
YEP. TIME TO REST NOW.
THERE'S SOMETHING VERY IMPORTANT TO DO TOMORROW.
TOMORROW, THERE'S A WAR TO BE WON.
CLICK

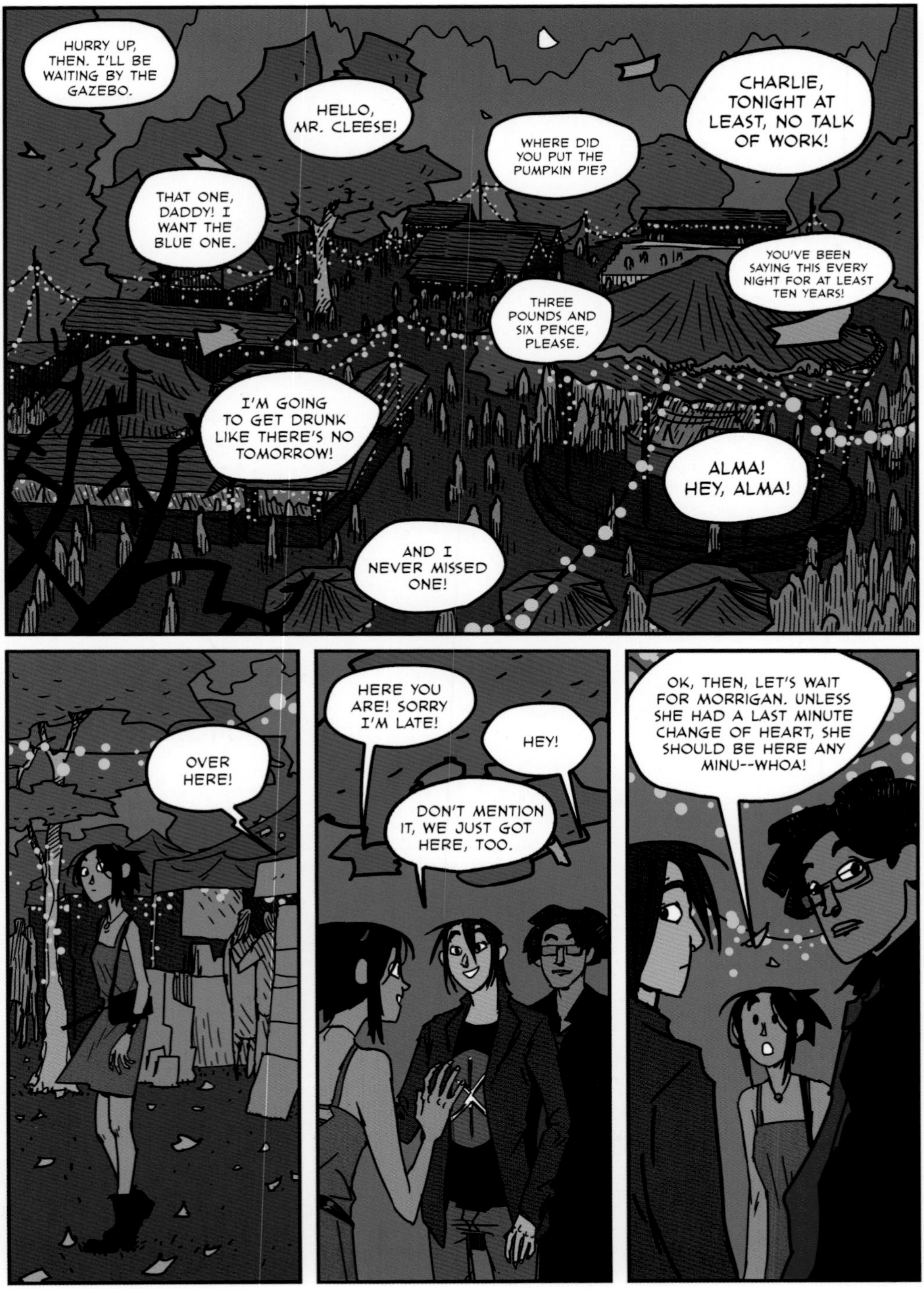

HURRY UP, THEN. I'LL BE WAITING BY THE GAZEBO.
HELLO, MR. CLEESE!
WHERE DID YOU PUT THE PUMPKIN PIE?
CHARLIE, TONIGHT AT LEAST, NO TALK OF WORK!
THAT ONE, DADDY! I WANT THE BLUE ONE.
YOU'VE BEEN SAYING THIS EVERY NIGHT FOR AT LEAST TEN YEARS!
THREE POUNDS AND SIX PENCE, PLEASE.
I'M GOING TO GET DRUNK LIKE THERE'S NO TOMORROW!
ALMA! HEY, ALMA!
AND I NEVER MISSED ONE!
OVER HERE!
HERE YOU ARE! SORRY I'M LATE!
HEY!
DON'T MENTION IT, WE JUST GOT HERE, TOO.
OK, THEN, LET'S WAIT FOR MORRIGAN. UNLESS SHE HAD A LAST MINUTE CHANGE OF HEART, SHE SHOULD BE HERE ANY MINU--WHOA!

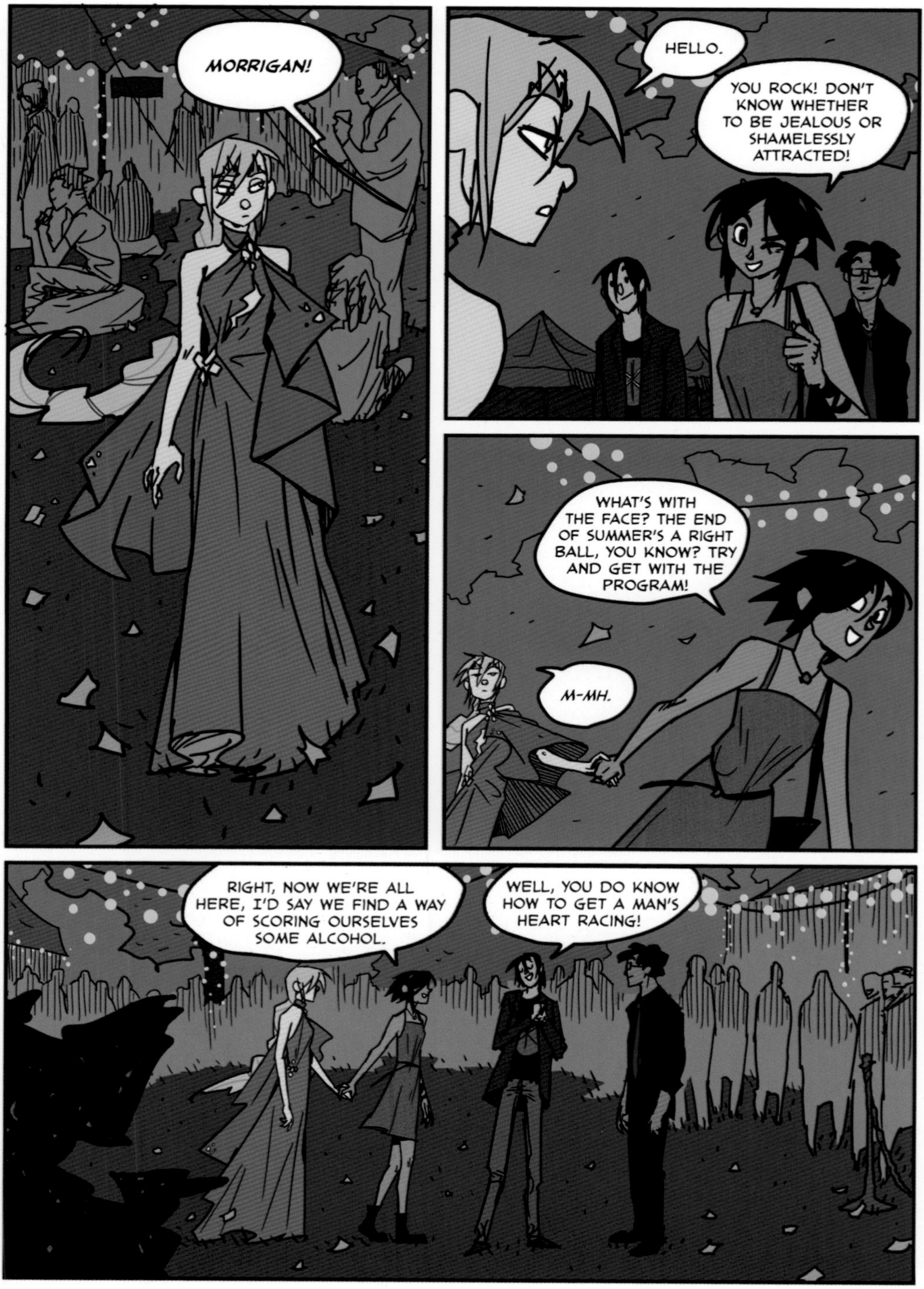
MORRIGAN!
HELLO.
YOU ROCK! DON'T KNOW WHETHER TO BE JEALOUS OR SHAMELESSLY ATTRACTED!
WHAT'S WITH THE FACE? THE END OF SUMMER'S A RIGHT BALL, YOU KNOW? TRY AND GET WITH THE PROGRAM!
M-MH.
RIGHT, NOW WE'RE ALL HERE, I'D SAY WE FIND A WAY OF SCORING OURSELVES SOME ALCOHOL.
WELL, YOU DO KNOW HOW TO GET A MAN'S HEART RACING!

CALL ME ORDINARY, BUT I THINK *LONDON CALLING* IS STILL THEIR BEST EFFORT.

COME OFF IT! WHAT ABOUT *GIVE 'EM ENOUGH ROPE*, THEN? THE TITLE ALONE...!

PERHAPS WITH "TOMMY GUN" AND "ENGLISH CIVIL WAR," BUT I'LL STICK TO MY OPINION. SUE ME!

DON'T TEMPT ME! I'LL BE LENIENT JUST BECAUSE THAT ALBUM HAS "SPANISH BOMBS."

YOU'RE FORGETTING "I'M NOT DOWN"! JUST WHO ARE YOU, EXACTLY?

DO YOU LIKE THE CLASH, MORRIGAN?

I RECKON SO, IF THE VOLUME'S LOUD ENOUGH.

THEN SHE'D LOVE YOUR SOLOS, ROBIN!

IF YOU REFER TO THE AMP THAT EXPLODED, SIMON, I HAVE NO REGRETS WHATSOEVER! "THE DAY THE WORLD TURNED DAY-GLO" CANNOT BE PLAYED ANY OTHER WAY!

HEY, MINE WAS A COMPLIMENT! SERIOUSLY, THOUGH, GIRLS, WE PLAY THREE TIMES A WEEK IN MY FOLKS' BASEMENT. CONSIDER YOURSELVES INVITED, WHENEVER YOU FANCY.

I'VE ALWAYS WANTED TO SEE AN EXPLODING AMP!

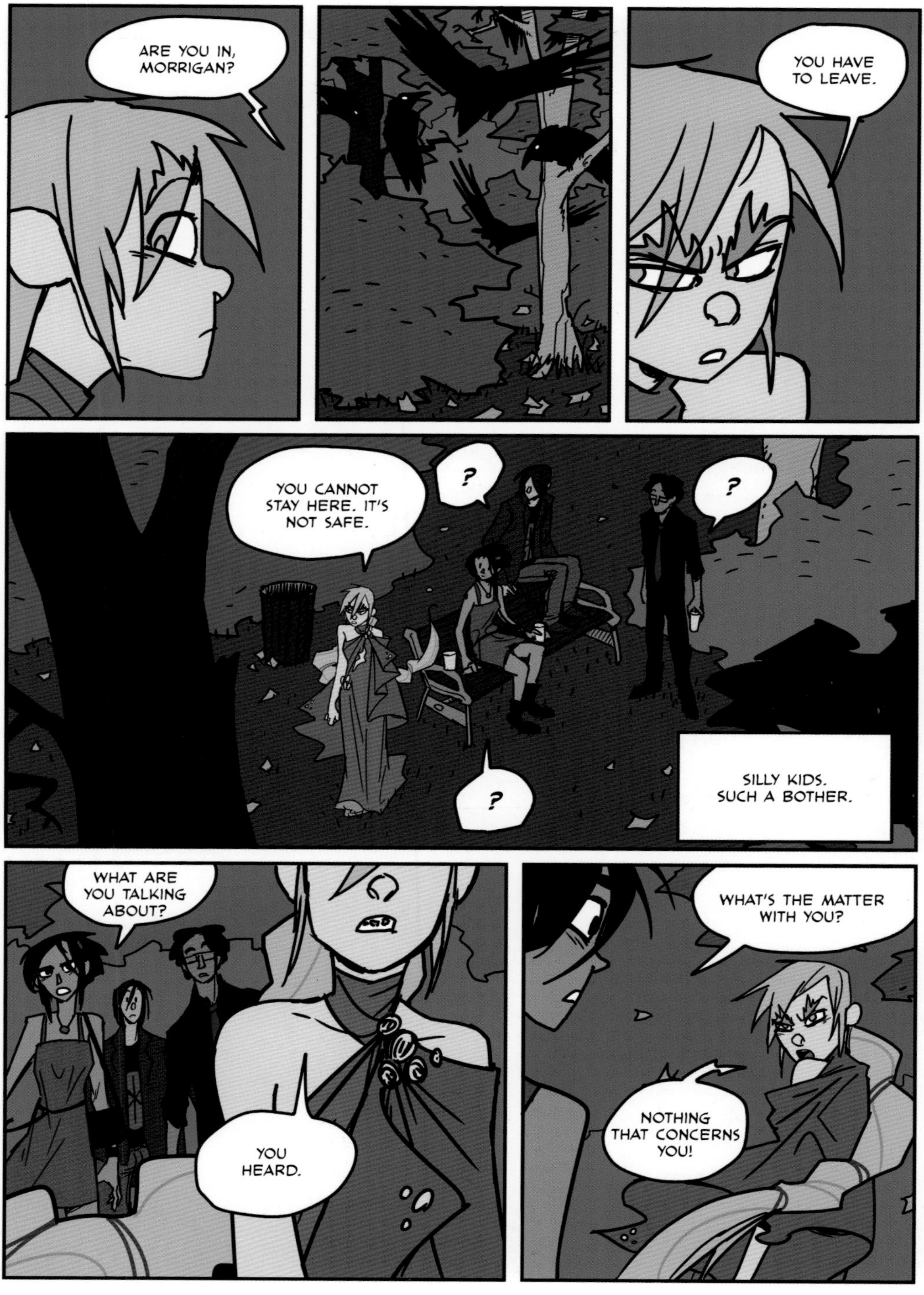
ARE YOU IN, MORRIGAN?
YOU HAVE TO LEAVE.
YOU CANNOT STAY HERE. IT'S NOT SAFE.
?
?
?
SILLY KIDS. SUCH A BOTHER.
WHAT ARE YOU TALKING ABOUT?
YOU HEARD.
WHAT'S THE MATTER WITH YOU?
NOTHING THAT CONCERNS YOU!

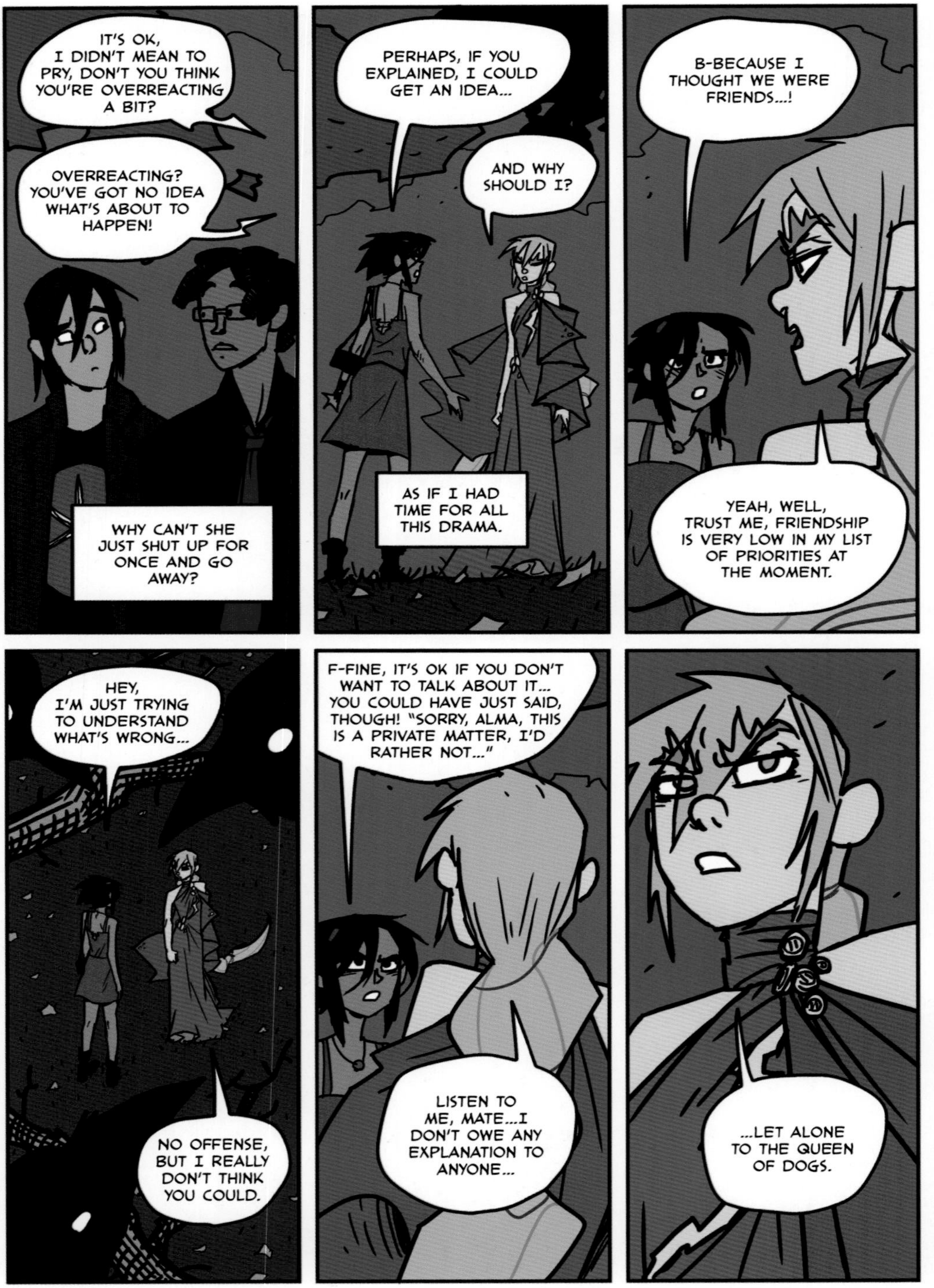
IT'S OK, I DIDN'T MEAN TO PRY, DON'T YOU THINK YOU'RE OVERREACTING A BIT?
OVERREACTING? YOU'VE GOT NO IDEA WHAT'S ABOUT TO HAPPEN!
WHY CAN'T SHE JUST SHUT UP FOR ONCE AND GO AWAY?
PERHAPS, IF YOU EXPLAINED, I COULD GET AN IDEA...
AND WHY SHOULD I?
AS IF I HAD TIME FOR ALL THIS DRAMA.
B-BECAUSE I THOUGHT WE WERE FRIENDS...!
YEAH, WELL, TRUST ME, FRIENDSHIP IS VERY LOW IN MY LIST OF PRIORITIES AT THE MOMENT.
HEY, I'M JUST TRYING TO UNDERSTAND WHAT'S WRONG...
NO OFFENSE, BUT I REALLY DON'T THINK YOU COULD.
F-FINE, IT'S OK IF YOU DON'T WANT TO TALK ABOUT IT... YOU COULD HAVE JUST SAID, THOUGH! "SORRY, ALMA, THIS IS A PRIVATE MATTER, I'D RATHER NOT..."
LISTEN TO ME, MATE...I DON'T OWE ANY EXPLANATION TO ANYONE...
...LET ALONE TO THE QUEEN OF DOGS.

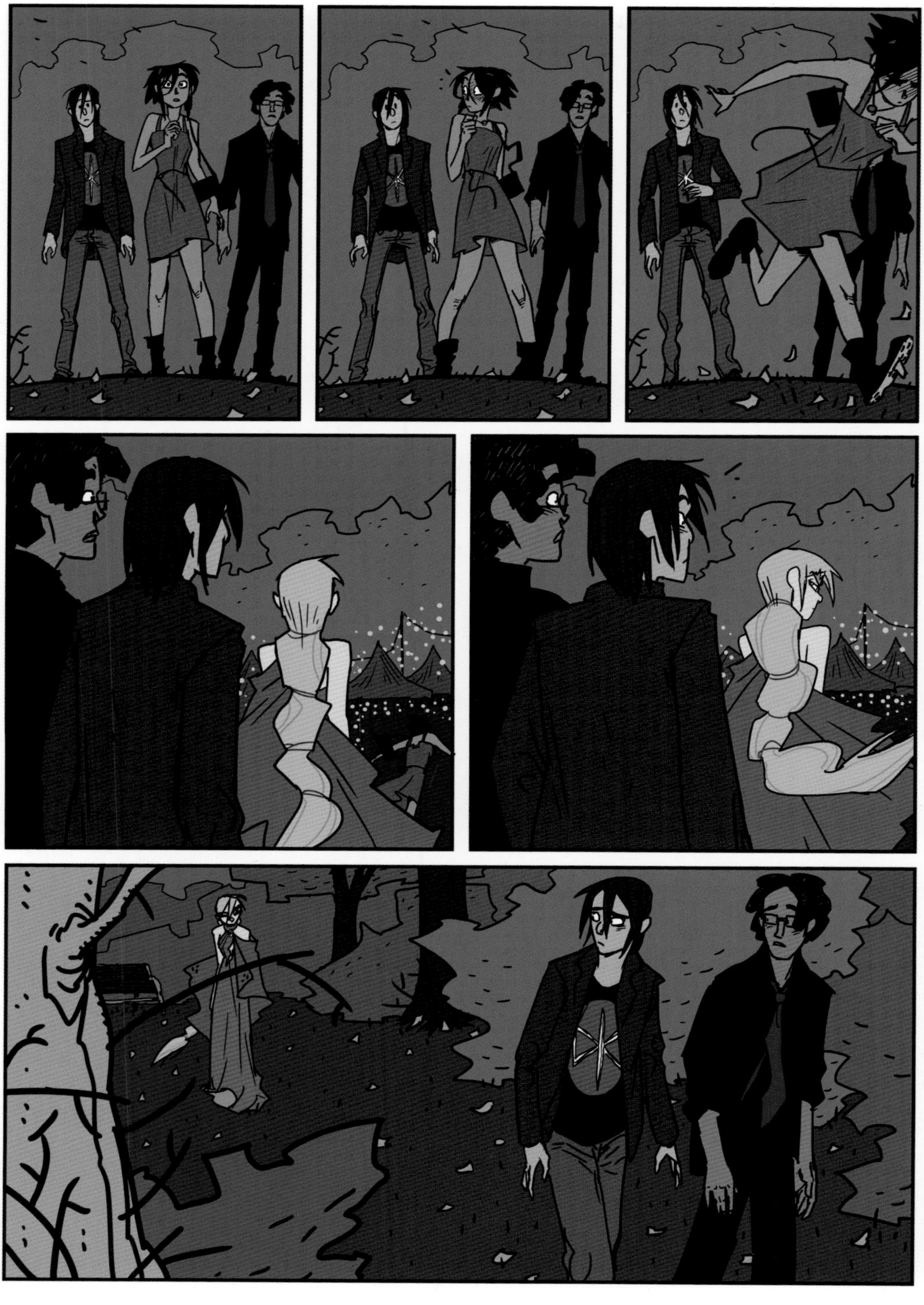

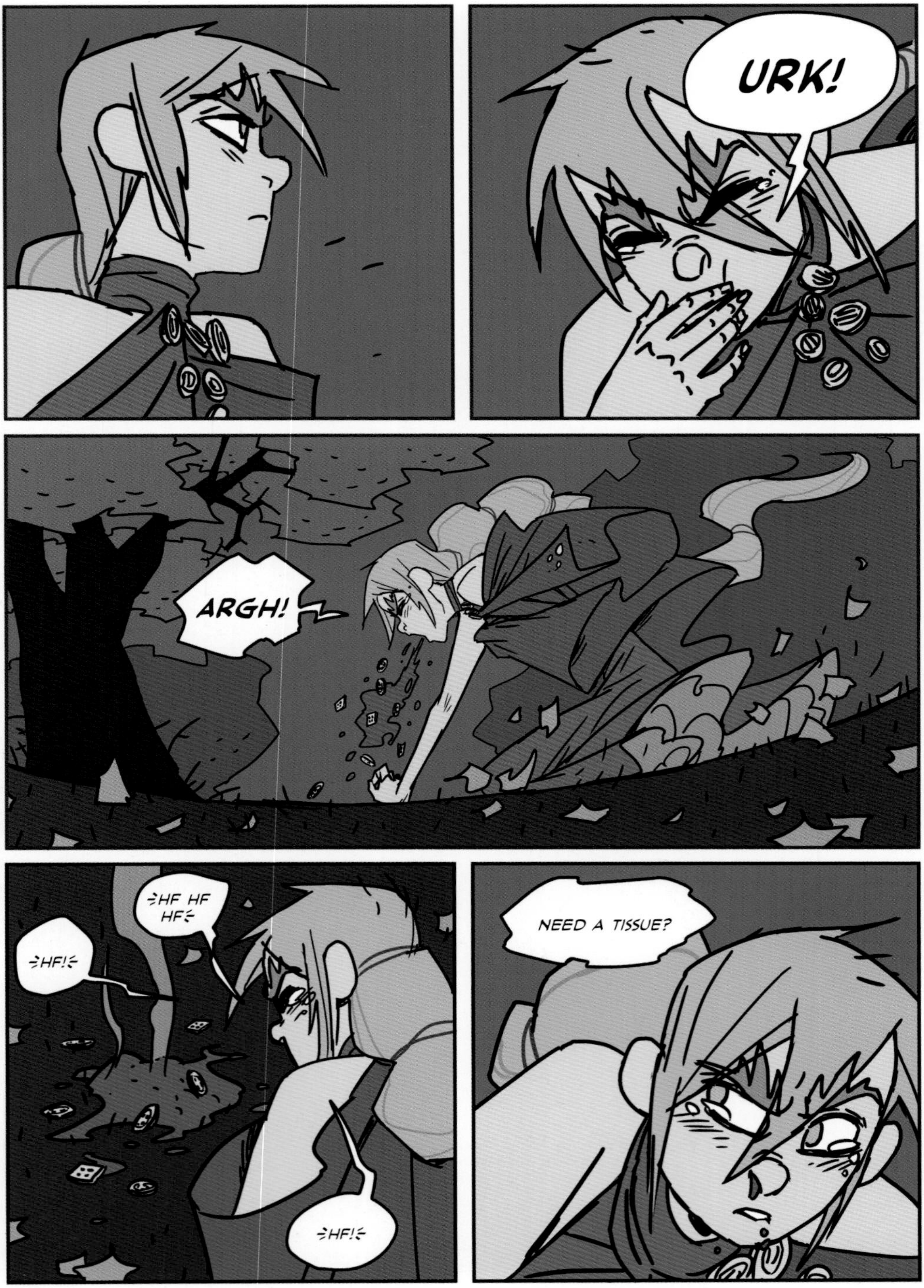
URK!
ARGH!
=HF HF HF=
=HF!=
=HF!=
NEED A TISSUE?

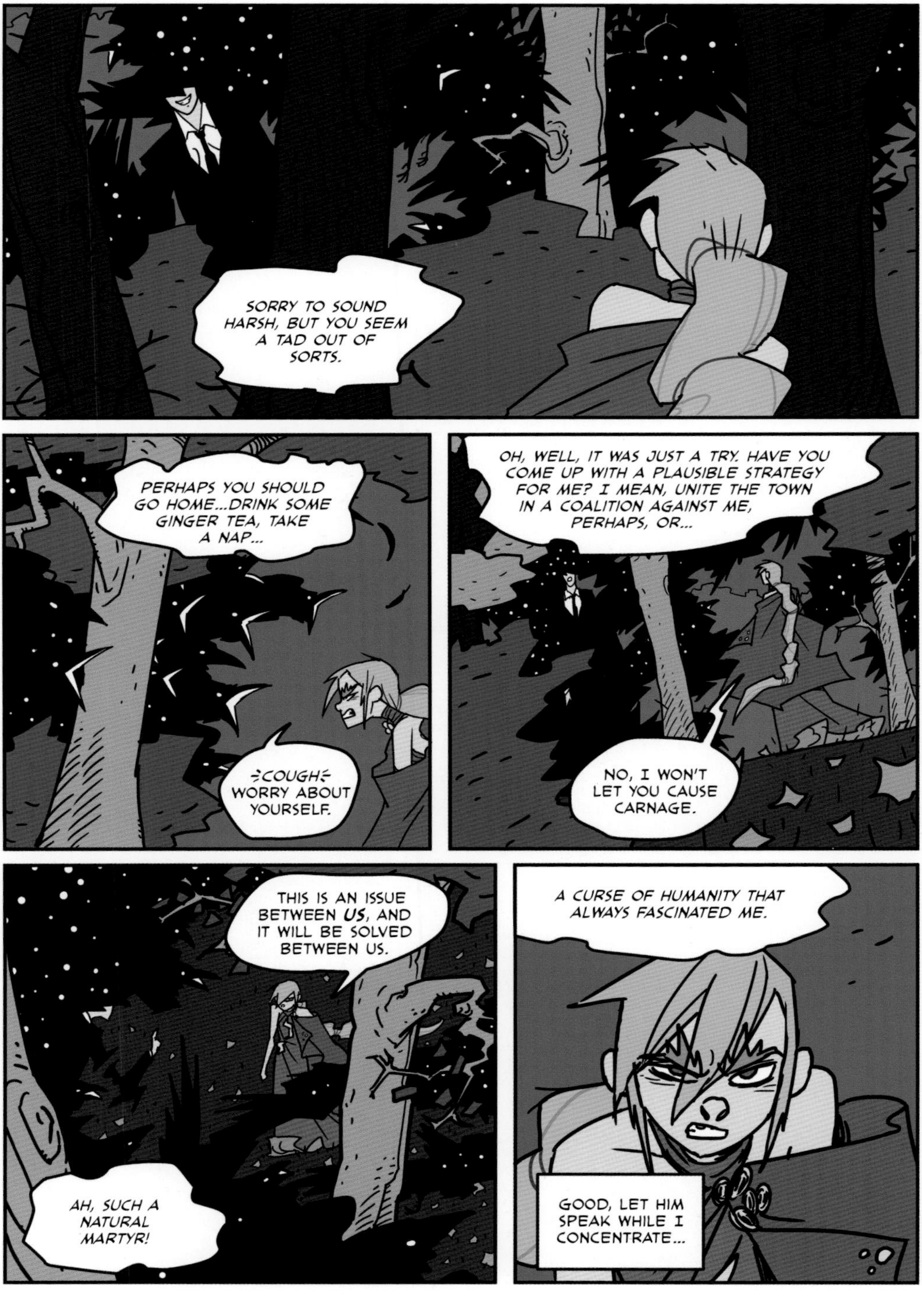
SORRY TO SOUND HARSH, BUT YOU SEEM A TAD OUT OF SORTS.
PERHAPS YOU SHOULD GO HOME...DRINK SOME GINGER TEA, TAKE A NAP...
COUGH WORRY ABOUT YOURSELF.
OH, WELL, IT WAS JUST A TRY. HAVE YOU COME UP WITH A PLAUSIBLE STRATEGY FOR ME? I MEAN, UNITE THE TOWN IN A COALITION AGAINST ME, PERHAPS, OR...
NO, I WON'T LET YOU CAUSE CARNAGE.
THIS IS AN ISSUE BETWEEN US, AND IT WILL BE SOLVED BETWEEN US.
AH, SUCH A NATURAL MARTYR!
A CURSE OF HUMANITY THAT ALWAYS FASCINATED ME.
GOOD, LET HIM SPEAK WHILE I CONCENTRATE...

KKT--

KKT--

KKT--

...TAKE CONTROL OF THEIR BODIES...

...AND GET THEM AWAY FROM HERE!

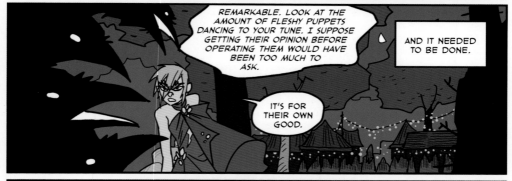

REMARKABLE. LOOK AT THE AMOUNT OF FLESHY PUPPETS DANCING TO YOUR TUNE. I SUPPOSE GETTING THEIR OPINION BEFORE OPERATING THEM WOULD HAVE BEEN TOO MUCH TO ASK.

AND IT NEEDED TO BE DONE.

IT'S FOR THEIR OWN GOOD.

IF SELF-FORGIVENESS IS YOUR ANSWER...ANYWAY, HUMAN MORAL DILEMMAS ARE NONE OF MY CONCERN.

WELL, MORRIGAN MOORE, IT'S BEEN A REAL PLEASURE BUT NOW'S THE TIME TO GET YOU OFF THAT CHESSBOARD.

I WOULDN'T BANK ON IT!

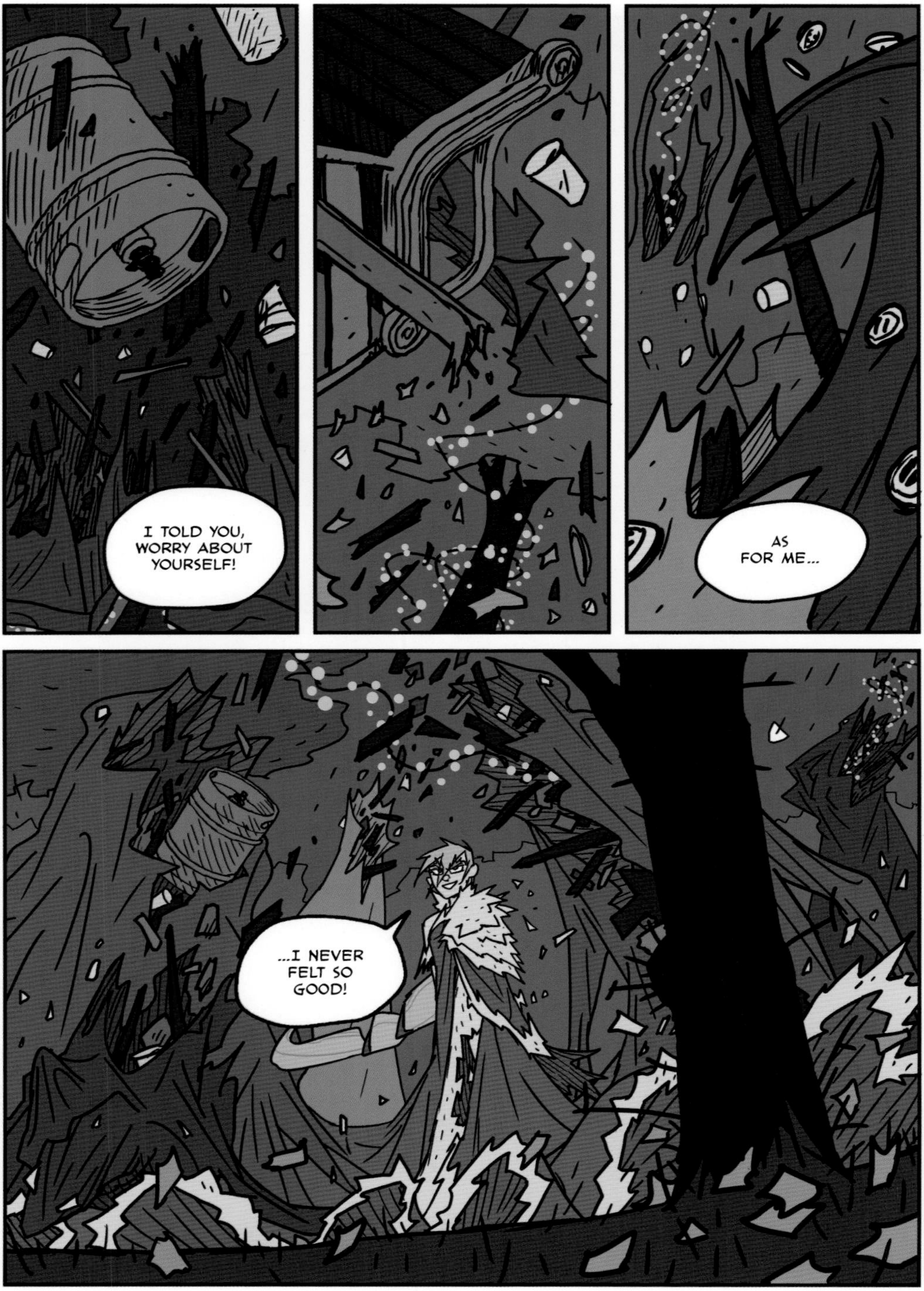
I TOLD YOU, WORRY ABOUT YOURSELF!
AS FOR ME...
...I NEVER FELT SO GOOD!

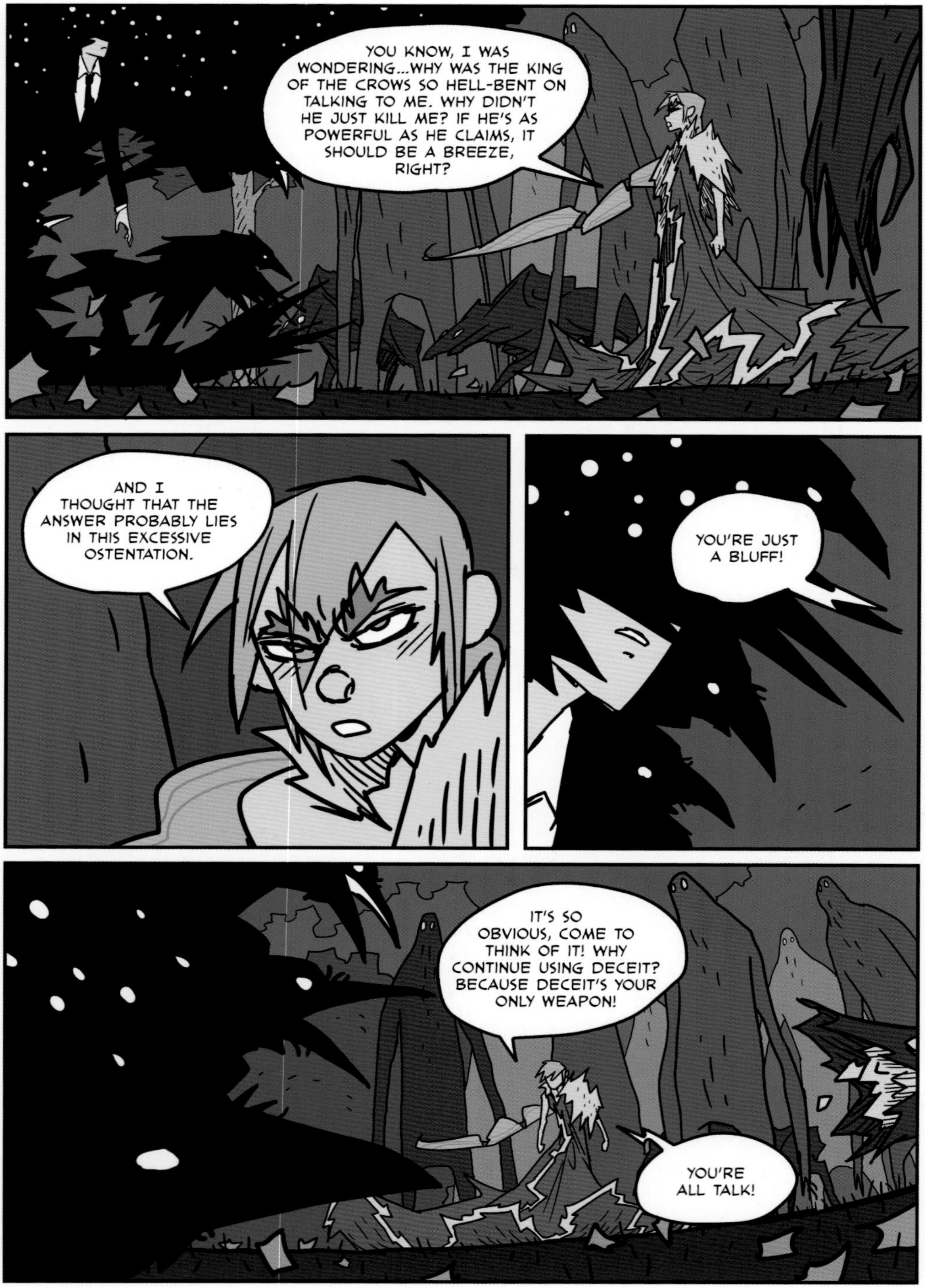
YOU KNOW, I WAS WONDERING...WHY WAS THE KING OF THE CROWS SO HELL-BENT ON TALKING TO ME. WHY DIDN'T HE JUST KILL ME? IF HE'S AS POWERFUL AS HE CLAIMS, IT SHOULD BE A BREEZE, RIGHT?
AND I THOUGHT THAT THE ANSWER PROBABLY LIES IN THIS EXCESSIVE OSTENTATION.
YOU'RE JUST A BLUFF!
IT'S SO OBVIOUS, COME TO THINK OF IT! WHY CONTINUE USING DECEIT? BECAUSE DECEIT'S YOUR ONLY WEAPON!
YOU'RE ALL TALK!

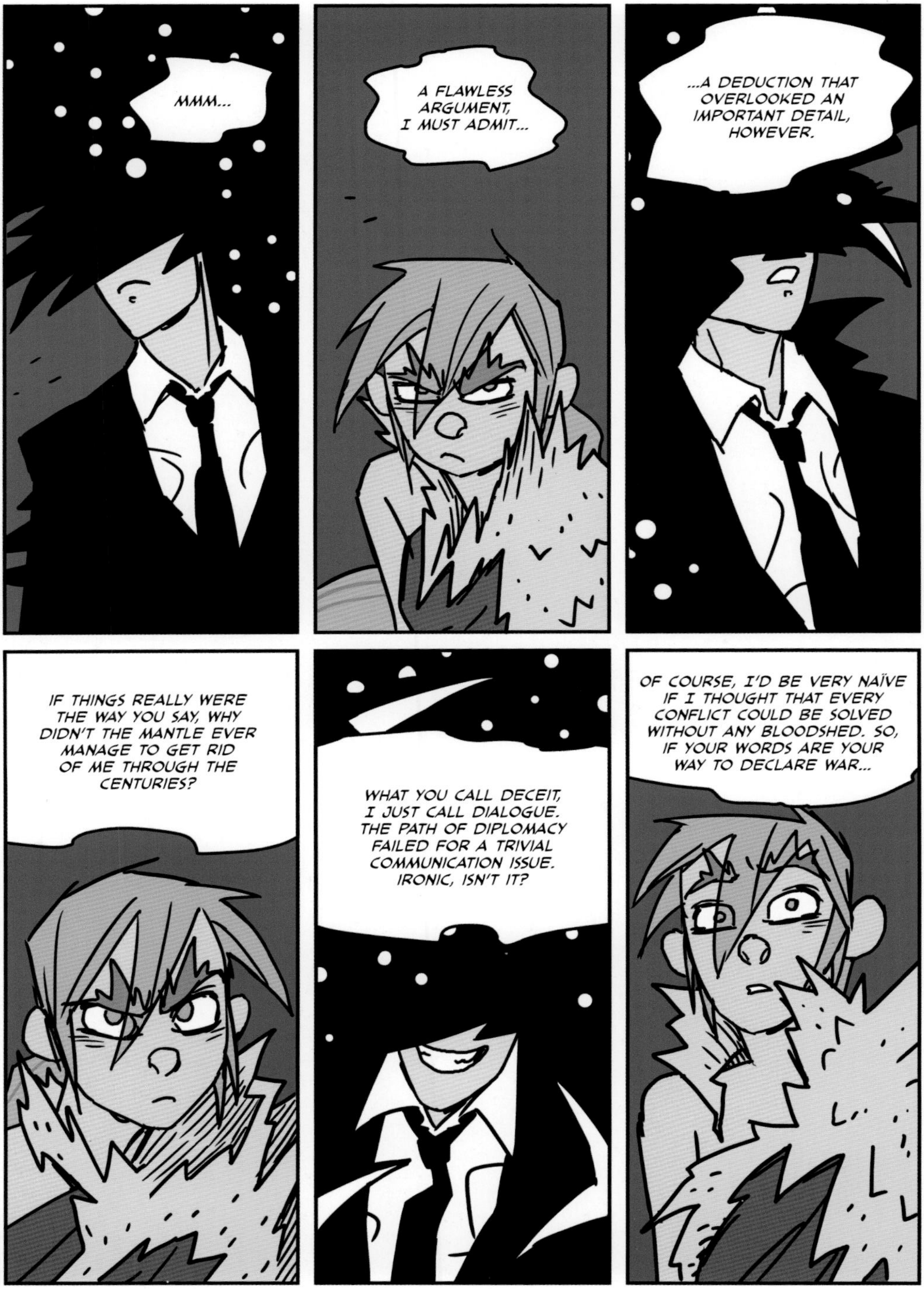
MMM...
A FLAWLESS ARGUMENT, I MUST ADMIT...
...A DEDUCTION THAT OVERLOOKED AN IMPORTANT DETAIL, HOWEVER.
IF THINGS REALLY WERE THE WAY YOU SAY, WHY DIDN'T THE MANTLE EVER MANAGE TO GET RID OF ME THROUGH THE CENTURIES?
WHAT YOU CALL DECEIT, I JUST CALL DIALOGUE. THE PATH OF DIPLOMACY FAILED FOR A TRIVIAL COMMUNICATION ISSUE. IRONIC, ISN'T IT?
OF COURSE, I'D BE VERY NAÏVE IF I THOUGHT THAT EVERY CONFLICT COULD BE SOLVED WITHOUT ANY BLOODSHED. SO, IF YOUR WORDS ARE YOUR WAY TO DECLARE WAR...

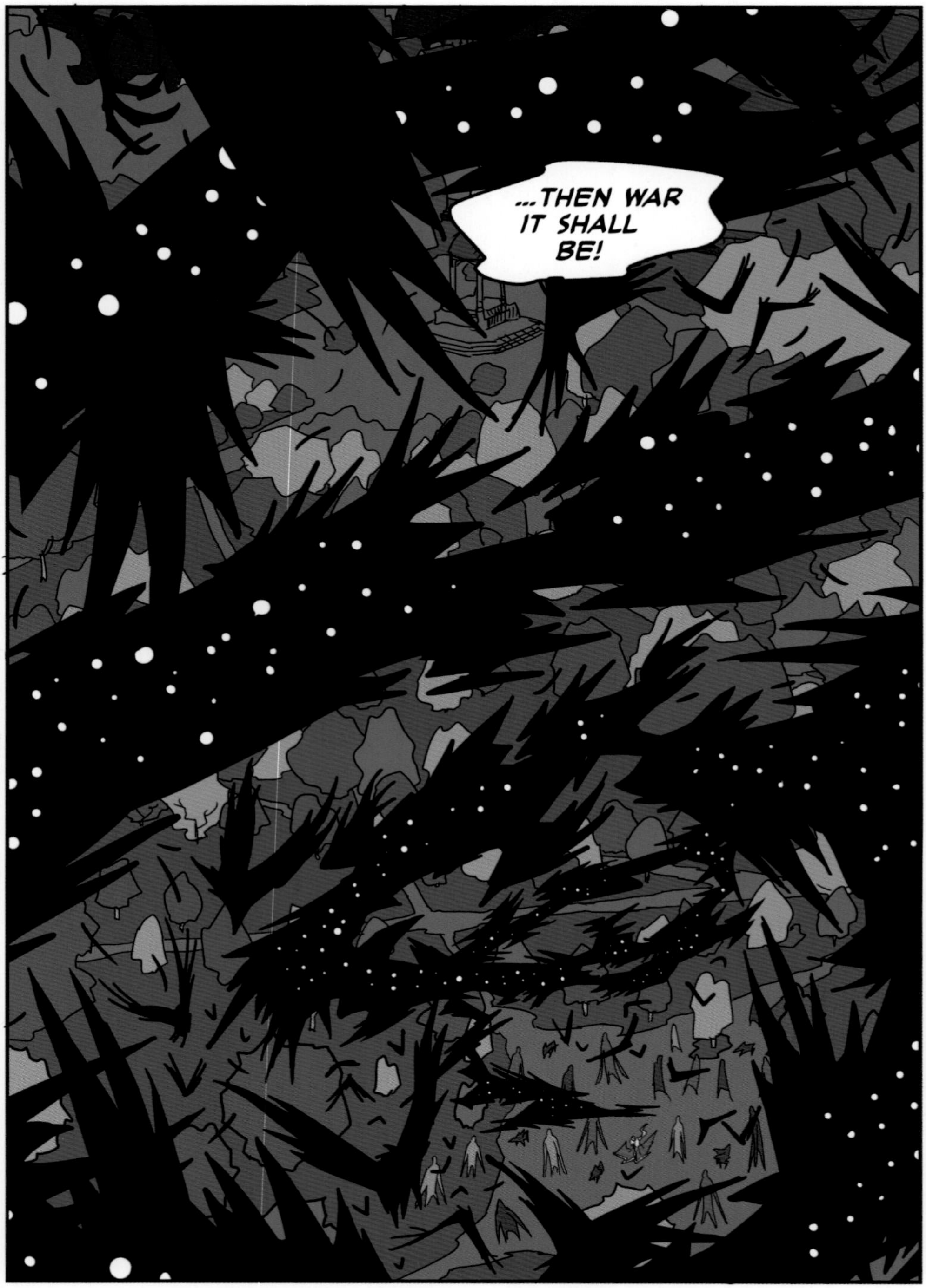
...THEN WAR IT SHALL BE!

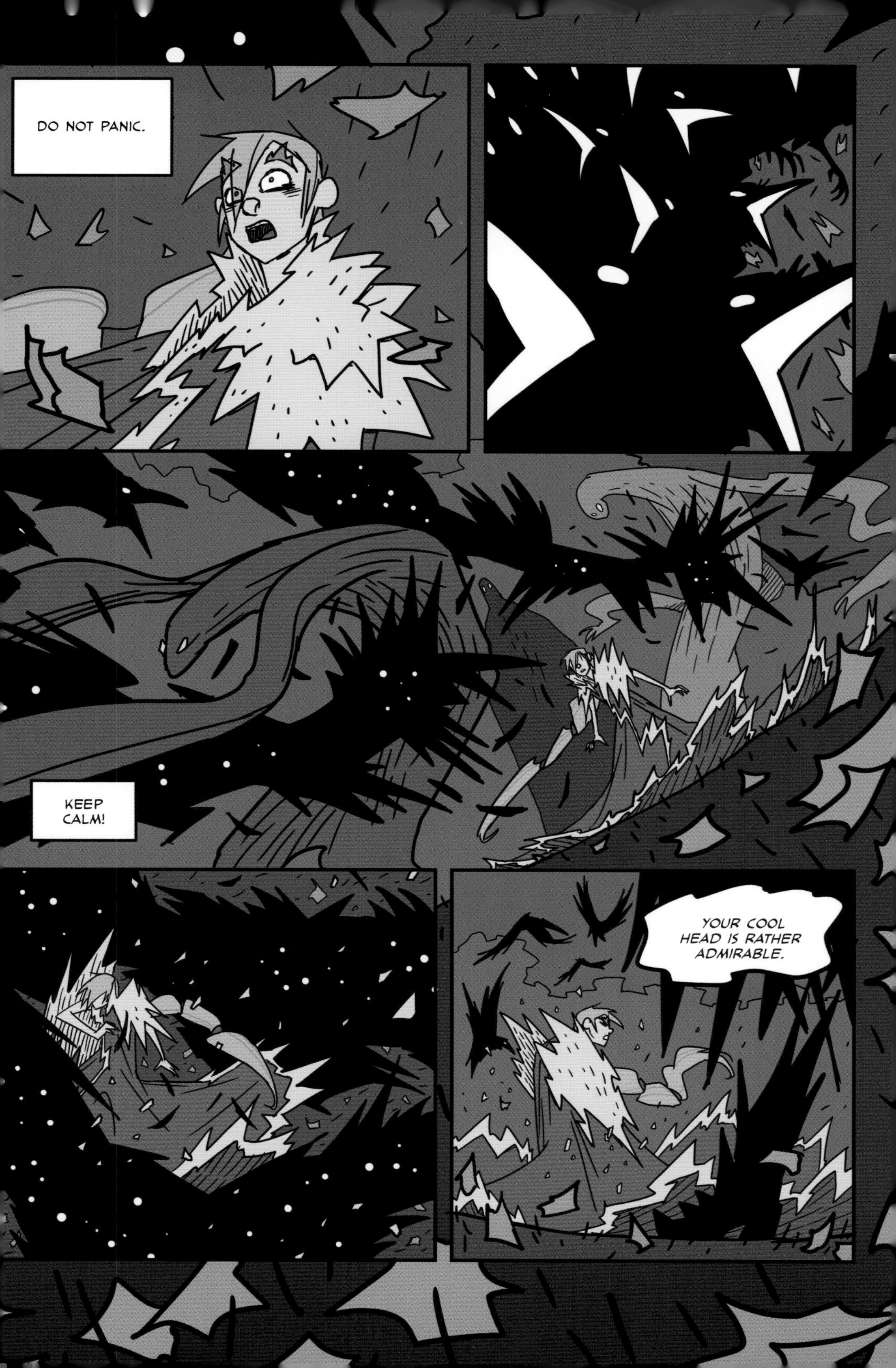
DO NOT PANIC.
KEEP CALM!
YOUR COOL HEAD IS RATHER ADMIRABLE.

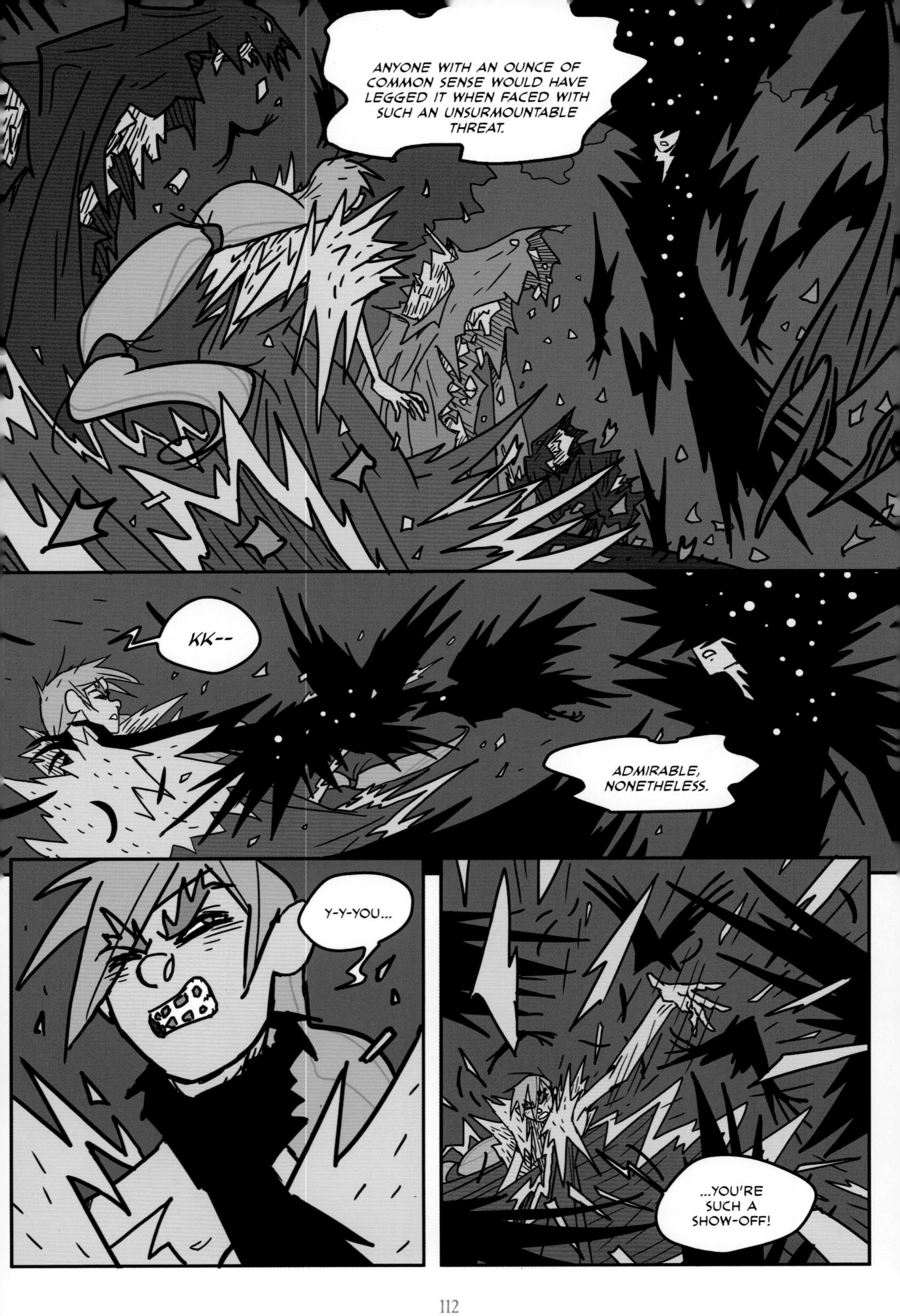
ANYONE WITH AN OUNCE OF COMMON SENSE WOULD HAVE LEGGED IT WHEN FACED WITH SUCH AN UNSURMOUNTABLE THREAT.
KK--
ADMIRABLE, NONETHELESS.
Y-Y-YOU...
...YOU'RE SUCH A SHOW-OFF!

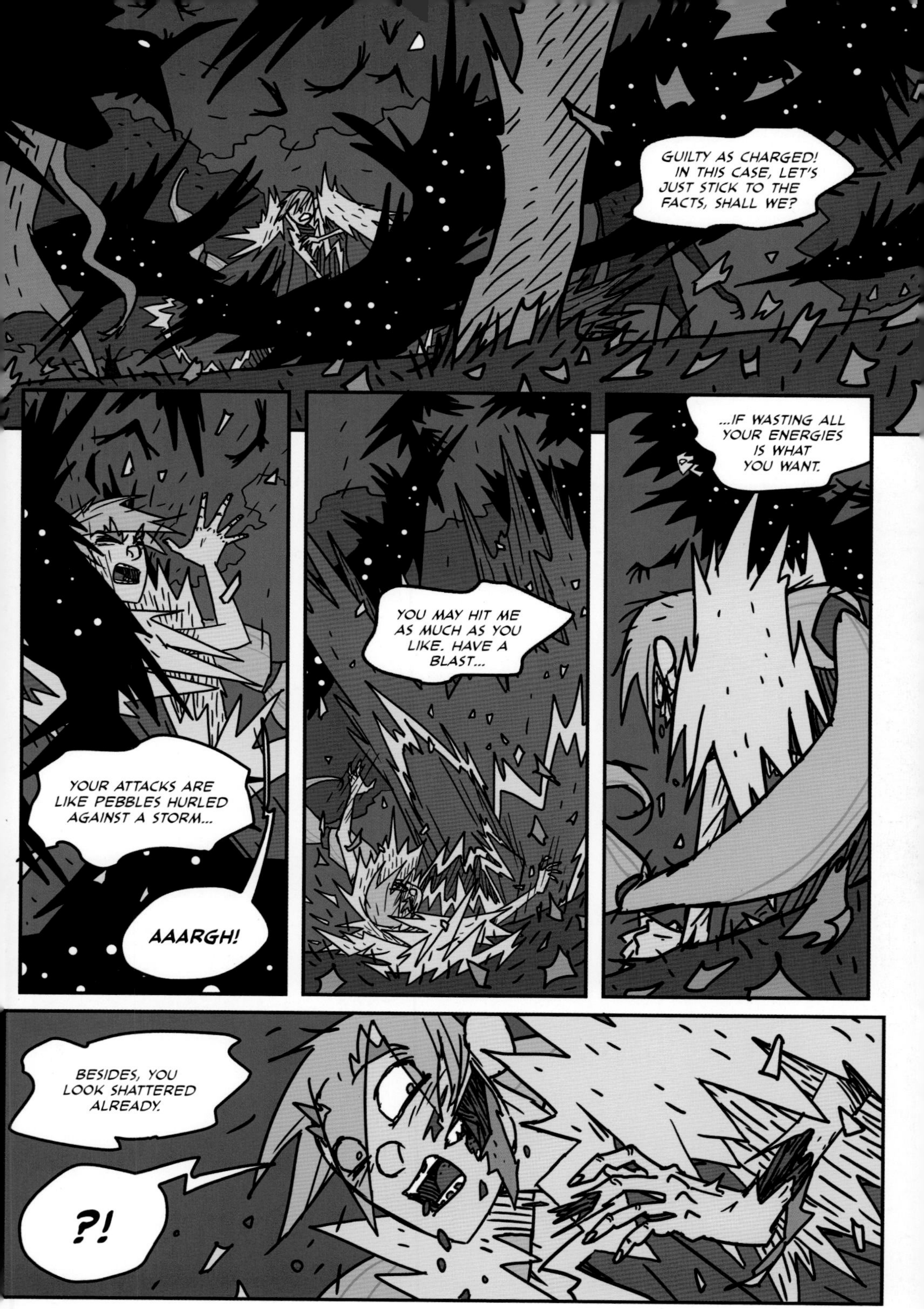

GUILTY AS CHARGED! IN THIS CASE, LET'S JUST STICK TO THE FACTS, SHALL WE?
YOUR ATTACKS ARE LIKE PEBBLES HURLED AGAINST A STORM...
AAARGH!
YOU MAY HIT ME AS MUCH AS YOU LIKE. HAVE A BLAST...
...IF WASTING ALL YOUR ENERGIES IS WHAT YOU WANT.
BESIDES, YOU LOOK SHATTERED ALREADY.
?!

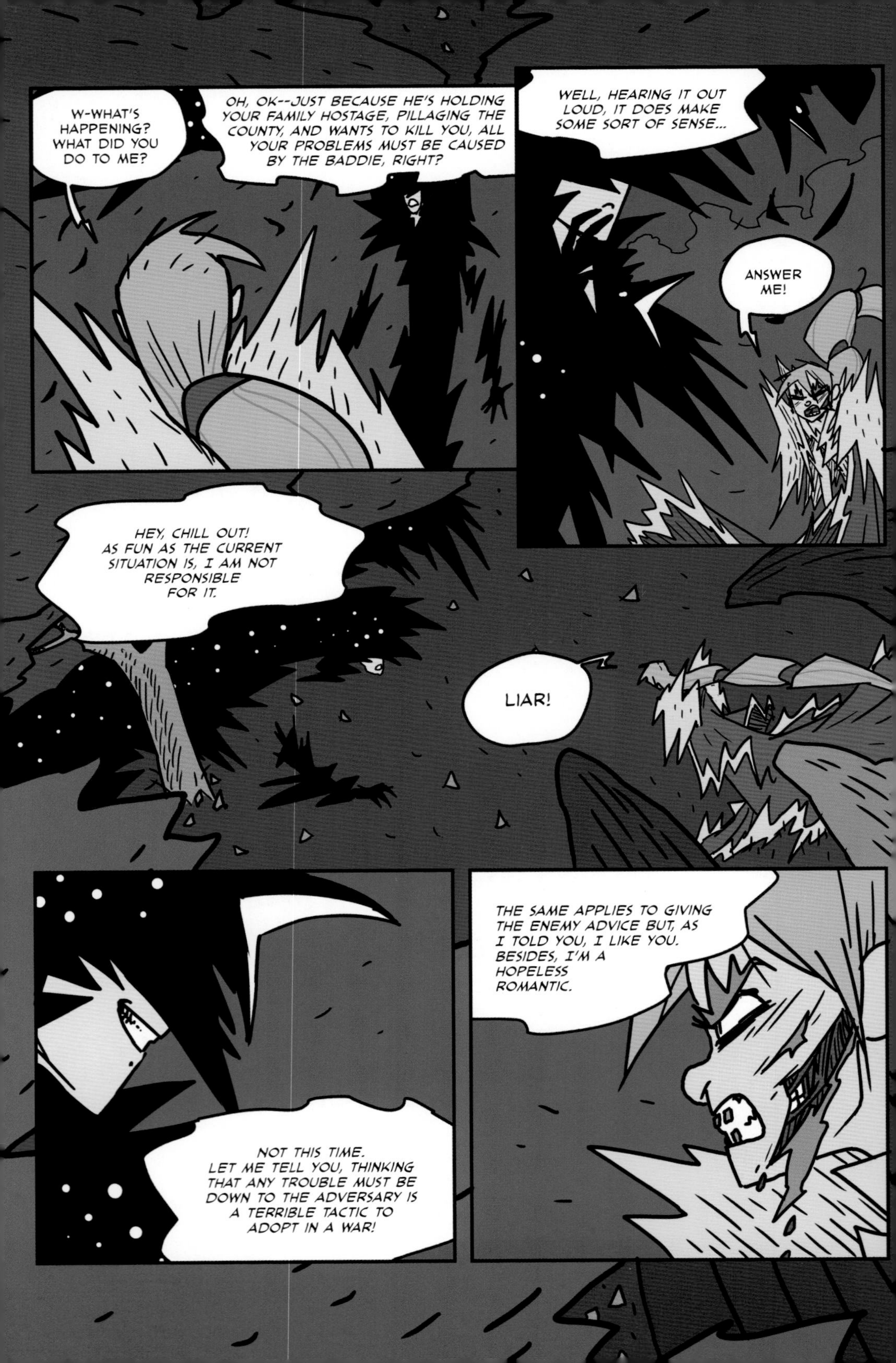
W-WHAT'S HAPPENING? WHAT DID YOU DO TO ME?
OH, OK--JUST BECAUSE HE'S HOLDING YOUR FAMILY HOSTAGE, PILLAGING THE COUNTY, AND WANTS TO KILL YOU, ALL YOUR PROBLEMS MUST BE CAUSED BY THE BADDIE, RIGHT?
WELL, HEARING IT OUT LOUD, IT DOES MAKE SOME SORT OF SENSE...
ANSWER ME!
HEY, CHILL OUT! AS FUN AS THE CURRENT SITUATION IS, I AM NOT RESPONSIBLE FOR IT.
LIAR!
NOT THIS TIME. LET ME TELL YOU, THINKING THAT ANY TROUBLE MUST BE DOWN TO THE ADVERSARY IS A TERRIBLE TACTIC TO ADOPT IN A WAR!
THE SAME APPLIES TO GIVING THE ENEMY ADVICE BUT, AS I TOLD YOU, I LIKE YOU. BESIDES, I'M A HOPELESS ROMANTIC.

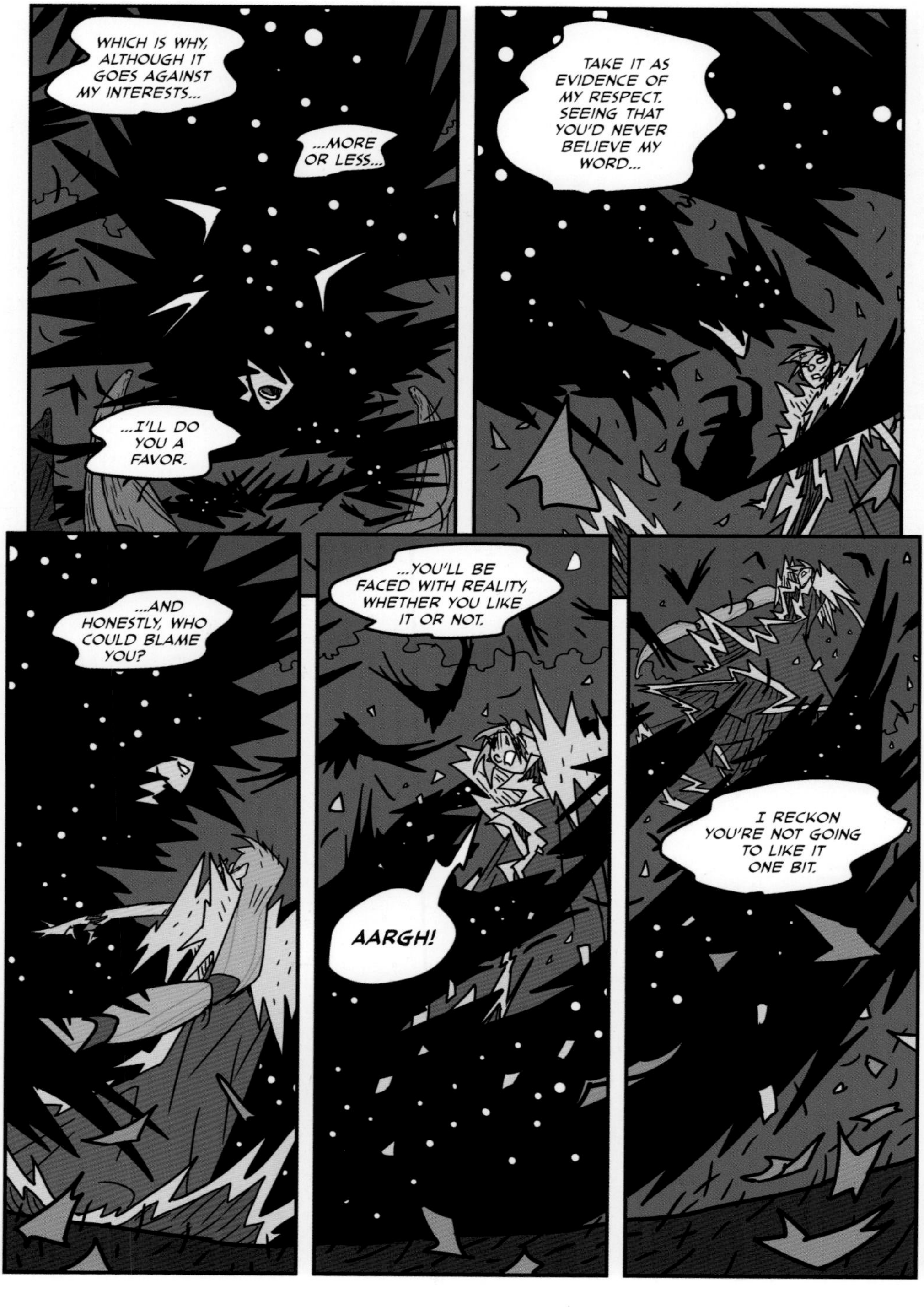
WHICH IS WHY, ALTHOUGH IT GOES AGAINST MY INTERESTS...
...MORE OR LESS...
...I'LL DO YOU A FAVOR.
TAKE IT AS EVIDENCE OF MY RESPECT. SEEING THAT YOU'D NEVER BELIEVE MY WORD...
...AND HONESTLY, WHO COULD BLAME YOU?
...YOU'LL BE FACED WITH REALITY, WHETHER YOU LIKE IT OR NOT.
AARGH!
I RECKON YOU'RE NOT GOING TO LIKE IT ONE BIT.

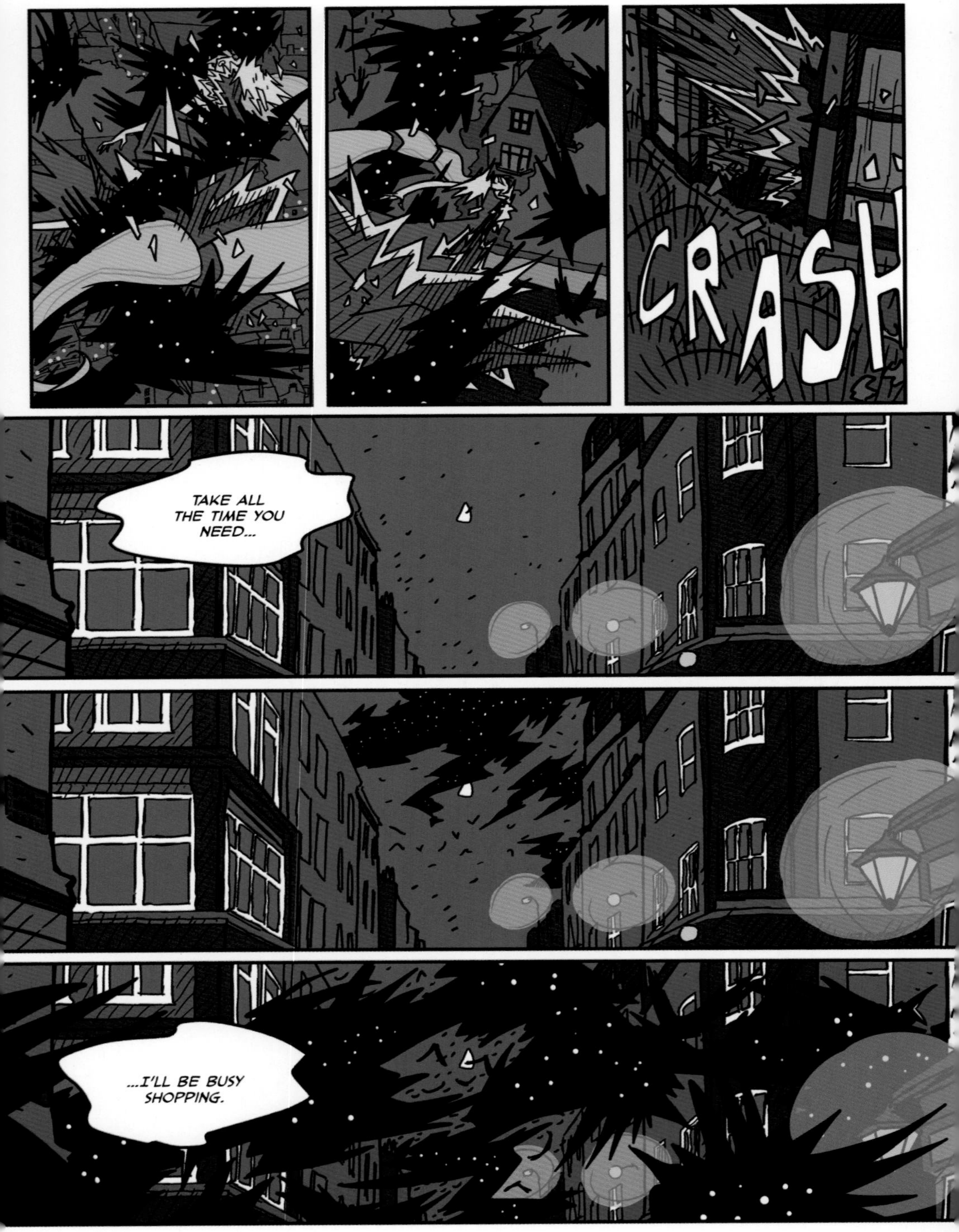
CRASH
TAKE ALL THE TIME YOU NEED...
...I'LL BE BUSY SHOPPING.

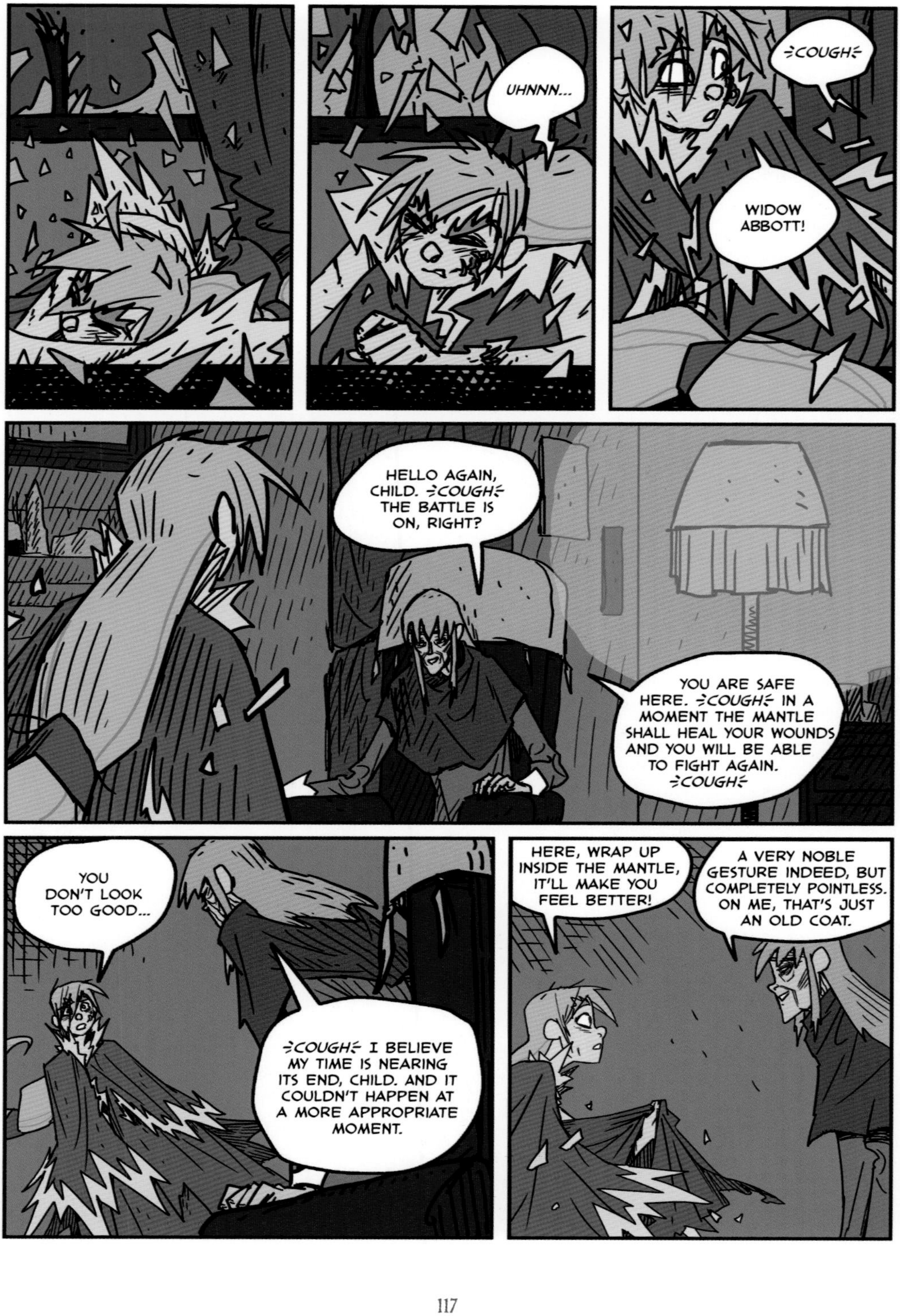
UHNNN...
≑COUGH≑
WIDOW ABBOTT!
HELLO AGAIN, CHILD. ≑COUGH≑ THE BATTLE IS ON, RIGHT?
YOU ARE SAFE HERE. ≑COUGH≑ IN A MOMENT THE MANTLE SHALL HEAL YOUR WOUNDS AND YOU WILL BE ABLE TO FIGHT AGAIN. ≑COUGH≑
YOU DON'T LOOK TOO GOOD...
≑COUGH≑ I BELIEVE MY TIME IS NEARING ITS END, CHILD. AND IT COULDN'T HAPPEN AT A MORE APPROPRIATE MOMENT.
HERE, WRAP UP INSIDE THE MANTLE, IT'LL MAKE YOU FEEL BETTER!
A VERY NOBLE GESTURE INDEED, BUT COMPLETELY POINTLESS. ON ME, THAT'S JUST AN OLD COAT.

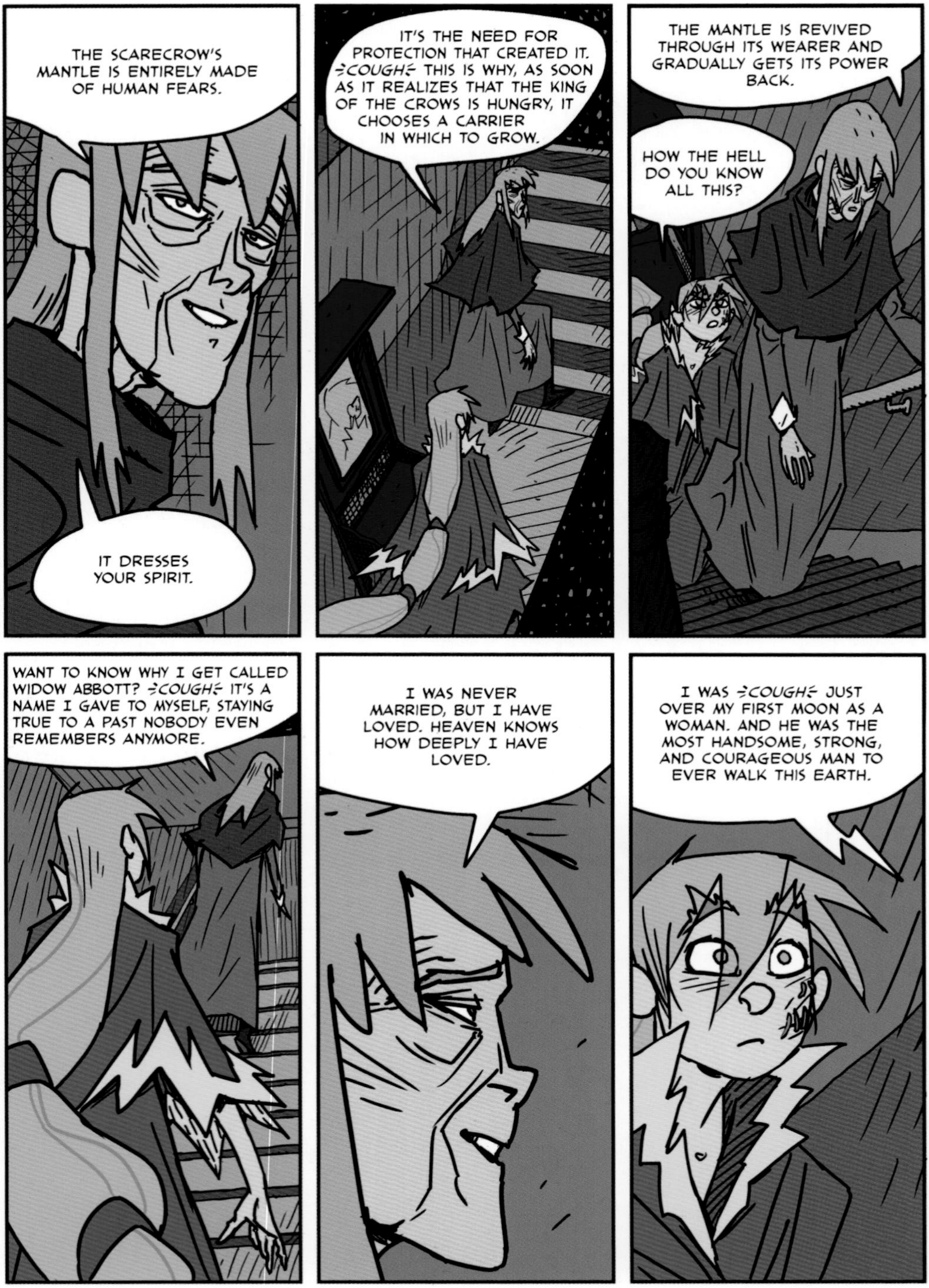
THE SCARECROW'S MANTLE IS ENTIRELY MADE OF HUMAN FEARS.
IT DRESSES YOUR SPIRIT.
IT'S THE NEED FOR PROTECTION THAT CREATED IT. ≑COUGH≑ THIS IS WHY, AS SOON AS IT REALIZES THAT THE KING OF THE CROWS IS HUNGRY, IT CHOOSES A CARRIER IN WHICH TO GROW.
THE MANTLE IS REVIVED THROUGH ITS WEARER AND GRADUALLY GETS ITS POWER BACK.
HOW THE HELL DO YOU KNOW ALL THIS?
WANT TO KNOW WHY I GET CALLED WIDOW ABBOTT? ≑COUGH≑ IT'S A NAME I GAVE TO MYSELF, STAYING TRUE TO A PAST NOBODY EVEN REMEMBERS ANYMORE.
I WAS NEVER MARRIED, BUT I HAVE LOVED. HEAVEN KNOWS HOW DEEPLY I HAVE LOVED.
I WAS ≑COUGH≑ JUST OVER MY FIRST MOON AS A WOMAN. AND HE WAS THE MOST HANDSOME, STRONG, AND COURAGEOUS MAN TO EVER WALK THIS EARTH.

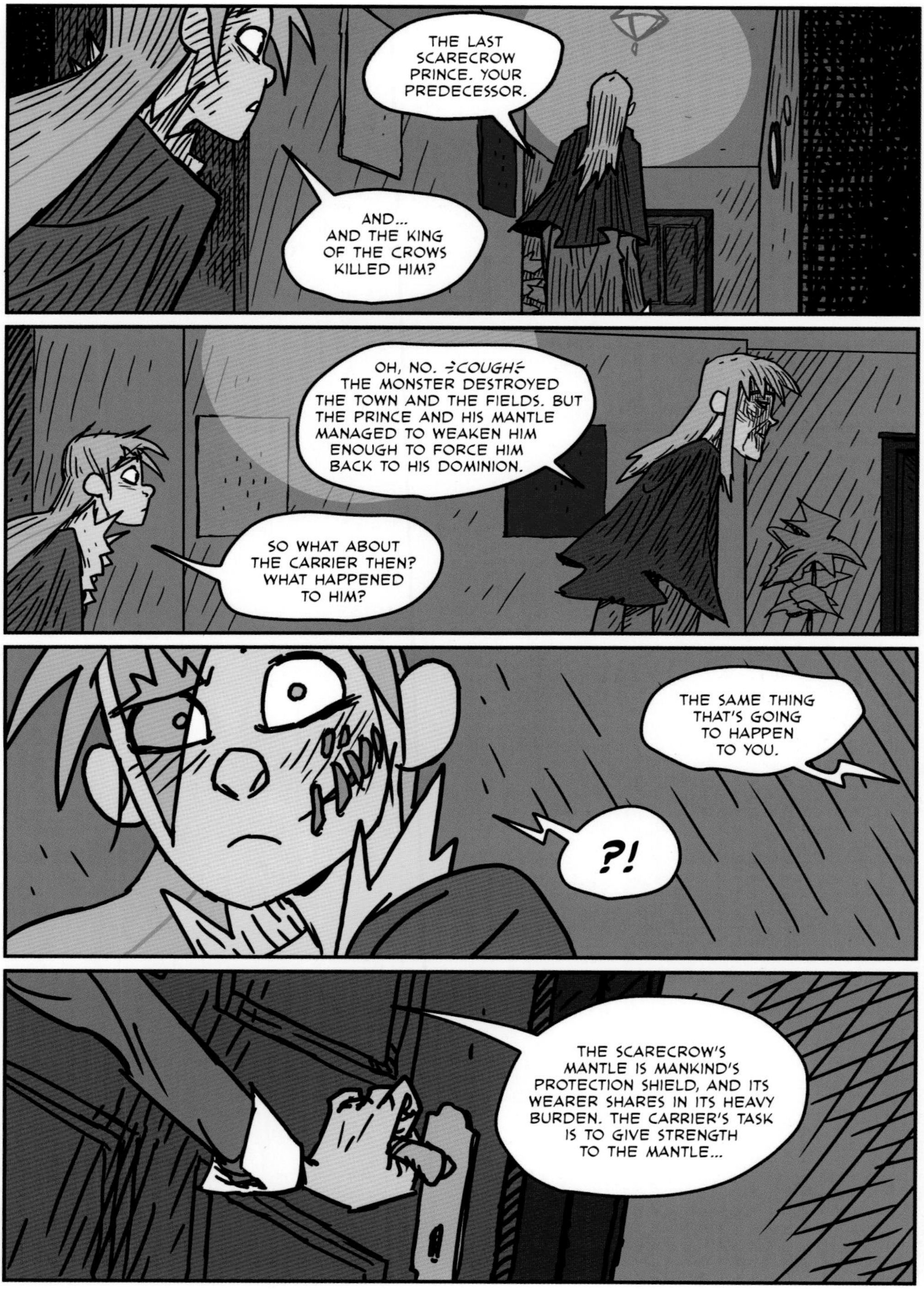
THE LAST SCARECROW PRINCE. YOUR PREDECESSOR.
AND... AND THE KING OF THE CROWS KILLED HIM?
OH, NO. ≈COUGH≈ THE MONSTER DESTROYED THE TOWN AND THE FIELDS. BUT THE PRINCE AND HIS MANTLE MANAGED TO WEAKEN HIM ENOUGH TO FORCE HIM BACK TO HIS DOMINION.
SO WHAT ABOUT THE CARRIER THEN? WHAT HAPPENED TO HIM?
THE SAME THING THAT'S GOING TO HAPPEN TO YOU.
?!
THE SCARECROW'S MANTLE IS MANKIND'S PROTECTION SHIELD, AND ITS WEARER SHARES IN ITS HEAVY BURDEN. THE CARRIER'S TASK IS TO GIVE STRENGTH TO THE MANTLE...

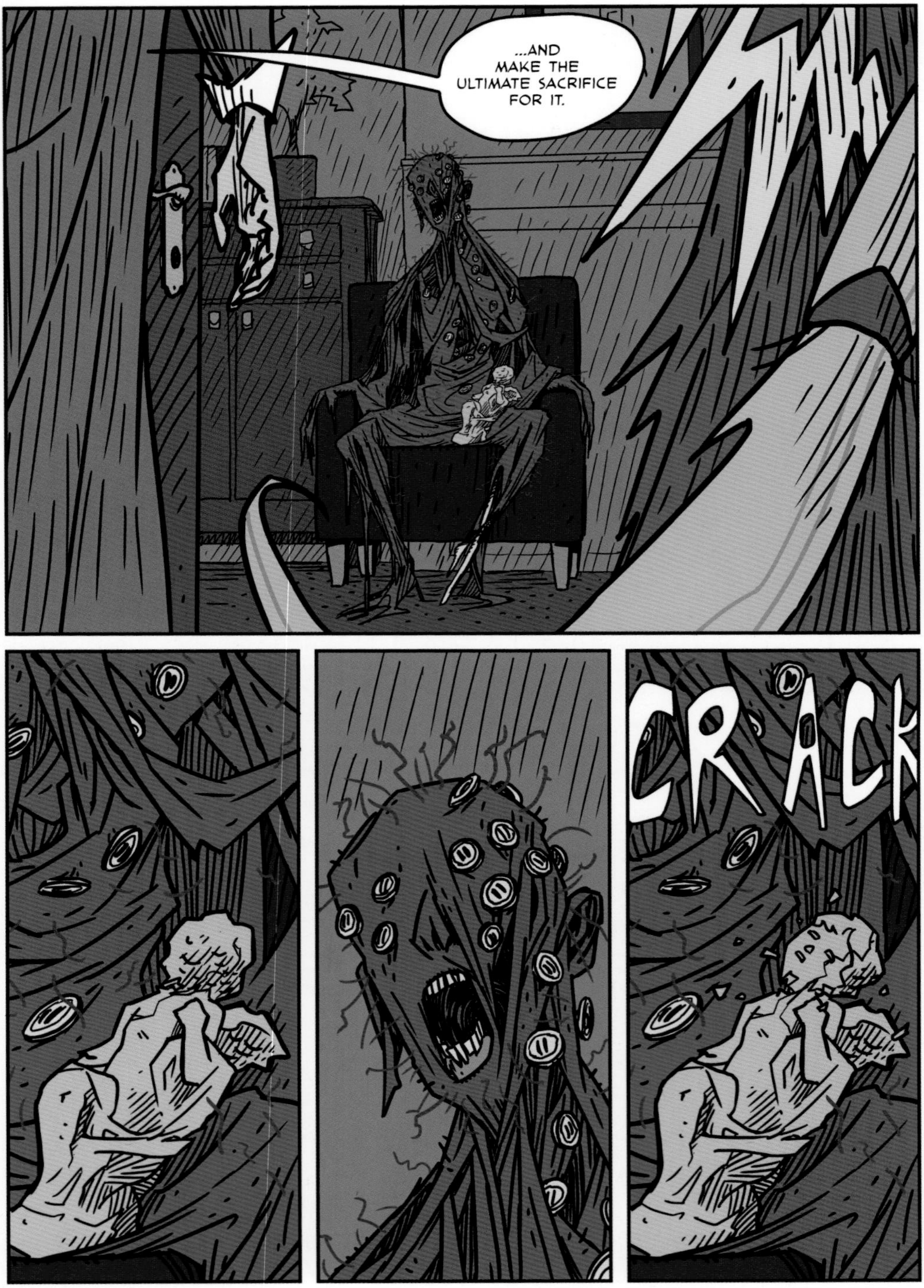
...AND MAKE THE ULTIMATE SACRIFICE FOR IT.
CRACK

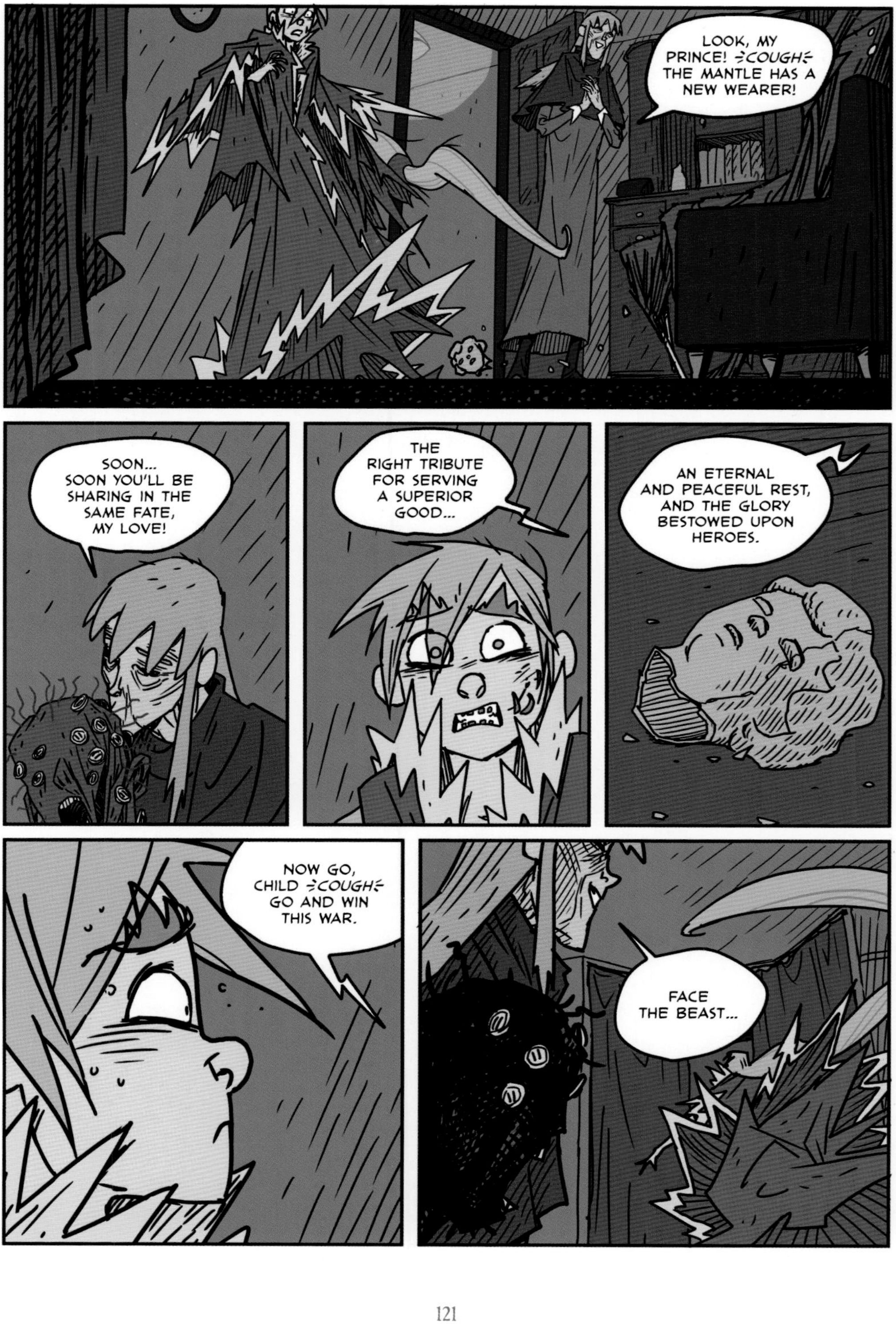
LOOK, MY PRINCE! =COUGH= THE MANTLE HAS A NEW WEARER!
SOON... SOON YOU'LL BE SHARING IN THE SAME FATE, MY LOVE!
THE RIGHT TRIBUTE FOR SERVING A SUPERIOR GOOD...
AN ETERNAL AND PEACEFUL REST, AND THE GLORY BESTOWED UPON HEROES.
NOW GO, CHILD =COUGH= GO AND WIN THIS WAR.
FACE THE BEAST...

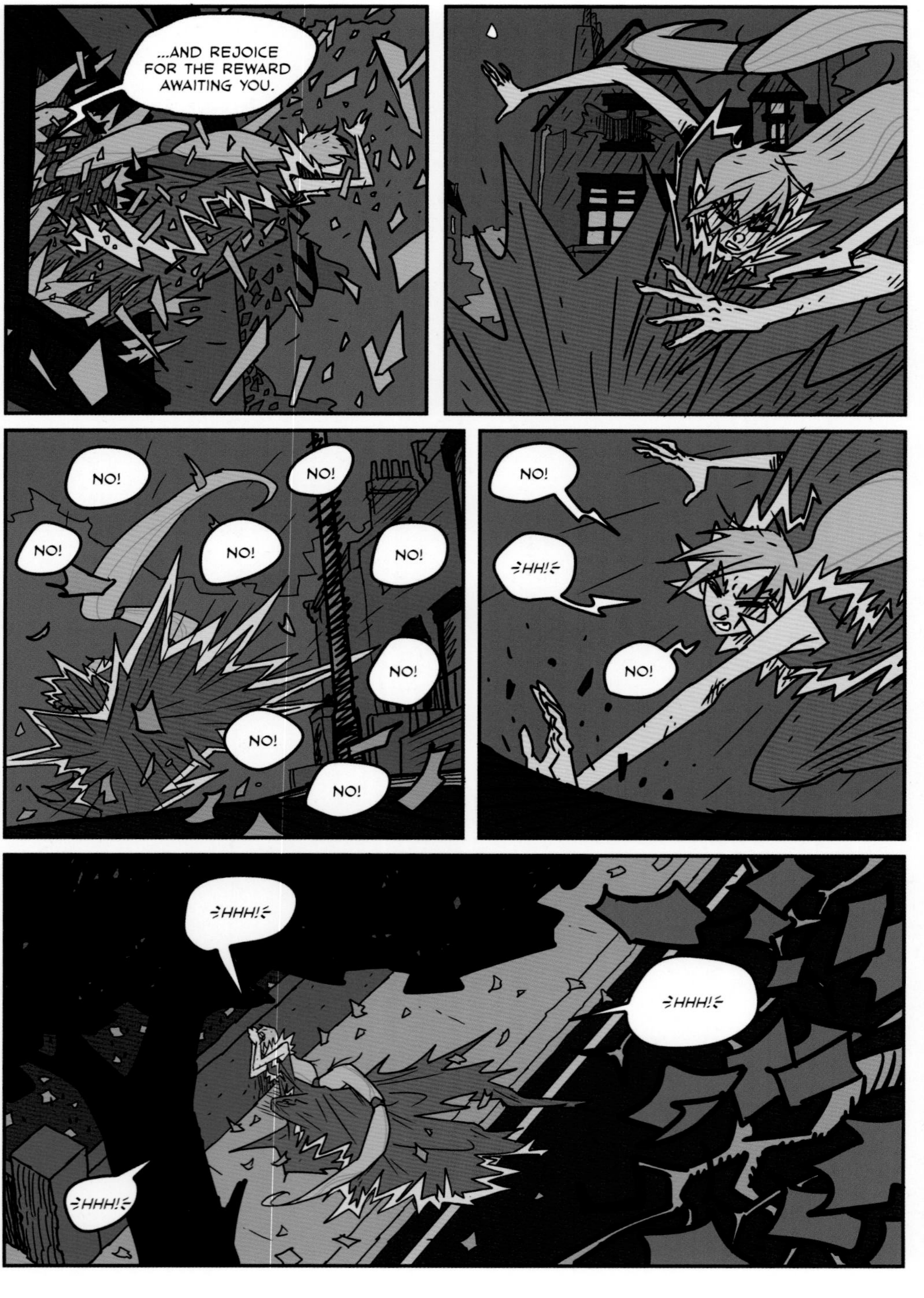
...AND REJOICE FOR THE REWARD AWAITING YOU.
NO!
NO!
NO!
NO!
NO!
NO!
NO!
NO!
NO!
HH!
NO!
HHH!
HHH!
HHH!

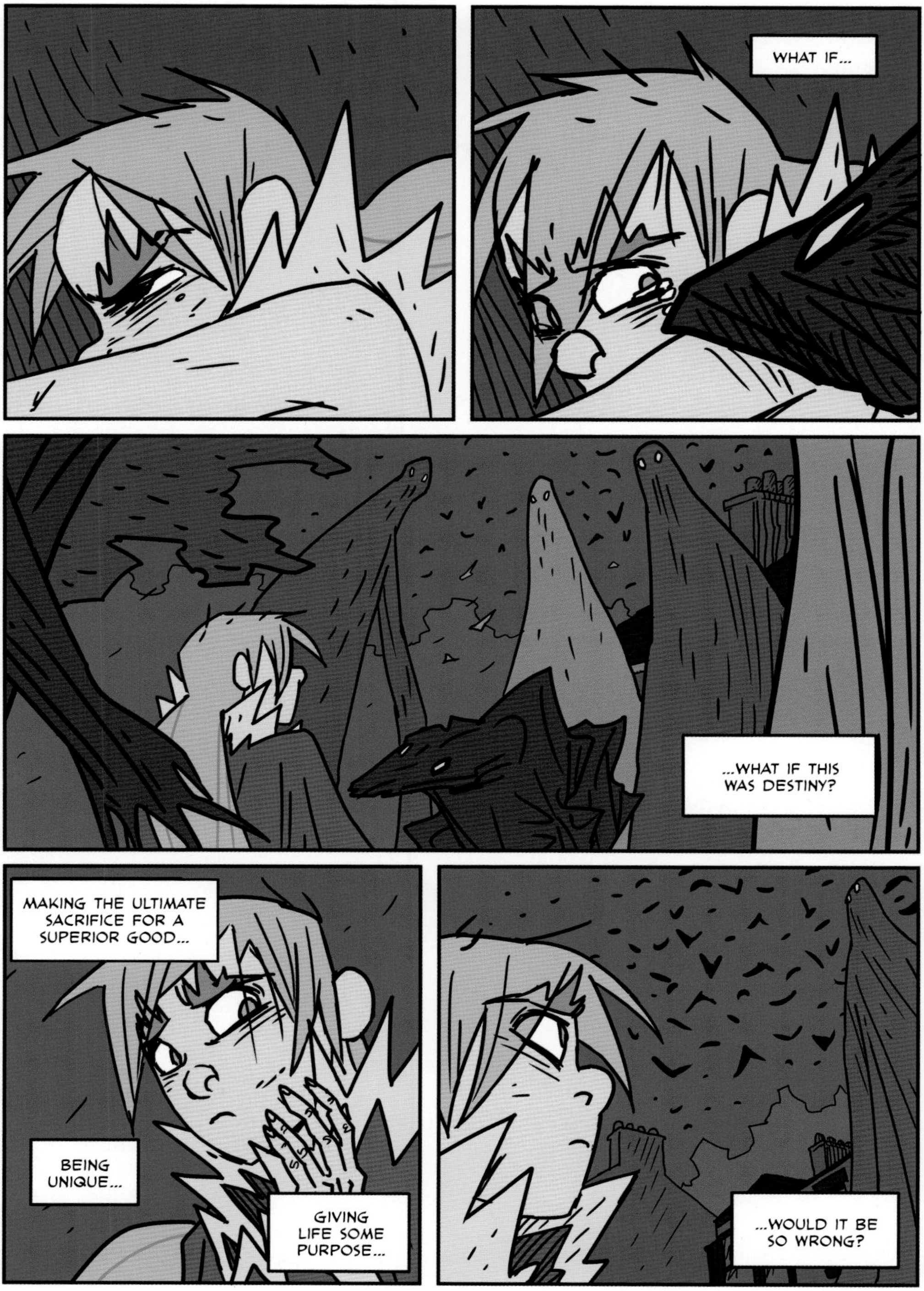
WHAT IF...
...WHAT IF THIS WAS DESTINY?
MAKING THE ULTIMATE SACRIFICE FOR A SUPERIOR GOOD...
BEING UNIQUE...
GIVING LIFE SOME PURPOSE...
...WOULD IT BE SO WRONG?

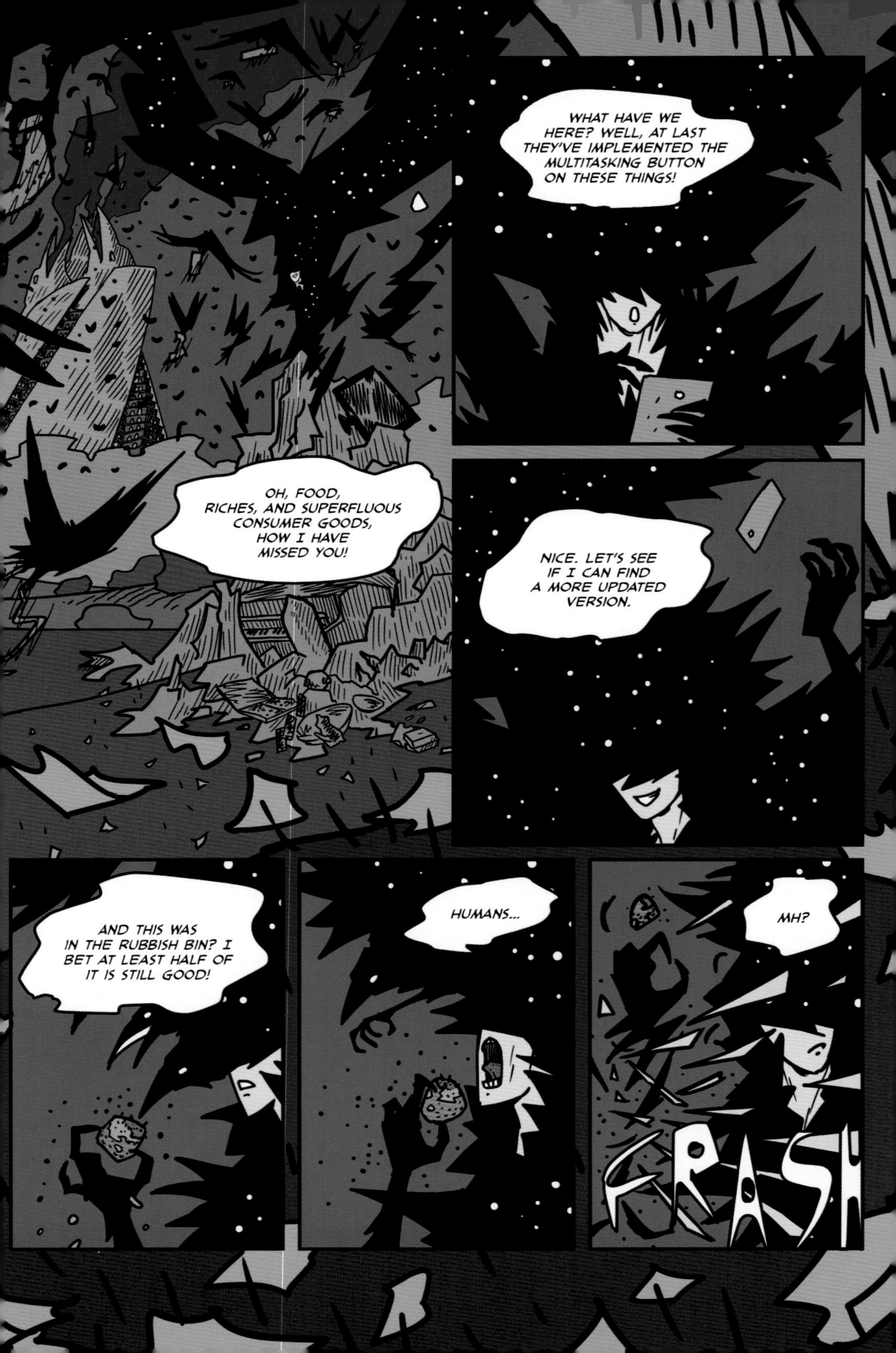
WHAT HAVE WE HERE? WELL, AT LAST THEY'VE IMPLEMENTED THE MULTITASKING BUTTON ON THESE THINGS!
OH, FOOD, RICHES, AND SUPERFLUOUS CONSUMER GOODS, HOW I HAVE MISSED YOU!
NICE. LET'S SEE IF I CAN FIND A MORE UPDATED VERSION.
AND THIS WAS IN THE RUBBISH BIN? I BET AT LEAST HALF OF IT IS STILL GOOD!
HUMANS...
MH?
CRASH

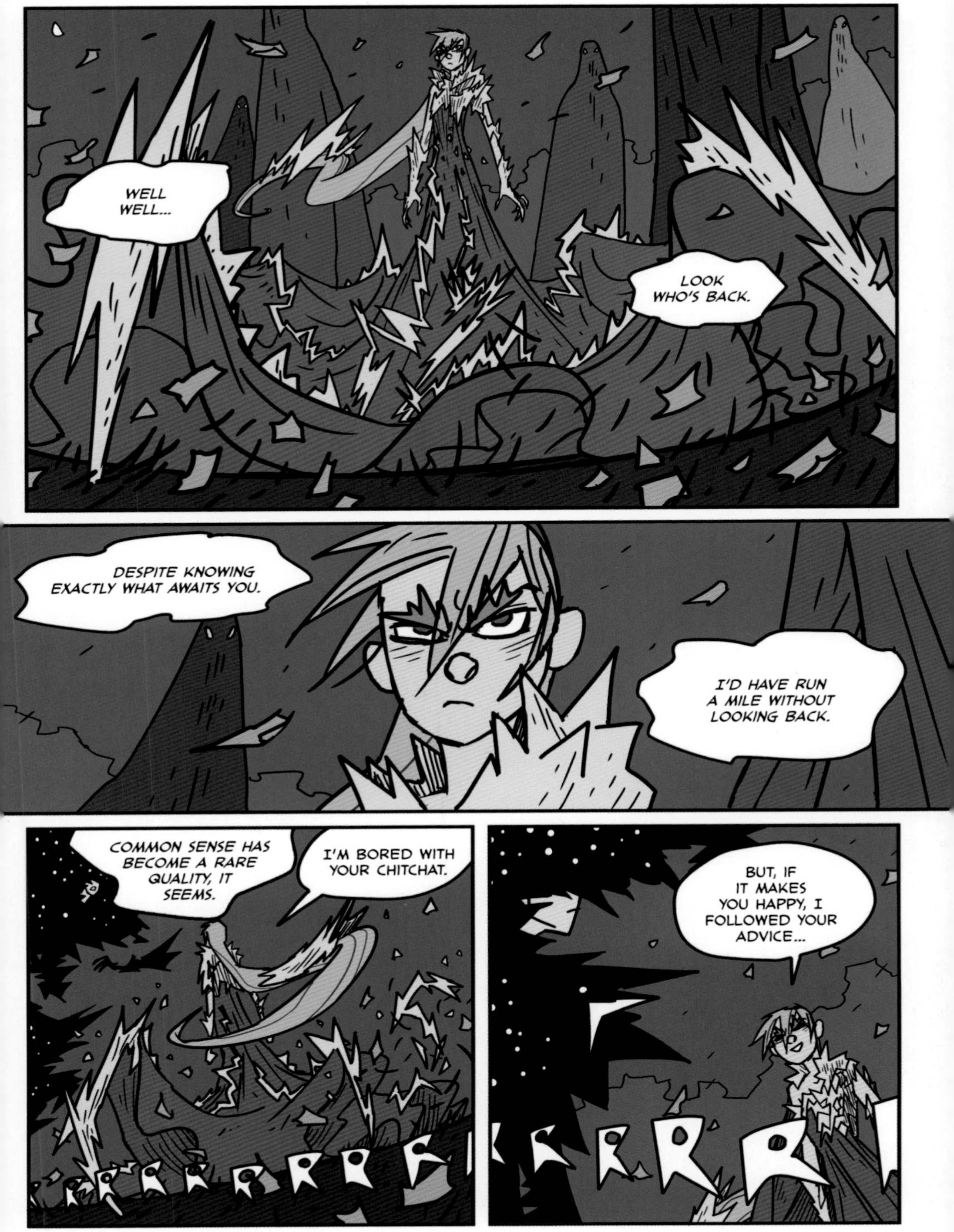
WELL WELL...
LOOK WHO'S BACK.
DESPITE KNOWING EXACTLY WHAT AWAITS YOU.
I'D HAVE RUN A MILE WITHOUT LOOKING BACK.
COMMON SENSE HAS BECOME A RARE QUALITY, IT SEEMS.
I'M BORED WITH YOUR CHITCHAT.
BUT, IF IT MAKES YOU HAPPY, I FOLLOWED YOUR ADVICE...

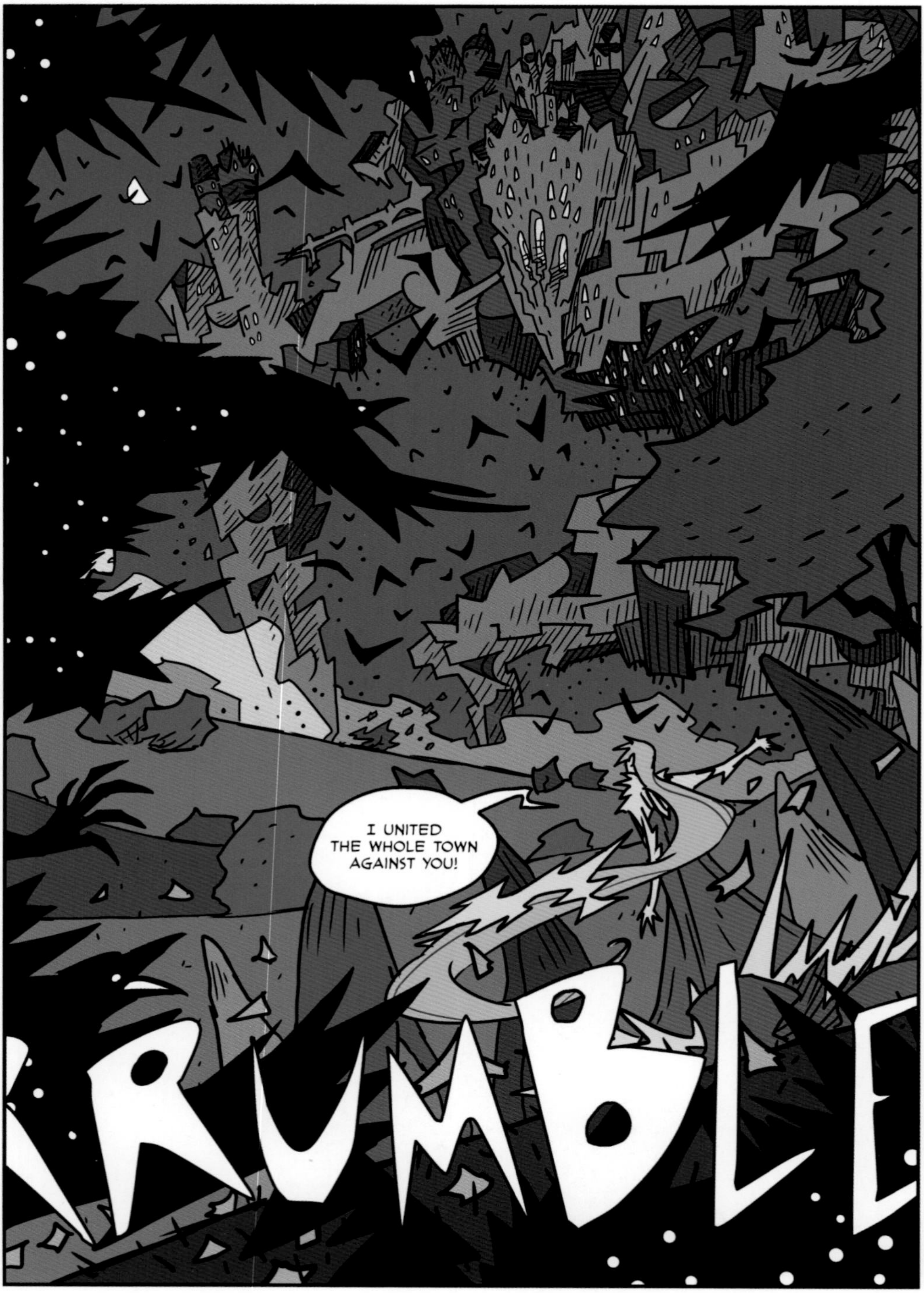
I UNITED THE WHOLE TOWN AGAINST YOU!
RUMBLE

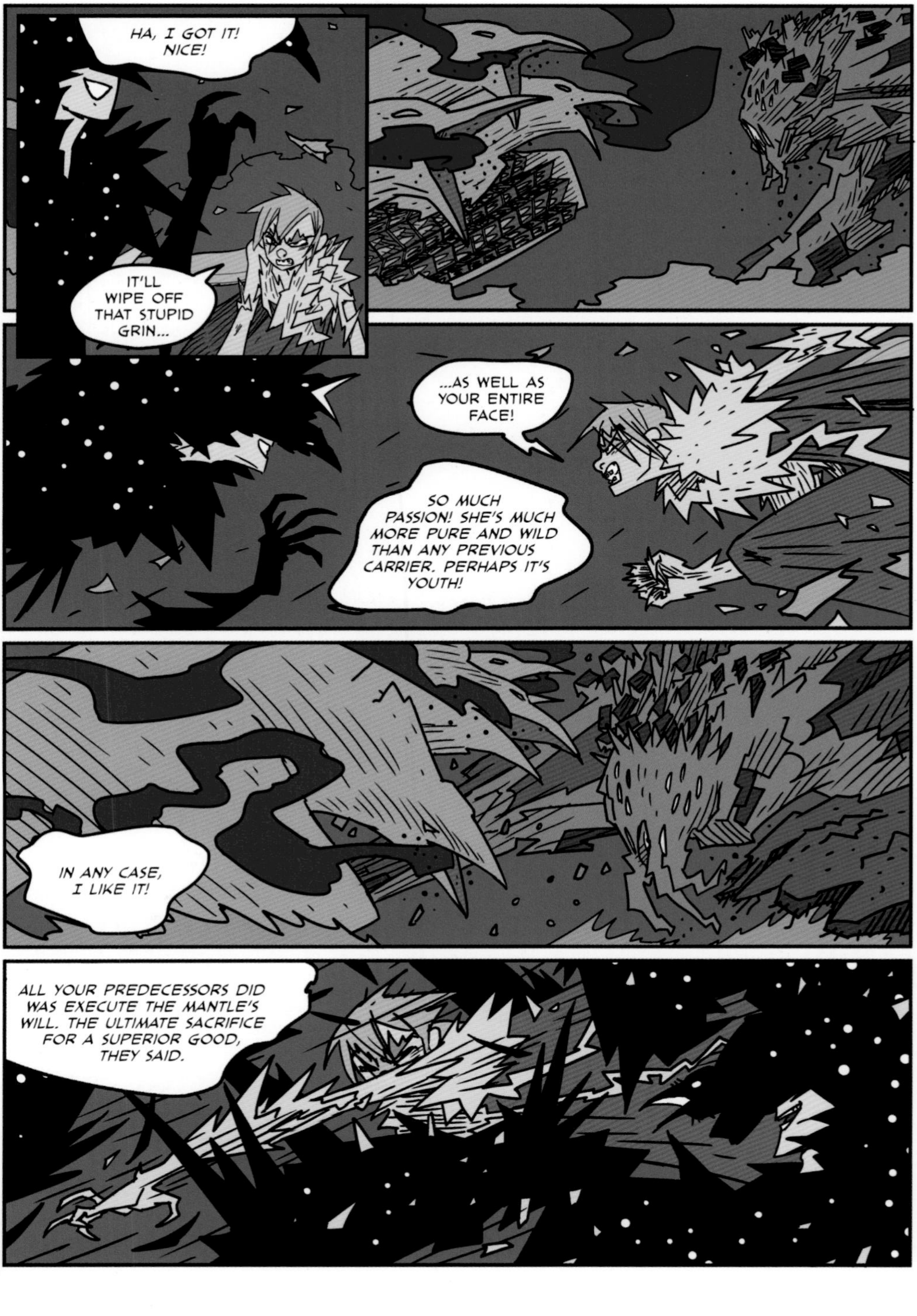
HA, I GOT IT! NICE!
IT'LL WIPE OFF THAT STUPID GRIN...
...AS WELL AS YOUR ENTIRE FACE!
SO MUCH PASSION! SHE'S MUCH MORE PURE AND WILD THAN ANY PREVIOUS CARRIER. PERHAPS IT'S YOUTH!
IN ANY CASE, I LIKE IT!
ALL YOUR PREDECESSORS DID WAS EXECUTE THE MANTLE'S WILL. THE ULTIMATE SACRIFICE FOR A SUPERIOR GOOD, THEY SAID.

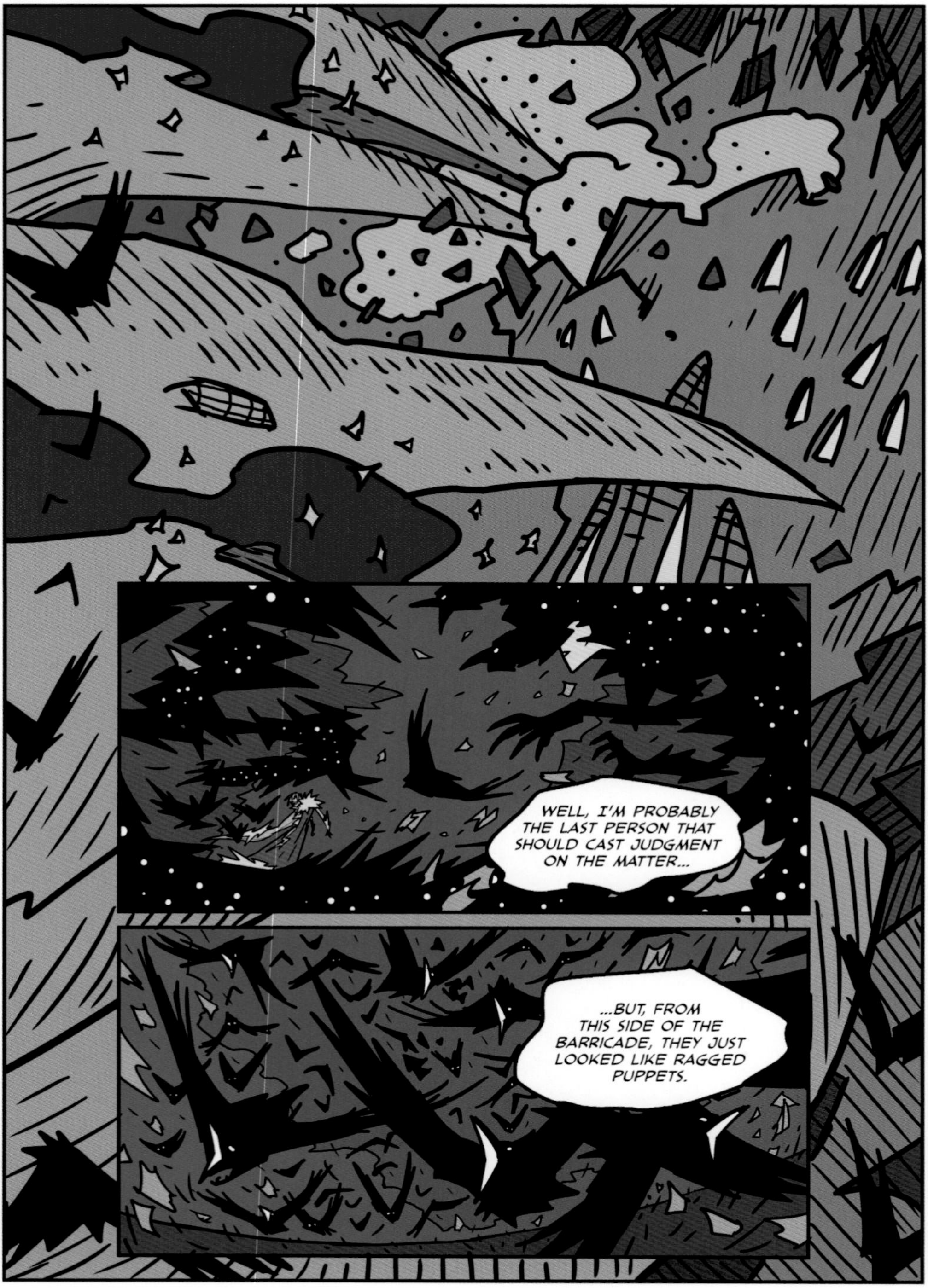
WELL, I'M PROBABLY THE LAST PERSON THAT SHOULD CAST JUDGMENT ON THE MATTER...
...BUT, FROM THIS SIDE OF THE BARRICADE, THEY JUST LOOKED LIKE RAGGED PUPPETS.

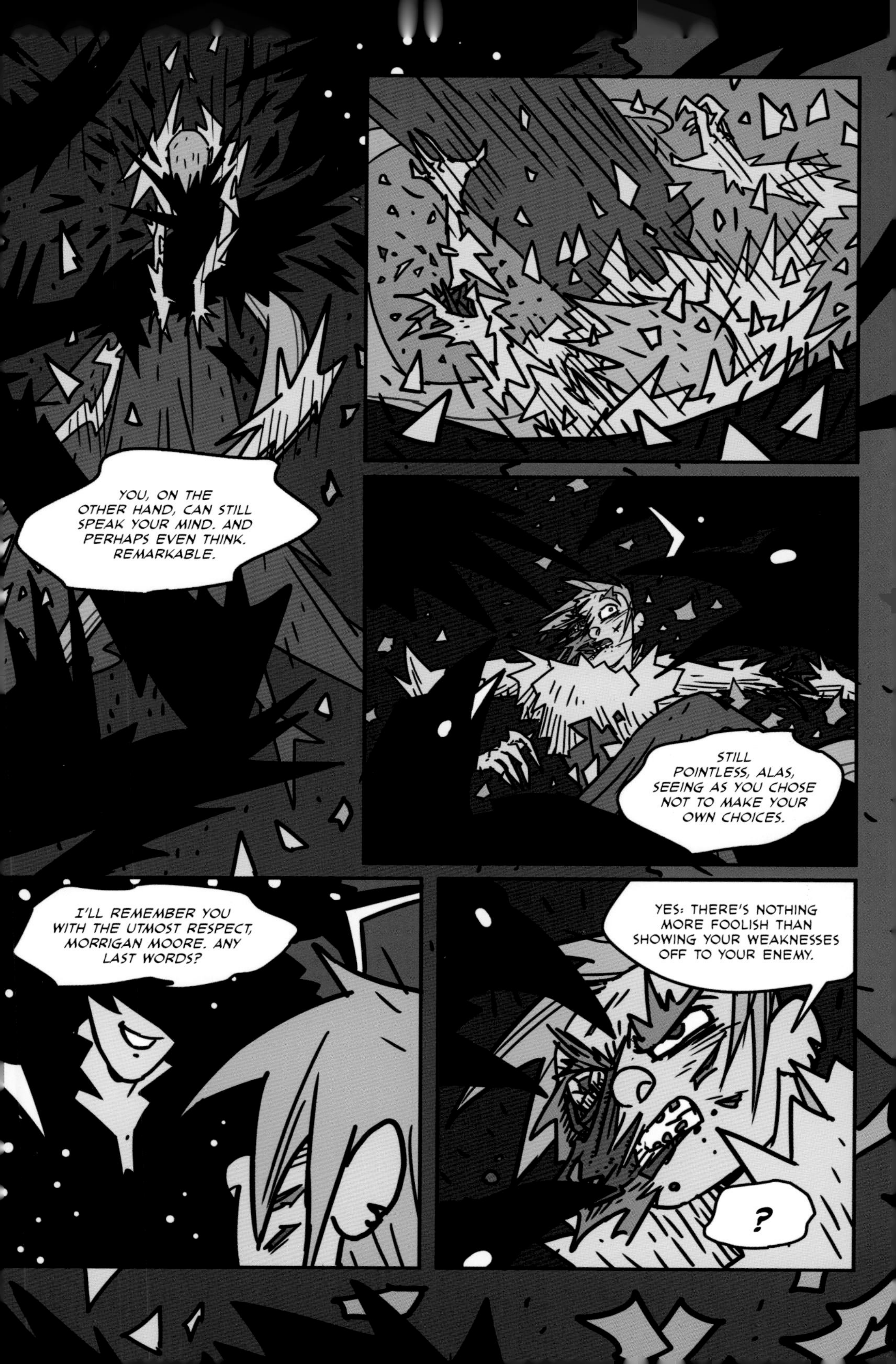
YOU, ON THE OTHER HAND, CAN STILL SPEAK YOUR MIND. AND PERHAPS EVEN THINK. REMARKABLE.
STILL POINTLESS, ALAS, SEEING AS YOU CHOSE NOT TO MAKE YOUR OWN CHOICES.
I'LL REMEMBER YOU WITH THE UTMOST RESPECT, MORRIGAN MOORE. ANY LAST WORDS?
YES: THERE'S NOTHING MORE FOOLISH THAN SHOWING YOUR WEAKNESSES OFF TO YOUR ENEMY.
?

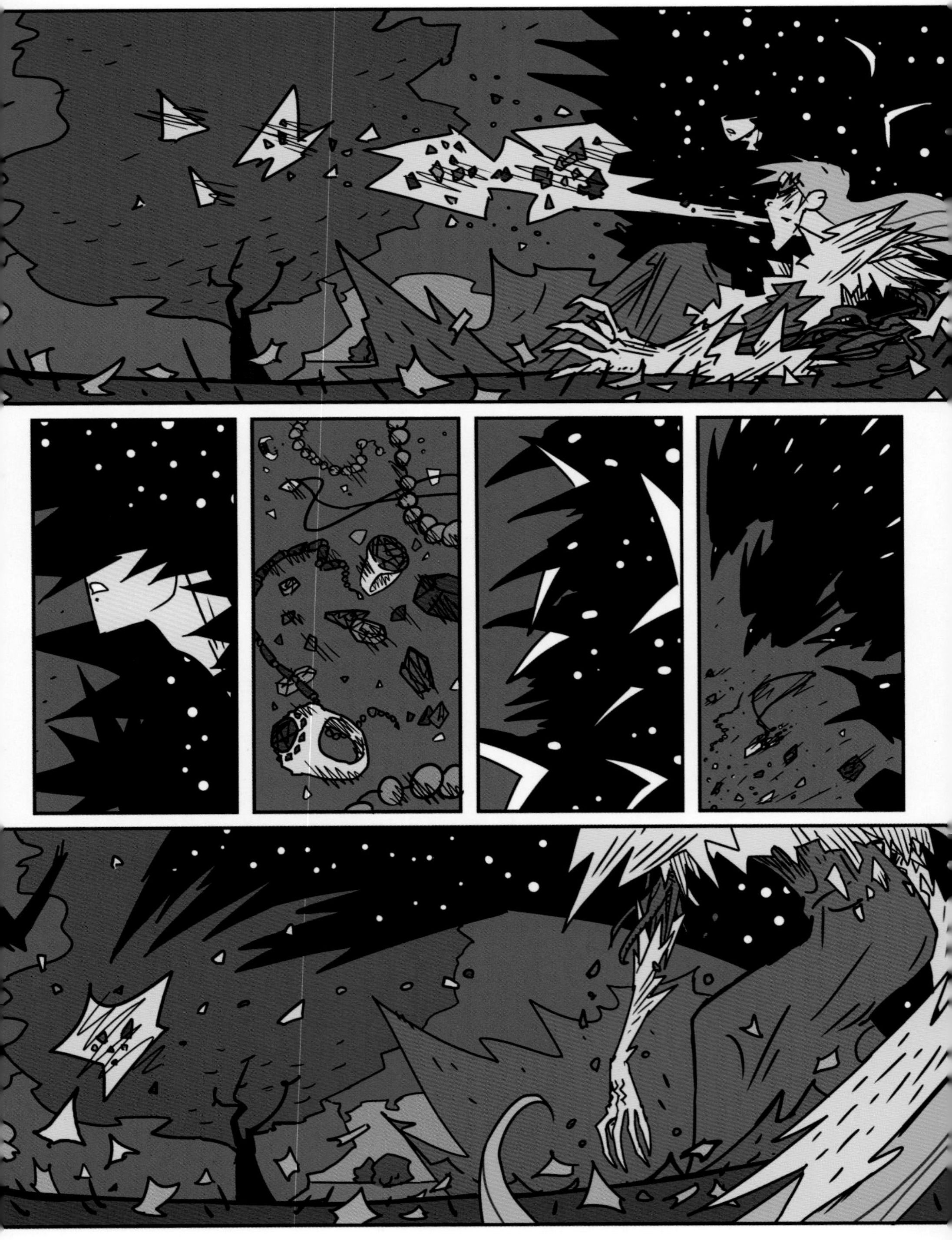

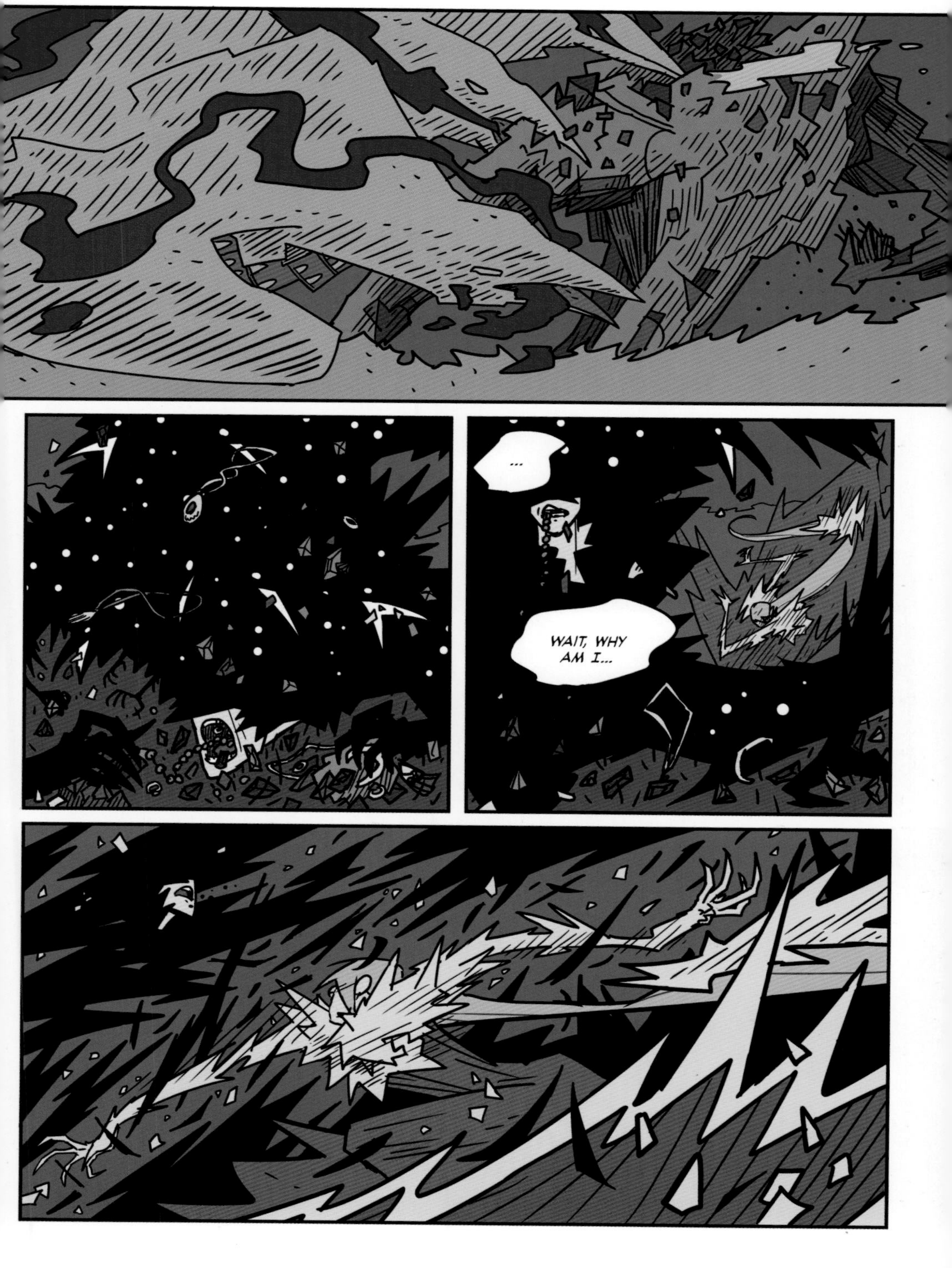
...
WAIT, WHY AM I...

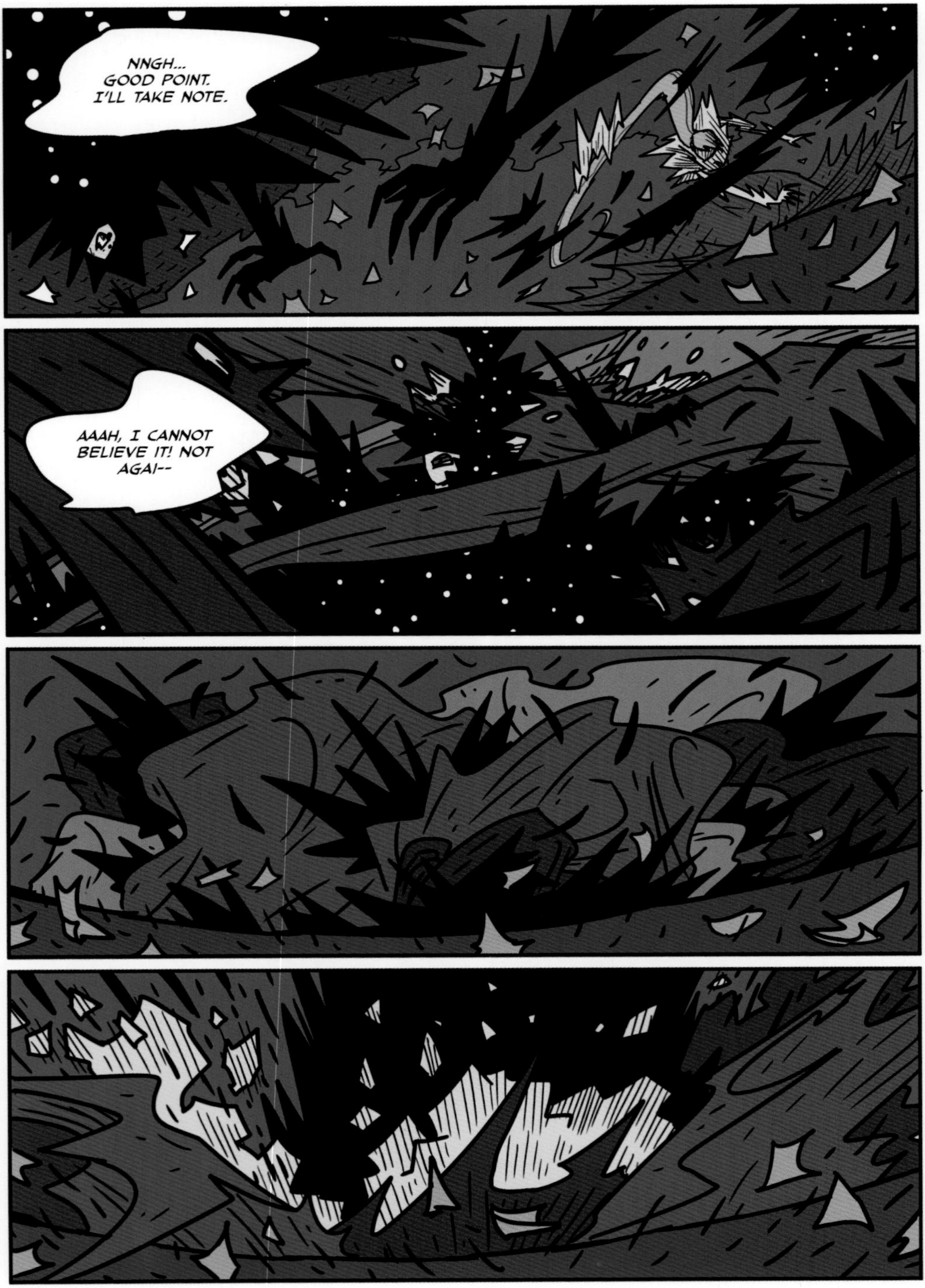
NNGH... GOOD POINT. I'LL TAKE NOTE.
AAAH, I CANNOT BELIEVE IT! NOT AGAI--

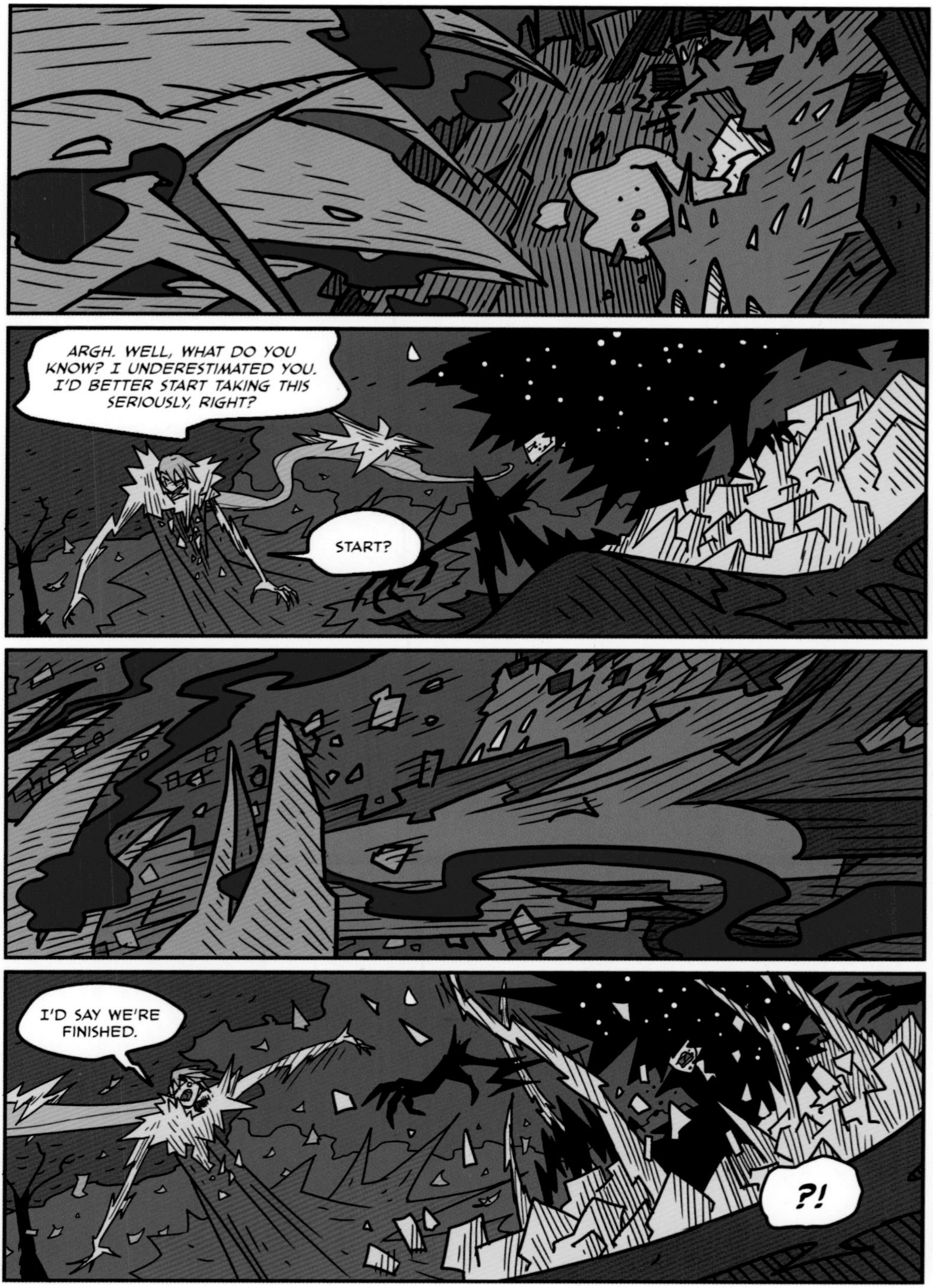
ARGH. WELL, WHAT DO YOU KNOW? I UNDERESTIMATED YOU. I'D BETTER START TAKING THIS SERIOUSLY, RIGHT?
START?
I'D SAY WE'RE FINISHED.
?!

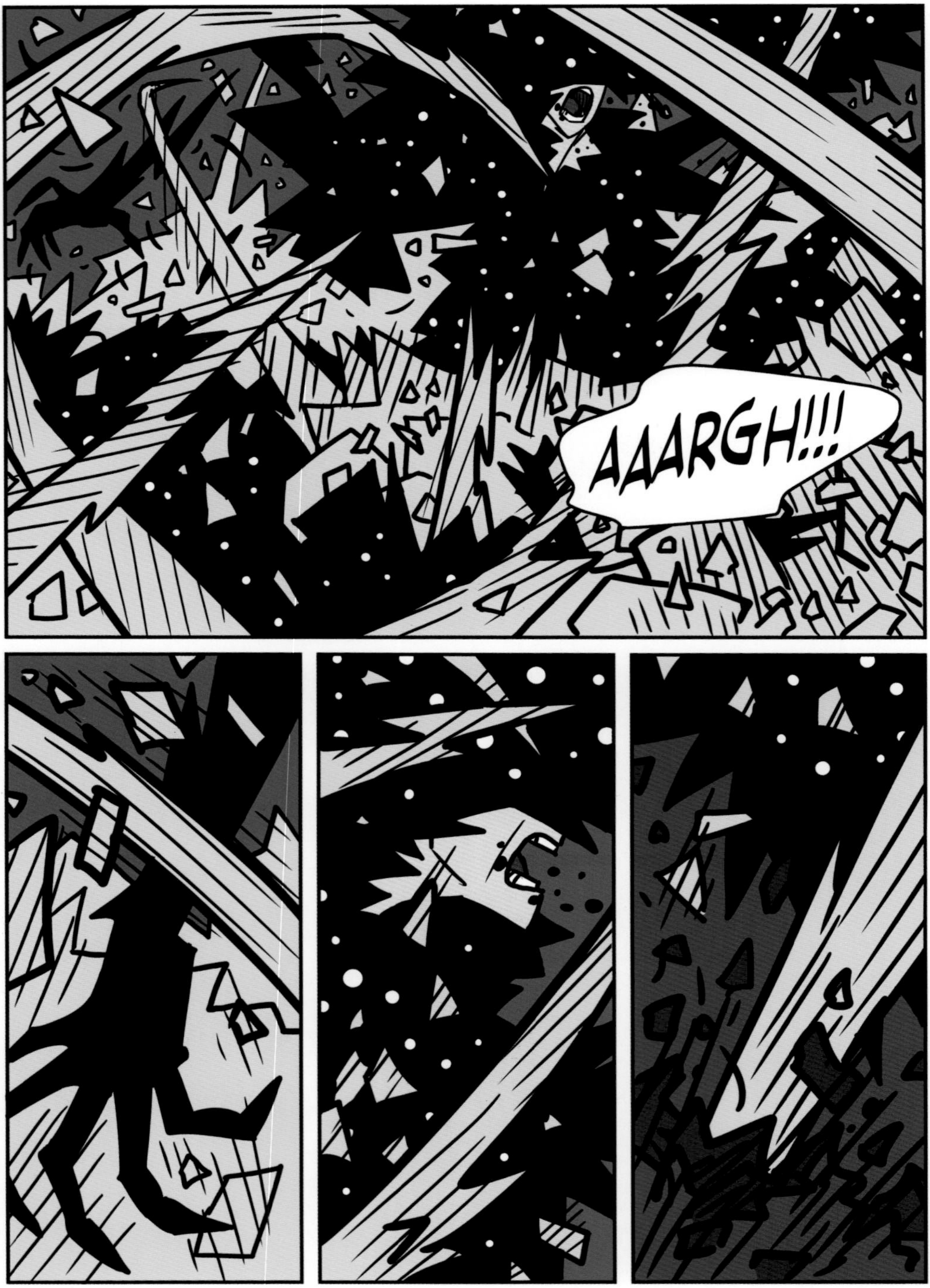
AAARGH!!!

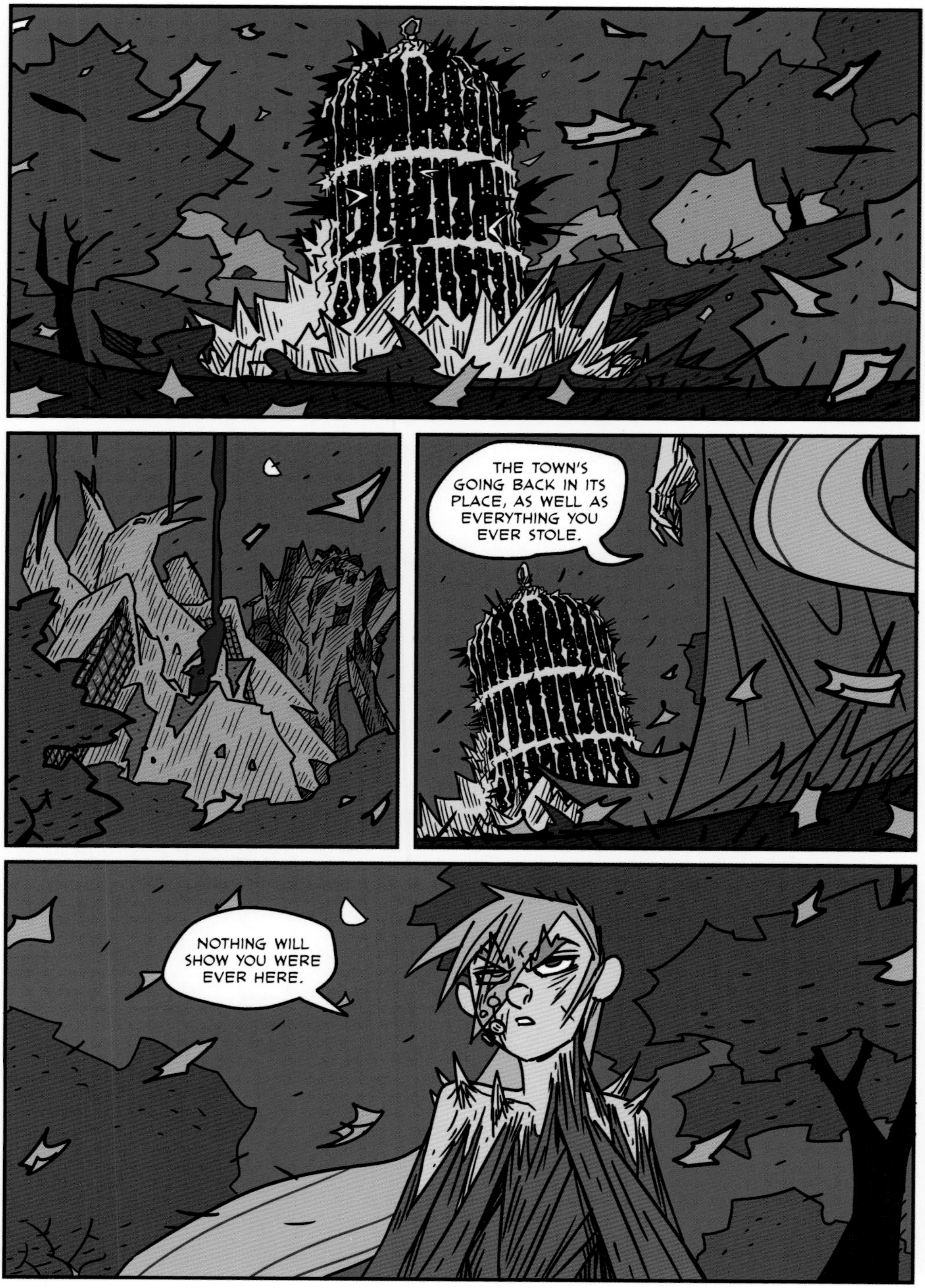
THE TOWN'S GOING BACK IN ITS PLACE, AS WELL AS EVERYTHING YOU EVER STOLE.
NOTHING WILL SHOW YOU WERE EVER HERE.

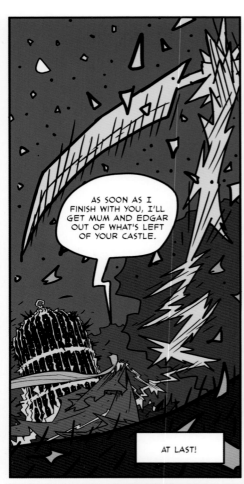

AS SOON AS I FINISH WITH YOU, I'LL GET MUM AND EDGAR OUT OF WHAT'S LEFT OF YOUR CASTLE.

AT LAST!

KILL THE MONSTER! ELIMINATE THE THREAT!

AND THEN...

KILL HIM, AND THEN...

...THEN...

...YOU'LL FINALLY BE ABLE TO REST!

...I'LL FINALLY BE ABLE TO REST.

REST?

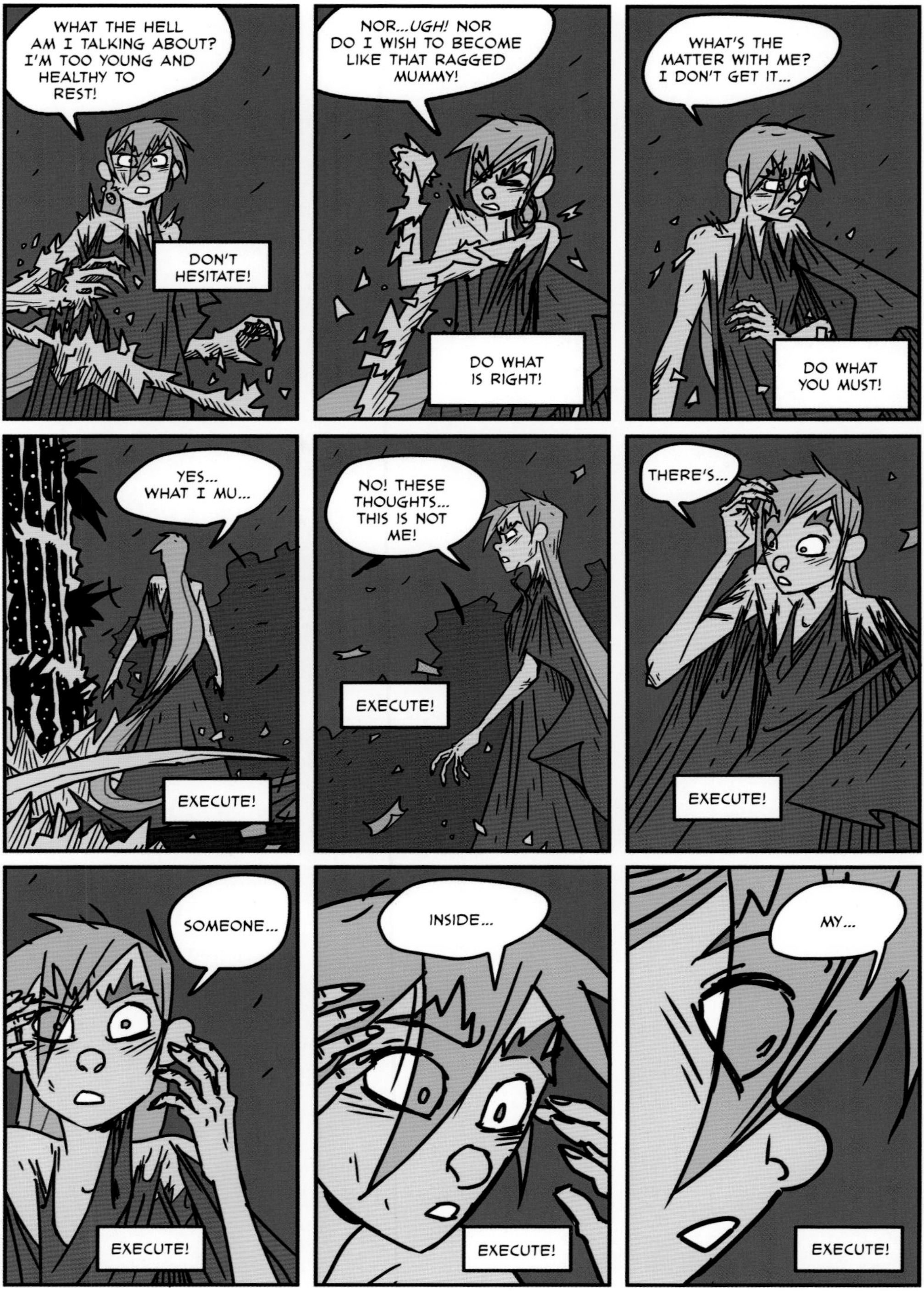
WHAT THE HELL AM I TALKING ABOUT? I'M TOO YOUNG AND HEALTHY TO REST!
DON'T HESITATE!
NOR...UGH! NOR DO I WISH TO BECOME LIKE THAT RAGGED MUMMY!
DO WHAT IS RIGHT!
WHAT'S THE MATTER WITH ME? I DON'T GET IT...
DO WHAT YOU MUST!
YES... WHAT I MU...
EXECUTE!
NO! THESE THOUGHTS... THIS IS NOT ME!
EXECUTE!
THERE'S...
EXECUTE!
SOMEONE...
EXECUTE!
INSIDE...
EXECUTE!
MY...
EXECUTE!

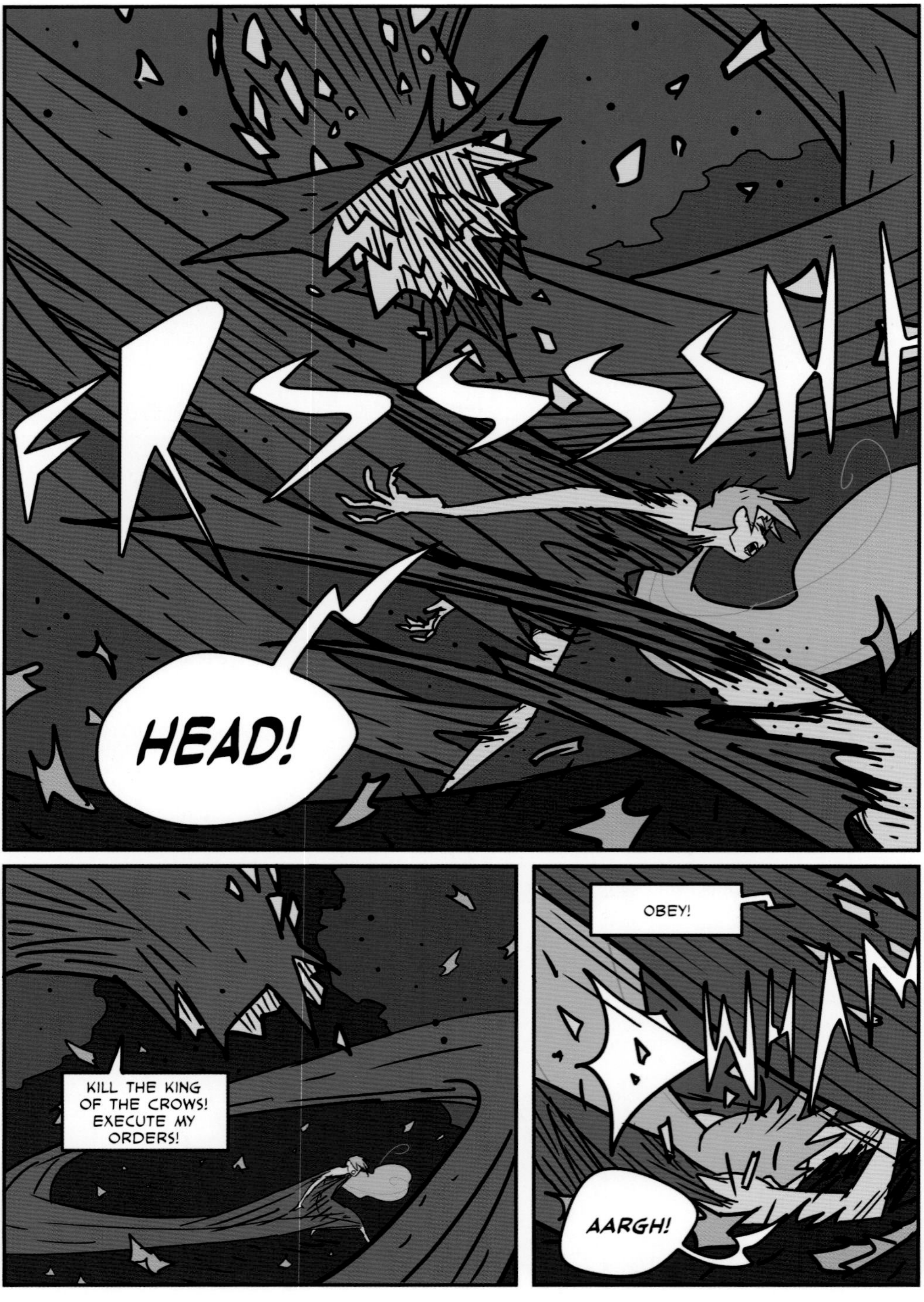
FSSSSH
HEAD!
KILL THE KING OF THE CROWS! EXECUTE MY ORDERS!
OBEY!
WHAM
AARGH!

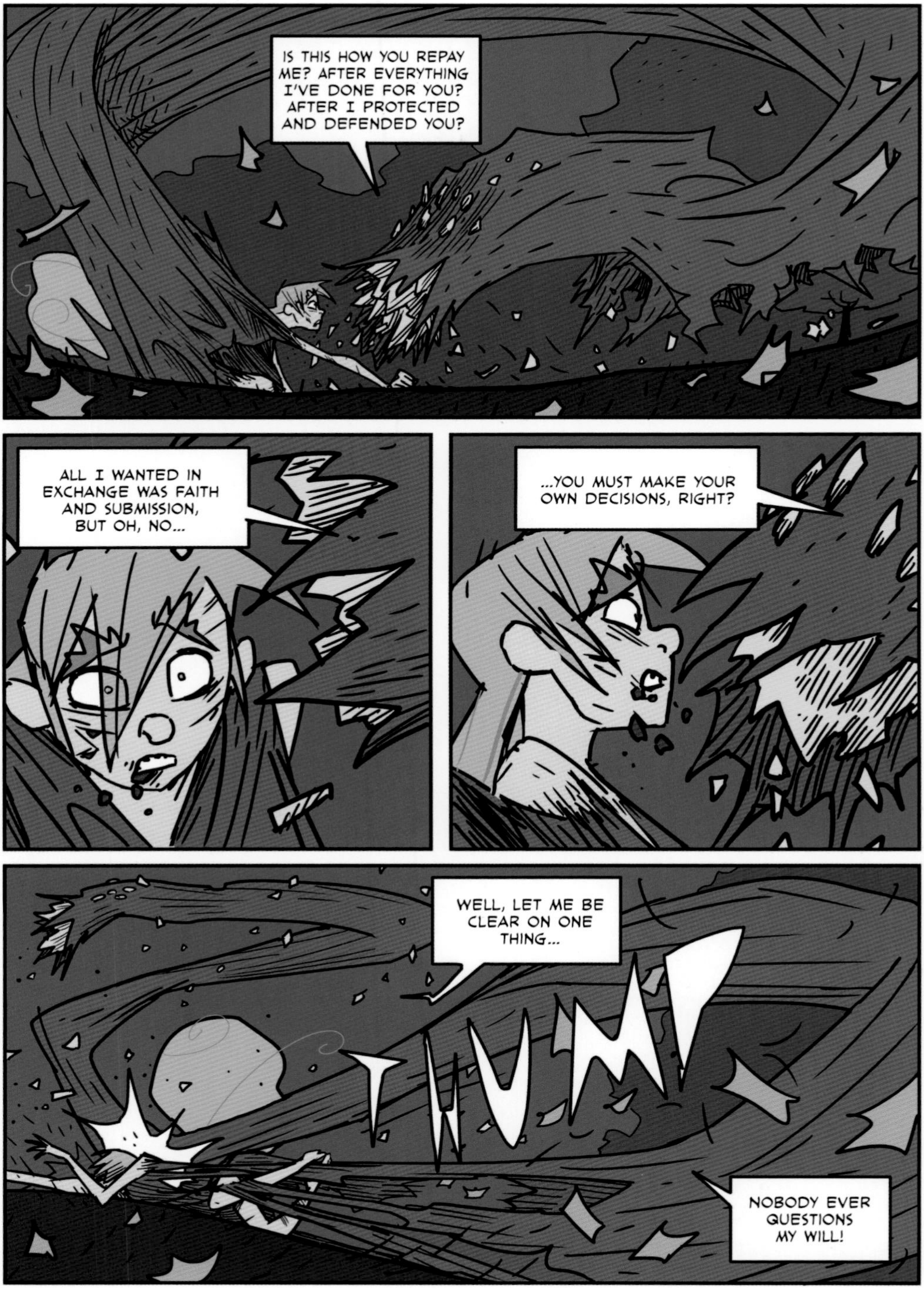
IS THIS HOW YOU REPAY ME? AFTER EVERYTHING I'VE DONE FOR YOU? AFTER I PROTECTED AND DEFENDED YOU?
ALL I WANTED IN EXCHANGE WAS FAITH AND SUBMISSION, BUT OH, NO...
...YOU MUST MAKE YOUR OWN DECISIONS, RIGHT?
WELL, LET ME BE CLEAR ON ONE THING...
THUMP
NOBODY EVER QUESTIONS MY WILL!

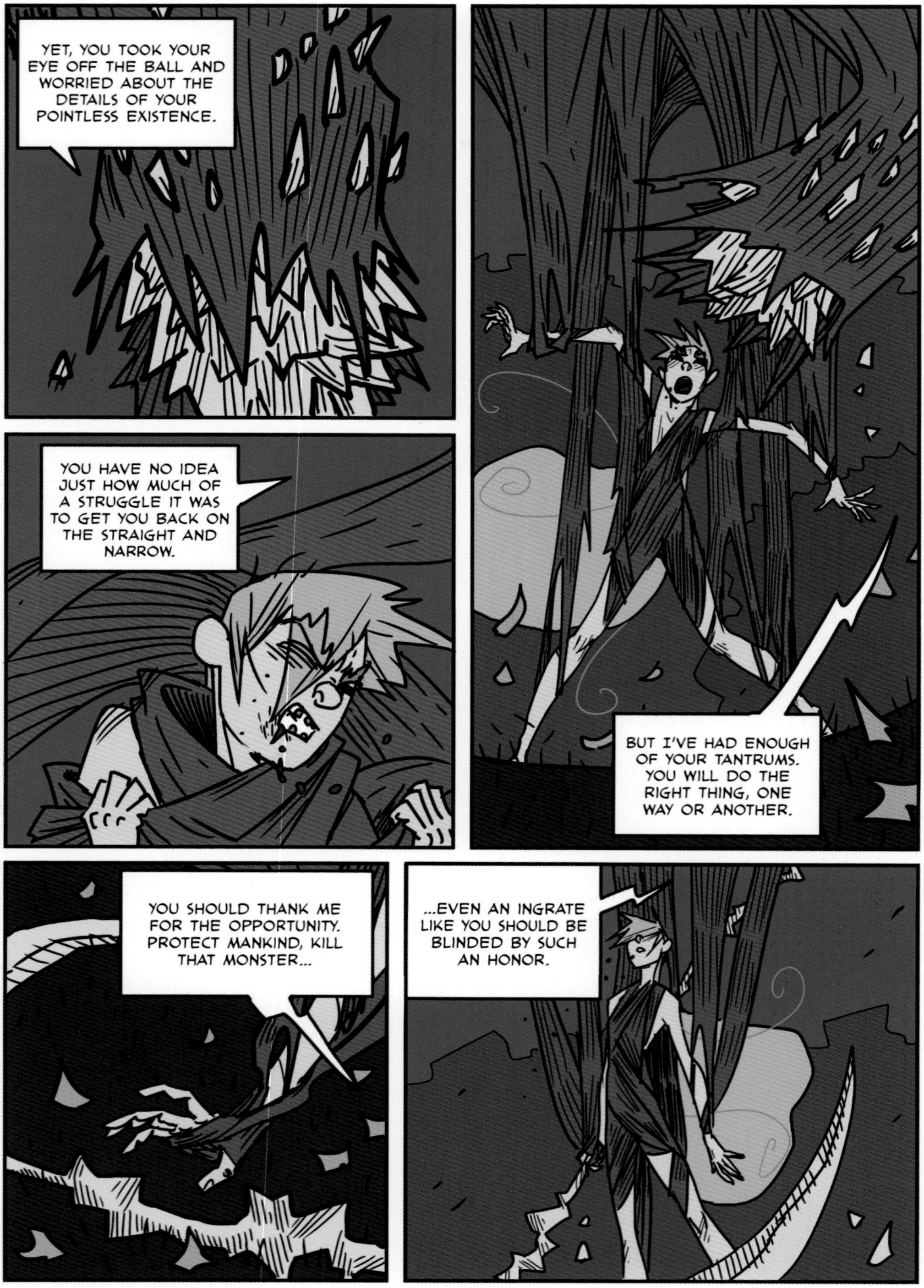
YET, YOU TOOK YOUR EYE OFF THE BALL AND WORRIED ABOUT THE DETAILS OF YOUR POINTLESS EXISTENCE.
YOU HAVE NO IDEA JUST HOW MUCH OF A STRUGGLE IT WAS TO GET YOU BACK ON THE STRAIGHT AND NARROW.
BUT I'VE HAD ENOUGH OF YOUR TANTRUMS. YOU WILL DO THE RIGHT THING, ONE WAY OR ANOTHER.
YOU SHOULD THANK ME FOR THE OPPORTUNITY. PROTECT MANKIND, KILL THAT MONSTER...
...EVEN AN INGRATE LIKE YOU SHOULD BE BLINDED BY SUCH AN HONOR.

ONE FINAL EFFORT IS REQUIRED.

ONE LAST STROKE OF THE SICKLE.

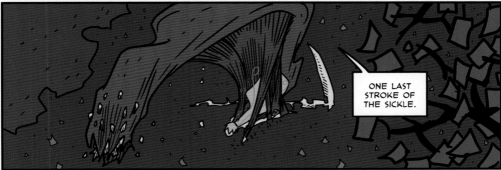

MANKIND WILL BE FOREVER SAFE...

AND ALL OF THIS THANKS TO YOU.

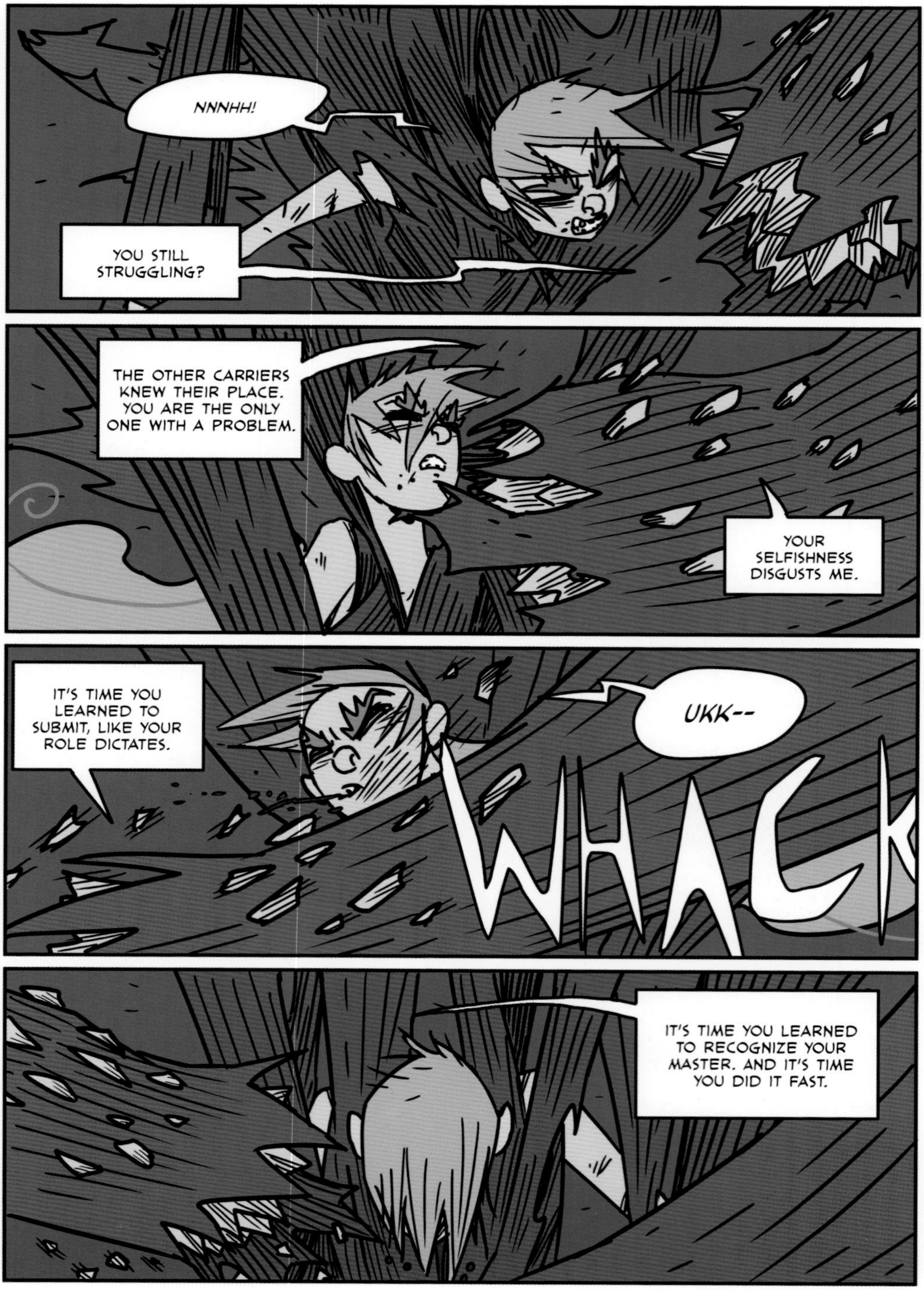
NNNHH!
YOU STILL STRUGGLING?
THE OTHER CARRIERS KNEW THEIR PLACE. YOU ARE THE ONLY ONE WITH A PROBLEM.
YOUR SELFISHNESS DISGUSTS ME.
IT'S TIME YOU LEARNED TO SUBMIT, LIKE YOUR ROLE DICTATES.
UKK--
WHACK
IT'S TIME YOU LEARNED TO RECOGNIZE YOUR MASTER. AND IT'S TIME YOU DID IT FAST.

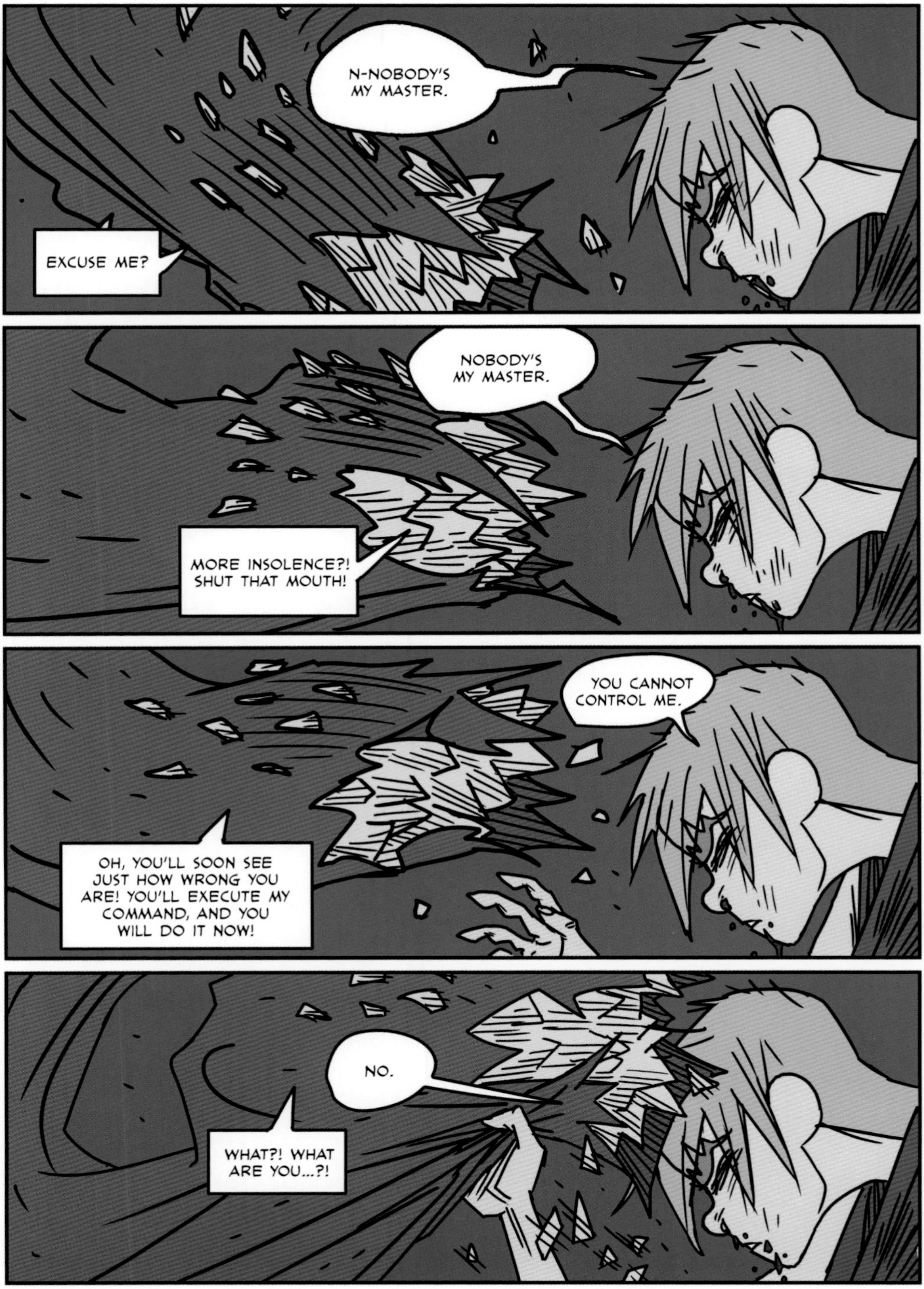
N-NOBODY'S MY MASTER.
EXCUSE ME?
NOBODY'S MY MASTER.
MORE INSOLENCE?! SHUT THAT MOUTH!
YOU CANNOT CONTROL ME.
OH, YOU'LL SOON SEE JUST HOW WRONG YOU ARE! YOU'LL EXECUTE MY COMMAND, AND YOU WILL DO IT NOW!
NO.
WHAT?! WHAT ARE YOU...?!

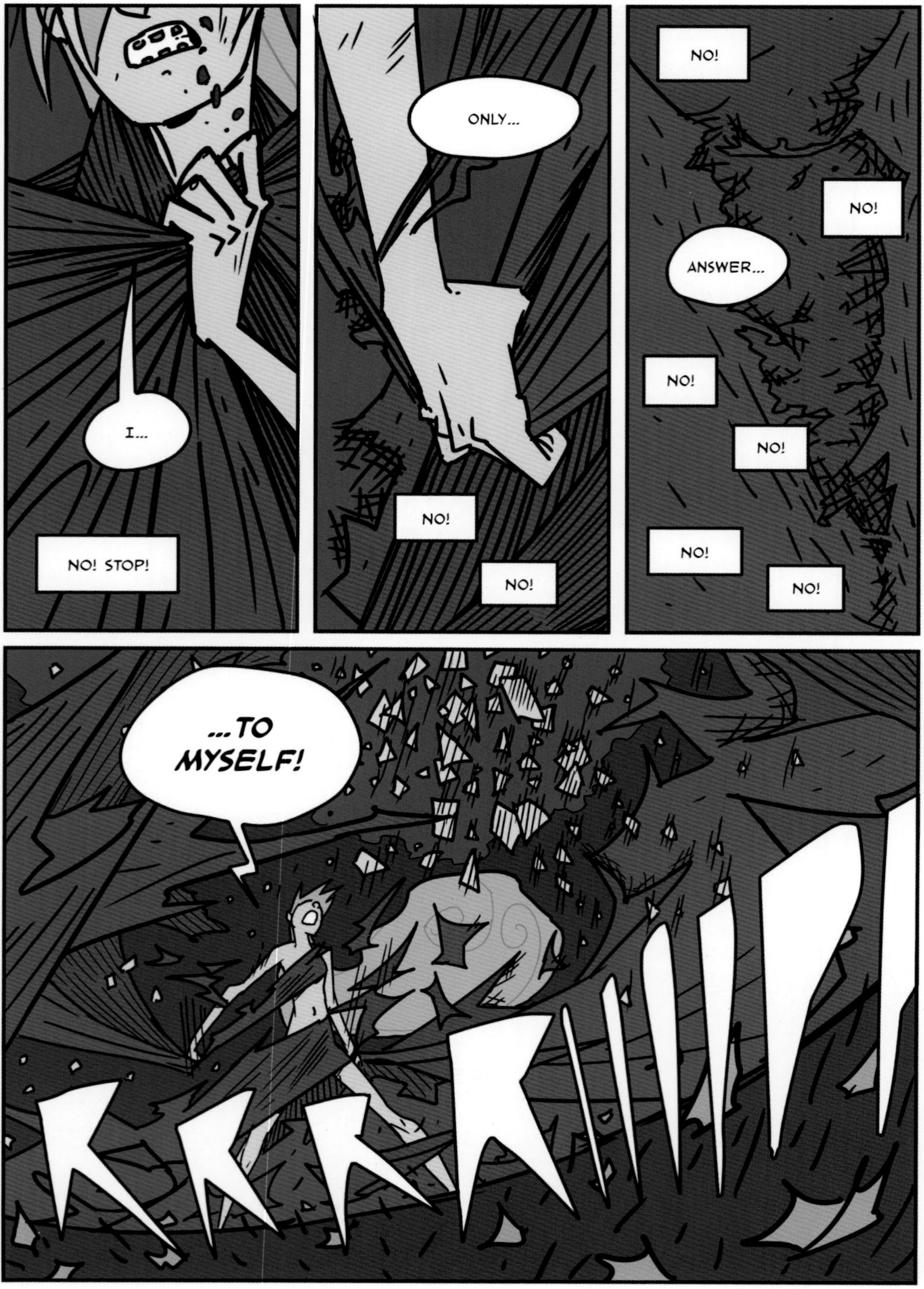
I...
NO! STOP!
ONLY...
NO!
NO!
NO!
NO!
ANSWER...
NO!
NO!
NO!
NO!
...TO MYSELF!

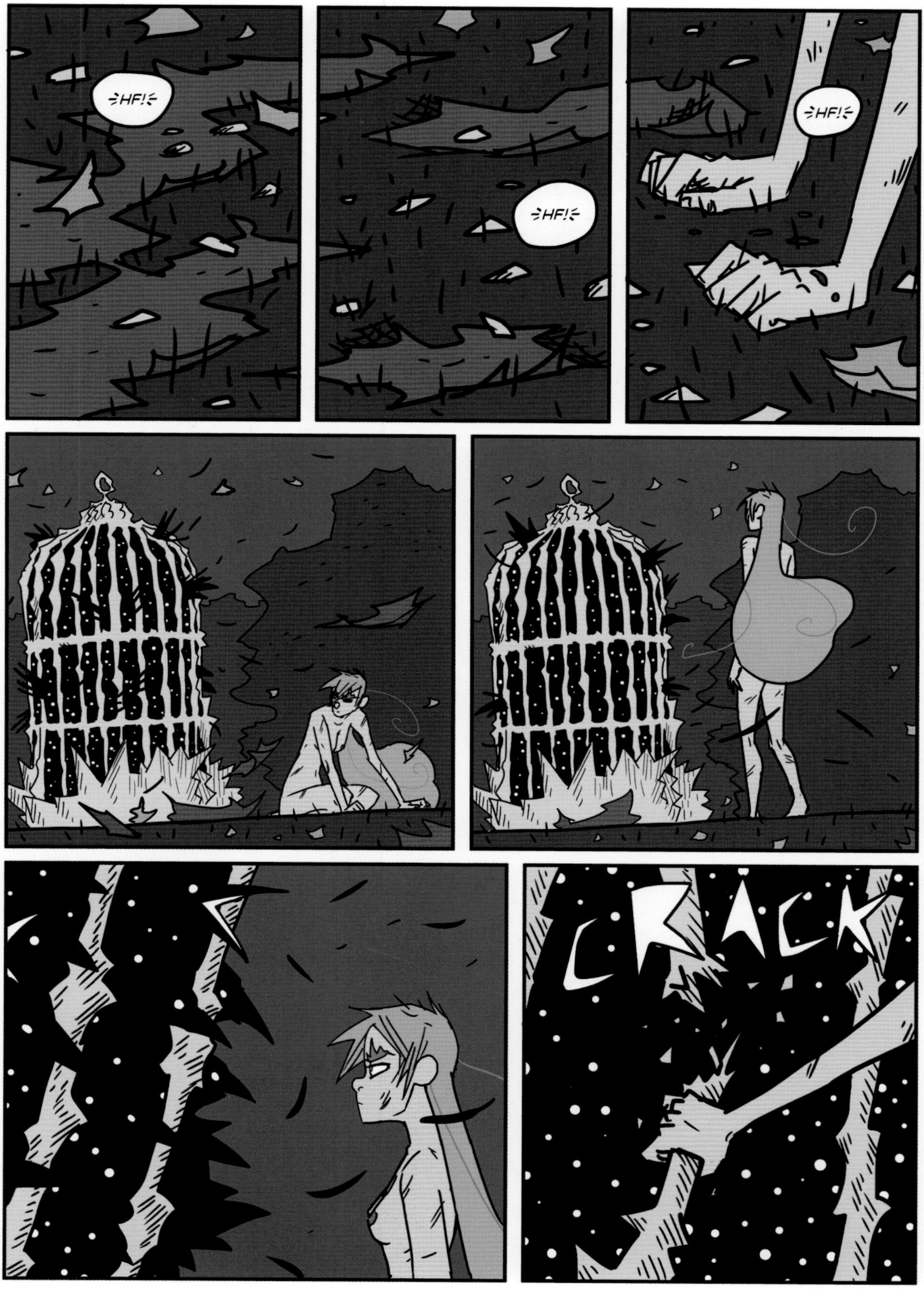
HF!
HF!
HF!
CRACK

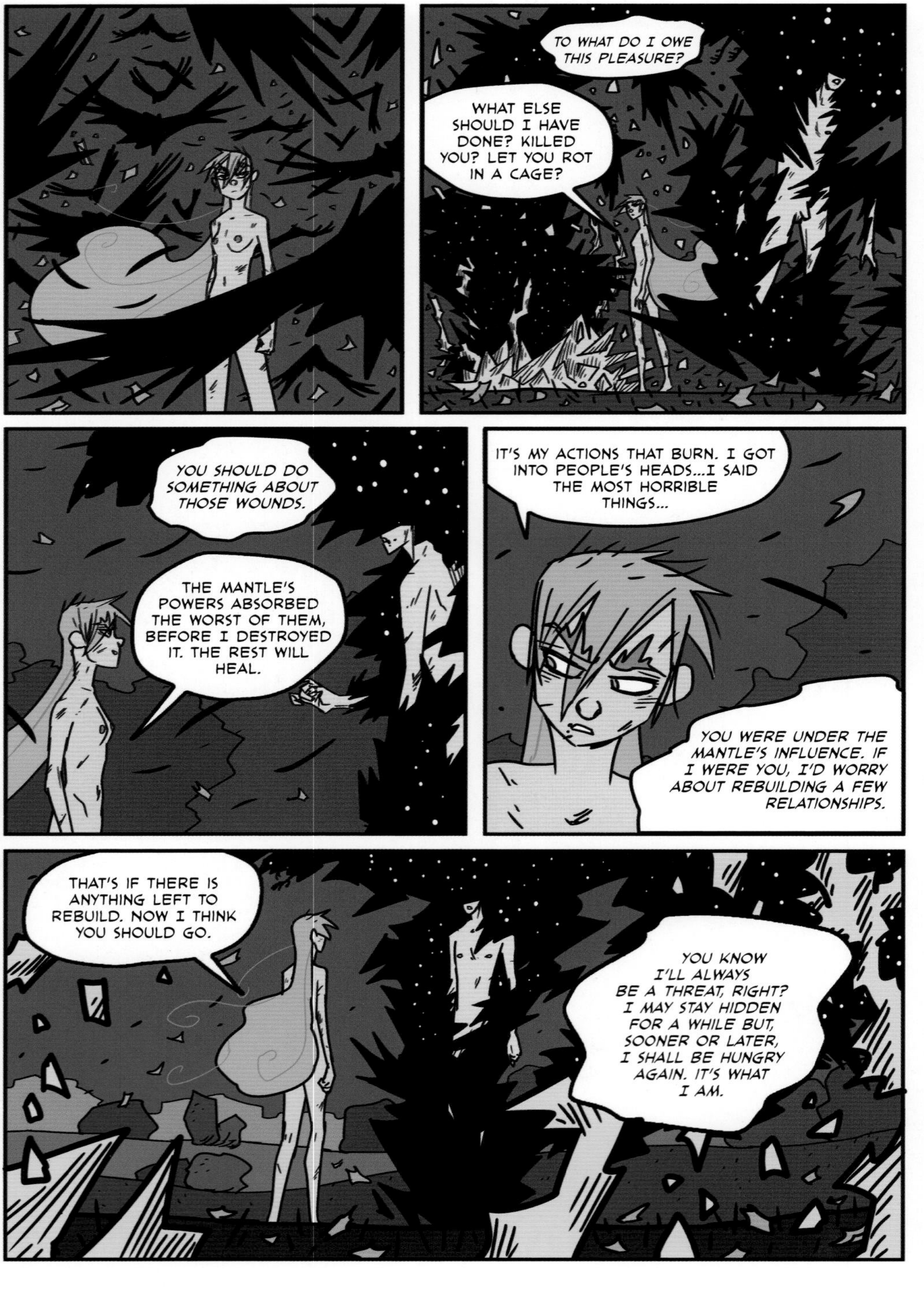
TO WHAT DO I OWE THIS PLEASURE?
WHAT ELSE SHOULD I HAVE DONE? KILLED YOU? LET YOU ROT IN A CAGE?
YOU SHOULD DO SOMETHING ABOUT THOSE WOUNDS.
THE MANTLE'S POWERS ABSORBED THE WORST OF THEM, BEFORE I DESTROYED IT. THE REST WILL HEAL.
IT'S MY ACTIONS THAT BURN. I GOT INTO PEOPLE'S HEADS...I SAID THE MOST HORRIBLE THINGS...
YOU WERE UNDER THE MANTLE'S INFLUENCE. IF I WERE YOU, I'D WORRY ABOUT REBUILDING A FEW RELATIONSHIPS.
THAT'S IF THERE IS ANYTHING LEFT TO REBUILD. NOW I THINK YOU SHOULD GO.
YOU KNOW I'LL ALWAYS BE A THREAT, RIGHT? I MAY STAY HIDDEN FOR A WHILE BUT, SOONER OR LATER, I SHALL BE HUNGRY AGAIN. IT'S WHAT I AM.

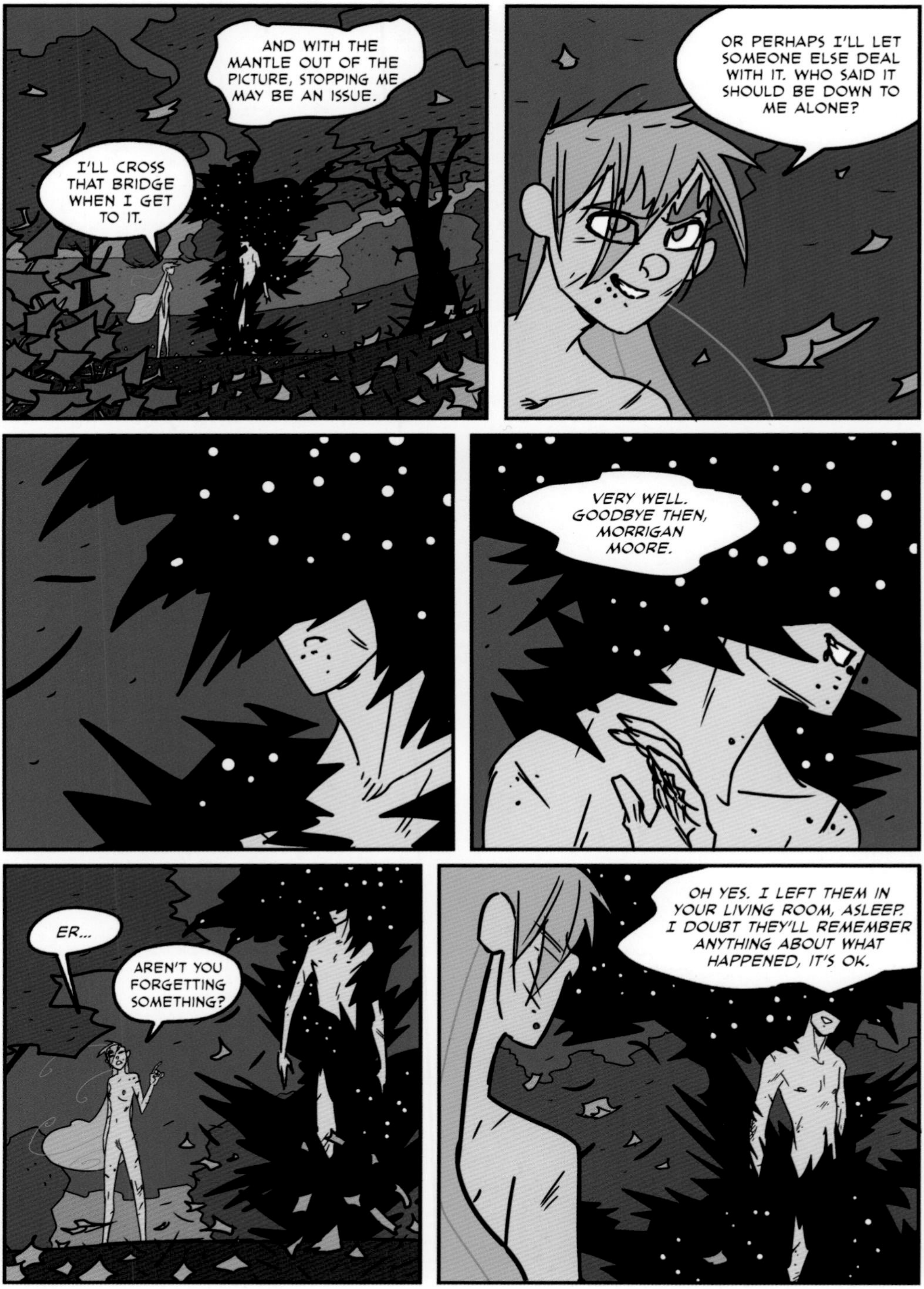
AND WITH THE MANTLE OUT OF THE PICTURE, STOPPING ME MAY BE AN ISSUE.
I'LL CROSS THAT BRIDGE WHEN I GET TO IT.
OR PERHAPS I'LL LET SOMEONE ELSE DEAL WITH IT. WHO SAID IT SHOULD BE DOWN TO ME ALONE?
VERY WELL. GOODBYE THEN, MORRIGAN MOORE.
ER...
AREN'T YOU FORGETTING SOMETHING?
OH YES. I LEFT THEM IN YOUR LIVING ROOM, ASLEEP. I DOUBT THEY'LL REMEMBER ANYTHING ABOUT WHAT HAPPENED, IT'S OK.

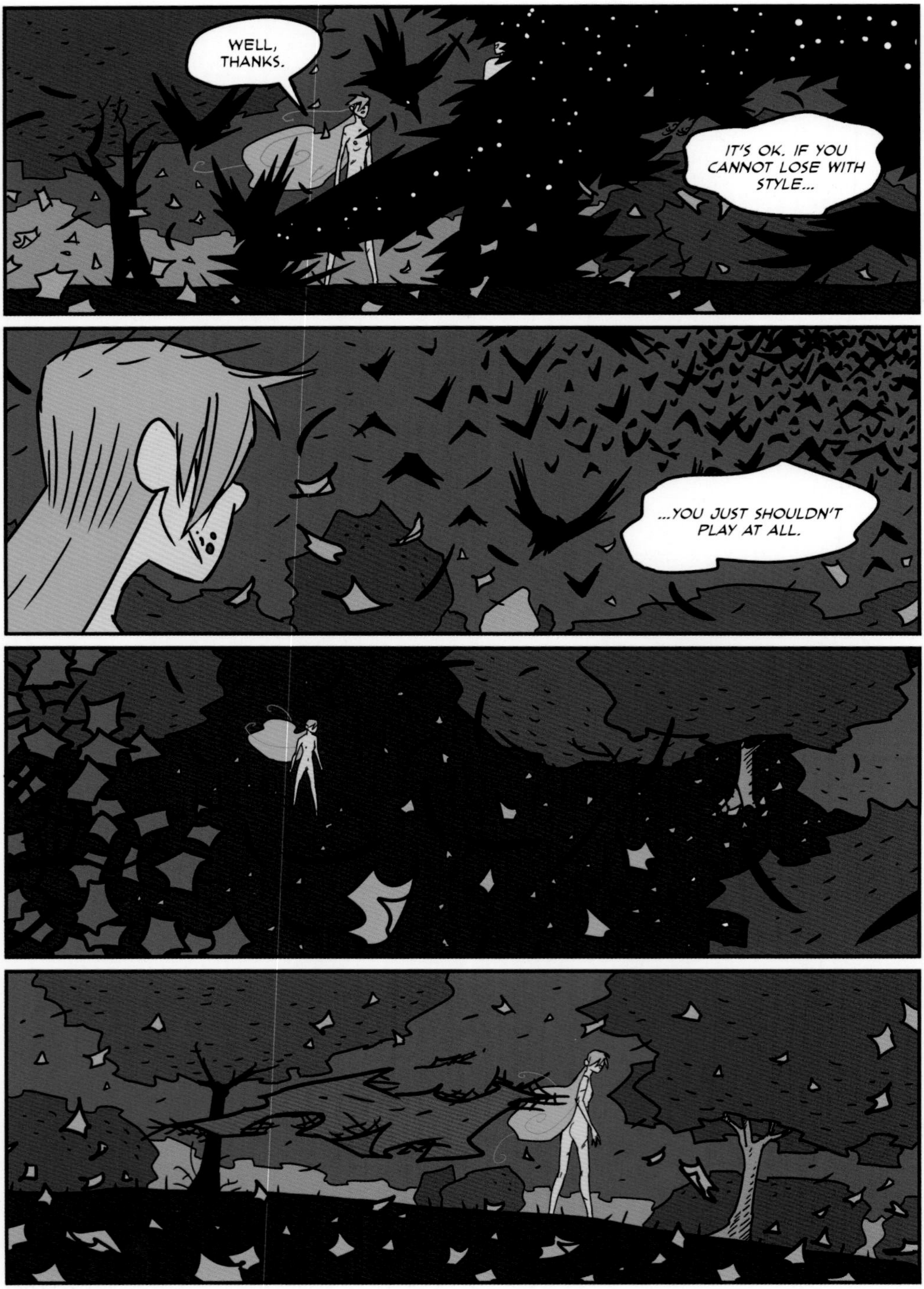
WELL, THANKS.
IT'S OK. IF YOU CANNOT LOSE WITH STYLE...
...YOU JUST SHOULDN'T PLAY AT ALL.

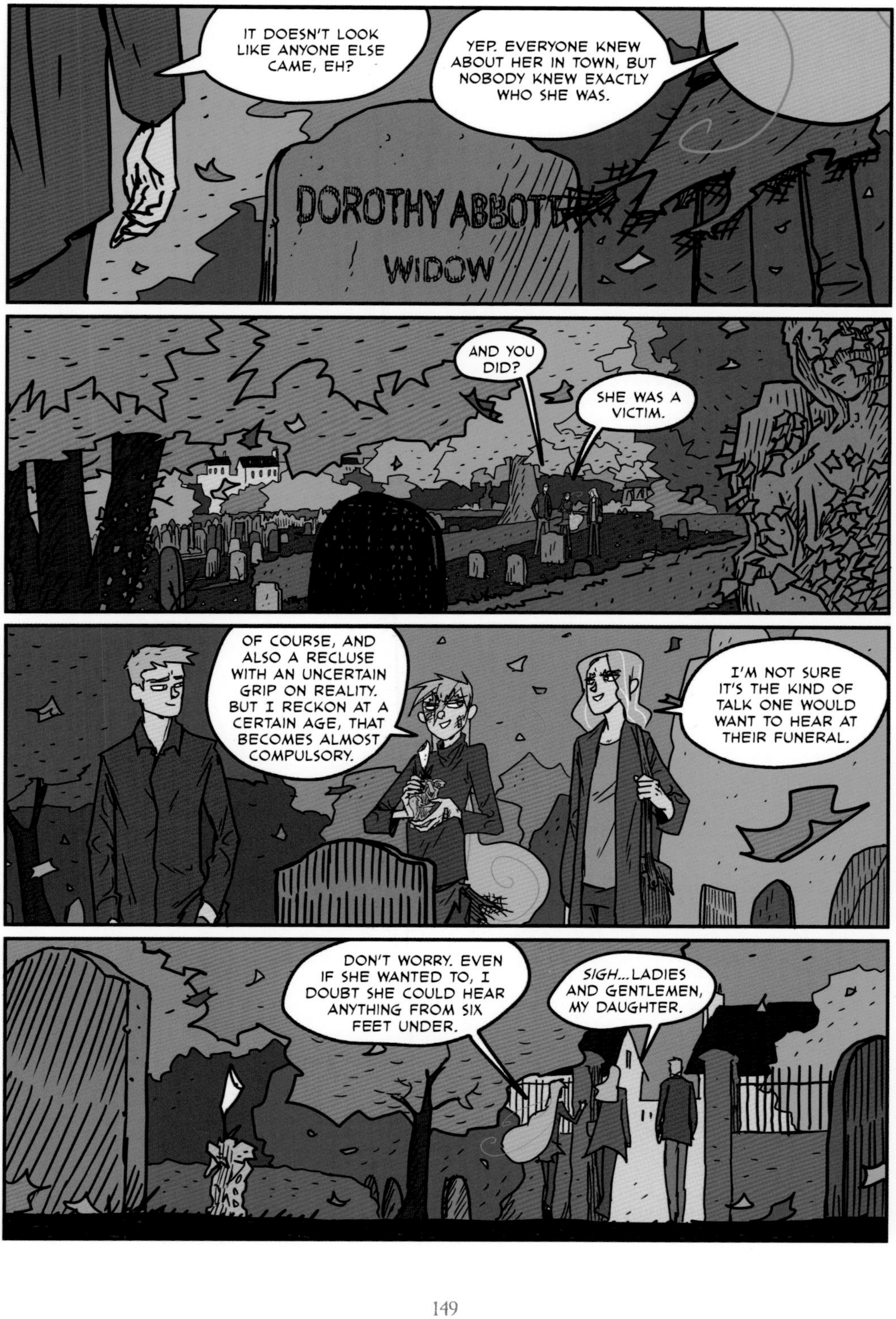
IT DOESN'T LOOK LIKE ANYONE ELSE CAME, EH?
YEP. EVERYONE KNEW ABOUT HER IN TOWN, BUT NOBODY KNEW EXACTLY WHO SHE WAS.
DOROTHY ABBOTT
WIDOW
AND YOU DID?
SHE WAS A VICTIM.
OF COURSE, AND ALSO A RECLUSE WITH AN UNCERTAIN GRIP ON REALITY. BUT I RECKON AT A CERTAIN AGE, THAT BECOMES ALMOST COMPULSORY.
I'M NOT SURE IT'S THE KIND OF TALK ONE WOULD WANT TO HEAR AT THEIR FUNERAL.
DON'T WORRY. EVEN IF SHE WANTED TO, I DOUBT SHE COULD HEAR ANYTHING FROM SIX FEET UNDER.
SIGH... LADIES AND GENTLEMEN, MY DAUGHTER.

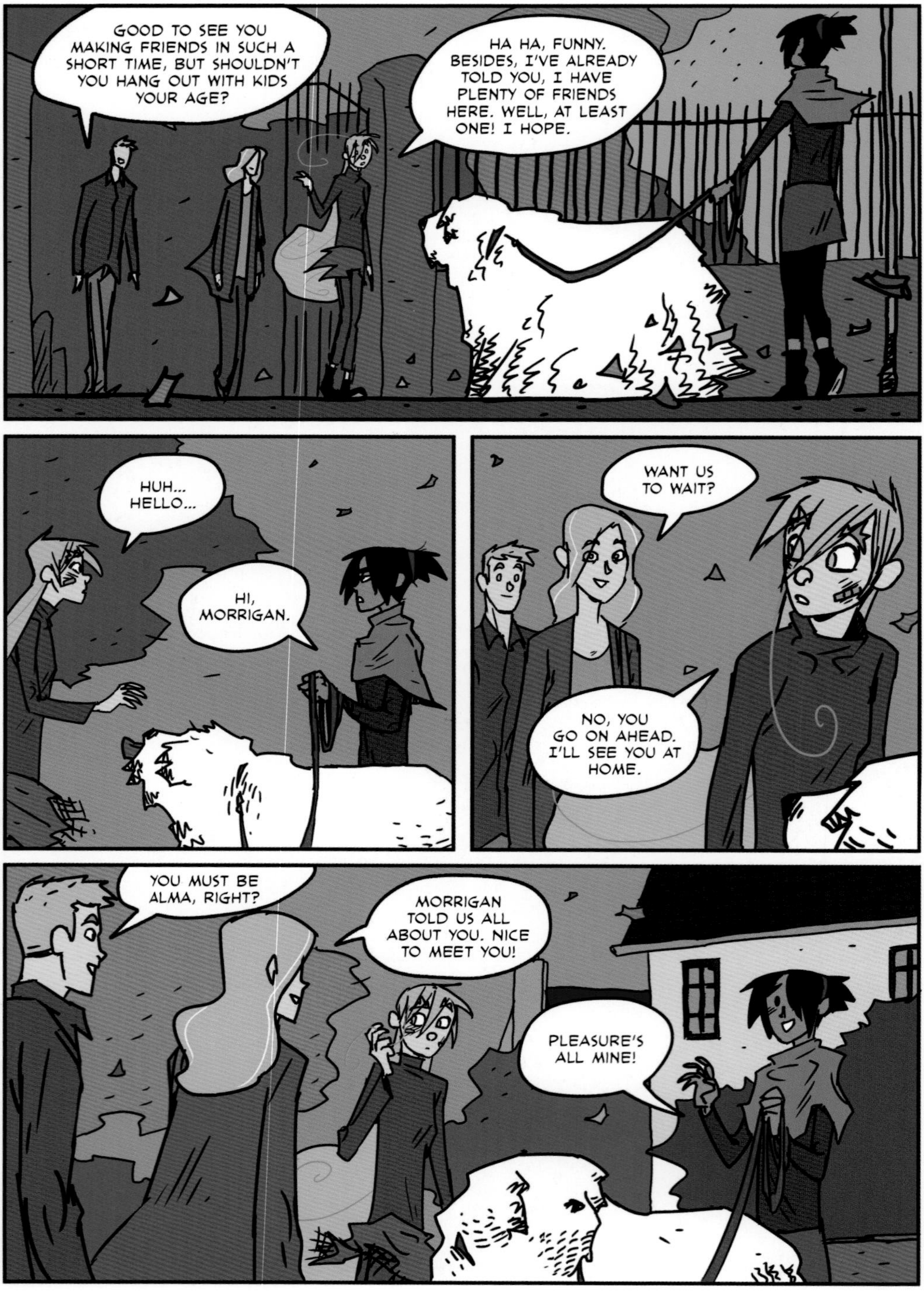
GOOD TO SEE YOU MAKING FRIENDS IN SUCH A SHORT TIME, BUT SHOULDN'T YOU HANG OUT WITH KIDS YOUR AGE?
HA HA, FUNNY. BESIDES, I'VE ALREADY TOLD YOU, I HAVE PLENTY OF FRIENDS HERE. WELL, AT LEAST ONE! I HOPE.
HUH... HELLO...
HI, MORRIGAN.
WANT US TO WAIT?
NO, YOU GO ON AHEAD. I'LL SEE YOU AT HOME.
YOU MUST BE ALMA, RIGHT?
MORRIGAN TOLD US ALL ABOUT YOU. NICE TO MEET YOU!
PLEASURE'S ALL MINE!

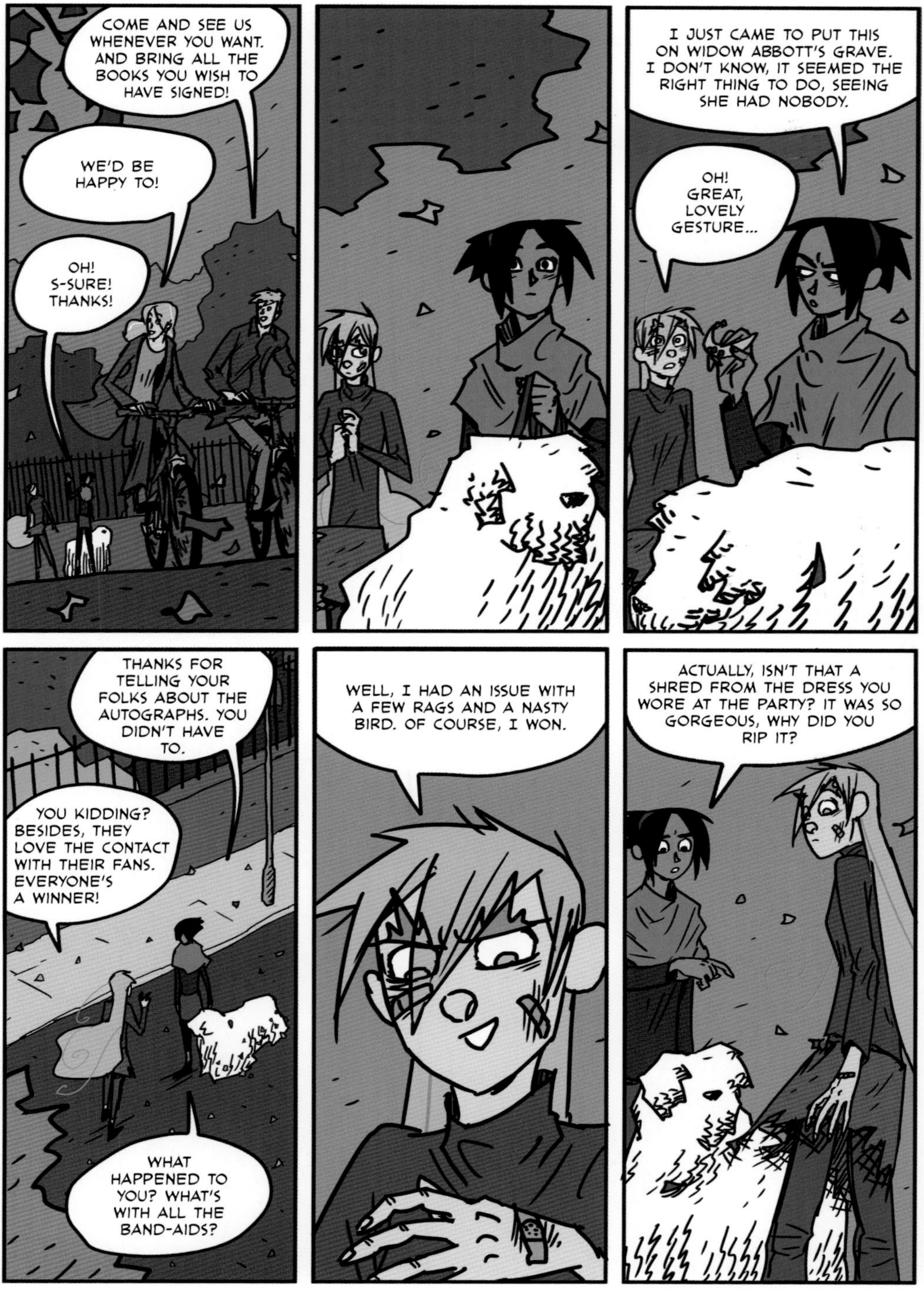
COME AND SEE US WHENEVER YOU WANT. AND BRING ALL THE BOOKS YOU WISH TO HAVE SIGNED!
WE'D BE HAPPY TO!
OH! S-SURE! THANKS!
I JUST CAME TO PUT THIS ON WIDOW ABBOTT'S GRAVE. I DON'T KNOW, IT SEEMED THE RIGHT THING TO DO, SEEING SHE HAD NOBODY.
OH! GREAT, LOVELY GESTURE...
THANKS FOR TELLING YOUR FOLKS ABOUT THE AUTOGRAPHS. YOU DIDN'T HAVE TO.
YOU KIDDING? BESIDES, THEY LOVE THE CONTACT WITH THEIR FANS. EVERYONE'S A WINNER!
WHAT HAPPENED TO YOU? WHAT'S WITH ALL THE BAND-AIDS?
WELL, I HAD AN ISSUE WITH A FEW RAGS AND A NASTY BIRD. OF COURSE, I WON.
ACTUALLY, ISN'T THAT A SHRED FROM THE DRESS YOU WORE AT THE PARTY? IT WAS SO GORGEOUS, WHY DID YOU RIP IT?

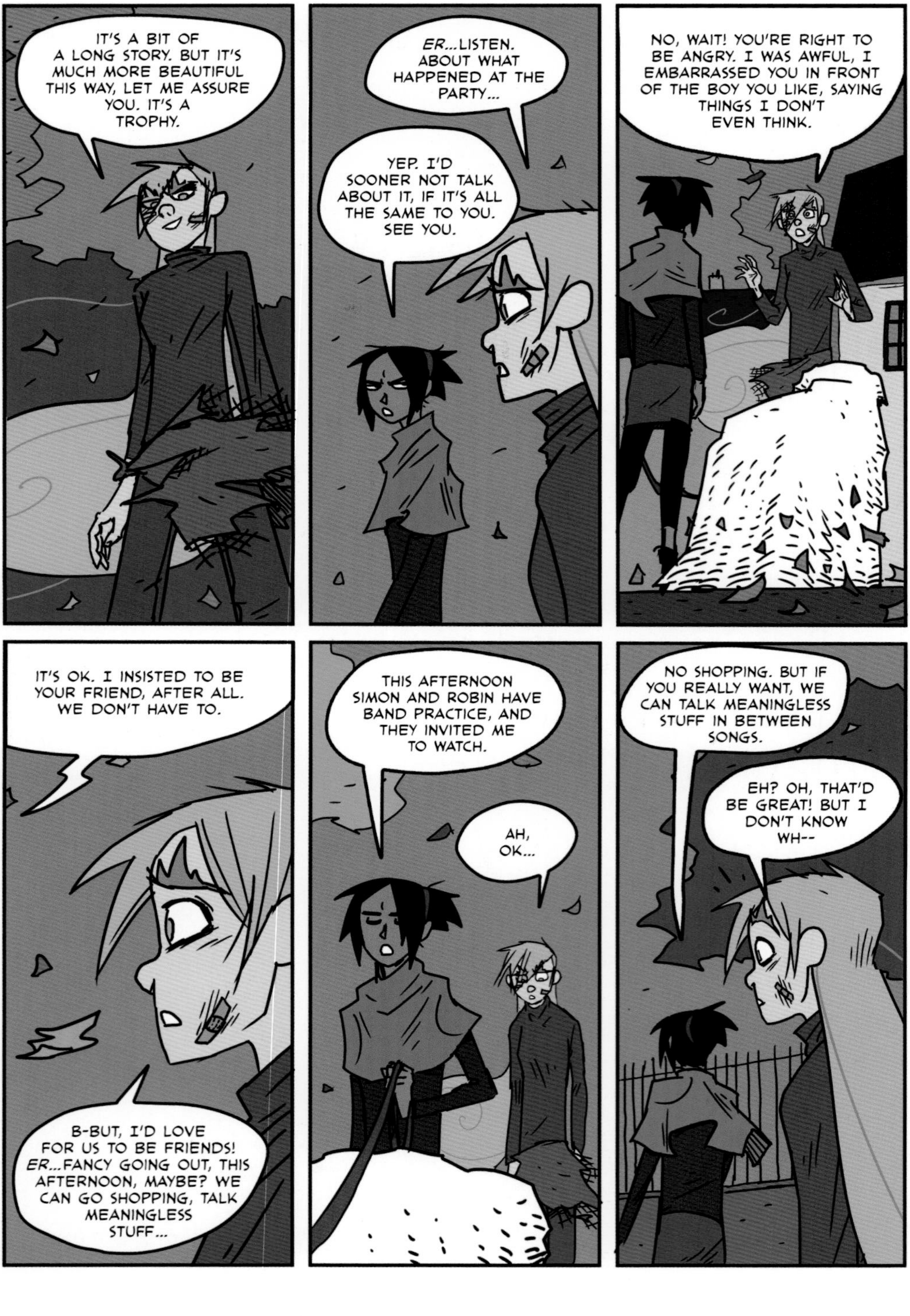
IT'S A BIT OF A LONG STORY. BUT IT'S MUCH MORE BEAUTIFUL THIS WAY, LET ME ASSURE YOU. IT'S A TROPHY.
ER...LISTEN. ABOUT WHAT HAPPENED AT THE PARTY...
YEP. I'D SOONER NOT TALK ABOUT IT, IF IT'S ALL THE SAME TO YOU. SEE YOU.
NO, WAIT! YOU'RE RIGHT TO BE ANGRY. I WAS AWFUL, I EMBARRASSED YOU IN FRONT OF THE BOY YOU LIKE, SAYING THINGS I DON'T EVEN THINK.
IT'S OK. I INSISTED TO BE YOUR FRIEND, AFTER ALL. WE DON'T HAVE TO.
B-BUT, I'D LOVE FOR US TO BE FRIENDS! ER...FANCY GOING OUT, THIS AFTERNOON, MAYBE? WE CAN GO SHOPPING, TALK MEANINGLESS STUFF...
THIS AFTERNOON SIMON AND ROBIN HAVE BAND PRACTICE, AND THEY INVITED ME TO WATCH.
AH, OK...
NO SHOPPING. BUT IF YOU REALLY WANT, WE CAN TALK MEANINGLESS STUFF IN BETWEEN SONGS.
EH? OH, THAT'D BE GREAT! BUT I DON'T KNOW WH--

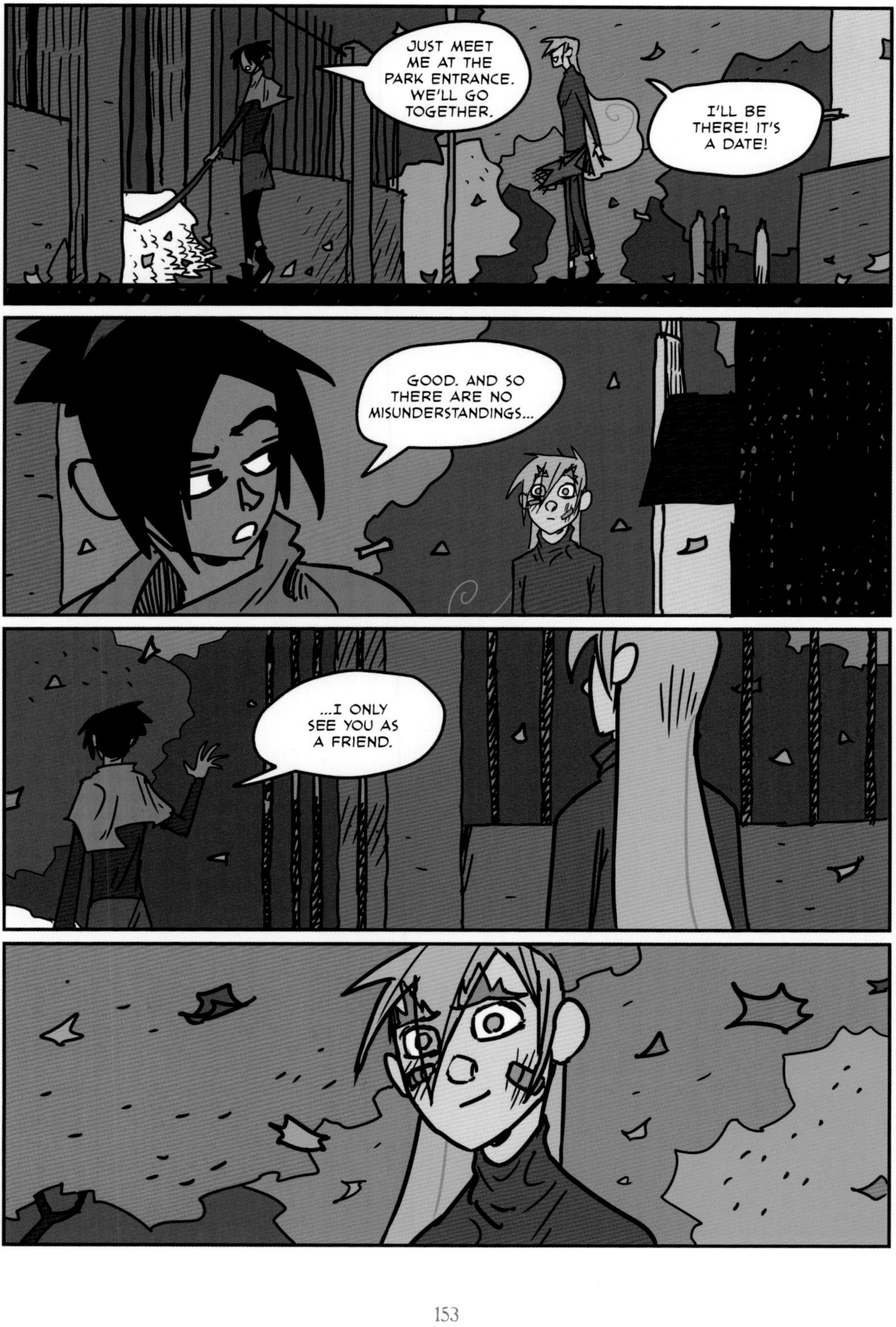
JUST MEET ME AT THE PARK ENTRANCE. WE'LL GO TOGETHER.
I'LL BE THERE! IT'S A DATE!
GOOD. AND SO THERE ARE NO MISUNDERSTANDINGS...
...I ONLY SEE YOU AS A FRIEND.

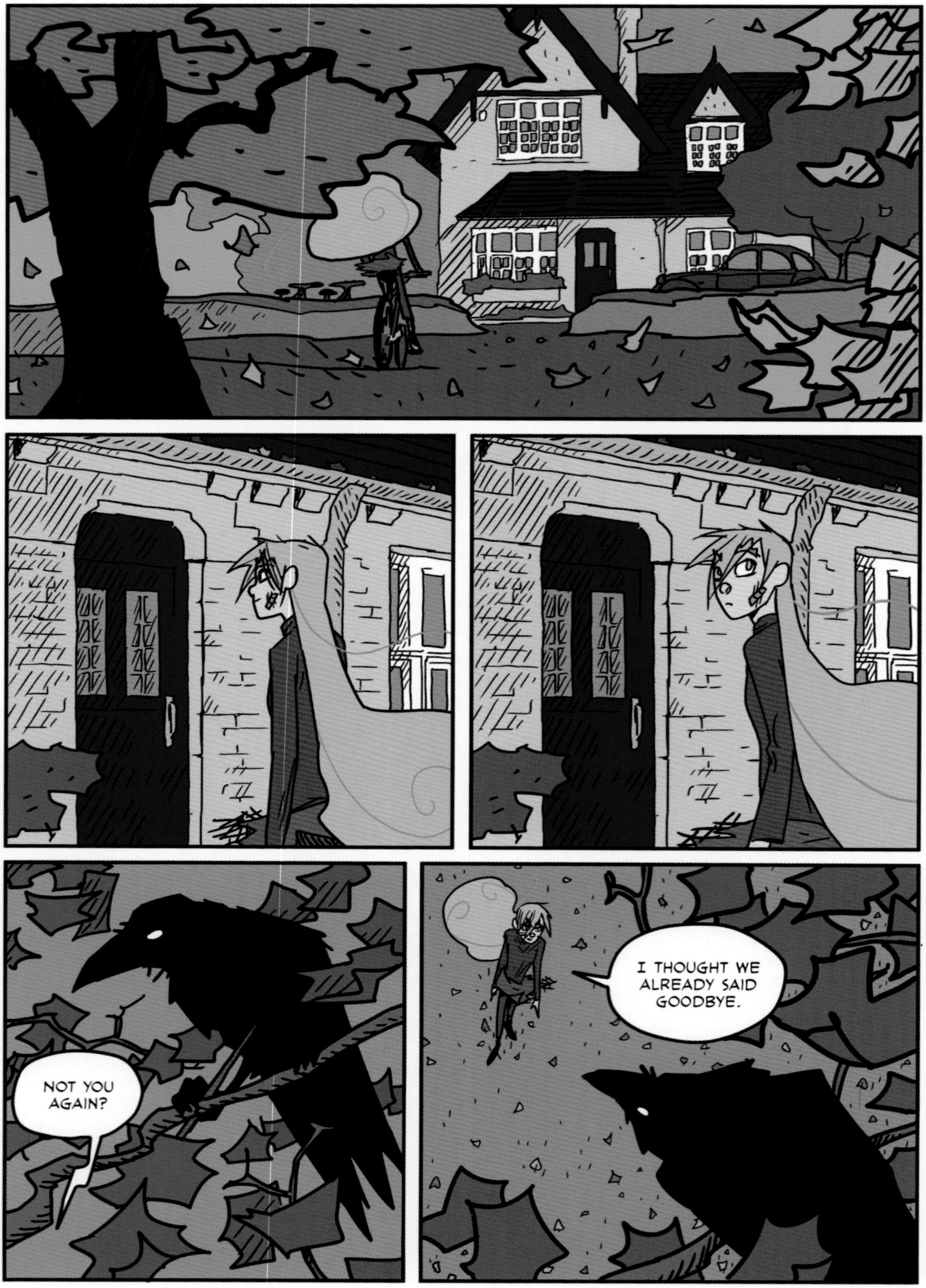
NOT YOU AGAIN?
I THOUGHT WE ALREADY SAID GOODBYE.

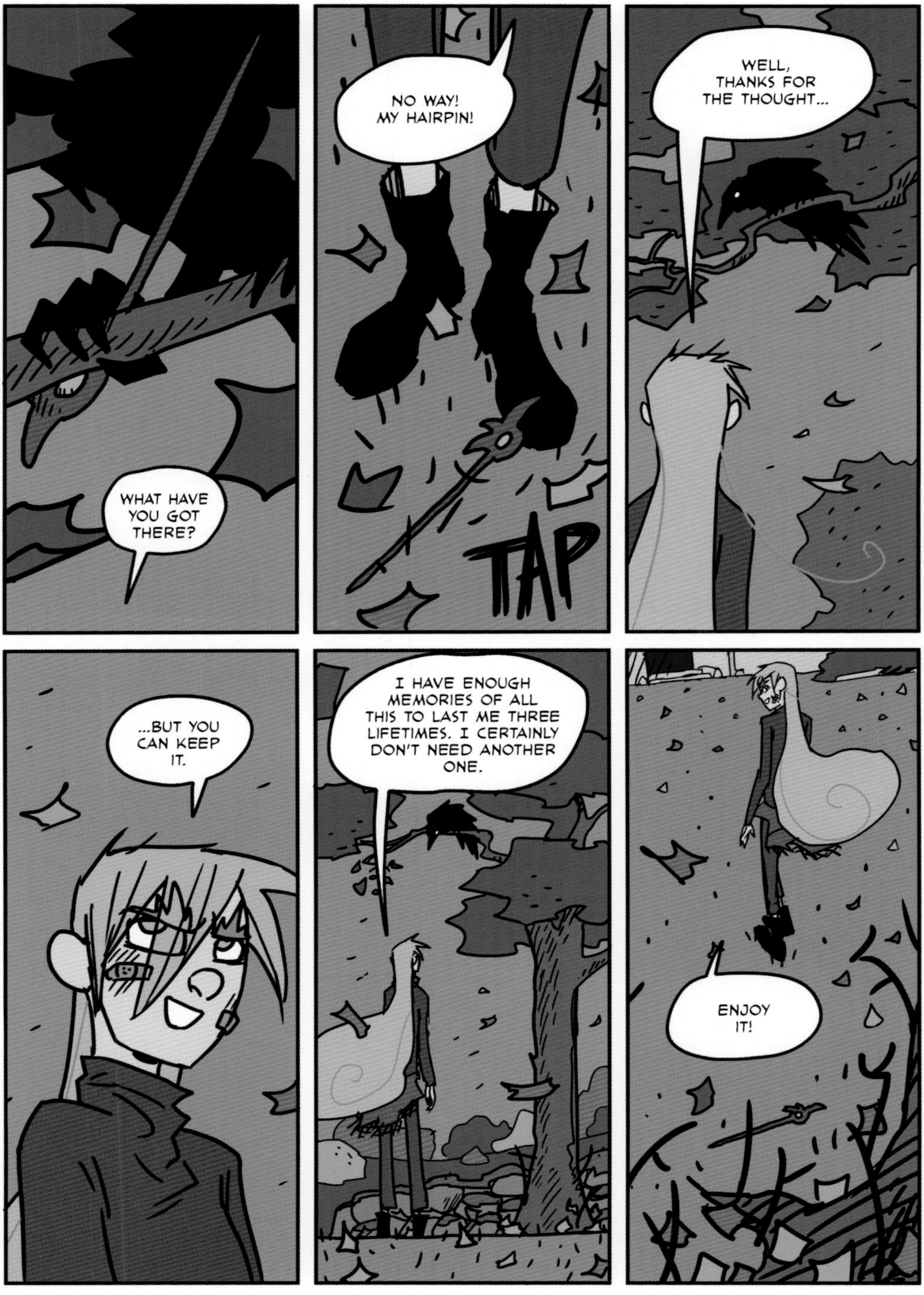
WHAT HAVE YOU GOT THERE?
NO WAY! MY HAIRPIN!
TAP
WELL, THANKS FOR THE THOUGHT...
...BUT YOU CAN KEEP IT.
I HAVE ENOUGH MEMORIES OF ALL THIS TO LAST ME THREE LIFETIMES. I CERTAINLY DON'T NEED ANOTHER ONE.
ENJOY IT!

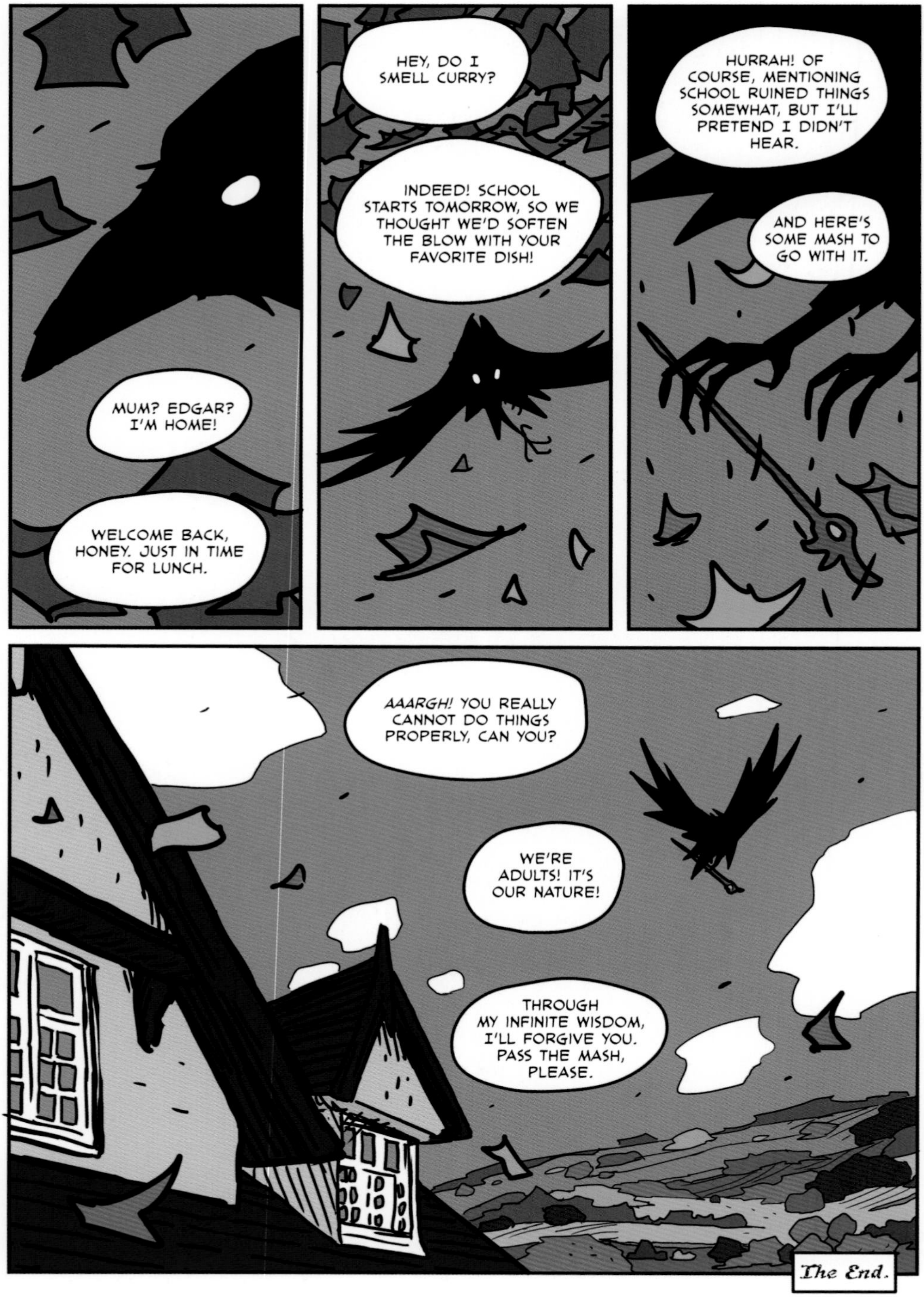
MUM? EDGAR? I'M HOME!
WELCOME BACK, HONEY. JUST IN TIME FOR LUNCH.
HEY, DO I SMELL CURRY?
INDEED! SCHOOL STARTS TOMORROW, SO WE THOUGHT WE'D SOFTEN THE BLOW WITH YOUR FAVORITE DISH!
HURRAH! OF COURSE, MENTIONING SCHOOL RUINED THINGS SOMEWHAT, BUT I'LL PRETEND I DIDN'T HEAR.
AND HERE'S SOME MASH TO GO WITH IT.
AAARGH! YOU REALLY CANNOT DO THINGS PROPERLY, CAN YOU?
WE'RE ADULTS! IT'S OUR NATURE!
THROUGH MY INFINITE WISDOM, I'LL FORGIVE YOU. PASS THE MASH, PLEASE.
The End.

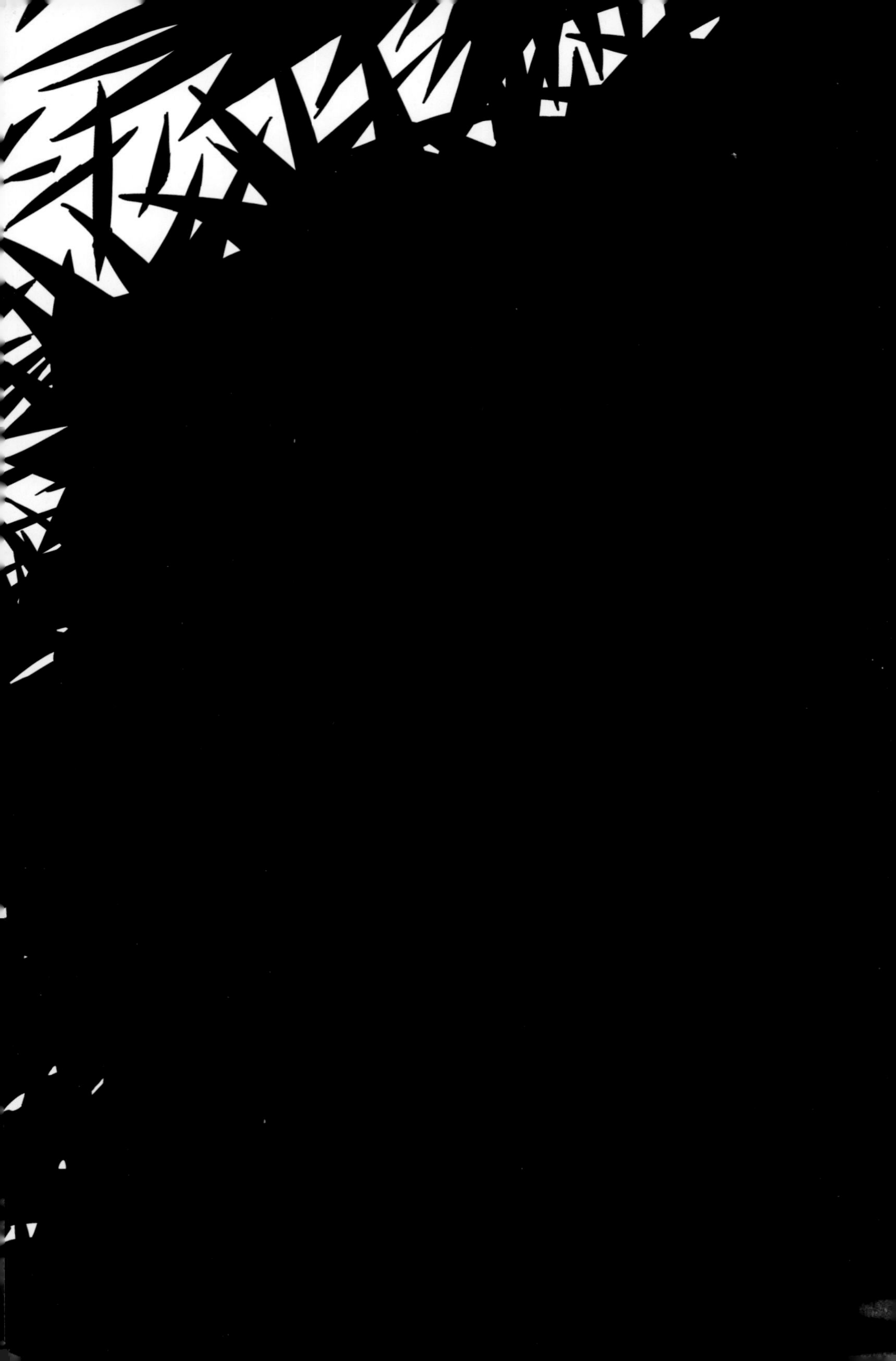

FEDERICO ROSSI EDRIGHI was born in Rome in 1982. Between 2006 and 2014 he worked on storyboards for feature films and TV series for studios such as Musicartoon and Rainbow CGi. He contributed to the fourth season of *John Doe* (Editoriale Aurea) written by Mauro Uzzeo and Roberto Recchioni, and to *Harpun* (GP Publishing) written by Giovanni Masi, reprinted by Verticomics in 2016.

In 2015 he illustrated the adaptation of *At the Mountains of Madness* for the series *Roberto Recchioni Presents: The Masters of Horror* (written by Giovanni Masi, published by Star Comics) and from the same year he has been working on the *Dylan Dog* series for Sergio Bonelli Editore.

In 2016 he published *The Scarecrow Princess* with BAO Publishing.